BENT OUT OF SHADE

A HUMOROUS PARANORMAL WOMEN'S FICTION

DEBORAH WILDE

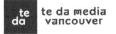

te da media
vancouver

1

GIVEN THE DEMON'S SMASHED-IN SNOUT, LARGE EARS sprouting dense, bristly hair, and pustules encrusting a flabby crab-shaped body, its anger issues were well warranted. That still didn't mean I was comfortable with it attacking my kid. Even if it was a practice fight in my ex's side of our duplex.

"Watch the pincers, Sadie." Eli Chu, my baby daddy, sat forward on his sofa, his elbows braced on his thighs, as glued to the action as a coach during the finals of the Stanley Cup. Well, a coach who flinched at every scuff imposed on his precious house, endured thanks to this home game, but who concealed his anxiety whenever his star player looked over for encouragement.

Sadie caught her dad's eye, and Eli flashed her a big thumbs-up.

Today's evil crustacean foe had come courtesy of Naveen Kumar, our demon wrangler extraordinaire, who presided over the event with all the dignity he could muster, despite clenching his jaw every time Eli flinched. Thanks to a small screw-up involving an angry goth girl and her overly enthusiastic fists, the practice fiend Nav had intended for Sadie to dispatch was no longer an option, so he'd brought this awful crab instead.

Apparently, it was the least lethal one he could get on short notice. I'd tried to call the session off because neither Eli nor I had a basement or rec room in our duplex, our garages were too cramped, and our backyards too exposed for our child to face down a demon with a two-foot leg span. However, here we were, because a certain other parent had broken down in the face of Sadie's puppy dog eyes and told her it was fine to proceed. I smirked. At least when she'd tried to guilt me into this mess, I'd protested.

The furniture in Eli's large living room had been pushed to the side, effectively turning this event into theater in the round. Perfect for my drama club daughter.

Behind her, Sadie's animated shadow poured out enough light to power a solar system. I winced, adjusting the sunglasses Nav had provided us with.

Nav flung the agitated demon toward the corner, wielding his staff made of solid light with the same calm awareness and infallible instincts he brought as leader of our local spawn-killing organization.

The demon skittered over the plastic sheeting on the floor, hissing and seeking an opening.

Eli dug the heels of his palms into his thighs, scrutinizing the tarps for any gap that would lead to his hardwood floor getting injured.

Nav boxed the demon in. "Deep breath, harness the magic, poppet." His posh British accent was all kinds of charming, though it would have been better if, when he placed a hand on his abdomen in demonstration, his admirable six-pack wasn't hidden by his shirt.

What? A woman could look.

Sadie did as instructed but her shadow oscillated.

Eli tsked. "You're going too hard, too fast. Pace yourself."

Nav arched an eyebrow, a muscle once more ticking in his jaw. "We agreed I was running this session."

"You are." Eli didn't take his eyes off Sadie. "What did I say about tight shoulders?" He shook his out in demonstration. "The more you tense, the more you flare."

Poor Naveen white-knuckled his weapon while I debated whether the demon or Eli had better odds of surviving.

My daughter flung a lock of lank black hair out of her face. "Daaad." I swear she rolled her eyes, but as they were jet-black pools—including the sclera—it didn't land.

It amused the crap out of me, though my grin turned to a gasp as the demon clicked its pincers together twice and they doubled in size, knocking a photo of Eli and Sadie off an end table.

Eli winced. "That was a nice picture."

"Glass is replaceable." Nav toed the broken frame closer so it wouldn't get trampled on, and the demon shot past him, crackling with blue light.

Sadie kicked the evil crab away with a screech, narrowly avoiding having her toes smushed.

"Sades!" I jumped out of the chair, my scythe in hand. One of the many, many perks of being a Banim Shovavim was that my magic could take the form of a sharp and deadly shadow scythe. Extremely good for slicing crabs and defending my child.

Eli had shot to his feet as well, but only to yank an armchair out of demon range.

"Ew! Ew! Ew!" Sadie did a little hopping dance, almost tripping over the large carrier crate infused with magic that the demon had been transported in. "I felt its pus jigglies."

I sank back into my seat, shooting Eli a warning look over the tops of my sunglasses. He returned it, stroking the top of his armchair entirely unrepentantly.

An electric sizzling sound was followed by the reek of cooking flesh, and Nav yanked his staff out of the demon's eye. "Stay put, you little bugger." He ignored the growling monstrosity flailing about with clacking claws and one blazing red eye to frown at his mentee. "Darling, what were our rules? We don't touch it directly, am I correct?"

Sadie hung her head. "Magic or run."

For reasons we had yet to confirm but suspected had to do with Sadie being an Ohrist baby carried to term inside her Banim Shovavim mom, my kid's magic didn't manifest like normal. My daughter was definitely Ohrist, albeit with rare nulling magic, yet she required an animated shadow to use her powers. That was a Banim Shovavim trick, though ours were normal where Sadie's was pure bright light.

Another key difference was that if a demon slashed her shadow, Sadie's insides wouldn't ooze out, nor would she feel pain like I did when anything hurt my shadow, Delilah, as we'd learned fifteen minutes ago.

"Your reaction was understandable, but 'magic or run' must become instinct," Nav said. "Unlike your mother, you don't get injured if your shadow does, so use it for all physical contact." He bonked the fiend on the top of its head to shut it up. "We'll double down on those drills."

"That's an excellent idea." I rested my scythe in my lap. "Let's practice running away."

Since Sadie's power and its unique manifestation would never be explained beyond conjecture, Sadie, Eli, and I had decided to focus on her mastering her abilities instead. Running away was top of the list as far as I was concerned.

Eli smoothed out the bunched-up plastic sheeting. "No drills. Nav has enough to do keeping the demon away from the walls."

Murder in his eyes, Nav swung his staff in my ex's direction.

I smacked the big dummy, who clearly wanted to never get laid again. "Sadie's had enough demon exposure for one day."

Sadie took a few deep breaths, her hands on her belly and her shadow's brilliance dimming from midday-sun-on-snow to flood-lights-on-a-soccer-field-at-night. "Stop helicopter parenting me."

I wagged a finger at her. "Or 'Thanks, Mom, for valuing my well-being over that of furniture.'"

"Mir." Eli draped an arm over my shoulders. "Sadie's got this."

4

She preened at his words. I, however, knocked the traitor's arm off me.

"Nothing is going to happen to her," he continued. "Especially if she doesn't ever touch the damn thing to see if she can null its magic."

"Oh my God!" Sadie snapped. "You touch it if you want it that badly."

Nav whistled loudly, shocking the humans into silence and the demon into rearing onto its long hind legs. It swiped a pincer along the mantel, hitting Eli's framed Canucks' jersey, which hung in the spot of honor above the fireplace and was signed by his man crush Henrik Sedin and Sedin's twin brother, Daniel.

The jersey thudded to the ground, the glass shattering.

Eli emitted a half swooning, half guttural cry that was almost operatic in nature, freaking out the demon, whose pincer then caught on the hem of the uniform.

Nav herded the creature away from the jersey. "It's merely a snag."

Eli grabbed his prized possession, examined it with laser precision, then clutched it to his chest with a sigh of relief.

"The stupid hockey jersey gets you more upset than the smashed photo of me?" Sadie's white shadow flickered wildly.

Her dad carefully folded the garment. "I mean, I have lots of wonderful pictures of you, pumpkin."

I slashed a hand across my throat.

He deflated back into his chair, the jersey out of harm's way. "Love you, baby girl."

"You suck!" Her shadow pulsed like a strobe light.

"Breathe, poppet," Nav drawled. "Let's try this again."

I slapped a hand over my sunglasses. "I can't watch."

"So you keep saying, and yet you remain," Nav said.

"Less sarcasm, more demon minding." I jerked a thumb at him.

"Amen," Eli said.

Making a snarky face at both of us, Nav herded the demon toward a corner where it bumped into a large planter.

"My ficus," Eli moaned, earning a huff from our child.

"Yes, darling," Nav said absently, raking a lock of platinum hair off his brown skin.

Smirking, I nudged my ex, who blushed.

"What happened to not watching?" Eli muttered.

He'd informed me about a week ago that he and Nav were giving a relationship a go. I was thrilled that my gay ex-husband had found bliss with the best friend of the man I was stuck in relationship purgatory with. Would Laurent and I be as entertaining as the two of them? My smile dimmed. Maybe a better question was: would we ever get a chance to go on a date?

Eli pried my fingers off his hockey jersey with a scowl, smoothing out the wrinkles I'd made.

Sadie cracked her neck from side to side. "Okay, hold that chump down, Nav. I'm going in."

He forced the demon onto its belly, pinning it in place with his staff. "Approach it from the side because its peripheral vision is rubbish."

The crab-demon broke into a high-pitched, distressed chittering.

While Sadie waved at it like a photographer attempting to get a baby's attention, her shadow sidled up next to the creature and laid its palm on a cluster of pustules.

Sadie shuddered.

"Gently," Eli said. "Don't break them."

"Or I'll die a painful death. Yup, I heard Nav the first thirty-seven times he warned me."

"I don't want to repaint," Eli said mildly.

Sadie didn't appreciate my smothered snicker.

Nav snapped his fingers. "Hush, the pair of you. What do you feel, Sadie?"

She narrowed her eyes. Unlike Delilah, her shadow didn't have its own vision she could utilize. "A buzzing under its skin."

"Can you catch its magic with yours?" he asked.

She bit her lip, her face screwed up in concentration, then shook her head.

"You said it was a long shot that she'd be able to null demon magic," I said. "She tried. It didn't work. Let's wrap it—"

Sadie, Nav, and Eli turned identical looks of exasperation on me. I swear, even the demon looked annoyed.

Resigned, I swept out an arm. "By all means. Carry on." I poked at a seam on a cushion, until Eli covered my hand with a look that said *cut it out*.

"Remember the visualizations I had you working on?" Nav said.

Sadie exhaled slowly. Her shadow moved its hand over the demon's back, pausing and hovering over a back claw. "Here."

"Now try," Nav said.

The shadow's light rippled like a wave crashing against the demon's hard shell.

I leaned closer, engrossed despite my anxiety.

Sadie planted herself in a low squat. Her shadow rippled faster, but the demon continued to struggle, kept in place by Nav's weapon. Finally, her shade fell apart, reforming on the ground like a normal one. "Its magic slips away. I can't null it."

Nav patted her head with his free hand. "It was a good try. Now we know that demons are a no-go for you."

Letting out a relieved breath, I pulled off my sunglasses.

Bouncing on her toes, Sadie swung around to her dad with a gleam in her eyes. "Can I?"

Eli rubbed a hand over the back of his neck, though Nav looked as confused as I was.

My shoulders crept up and I turned slowly and menacingly to Eli, who'd once again fallen prey to Sadie's puppy dog eyes. "Can she what?"

"I might have promised her a feel-better treat if she couldn't null its magic." He tossed his shades onto the couch.

"What kind of—" I put two and two together and groaned. "Not Phoebe."

My kid had whipped the mini flamethrower out from the back of her loose shirt with a flourish.

"Our duplex is not insured for inside use of that weapon." I'd checked.

"It's on the lowest setting, Mother." With a dramatic sigh, Sadie uncapped it, her finger on the trigger.

"Don't 'Mother' me, child. Not committing arson is a perfectly reasonable request."

"Dad promised."

I ground my teeth together hard enough to take off a layer of enamel. Oh goody. Now I was somehow Bad Cop for telling our daughter not to incinerate her father's home. "A little support here?"

"Sadie," Eli said, "your mom is right."

I leaned back into the couch and crossed my arms smugly. "Thank you."

"You have to use it on the patio."

I face-palmed.

"Yay! Come on, Nav! Let's flambé this puppy." Sadie flung open the sliding door and bounded into the yard.

"By all means," Nav grumbled, poking the crab-demon with the light staff. "Allow me, a respected and formidable demon hunter, to do all the grunt work while you sit there, Your Majesty, and bask in the glow of your child's love."

Eli blew him an air kiss, and Nav whacked the demon in response.

Stunned from all its up close and personal time with the light staff, the demon wove precariously as if drunk.

"You are so making it up to me later," Nav said.

"Gross!" I yanked my feet onto the sofa before the demon crashed into them.

At Nav's prodding, it slid across the plastic, but he prevented it from bashing into the dining room table and spewing venomous pus. Or was that poisonous? Whatever. Dead was dead.

"'Gross' says the woman sleeping with my best friend." Nav pushed his sunglasses into his hair. "None of us are overjoyed at the incestuousness of this situation."

"Not you and Eli, dummy. The demon. Its pus bubbles were vibrating." I threw a hand over my face. "Look out!"

The demon spun like a tornado, knocking Nav's feet out from under him, then scampered nimbly outside.

I jumped up to run after it, but Nav was already halfway out the sliding door, staff held aloft like a spear. Remarkable reflexes, that man.

Eli lifted a corner of the sofa to release the tarp. "Thank God that's over."

What an adorable optimist.

2

"IS THE DEMON DEAD YET?" I CALLED OUT, TWISTING around to glance through the open sliding door. No one answered me, and I couldn't see down to the patio.

"Nav will handle it," Eli said, balling up the plastic sheeting.

"Sadie!" I yelled.

"What?" Her bellow from outside could be heard two blocks away.

"Stay on the tile," her useless father called out. "And careful of the demon," he added at my glower.

"I think I liked you better when you had issues with magic," I said.

"A flamethrower isn't magic, and you're the one who gave it to her."

I buried my head in my hands. "I did, didn't I?"

Eli patted my back. "I've trained her on its proper use."

Outside, Sadie gave a jubilant shout and started singing "Step in Time" from *Mary Poppins*, her happy dance song. What a weirdo.

I sniffed the air wafting in through the open sliding door, and my stomach lurched at the putrid odor of old fish. "That's rancid."

Nav strode back inside, his bootheels ringing against the floorboards. He had a look of disgust on his face. "Your excitable child took a selfie with the oil stain that was left after she torched the bugger."

"She stained the flagstone?" Eli ran out in his bare feet.

Nav snorted. "The man frames a hockey jersey like a Van Gogh and gets upset about a little demon stain?" He shook his head. "His priorities mystify me."

I stood up, stretching out my back. "He's not even distractable during hockey games."

"Trust me," Nav said darkly. "I know."

I laughed and grabbed my cardigan off the back of the chair, wondering if Laurent was back from his dybbuk hunting trip. It would be nice to have something distract me from the boxes of material I still had to catalogue for Tatiana's memoirs. Something other than obsessing over how next to track down my parents' murderer. "You two have plans tonight?"

Had they woken up this morning together? Done the crossword in bed? I didn't miss doing that with Eli, but I craved the intimacy of a lazy Sunday with someone I cared about.

"Eli made a reservation at the new restaurant in the casino downtown, but the stench of that dead demon has put me off seafood." Nav pushed the sofa back into place. "Luckily, it wasn't that old, because once its kind gets into the hundred, hundred fifty year range, you need a gas mask when you kill it."

I slung the sweater over my shoulder, then stilled. "Casino."

He snagged one end of the rolled-up area rug and shook it out. "Yes, Miriam. With the bright lights, overpriced food, and strange architecture to coerce one into losing one's sense of time and everything. Perhaps even a hand or two of blackjack."

"No." I moved out of his way. "The raven shifter's casino. When Laurent and I went there it was hit by a blind spot." It wasn't a normal blind spot. Not only had it blown up to enormous proportions, fighting back when I attempted to protect the shifters, but it was a directed attack on the casino itself, a magic force. The birds hadn't known who was behind it. "Poe said some Ohrists can manipulate ohr, but it's rare. But now, combined with what you said about how long demons live, it's got me wondering. Could a demon manipulate ohr? Throw up a blind spot?"

Nav smoothed the carpet edge down with his foot. "Not a blind spot, but some varieties with certain fire capabilities could produce something similar."

My eyes widened. "Fire? Do they have other powers? Like snapping someone's neck from a distance?"

"Doubtful. It's not compatible magic."

"Okay, what about working with someone who could kill that way?"

"Demons don't generally play nicely together." He lifted the coffee table with a grunt and set it in front of the sofa. "And they wouldn't partner up with a human unless they were bound."

"Are fire demons easy to bind, like kargh thurt demons?"

"Why do I sense there is more to this question?" Nav dropped onto the couch.

"Whoever killed my parents snapped their necks and set a very controlled fire to burn any trace of evidence. Same with the murder of the Lonestar who covered their deaths up. I thought it was the same person, but the assassinations happened almost thirty years apart."

"A demon bound to different humans?" He shook his head, resting his boots on the coffee table. "The binding would dissolve after they completed the task, or when the person who bound them died. Though it is possible that an Ohrist bound a fire demon the first time, then a family member or someone with a vested interest did the same thing years later."

I smiled widely. "You're so smart."

"Thank—" He cut himself off, narrowed his eyes, and then chucked a pillow at me. "No to whatever you're thinking of asking me to do. Your requests are annoying."

"This one is simple. Find a fire demon who would have been

active in Northern British Columbia back when my parents were killed and a few months ago with the Lonestar."

"I'll just check the sign-in sheet, shall I?"

I winged the pillow back at him. "No need to get snotty."

His expression softened. "You're right. It's an important factor to rule out, but that request is impossible. I might—*might*, mind you—be able to ascertain which demons were around at the time of McMurtry's death, but not if they'd been bound. And your parents were killed too far back to cross-reference it. I'm sorry."

"Thanks anyway." I paused. "You know Eli'll kill you for putting your boots on his coffee table."

Nav winked at me. "He's fun to rile."

"And with that, I'm out." I waved and headed into Eli's backyard. "Sadie, I'm going home."

She sat on the bottom stair of the balcony, texting, and totally ignoring her father, who was hosing down the flagstones by her feet.

"Yo. Princess," I said.

"I heard you." She didn't lift her eyes from the screen.

Her father mimed strangling her, but I frowned.

Sadie was still in the very new stages of dealing with the existence of magic, which had been compounded by our shocking discovery about two weeks ago that she had powers of her own. She found it isolating not to be able to discuss her powers with her Sapien friends and boyfriend. Much as she loved having magic, this was a million times harder to go through on her own, so I was trying to remain sympathetic.

I took a deep, steadying breath.

She looked up. "Can I go out with my friends?"

"You have until tomorrow," I said. "Besides, I thought Nessa and the gang were busy."

"They are. These are some Ohrist kids."

Eli twisted off the tap, water dribbling from the hose. "What Ohrist kids?"

Sadie shrugged. "Some people Tovah knows."

My friends' niece, Tovah, seemed like a nice young woman the one time I met her, but this was the first I was hearing of these other Ohrists. As happy as I was that Sadie was connecting with other kids like her, I was still her parent.

"I'd like more information than that," I said.

Sadie stood, sliding her phone into her pocket. "First you say you want me to meet Ohrists my age, now I get the third degree when I try?"

"This is hardly the third degree." Eli smiled evilly. "You want me to really bust that out, I will."

She threw up her hands. "I don't know more than that. They're meeting at a coffee shop nearby. Can I go or not?"

A large part of me wanted to say "not" because she was being a little cow. However, that meant I'd get to hang out with Miss Moody all night. I twisted my cardigan into a ball. She had no idea how lucky she was to have two parents to guide her through her teen years, never mind have the privilege of acting out, instead of feeling the pressure to be perfect. It took me years to believe that Goldie would keep me if I got angry or snippy.

I can't remember what I was so mad about the first time I actually talked back to my cousin, but I didn't just blurt out my feelings. I spent several nights practicing mouthing the words silently to myself, building up to voicing them in the safety of my room. That part was still far too clear, as was Goldie's confusion when, instead of my prepared rational speech, my emotions got the better of me and I blew up at her well after the initial conflict.

I leaned against the stair rail. None of that was Sadie's fault, and considering how much anxiety she'd had over the years from self-imposed perfectionist tendencies, it was a relief and a gift that she felt confident enough to test her limits.

"Go," I said. "But be back by dinner."

"Thanks." She hugged me and her father, her spirits instantly restored, and hopped through the door in the fence connecting his yard to mine.

"Her mood swings are bad enough," I said, "but she jumps between them so fast. I get she's acting out because so much has happened, but it's exhausting."

Eli wrapped the hose up on its mounted holder. "Careful, babe. If she gets really pissed off, she could null your magic."

"You're loving this, aren't you? I'm the one she could go all Mr. Hyde on while you, the one who passed down her magic gene, is exempt?"

He spread his index finger and thumb apart. "A little bit, yeah."

I made the sign of the evil eye. "I hope you go into one of your food comas after dinner tonight and can't perform."

Eli gasped. "That's cold."

"Truth hurts, baby." I ducked through the door in our fence and headed into my house, beelining directly for my office. A bland space with functional furniture, it wasn't used for much more than a dumping ground. When I'd brought work home as a law librarian, I'd done it from the comfort of my living room sofa.

I kept meaning to transform the office, along with the rest of the beige void I lived in, but with so many more pressing issues, I hadn't even gotten around to painting a single room. The only thing I'd done was install a giant whiteboard on one wall. At the top, I'd taped a photo of my parents with "Who killed them?" written above it.

I sighed. My murder board was another reason for Sadie's current mood. I'd told her the truth about my parents' deaths at our last therapy session. Her anger at me hiding magic from her was nothing compared to the thundercloud that had descended upon learning that I'd lied to her about her grandparents dying in a fire.

After two days of Sadie slamming my office door closed so she didn't have to see the board, I learned my lesson and kept the door permanently shut. She was working through the whole sordid story in her own time; I'd seen her standing in here studying the board the other night, but we had yet to discuss it.

Sitting down in my creaky chair, I pushed that aside to focus on the facts of Mom's and Dad's deaths. A line led from their picture to a grainy photo of Calvin Jones with bullet points written underneath. Ohrist. Hired my parents to cause Tatiana's car crash and steal Ascendant.

Calvin hung on to the amplifier for two years before Tatiana tracked him down. She also killed him in retaliation for her car crash, but before he died, he mentioned a buyer he had lined up for the artifact.

We'd discounted the buyer being involved in my parents' murders because they wouldn't have waited two years to get the Ascendant from Jones. Especially not if it was a demon.

I uncapped a blue dry erase marker and drew a line from Calvin to a new box that I labeled "demon accomplice?" along with: long life spans, murders happened almost thirty years apart, ability to manipulate ohr/fire, difficult to track down.

Calvin could have snapped my parents' necks from a distance and then a demon set the fire, since Nav didn't believe it likely that the demon had done both, but did Jones have any children or grandchildren? Had they been tasked with keeping the truth of the original murders suppressed and killed McMurtry?

After adding "kids?" to the board, I popped the cap on and off the marker. Calvin had died years ago. Any role in my parents' murders couldn't be proved, and even if it could, it's not like he could be put on trial. He didn't need to bequeath some grand plan to keep his name clear.

I struck an X through Calvin's name. Was this all down to some demon agenda? Around the time my parents died, McMurtry was taken into the demon realm and infected with a demon parasite, which cured his terminal cancer. That Lonestar was the link that spanned almost three decades, before he too was executed. I gnawed on the marker cap. If a fire demon had teamed up with an Ohrist, why kill my parents? Mom and Dad didn't have the Ascendant, Calvin did. Also, a demon wouldn't have bothered to cover up the murders.

Cursing, I threw the marker onto the desk.

The only other photo on my murder board was taped to the right side. It was an old picture of Arlo Garcia, the Banim Shovavim currently being tortured in the Kefitzat Haderech. He'd earned a special damnation at the hands of three Banim Shovavim–hating angels—Senoi, Sansenoi, and Sammaneglof—for using the Ascendant.

I'd managed one visit with him, but the KH had made it clear no further ones were permitted. I rubbed my temples. Very clear.

Arlo had been Tatiana's client, hiring her to find and steal the Ascendant. She'd spent three years tracking it down, finally snatching it from a shadowy group called the Consortium. They'd used it to open a portal to Gehenna to let dybbuks out, in aid of their experiments on Sapiens to turn them into hosts. Luckily, they hadn't had a full-strength Banim Shovavim on the job, and so those malevolent spirits weren't unleashed on the entire world.

Even though Arlo's name hadn't been erased, I'd crossed him off my list of suspects. That left the Consortium as the only other human players on the board, but my gut said they weren't part of this. Plus, I'd done a bit of surreptitious digging into them with the help of Ryann Esposito, the head Lonestar in Vancouver.

Officially, she wasn't allowed to go after the Consortium. It was too big and too powerful, and Lonestar leadership had deemed it a Sapien problem, but Ryann and I had channeled our mutual frustration into a covert investigation. Sadly, we hadn't learned anything beyond what we already knew. The other reason that organization didn't work as a possibility? I'd been with McMurtry when he was killed. Even if the murderer hadn't known who I was at the time, anyone with half a brain would have found out my identity and my connection to all of this and gone after me to shut me up.

Yet, no one had.

Why was I allowed to live, and why were great pains taken with the other murders to cover them up? I kept circling back to those questions.

I'd reached out to the gargoyles who played intermediary between supernaturals, hoping to find someone with answers. The one in Northern BC back when my parents died was no longer alive, however, if a new gargoyle had taken the old one's place, maybe they'd been brought up to speed on past events.

Harry, a speakeasy bartender and the go-to gargoyle here in Vancouver, was looking into this for me. Generally, I pestered him for meetings with Zev BatKian, but for better or worse, I'd graduated to making direct contact with the bloodsucker.

Sighing, I rubbed a smear of blue marker off my hand. My leads were slim, and the group working on this with me was comprised of a mouthy golem, a wolf shifter with a somewhat dimmed yet not depleted death wish, an elderly woman with powerful magic and a massive thirst for vengeance, and me.

Yeah, I couldn't see anything possibly going wrong.

3

SADIE BABBLED HAPPILY THROUGH DINNER ABOUT HER new buddies. Genuinely pleased that she was expanding her circle to kids with magic, I enjoyed her insights on her friends' personalities. Still, I was relieved when she went to call her boyfriend, Caleb, after we'd cleaned up the remains of our pasta primavera. He was in grade twelve to Sadie's grade eleven, but both Eli and I had thoroughly vetted the boy and deemed him a good kid, and I'd hate for Sadie's first relationship to crash and burn over magic.

I was wiping down the counter listening to the radio when the music cut away to the top local news stories. Apparently, it had been a slow weekend, because they were still reporting the headline from Friday about Sabrina Mayhew's big legal victory.

The young hotshot Crown Counsel prosecutor had taken down Paxton Craig, a local crime boss who'd proven slippery beyond belief. No one had ever gotten charges to stick to the leader of the Hastings Mill gang, much less managed to convict him on money laundering and fraud with a unanimous guilty verdict from the jury.

Sabrina was barely in her thirties; this win allowed her to write her ticket and either have her pick of prosecution cases or jump into the more lucrative criminal defense attorney arena. Good on her. She had to be smart, savvy, and ruthless to have defeated the team of high-priced lawyers that Craig had on staff.

My phone rang.

Speaking of smart, savvy, and ruthless...

"Hi, Tatiana," I said into my cell to the crisp strikes of a manual typewriter on her end. "Tell me that's your first chapter and not more emails."

My boss had recently purchased a Bluetooth keyboard that simulated the look and feel of a vintage typewriter, claiming she'd get more done on her memoirs that way. Except she was so excited by it that she'd decided to send letters to all her old friends with whom she'd lost contact.

"Don't ask and you won't be disappointed," Tatiana said sardonically in her raspy New Yorker accent. "You busy?"

Sadie and I had finished our Sunday night *Buffy* rewatch last week and had yet to pick our next show for tonight since my kid hadn't been sure if she'd be up to it after the demon session earlier.

"No, why?"

"You need to go to Vegas," she said. "A potential client requires our expertise."

"Yeah?" I transferred the cell to my other shoulder so I could rinse out the rag I'd been using to get grit off the stove. "What's the gig?"

"Missing person. Vincenzo BatXoha will fill you in when you get there."

The cloth splatted into the sink. "Since when do we work for vamps?"

When estries, the demons who originally sired vampires, turned humans, their children took on a new surname. It was comprised of the demon's name plus "bat," which was Hebrew for "daughter of," because to estries, all their children were daughters. Even though estries hadn't been seen in hundreds of years (well, not most of them), and nowadays only the undead created more of their kind, they kept the name of their founding demon in tribute.

Tatiana scoffed. "Did I miss a memo about the devaluation of vampire-owned currency?"

I dried off my hands, raising an eyebrow at her snippiness. "Laurent hasn't contacted you yet, huh?"

My boss's snark amped up in direct proportion to her concern, and ever since she and her nephew had exchanged "I love yous," she'd hovered over him protectively.

Just before he left on this dybbuk hunting job, Laurent had confessed he was fleeing town more to get away from this weird new dynamic between the two of them than to kill the dybbuk. And with him, that was saying something.

"Hmph," Tatiana said. "He should check in."

"You're right." I grabbed a pen and paper. "He should, but back to the case. Who could a vamp need us to locate?"

"Vincenzo declined to elaborate over the phone." She paused. "If he wants us to find anyone of interest to Zev, tell him we can't take him on as a client. He understands that you have authorization to speak on my behalf."

This was a major victory and I preened. Tatiana was trusting me big-time. Compared to last month when she'd impaled me with a tree root and left me to die, it was also a massive improvement.

I rubbed my gut where the wound had been. Trust aside, it would take time for me to truly forgive her.

And I'd never forget. I wasn't the same woman who'd reclaimed her magic a few months ago.

I wasn't even the same woman I'd been two weeks ago. My thirst for knowledge had sent me into the fire, and while I'd come out of the forge hardened, I missed the soft, naïve parts of me that I'd shed and wondered what else I'd lose before my quest to find my parents' killer was over.

My pen tore through the paper, the heart I'd been tracing and retracing shredded. "Anything about Vincenzo I should know going in? How powerful is he? Zev levels?"

"Hard to say. He's not as old as Zev, but he was an Ohrist when he was turned, so he'll have kept that magic. No idea what it is."

To my knowledge, the only other Ohrist vamp I knew was Zev's descendent Celeste BatSila, who he'd had turned by a different vampire line. Lonestars had banned changing Ohrists some time ago, but Zev had his ways. Well, I handled Celeste just fine, so maybe Vincenzo's additional powers wouldn't be an issue.

"Is he expecting me at a specific time?" I snapped off the radio midway through breaking news about another gang member found dead.

"Yes. In an hour." She gave me the address.

"Thanks for the notice."

"You're welcome. Take Emmett along as muscle." She disconnected in typical Tatiana fashion without saying goodbye and before I could ask any further questions.

Without any inkling of the vampire's Ohrist magic, it would be good to have backup, but why did BatXoha want us? Surely there was a magic fixer in Las Vegas.

More importantly, how should I dress to impress? This was my first client meeting in my new exalted position as one of the associates in Cassin & Associates.

I opted for a black pantsuit, my hair pulled back into a severe bun, and dark red lipstick: a look that my friend Mara at the law firm swore terrified the lawyers, visions of library hell dancing in their heads.

"Hey, Sades." I poked my head in her bedroom. It was better for her to know the truth of my magic jaunts than worry that I was lying when I ventured to the grocery store.

My kid looked up from her laptop and made a face. "New bedtime look?"

"I have to meet with a prospective client. Lock up tight before you go to sleep or stay at your dad's."

She returned to her computer.

I braced a hand on the doorframe. "Did you hear me?"

"Yeah. You're off running around with strange magic people, but I have to ask permission to play with new kids like I'm in preschool."

My hand tightened on the wood. Her acting out was a relief and a gift. "Your dad and I want to know who you're hanging out with, especially when they have magic."

She rolled her eyes. "Why? You think I'm going to go all Bad Willow because of peer pressure?"

I do not want to regift my child. I do not want to regift my child. "Enough, Sadie," I said in a hard voice.

She shrugged and started typing.

"I'll see you later." She didn't answer. I didn't expect her to.

I sat on the bottom stair for a few minutes. Then I got ready to meet a vampire.

Given I'd have to debrief with Tatiana afterward, I drove to her house in the swanky Shaughnessy neighborhood. For a world-renowned artist, her rustic Tudor Revival mansion in sedate colors evoked tea and cucumber sandwiches with the crusts cut off, not a passionate spirit and a wicked eye for detail. Her late husband, Samuel, had purchased it since his Jewish parents had been denied owning a home in this historically WASP-y neighborhood, but it was also excellent camouflage for the magic fixer.

Tatiana's assistant, Marjorie, opened the door for me. A smart, sweet girl in her early twenties with a tendre for my golem partner, she put up with a lot of attitude from our boss, but after Tatiana had made her cry recently, the artist had been more respectful of the young woman.

"Hi, Miri. She's in the kitchen."

"Thanks, I'll follow the sound of the typewriter." I stepped inside, my flats slapping softly against the floor. The stilettos I'd purchased to originally go with this outfit would have completed the dominatrix vibe, but I could run in flats. Function over fashion. "Is the clacking driving you crazy?"

"Mildly. I've been stretching canvases and it's not as noticeable up in the studio."

"Is Emmett in the kitchen?"

"He's getting ready." Marjorie's cheeks pinked and her eyes sparkled. "He's been telling me all about his adventures with you." Okay, this was too adorable. "He's so brave."

There was no follow-up comment of "You're so brave too," which told me everything I needed about what role I'd been relegated in these adventures. Well, we all exaggerated to impress our crushes. Emmett was pretty courageous, and hopefully he'd never be exposed like I was when I told Eli that I'd love to run a five-kilometer race with him on no notice because running was the best high ever.

"He really is." I headed down the hallway.

Dusk had fallen outside the windows of the kitchen, and the mint-green cabinets, cherry-red furniture, and bold checkerboard floor were a cheerful haven against the darkening overcast sky.

Tatiana sat at the large table, a pen in her mouth and her brows furrowed behind her oversize red glasses, typing using only her index fingers. Oy vey.

"Greetings and salutations," I said.

She glanced up and snorted a laugh that spat the pen out of her mouth.

I crossed my arms. "What's so funny?"

"Emmett," she called out, "Miriam's here."

"Coming." There was the clatter of heels and the golem entered the room.

My eyebrows shot into my hairline. "What the fuck? No way. No. Noooo. Nope."

The golem was dressed eerily similar to me, except with a bald head, and a pair of heels that I'd break an ankle in.

"A good power suit is a wardrobe staple." Tatiana smiled

indulgently at him, before nodding at me. "Though I'm surprised you know that."

"You bought it for him?" I crossed my arms. "Order him to take it off."

Emmett stroked his lapels. "Get real. I'm clearly the winner in the 'who wore it better?' competition. Go change into your regular sadness clothes, toots."

"First of all." I shot him the finger. "And B, you're supposed to be my muscle. Dress menacingly."

He sneered. "You think I can scare a vamp in bouncer black? This way, I'm formidable because of my unpredictability." He flexed his biceps. "Will I use my brawn? My shoe? Who can say?" He touched his lip then snapped his fingers at me. "Got any more lipstick? I'm out and I need a little coverage."

I lunged at him, but he dashed behind Tatiana.

"She's not letting me live my truth," he whined.

"You can live your truth all you want! But not like this. I've never even gone twinsies with my kid, and I'm not about to start with you."

"How was I supposed to know you'd finally wear something interesting?"

"Kindeleh, sha!" Tatiana wagged a finger at us. "You both look very fetching."

Emmett and I narrowed our eyes at each other, our lips curled in disdain.

"Go, meet with Vincenzo or you'll be late. And if you make me look bad, I'll make you have a terrible day."

My co-associate and I ducked our heads. "Yes, Tatiana," we muttered.

"Come on." I grabbed Emmett's elbow and hauled him into the Kefitzat Haderech.

The shadows rippled outward like splashing through a warm, shallow pond, and the ground turned spongey for the long, slow blink that it took to transition to the magic space. I kept my gaze firmly forward, convinced that if I looked down, gravity would rear its head and I'd plummet Wile E. Coyote–style into a bottomless chasm. Once we landed in the cave, I tugged Emmett and myself free with the same gentle pull as exiting waves on the shore, shadows falling off us like droplets.

Pyotr, the gloomy gargoyle guardian, was crouched in front of a large grow light, testing the soil for his Chinese evergreen. During a recent garden store visit—that I still couldn't believe we'd gotten away with—Pyotr had fallen in love with these leaves edged in red, named the plant Scarlet, and clutched it to his chest like a teddy bear.

As soon as he got back to the KH, he'd replanted Scarlet into a fancy and far-too-large ceramic planter that he kept next to his table.

"Scarlet's looking good," Emmett said. He'd also been with us on the garden store outing.

Pyotr lumbered to his feet with a creak, his large stone hand on his lower back. "Ooh. Best friend Sadie give team outfits for us?"

My daughter had dressed him and Emmett on our garden store jaunt, earning Pyotr's everlasting adoration.

I hated to dash the hope shining in his eyes, but dressing like Emmett was bad enough. I wasn't adding this lanky stone creature into our wardrobe mix. "Sorry, buddy. It's a work thing."

Pyotr shrugged, his bulbous eyes drooping farther down his face as if this was exactly what he expected from the universe. "Take sock."

Emmett almost sprained an ankle over the uneven cave floor, hurrying to the stone slab to pick a sock off the pile. He was like a little kid insisting on pressing the elevator button—which he also did. He circled the pile, his finger on his lip, muttering under his breath.

"Pick one and let's go," I said.

"This one." His hand shot out, paused, then jumped two socks over to a bright yellow ankle sock with bumblebee stripes on the pompom.

The narrow green door that always led out of this section appeared in the rock face. The KH had never acknowledged Emmett's presence, processing him as any other inanimate object with Ohrist magic on it. We exited, following the dimly lit path, but walked for only a couple of minutes before a purple door revealed itself and we stepped into the warm Vegas night.

I blinked my eyes against the riot of neon on the strip, an acid trip–inspired global journey from the Statue of Liberty to the Eiffel Tower, past an Egyptian pyramid, and along Italian fountains.

The streets thronged with tourists flitting from one casino to the other, kids with balloon hats taking photos with beloved fictional characters, and couples perusing brightly lit billboards for a celebrity act or a famous restaurant.

Emmett had stopped dead, his eyes wide and his mouth falling open.

I tugged on his arm, glancing around nervously, but this was Vegas, baby. Everyone assumed he was part of some schtick. Still, the clock was ticking. "This way."

We darted down a side street, stopping in front of the entrance to Tempest. The neon sign had a palm tree for the T, but otherwise little to telegraph what to expect inside this nightclub.

"Let me do the talking," I told my partner.

The bouncer's impassive expression didn't twitch a muscle at the sight of Emmett and me.

"Hi," I said. "We—"

"Get in line," he grunted and jerked his chin at the velvet rope with no one behind it.

A group of young, beautiful twentysomething men and women with glowing skin, salon-ad hair, and clothes that hugged their lithe bodies like a long-overdue reunion sailed past us into the club.

Emmett reached for one dude's electric-blue velvet suit as he passed by, but I slapped his hand down.

Part of me wanted to absolutely destroy the bouncer with some viciously witty remarks on ageism, but I had a better card to play.

"We have an appointment with Mr. BatXoha." I handed him a business card. "Still want us to get in line?"

Turning away, he touched his Bluetooth earpiece, talking softly into it. With a final, doubtful look, he allowed us entrance. "Head for the VIP area at the back. Boss will find you."

"Welcome to Tempest," I said, marching inside. "Have a great night."

The sound of waves washed over us, timed to the pulsing of the glittering star show projected overhead in the wide foyer. Curving around the coat check, smoky glass doors slid open at our approach, leading to a manmade beach.

Revelers drank, danced, and flirted to the scent of coconut- and salt-tinged sea air artificially pumped in, while Latin music throbbed through speakers inset among the palm trees. It took a moment to figure out where the reality of this "tropical island" stopped and the nonmagical light of the moon casting a smudgy white glow on the horizon began because it was so cleverly done that I swore I was outside and across the water from the far-off lights of civilization.

I kept a tight hold on Emmett, who watched the proceedings with naked longing. Maybe he and Pyotr could go to Blood Alley or some other Ohrist nightlife space. Ooh, or he could take Marjorie somewhere safe on a date. I made a note to discuss that with him at some point.

For now, we pushed our way through the crowd, dodging servers carrying trays of huge colorful drinks and overly enthusiastic dancers on the sand.

The VIP lounge was nothing more than a large raised wooden floor dotted with private gazebos, their filmy curtains fluttering in the breeze. A female bouncer with a flat, hard stare and heels that made Emmett's look like old lady slippers guarded another velvet rope.

I shivered involuntarily, keeping my gaze on her chin, instead of provoking her with direct contact. Her lips quirked up.

"Valentinos?" Emmett motioned at her shoes.

She gave an approving nod. "Good eye."

Emmett shrugged. "A girl's gotta know her shoes." He frowned and pointed at my flats. "Strictly bargain bin, but we're just work colleagues."

After the number of times I'd saved his ungrateful ass, he was disavowing me? Emmett's need to pump up his own confidence at the expense of others wasn't exactly news to me, but it still grated. I unclenched my fists, reminding myself that he'd grown a lot in his short life and not to take too much offense at the areas still lacking in self-awareness.

"Can't pick your coworkers." The bouncer unclipped the rope.

My partner nodded. "Amen, sister."

"Vincenzo awaits you in the gazebo on the far left," she said.

Emmett gave an annoyed huff because I was still gaping at him. "Newbies. Come along, Miriam. Don't keep our client waiting."

I followed hot on his heels. "Disrespect me like that again and I'll have Jude turn you into a paperweight."

He shrugged it off with "Then dress better," walked into the gazebo we'd been directed to, and stiffened. I thought it was from my sweet burn, but when I rammed into his back and he didn't move an inch, I inwardly groaned. Great. Hit with magic before we'd even spoken. This meeting was going to go swimmingly.

A handsome thirtysomething man with bronze skin and tawny hair awaited us. His simple white linen shirt and slacks displayed the strong line of his shoulders and well-muscled thighs without being showy.

"Are you Mr. BatXoha?" Was it better if magic man was our vampire client or just another minion to get past? So hard to decide.

"Sí. Call me Vincenzo." His white, even teeth flashed against his skin when he smiled, free of any hint of fangs. "Tatiana did not mention anyone else would be at this meeting," he said with a light Spanish accent.

"Bringing a partner is standard procedure," I said.

The vampire raised an eyebrow. "Is it?"

A compulsion nipped at my brain with sharp teeth. I winced but was able to withstand the directive to blurt all my secrets out and give this vampire the keys to my vulnerabilities.

"It is," I said, glancing at said backup to see if the compulsion had affected him. Last time that happened, it hadn't gone well for either of us.

Emmett remained totally still. He appeared to be powered down, the light in his eyes dimmed.

I rested my hand on the golem's shoulder and prayed it looked casual. "Did you kill him?"

"That would be inhospitable," BatXoha said.

An inch and a half to our left was a shadow that would get Emmett and me back to the KH. I tightened my grip, ready to shove us to safety if necessary. This was a ridiculous amount of fuckery for the first fifteen seconds of a meeting where the client should have been trying to impress us, not piss us off. Poor Emmett.

"Please unfreeze him."

Vincenzo trailed a finger almost absently along his throat and I swallowed. "We will speak while your partner waits here." He extended a hand to a seat. "No harm will come to him and he will leave in good health."

At my hesitation, the vamp's eyebrows rose.

I had to follow him. That much was clear. But two could play games on multiple levels, so I walked toward the chairs, sucking in a sharp breath when I "accidentally" brushed against him. He generated body heat. A tan could be faked, even some other details of being human could be replicated by your garden variety bloodsucker. But to actually generate heat when you were undead?

Who was this guy, and how powerful did he have to be to do that?

Unlike the other gazebos, which contained L-shaped cushioned benches and were strung with fairy lights and flickering candles in glass holders, this one had two white rattan chairs angled to make the most of the ocean view. The enchanting vista aside, this gazebo was designed for meetings, not socializing.

I settled myself into a chair and thought it out. It had to be part of his Ohrist powers. Their magic was rooted in the ability to manipulate light and life energy. If Vincenzo could reduce someone's life energy to the point where they were frozen and dead-looking (Exhibit A: Emmett), then he could probably do the opposite and enhance his own appearance despite being a vampire (Exhibit B: himself).

My nails tapped out a nervous rhythm on the chair's armrest, and I willed myself to stop it. It would be lovely to swing my feet up onto the scuffed white railing, lulled by the motion of the waves and the sensual salsa music, but I sat too stiffly to even enjoy the plush padding.

What would happen to me if I didn't complete his assignment? Or worse, what if I had to refuse it altogether?

I glanced at Emmett and I shuddered.

Vincenzo regarded me frankly, leaning forward with his elbows draped on his thighs, prisms of white light from a small chandelier overhead washing over his almost-pretty features. He tapped the toe of a burgundy sharkskin shoe while I tried not to fidget, but the hairs on the back of my neck stood up under his scrutiny.

What was I being judged on? Age? Appearance? My outfit that projected law firm confidence in a law firm was laughable on this beach. I couldn't even curse Tatiana for setting me up, because it was entirely possible she hadn't known about the club either.

Vincenzo was still evaluating me with that cool and even stare. I smoothed out my extremely out of place suit and formed a list of all my credentials. I was damn good at this job, despite whatever he may have to say about my wardrobe.

But then he spoke, and it wasn't a snide comment or a dismissal.

"My fiancée is missing."

4

WELL, SHIT. I NODDED, MOSTLY TO COMPOSE MY thoughts. *Please don't let his fiancée be one of Zev's vamps.* Things were so strained between Zev and Tatiana that there was no way we could encroach on his territory without getting his permission, even to investigate this case. "Are they a vampire?"

"No. She's Sapien."

Not a search for a wayward vampire bride, and thus of no concern to BatKian. My shoulders descended a notch. But only a notch. "May I ask your intentions once she's found?"

His brow furrowed. "I'm going to marry her."

His genuine confusion over the question eased my fears that he wanted her located to enact vengeance. Much as I really didn't want to ask the follow-up, I had to. "Could she have gone missing of her own volition?"

It was a woman's prerogative, after all.

"No." His fangs descended, his eyes blazing red, and I flinched, calculating how fast I could tip my chair into the shadows and escape. The vampire wrestled his anger under control, his fangs retracting first and his irises flipping between red and brown before settling into their regular chocolate color. "I'm not used to being questioned."

I almost snorted. I'd never have guessed.

"We've kept our relationship secret for a number of reasons," he said.

"A vampire marrying a Sapien is unusual," I conceded, "but it's not illegal. Even if you were planning to turn her, that's permitted." Much to my disgust.

"Bree has no desire to stop being human. Not now, at least. Maybe in the far-off future she'll choose differently..." His gaze went soft and his hand flitted to his left ring finger.

I gentled my tone. "You love her a great deal and I'll do everything I can to find her, but I need more details. Why else did you keep the relationship secret? Would your public persona as a club owner be problematic for friends or family?"

"Bree doesn't have any family and very few close friends. They don't know that I'm a vampire, but they are aware of our relationship and that I'm a businessman from Vegas." He shook his head. "She's in a job that is rife with conflict. I expect someone in her professional life has come after her."

This was getting more interesting by the moment because *my* first assumption was that a fellow vampire had gone after her as Vincenzo's weak link. "Do you have any enemies who would strike at you through Bree?"

He broke the arm off his chair like he was snapping a pencil in half. "She is not missing because of me."

I bowed my head so he didn't see my eye roll. Typical arrogant vampire, refusing to entertain that he might be at fault. "Apologies. I didn't mean to suggest that was the case. However—"

He growled and I quickly changed the topic.

"What does Bree do?" I checked in on Emmett, but he was as well as could be for a giant paperweight. I just had to hope that Vincenzo made good on his word and restored him.

"She's a lawyer. You might know her as Sabrina Mayhew."

"Fuck me!" I clapped my hand over my mouth at my impropriety, my eyes wide and my heart hammering. "I, uh, mean,

Sabrina is your fiancée? But she was all over the news two days ago when the verdict came out."

"She nailed that pendejo." The pride in his voice was unmistakable.

"Did Paxton Craig have magic?"

"No."

"Is that why you contacted Tatiana instead of a fixer here in Vegas? Sabrina lives in Vancouver and we give you the home turf advantage?"

"That and because very few of the older generation of machers have survived to Tatiana's age. It speaks to a certain..." He drew his brows together as if searching for the right word. "Resiliency."

No kidding. A macher was the Yiddish word for both a big shot and a fixer. It was a testament to Tatiana's skill and intelligence that she'd hadn't merely survived, she was still in the magic fixer game.

"When was the last time you spoke with Sabrina?" I said.

"After the trial's end," he said. "Bree was taking her staff out for dinner and drinks Friday night in thanks, then she was supposed to fly here yesterday for our private ceremony. There's no way she would have missed it." He held my gaze a beat too long as if daring me to refute that point. Not being suicidal, I didn't. "I'm unable to get hold of her now."

"Assuming she wasn't in an accident—"

"It's Craig's people," he said. "Find Sabrina. And her abductors."

He'd kill them. Presuming Vincenzo's hypothesis was correct, and it was another human who'd targeted Sabrina? I worried at my bottom lip. She had a solid conviction rate under her belt, and along with that came enemies.

Did any of them deserve to die if they'd gone after her?

Did I care?

A group of women danced onto the sand along the shore,

drinks in hand. Did Bree make it to dinner, flush with triumph, and accepting well-deserved toasts?

"Okay," I said.

"One other condition. No one outside your firm is to know she's missing." Vincenzo's eyes glowed a burnt crimson.

A human bride would be seen by many in the supernatural community as a huge weakness on BatXoha's part. His power and reputation would stave off all but the most foolish or arrogant taking him on, but if his fiancée was missing? It wouldn't matter if it was because she did a runner or was kidnapped, others would take it as a rallying cry to attack the vampire who couldn't even babysit a human.

I nodded. "Provided the case doesn't run us up against Zev BatKian, in which case he'd have to be briefed. Otherwise you have my word."

"Your word isn't enough. You will swear a blood oath."

A what now? Nope. Didn't need to know. Wasn't happening. I wasn't about to sacrifice my free will with a magic promise to some unfamiliar vampire. Correction: anyone familiar or not. "I'm more a pinky swear person."

"It's nonnegotiable," he said.

"You should have thought of that before you gave me the details. I won't swear a blood oath, and if you kill me, you'll upset my boss. She'll probably drag the Lonestars and Mr. BatKian's crew into it." I shrugged. "You have my word, and now I'd like my partner—fuck!"

Faster than I could process, he'd bit my wrist. The pain was a quick sting; far worse was that my magic had gone dormant.

The tied-back curtains fluttered free to enclose the three of us in the gazebo, and struggle as I might, Vincenzo was too strong to pull free of his grip.

His eyes flashed and his fingers bit into my flesh. "Say you swear you will do everything in your power to find Sabrina and only share information about her disappearance with Tatiana."

My foot twitched. I longed to kick him in the shins, bite his hand, or play dirty in any way to free myself, but Emmett was still frozen, and while hurting the vampire would feel great, there was a lot to be said for biding my time. I'd make him pay for this, but it would be at a moment of my choosing, when he least expected it.

I brought my emotions under control with steely determination. "I swear to do everything in my power to find Sabrina and only share information about her disappearance with my *team*," I said coldly.

Vincenzo glanced at Emmett. "Very well." After I made the vow, the vampire impatiently prompted me to finish it with *May the binding magic bleed me dry should I break this oath.*

"Bleed me dry?" When his fingers pressed hard enough into my flesh to bruise it, I repeated the rest of the phrase like a good girl. My body tingled and the skin around his bite turned red and painful enough to make my eyes water. I pressed my lips together. Just when I thought a cry would burst out of me, the ache disappeared.

"If your intentions weren't pure, you'd have died." Vincenzo released me, the tight lines at the corners of his eyes and mouth easing and his shoulders relaxing. "I had to be sure. Bree is everything to me."

I shook out my arm. The mark had faded but not disappeared. Just like my resentment. If I was in his position, I'd also want an iron-clad guarantee, but he'd stolen my consent. I probably would have agreed! This just made things between us feel sour from the start.

I couldn't do anything about it because the asshole had suppressed my magic when he'd bitten me, and it was only the faintest tingle now. "How long will the bite last?"

"A few hours. However, the oath stands for all time."

"I figured." Why should any of this be easy? I folded my sleeves over my hands.

"You will keep me continually updated." He paused. "Please."

I sighed. "Of course."

Vincenzo clapped Emmett on the shoulder, and the golem shook himself like a cat rousing from a nap. "Tatiana has a reputation for being the best. Don't make me doubt the veracity of that. Find Bree quickly." He strode off, a deceptively lithe powerhouse in top-dollar threads.

"He turned me into a goddamned statue." Emmett clenched his fists.

I placed my hand on his shoulder, putting any lingering resentment at his earlier assholeness aside. "Yeah, but it's because he perceived you as a threat."

Emmett pressed his lips into a tight grimace and shook me off. "I need a drink."

"No, you—" Argh. I pushed through the crowd after the stubborn ass who knew damn well that drinking could send him into a prophecy state from which he might not return.

Conscious of the looks we were attracting as Emmett elbowed his way through the patrons, I hauled him outside, dragging him down the block and away from the lineup that had started outside Tempest. "We're still on company time. Act professional."

He wiped the lipstick off his mouth with the back of his hand. "I'm a joke. The lump you haul out when you need me to get past a heartbeat alarm because otherwise I'm useless."

A prickly sensation raced across my shoulder blades, but no one in the line was paying attention to us and the rest of the block was empty.

"Even Laurent gets compelled by vamps," I said. "That doesn't make you useless."

"I've had my leg torn off, been passed around from boss to boss like cheap wine, almost got us fried by a magic booby trap, and you keep having to rescue me."

I rubbed my sore wrist, tempering my desire to tell him to snap out of his pity party in the face of his glum resignation. "That's not true. When we were in the Human Race—"

"You mean well, toots, but forget it."

The sensation that we were being watched grew stronger, so I summoned Delilah. "Let's discuss this at home."

At the sight of my animated shadow, Emmett slumped his shoulders. "Why? Are there more bad guys for you to defend me from?" He shuffled off around the corner back to the strip.

There was a loud bang from the alley nearby that sounded eerily like a body getting thrown into a wall. I didn't want to leave Emmett, but I couldn't not help if someone was hurt. But no, when I hurried over to investigate, it was just an employee tossing garbage bags into a dumpster, and by the time I made it to the strip with Delilah curled around my feet, Emmett was gone.

I pushed through the crowds that had gotten less family friendly, with boisterous people openly drinking in the streets, and swore. Just because people had so far assumed he was part of some act didn't mean he could get away with publicly flaunting his supernatural appearance.

If the local Lonestars got wind of this, we'd both be screwed.

I jumped up, trying to see over other people's heads for a glimpse of him. Usually, I loved neon signage, but there was so much of it that everyone was bathed in a red wash that made it hard to find the golem's red clay skin. I whipped out my phone and called him, but it went to voice mail.

"Damn it, Emmett," I muttered.

"You have been summoned." A baby-faced young man with Jesus hair intercepted me holding a crudely made amulet with three cartoony figures engraved on it. Near as I could tell, the center image was a wingless bird. Great. Another weird street recruiter for some wacky religion.

"No, thanks." I pushed past him, phone in hand, but he grabbed my arm, his eyes gleaming fervently, and a warning siren went off in my head. Was he the one I'd sensed watching me earlier? I jerked free. "What do you want?"

"It is a great honor to be summoned." He showed me the amulet again like that would clear everything up.

Was he trying to serve me with that thing like it was a legal summons?

I flicked the artifact with a finger. "Did the judge send you?" I mocked.

A painfully wide smile cracked over his face. "Judge, jury, and executioner." He bounced on his toes. "But no, this is a summons."

He wasn't dybbuk-possessed and there was no hint of fangs, but his delirious gleam sent shivers up my spine. I stumbled backward, knocking into a couple who reeked of beer.

Regaining my footing, I sprinted across a road as the light changed from red to green and was almost mowed down by a stretch limo. The cacophony of music and chatter, lights and flashing billboard images was overwhelming and disorienting. Zigzagging, my heart in my throat, I wove through the crowded streets as fast as I could, but every time I glanced over my shoulder, dude remained on my tail, waving the amulet.

I slipped inside a crowded casino. Slot machines jangled, coins clanked, and chips were shuffled in a discordant wash of sound. I veered down a row of video poker machines, hid behind a group of showgirls, and called Emmett again.

Thankfully, he picked up.

"Where are you?" I said urgently.

"Answer the summons," an unfamiliar female voice said.

I shivered, despite a hot flash making me schvitz. Do as the weird strangers commanded or endanger my friend? I stepped out from my hiding spot. Screw that. We'd had a few bad hands with Vincenzo, but it was time to turn our luck around.

We were in Vegas, after all. And if I had to bust out my magic? I smiled coldly. Well, what happened in Vegas, and all that.

5

STILL ON THE PHONE WITH THE WOMAN, I HURRIED TO the exit, dodging a group of excited newcomers ready to hit the jackpot. "Is my friend okay?"

"Of course. But you must answer the summons."

"Where?"

She gave me an address, ordered me to be there in ten minutes, and disconnected.

Who were these people? I opened a maps app. It made no sense for them to be affiliated with Vincenzo. Could they be behind Sabrina's disappearance? They might be part of the Consortium, but that didn't feel right either.

Was "summoned" a euphemism for "blackmailed"? James Learsdon had intended to coerce me into helping him locate the Ascendant, and Zev had done the same. Had someone new shown up to make me find the artifact for them? Well, they were shit out of luck.

The app showed an eight-minute walk to get to the location. That woman had given me ten minutes, but I could get there in seconds using the KH. She probably didn't know I was Banim Shovavim. That was a plus, but it made this situation even more confusing. Why did they want me so badly?

I raced to the bathrooms, locked myself into a dimly lit stall, and stepped through the shadows. Poor Pyotr barely got a hello, but he nodded sympathetically when I rushed to the sock pile, grabbed a silky thigh-high stocking, and spun for the exit, explaining I had to rescue Emmett.

My destination was Ye Olde Wedding House, a cute yellow bungalow with a sign in fancy script out front.

Remaining cloaked, I circled the house, peering through stained-glass windows into a pink and white foyer. Through the next set of windows, I made out an airy room containing several rows of pews. Emmett sat at the end of the petal-strewn aisle, on the stair leading to a wedding arch covered in flowers.

The Jesus-haired dude I'd encountered sat in profile in the first pew while a young woman with a sweet face and blond hair to her waist burned incense in a pewter stand next to the arch. Like the man who'd first accosted me, she appeared human, but best to assume they had magic.

Had I been targeted by some hippie cult?

I weighed my options. The easiest plan would be to rush in cloaked, grab Emmett, and jet out through the shadows. Except that wouldn't get me answers, and if I didn't know who was after me, then I couldn't formulate the best plan for survival.

The bells over the front door rang jauntily when I entered, but I stepped into the inner sanctum with my hands up, my eyes wide, and my breath coming in shallow pants.

"I'm here," I said in a quivering voice. My nose twitched at the incense fogging the air. "We'll do whatever you want if you let us go unharmed."

Emmett glanced at me sharply, then snorted quietly.

The woman stepped out from behind the pulpit, flicking a lighter on and off. "You won't be disappointed."

"Who wants to see me?"

Her smile faltered. "Don't you know?"

"I really don't," I said. "Is this about Sabrina?"

"Who?" She shot an uncertain look at her partner.

He stood up with the amulet outstretched. "It doesn't matter. You have been summoned and must answer. It is a great honor."

"Yeah, you've said. Over and over again." Emmett jerked his chin at me. "Next time I'm used as bait, at least let it be by a top-tier supervillain. Someone Vincenzo level, ya know?"

"I'll do my best," I said dryly.

"Let us proceed." The man shook his wrists, and two blades appeared in his hands, the amulet gone. Nice sleight of hand—not actual magic—but hell no.

Shadows swirled over my skin while Emmett roared and rushed the woman, tackling her.

"That's for lying about seeing the wax museum," he said.

I rolled my eyes. That's how they got him to go with them? Did I really need to warn the golem to stay away from promises of puppies and candy?

Her partner had dropped to one knee, carving a swirly pattern into the wood floor with the blades, his eyes darting to the ceiling continuously.

Huh. I sidled closer to him, ready to call up Delilah. "Being given directions for the summons, are you?"

He grinned, and that cult-like zeal from one so young unnerved me. "It's exciting, isn't it?" he said.

For you, maybe. "Who should I address my greetings and salutations to?"

He laughed like I was a toddler who'd asked to drive a car. "You haven't earned first-name privileges."

I ruled out a demon because their minions didn't come off as sugared-up toddlers hyped for playground time, plus, I'd totally have been given some evil moniker. "How about you let me hold the amulet, since I'm being summoned and all?"

He clapped his hands together, thrilled I was finally on board with the plan, and with great reverence, he deposited the amulet in my palm.

"So." I tapped the three figures engraved on it. "Want to chat about these?"

"The less said the better." He yanked the blades out from the floor to resume carving, but the pattern was too abstract to identify. Was he making a tiny landing pad? A *Star Trek* "beam me up" circle?

Before I could inquire further, Emmett grunted, using some crazy wrestling move to get the woman in a headlock. She was fighting back but only to escape, not to hurt the golem.

"I must light the candles!" she cried, stretching for the fallen lighter. "It is my sacred duty! And I get to use the scented ones."

I sighed. Time to leave Planet Crazy. "Uh, Emmett?"

"Tap out, bitch," he snarled, knuckling blondie's head. "I dare you."

"That's enough, Hulk Hogan." I pulled him off her.

Jesus-hair dude was oblivious to these antics. His intricate floor art was very pretty but sadly we wouldn't be here to see it to completion.

I ran down the aisle, trusting Emmett to follow, but out of nowhere, the door to the foyer slammed shut and a lock was engaged.

The woman dropped her outstretched hands, nodding in satisfaction, while her partner glanced up, his brows drawn together, and pushed to his feet. "Wait! It's almost time." He waved at us with the blades.

Emmett took that as a threat, grabbed the man, and threw him to the ground.

Dude lost his hold on his weapons. Typical hippie. Then one whistled past me into the wall, and a sharp pain seared through my body.

Something had happened that was bad. I doubled over. I didn't want to look, didn't want to know the horrible specifics, but my vision was blurry. Colors blended into sweaty smudges, and I squeezed my eyes closed, my heart hammering in my ears. No. This couldn't be the end.

"Emmett..." I gritted out through my teeth against the pain.

The golem caught me before I listed totally sideways and hit the ground. Scooping me up, he kicked down the foyer door and ran into a shadowy corner.

"Knives hurt," I mumbled.

He slapped my cheek. "Come on, toots. You're our only way home. Go into the Kefitzat Haderech." He slapped me harder. "That's an order."

I reached for the shadows to part them, but they slid out of my hands like beaded curtains. My entire left side where the blade was embedded had gone numb, and when I tried to reach out for the KH again, I couldn't move that arm.

"Taxi?" I slurred.

"Please come back! You don't want to miss this." The blonde ran toward us with a fat lit candle reeking of vanilla in her hand.

Emmett pinched me hard.

Delilah shot out of me and grabbed him by the throat.

"KH," he croaked.

She tugged and the three of us fell through the shadows.

There was no sock pile, no Pyotr, and not even Emmett. There was me, standing on a rocky ledge in a vast underground grotto with turquoise waters so vibrant they lit up the room.

A serpentine shadow as wide as my car slithered beneath the surface. It raised its scaly armored head partway out of the water, the fathomless gaze of its obsidian eyes boring into my soul.

Two razor-sharp fangs protruded from its upper lip and smoke belched from nostrils the size of tires, forming into a familiar phantom skeleton face.

"I am Leviathan," Smoky intoned. The rest of the sea monster silently stared at me. Ah. They were one and the same.

That said, I took a very large step back, because Smoky was no less terrifying for learning that it was nasal exhaust. "I am Miriam."

The corporeal portion of the sea monster submerged itself until only Smoky and the crown of the monster's head remained visible. "I was deemed an abomination and exiled here."

"You and me both." I blotted sweat off my chest. Add some

45

eucalyptus to the hot, humid air and I could have a proper cleansing schvitz. "Okay, not so much exiled, but as a Banim Shovavim, Senoi, Sansenoi, and Sammaneglof had high hopes of my eternal damnation." Oh. Hang on. Despite my previous assumption, Smoky-Leviathan wasn't the one in charge of the KH. "Was it the three angels who exiled you? Do they run the Kefitzat Haderech?"

Both the skeleton face's expression and the waters darkened, frost skirting out to tendril up the cave walls. "The Kefitzat Haderech is a Banim Shovavim space. Those intruders imposed their vile magic upon it."

When Senoi, Sansenoi, and Sammaneglof couldn't kill Lilith's second batch of children, the Banim Shovavim, they fed us a story about how we were wicked and doomed to eternal damnation. Unless we realized that it was just a story, not an inevitable outcome, our self-judgment often doomed our spirits to eternally wander the KH's paths.

"I didn't realize that the KH was initially separate from the magic torture inflicted by the angels. This is why we can't have nice things." I kicked at a rock, sending it bouncing into the cave wall.

"They despise Lilith's progeny," Smoky said. "The story of your wickedness is not merely recounted, it magically takes root in you, infusing the listener with doubts as to their true nature. Should a Banim Shovavim not see through it in time, condemnation is assured, and the angels' torture carried out."

"Judge, jury, and executioner," I said bitterly. My hand flew to my mouth. Were Senoi, Sansenoi, and Sammaneglof the ones who had summoned me? Were they looking to get me in their clutches some other way since I'd called bullshit on the story? That would never happen.

"They stuck you here as well," I said. "Another abomination locked up with the damned Banim Shovavim for company."

"Should I fail to do their bidding, I shall be smote," the monster intoned.

Smoky didn't harbor antipathy toward Banim Shovavim like the angels did. In fact, he deemed Ohrists the abominations, declaring Banim Shovavim superior.

"The enemy of my enemy is my friend?" I said. "Is that your deal?"

"Just so."

"I'm happy to play on the same team, but why did you bring me here?"

"You have been poisoned. I can heal you."

Until the phantom skeleton face spoke those words, I'd forgotten that I had a knife sticking out of me because I didn't feel any pain. "Did you treat me when I was impaled on the tree?"

"Yes."

"Well, thanks for that and please heal away now."

"You will promise to free me," it said.

I spread my hands wide. "Look, you have my deepest sympathies for your plight, but I'm full up on tasks."

Smoky whipped around me, scattering pebbles and dirt, the lake water crashing angrily onto the rocky strip of land. "You have the Ascendant."

Squinting, I protected my face with my forearm, the wet air acquiring an acrid tinge. "I had it. Past tense. It's gone."

Everything went very still.

I cracked an eye open. Smoky hovered over the water with a defeated expression.

"Pyotr has told me of the outside world," it said. "It has changed much since I roamed free." It turned its face to the ceiling as if seeking out the sun. "I had hoped to see it once more." Then, as though realizing it was being awfully genuine with someone it was supposed to intimidate into serving it, the creature's expression went back to neutral. "I have wasted your time. I shall heal you now."

I had way too much on my plate, and besides, the Leviathan was a sea monster. It lived in the depths, so it wasn't as if it was missing out on beach vacations and a European tour. What did it expect me to do? Sneak into Gehenna, find and steal the Ascendant back, and hand it over to set it free?

At the same time, it didn't deserve to be stuck in here any more than the trapped Banim Shovavim did. Wasn't I constantly working to make sure my people weren't absolutely hated on for no reason? Could I really leave someone in a similar position?

A voice in my head started cackling hysterically.

I sighed. "I'll work on it."

Smoky beamed, exposing all its pointy teeth, and the Leviathan raised his head to turn wide, shining eyes on me.

I ducked my head, rubbing the back of my neck under the weight of all that joy—and monster. Smoky was an extension of the Leviathan and more than enough to deal with on its own. The serpent could remain out of sight, please and thank you. Oh well, at least they both liked me.

A giant claw rose from the water, each of its nails the length of my forearm.

Yelping, I stumbled back. Had I read this wrong?

The Leviathan scooped me up and dunked me in the warm water.

I plugged my nose, closed my mouth, and tried not to think of fecal counts.

Black and purple tendrils oozed from my body to mix with the blood being cleansed from my stab wound. The blade dislodged from my flesh, falling away to the dark depths.

The sea monster deposited me back on the shore, dripping wet, but fully healed and able to take the first full breath since I'd been stabbed. Too bad Vincenzo's puncture wound remained.

"Got a hair dryer?" I said.

The monster raised its head from the water and blew on me. Its breath caressed my skin like a hot desert wind, drying all of me in seconds, unlike every hand dryer in every women's restroom I'd ever used. Then Smoky dissipated and the Leviathan sank beneath the surface, lost to sight.

6

A MOMENT LATER, I FOUND MYSELF ON THE SOCK PILE, dazed but alive and dry. "Pyotr?"

The gargoyle ran over to me, wringing his hands. "Where you go?"

"I met the Leviathan." I mimed a scary face and Pyotr's eyebrows shot up.

"Is shy. You're lucky. And no scar." The gargoyle gently touched my side. "Does it hurt?"

"Not at all."

Emmett yelled out in triumph to the sound of explosions. The golem sat at Pyotr's table playing some old game involving alien spaceships.

"Don't disturb your space battle to worry about me," I said.

His thick clay fingers jabbed the controller buttons rapidly. "I knew you'd be back."

His utter confidence in me eased a knot of tension in my chest. A very small knot because apparently, I was going to attempt my half-assed plan to retrieve the Ascendant.

I swung my feet onto the ground, dislodging socks, lifted my torn jacket, and inspected my camisole. Damn it, I liked this suit.

Podium music played from the television.

"All right. Emmett, time to go."

"One more game," he whined.

"Now," I snapped. My day wasn't over and it had already lasted two lifetimes too long.

"Sorry, Miri."

Nodding at his contrite tone, I snagged a sock off the pile for the trip home.

Emmett gave Pyotr the controller back. "Come see me sometime. Bring the game."

Pyotr swung his stone head back to me. "Miriam, you arrange, yes?"

"Sure thing," I said wearily. They could provide their own snacks, though.

A couple minutes later, Emmett and I entered Tatiana's foyer. I kicked off my shoes and took off my ripped blazer.

"We're back," I called out.

"I'm in the kitchen."

Emmett went to his room to quickly change since the heels were killing his feet, so I headed in by myself, hoping the typewriter keyboard had been retired for the night.

"The triumphant associates return with news of our new client." An asshole one. Rubbing my throbbing wrist, I stepped into the kitchen and pulled up short.

The first thing I saw was my boss standing at the island in a 1950s-style shirtdress with a white ruffled apron over it.

The second was a very fine male denim-clad ass sticking out from under the sink. Next to him was a wooden toolbox, the tools all jumbled together. My fingers twitched, longing to organize it properly. At least that's the story I was going with.

"You've got drain trap problems?" I said. The oath's warning signal fell dormant. "I could have fixed that for you." I may have let Eli deal with my garden, but I'd learned to do small home repairs back when we were still married.

"Always nice to see a woman fending for herself," Tatiana said.

The man's upper body was wedged into the cupboard, the rest of him sitting back on his calves.

"C'est moi," Laurent said in a muffled voice.

Oh, good, because I'd felt vaguely guilty about how hard I was ogling this stranger. Let the guilt-free ogling commence! On second thought, I wrested my gaze away from Laurent's butt, thinking only the chastest of thoughts in front of his aunt.

Like how I wanted to curl up against him, my cheek pressed to his chest, wrapped up in a hug, and let all my stress wash away.

"Hey, Huff 'n' Puff." I pulled my hair free of its messy bun and ran my fingers through it to fluff up my curls.

Tatiana peered into a mixing bowl containing a brown gloopy mess, holding a wooden spoon over it like a wand that would transform the mush into something edible.

"You cook?" I leaned across the island from her.

Tatiana stabbed the concoction before yanking the spoon out. "How do you think I feed myself?"

"Sucking the marrow from the bones of your enemies? Takeout?"

Laurent barked a laugh, hit something hard enough for us to hear the thud, and then swore.

I almost offered to kiss it better. Then I could work my way down to the ticklish divot on his right hip and— *Chaste thoughts, Feldman.*

"This isn't cooking," Tatiana said. "It's baking."

"It is?" I scrunched up my face.

Laurent emerged from the cupboard, rubbing his head, ratchet in hand. He was deliciously rumpled, his brows furrowed in a tiny scowl and his lush lips in a pout. There was a smear of dirt across one bicep. "She offered to make me cookies in exchange for dealing with the sink."

"Should have asked to read the fine print beforehand," I said. "Like whether she could bake."

He dropped the ratchet into the toolbox and wiped his hands

on a rag. "I thought she'd have Marjorie make them as usual. Marjorie makes very good cookies."

"Not as good as mine," I said snippily.

Tatiana snorted, dumping the bowl's contents into the trash. "You weren't supposed to know it was Marjorie all those times."

"No wonder your assistant doesn't make you cookies, Tatiana," I said. "You force her into ghostbaking yours. Shame on you."

"It's the thought that counts." Tatiana tossed the bowl and spoon into the sink.

"Not when it comes to cookies," Laurent said sulkily. "Alors, your drain is unclogged."

"Thank you, Lolo." She sat down at the table, rubbing her temples. "Oy. That was exhausting."

I stifled a laugh. This entire exchange had done wonders to elevate my mood. I'd still take a Laurent hug, though.

"Leave the toolbox," she said. "Emmett can put it away."

"Walk me out?" Laurent raised an eyebrow at me.

"Sure." That sounded appropriately casual for the modern, sexually empowered woman I was, and oh dear Lord, did I want to jump him. I followed him down the hallway. "Did you find the dyb—"

He nudged me up against the wall, bracing a hand to one side of my head. With his other, he traced along the gash in my camisole. "Trouble tonight?"

My heart pounded and I took a deep breath, my chest rising and falling and the fabric settling back into place with a soft swish. "Nothing I couldn't handle. I'll fill you in when I have more time."

Laurent ripped open portals to Gehenna when he tossed dybbuks back in, though it was a one-way deal, thankfully, and more didn't fly out when he dispatched them back there. That ability, however, plus my sneaky Banim Shovavim ways might be enough to get me to the Ascendent, but I wanted to bask in his concern right now, not deal with his anger when he learned of my bargain with the Leviathan.

"Okay." His eyes darted to my décolletage, but he dropped his hand with a quick head shake. "I owe you a date."

"You do." Inhaling his rich cedar scent, I wrapped my arms around his chest.

He hugged me back, resting his cheek on the top of my head. "Are you free Tuesday night? I know it is not a typical date night, but Friday is too far away."

I smiled, my breathing slowing to match his, and snuggled in tighter. "It's my week with Sadie."

He groaned.

"But I'm sure she can spare me for an evening."

"Good. Wear stretchy clothes. You like to eat."

I jolted up stiffly, my arms crossed. "I beg your pardon?"

The doofus nodded enthusiastically. "Oui. A family that I helped a couple years ago have a restaurant. They're hosting some celebrity New York chef who's doing a tasting menu that lasts several hours." He rubbed his hands together. "Lots of courses and lots of time to spend together."

Ah. He wasn't being insensitive. Just clueless. Shifters needed to consume a lot of calories, while for me, it was more a choice than a requirement. "I'll wear my snazziest stretchy clothes."

A tiny crease appeared between his brows, and I could tell he was wondering if he'd screwed up, so I grinned.

A long, lingering dinner with lots of wine and conversation and the building up of sexual tension? Hell, yeah. I pressed a hand to my flushed cheek, my insides fizzing in anticipation. "It sounds lovely."

"It does." His eyes bored into mine.

I bit my bottom lip, savoring the energy crackling between our bodies.

"Move it, wolf," Emmett said, clomping down the hallway

toward us. "We have a debrief and you're not invited." He'd changed into a blue smoking jacket and black boxer shorts.

Flirting interruptus.

Laurent stepped back. "I'll pick you up at seven. Until Tuesday."

"Until then."

He bared his teeth at Emmett as they passed each other.

The second the front door closed, Emmett shook his head. "What you see in that dude is beyond me. I know it's hard for old women in the dating pool, but—oomph."

I dug my elbow into his gut.

"Which totally doesn't apply to you, you spring chicken," he said.

"Just shut up." I stomped back into the kitchen, the golem chortling softly as he followed.

We sat down at the large round table, and Tatiana pushed her laptop and retro keyboard to one side.

"Nu?" she said. "This job with Vincenzo won't encroach on Zev's territory?"

"Not unless a vampire is responsible for his missing Sapien fiancée." I held up a hand to cut off Tatiana's protest, and her immediate switch to hear me out was a nice change from the days I'd tiptoed around her power. "I made it clear that we'd need Zev's permission to hand that person over should that be the case." I paused. "He doesn't intend to turn her. She isn't interested."

Emmett grimaced. "Gross. She'll grow old and wrinkly while he stays hot. Why would a vamp agree to that?"

Tatiana fiddled with her large onyx cocktail ring, her expression wistful. "Vampires can be surprisingly romantic."

"Is this based on personal experience?" I said super casually.

She speared me with a flat look. "I've met lots of vampires, Miriam. They have a wide range of personalities."

That wasn't an answer, and from her supercilious raised

eyebrow, she was enjoying withholding her history with Zev from me. Eh. I'd break her. Eventually.

"Where do you intend to start?" Tatiana said.

"With a woman who knows everything." I plucked a grape from the fruit bowl in the center of the table and tossed it in my mouth.

"An oracle?" Emmett said.

"The administrative assistant at my old law firm. So pretty much." I drummed my fingers on the table. "Also, you should know that Vincenzo doesn't want anyone other than us to know about Sabrina's disappearance." I flashed the puncture marks.

Emmett leaned in for a better look. "He bit you?"

"Blood oath," I said.

"If we break it, do you suffer?" His brows drew together. Aw, look at him being worried for me.

"Unfortunately, yes," Tatiana said.

Her mild tone provoked a hot rush of anger inside me. "Thanks so much for alerting me to that possibility. He just grabbed me and bit. Took my magic in the moment too, so I couldn't even fight him off."

She opened her mouth to reply, but Emmett cut her off with a chuckle.

He rubbed his hands together. "So all I have to do is get a little chatty and we can watch you squirm. Epic."

Delilah had him in a chokehold in the blink of an eye.

Tatiana frowned. "That's a bit extreme."

"Emmett threatened me first," I said.

"Not that." My boss pulled out her phone. "I'm going to have a word with our client about him not trusting my impeccable reputation vis-à-vis confidentiality and success rates."

I took her cell away. "Missing the point."

Emmett pounded on the table for mercy and my shadow released him. "You're no fun," he sulked.

"Vincenzo's fiancée vanished," I said, ignoring him, "and he not only refuses to even consider one of his enemies might be behind it, he went to this extreme to keep it all hush-hush. How hard would it be to dig deeper into our client without alerting anyone to the facts?"

Tatiana swept some dead flower petals off the table and dumped them into a vase containing a wilted bouquet. "Difficult, since one of my prime sources is dead to me, but not impossible."

"Undead," Emmett corrected. "Mr. BatKian."

Tatiana narrowed her eyes and I kicked him under the table.

Emmett mimed zipping his lips.

"It's a red flag that our client doesn't want to pursue every angle to find her." Tatiana infused her magic into the flowers, and the blooms perked up into their full glory. "Leave that with Emmett and me while you investigate Sabrina's movements. Anything else?"

I removed the amulet from my trouser pocket and set it on the table.

She picked it up, running a finger over the clay edges. "What's this? Some chachka Sadie made when she was little? I wouldn't advise wearing it as jewelry if that's what you were wondering."

Emmett snickered.

Splaying my hands on the table, I silently counted to ten. "I took this from a couple of randos who kidnapped Emmett to force me to answer some summons."

"Which would have been a great honor," Emmett snarked.

"Yeah, well. Any thoughts?"

Tatiana tossed the amulet onto the table. "I'd get better branding if I were them. Those figures have absolutely no sense of style."

"That's your issue right now, is it?"

Tatiana shrugged. "Branding is everything. And no, I've never seen anything like this. Do you think whoever summoned you also took Sabrina?"

"I doubt it. Her name didn't spark any recognition and they

were pretty focused on me." I flipped the amulet over, hoping for some clarification, but the back was unmarked. "The last person who showed this much interest was James Learsdon, hoping to blackmail me into finding the Ascendant for him. Could this amulet be related to it? You think these engravings are demons?" I paused. "Or the three angels who damn Banim Shovavim?"

Either instance was terrifying, but neither felt right. Two of the figures resembled cartoonish birds, while one was sort of a headless upside-down hockey stick shape stuck on a rectangle with legs.

Plus, the pair at the wedding venue hadn't attempted to kill us. Demons trafficked in pain while the three angels harbored no love for my kind. I sighed. The only way to know for sure was to stay vigilant while investigating further.

Tatiana traced the figures with her finger. "There are three of them, but the figures are so crude, it's hard to say."

"Can I show it to Naveen? See if it ties to any demon complicit in my parents' or McMurtry's murders?"

She jabbed her bony finger into my chest, and I winced. "If any mention of my involvement with the Ascendant gets out," she said, "I'm burning your precious business cards and using you as fuel. But do as you must."

Nothing like a clear directive.

7

MONDAY STARTED WITH A VISIT TO MY FAVORITE former colleague, Mara. My crashing hard in the wee hours and sleeping in late made my timing perfect for her midafternoon coffee break.

The steely-eyed sixtysomething greeted me at reception with a huge hug. "Miri! I was so glad to get your text. Is it okay if we grab coffee in the lobby? Daniel starts a trial next week and he's in his usual tizzy."

Her boss, the Shechtman in Chan Wilkins Shechtman LLP, was usually extremely good-natured. The notable exception to this was in the week before a trial when his fierce moods and perfectionist tendencies had broken more than one young lawyer. Mara, who'd been with Daniel for years, was the only one who dared tear a strip off him.

We cut through the large atrium's open art gallery whose current photography exhibit featured Vancouver's neon signs from the 1950s onward. My favorites were tied between the one for a children's clothing store featuring a girl swinging on a swing and the sign for a long-defunct nightclub called the Smilin' Buddha Cabaret.

Mara grabbed us a table at the café in the back while I

purchased our lattes. Once we settled in, we chatted about working on the memoirs of a famous artist. I passed on art world gossip that Tatiana had shared, and Mara told me that my replacement was nowhere near as good as I'd been and that I was sorely missed.

It was the opening I'd been looking for.

"I bet the partners regret that Sabrina Mayhew never took them up on their offer out of law school," I said. "That woman is on fire."

Although Vincenzo's bite mark was gone, my wrist throbbed at the very mention of Sabrina. *Give it a rest, you dumb oath.*

Mara chuckled. "Their only consolation is that since she went to Crown Counsel, she's doing it for the cause, and no amount of money would have swayed her."

Prosecutors in British Columbia, known as Crown Counsel, were appointed and assigned to cases by the Criminal Justice Branch of the Ministry of the Attorney General.

Mara licked foam off her lip. "She's good to her paralegals and juniors," she said approvingly. Far too many lawyers were not. "I heard she went all out for them at Mauro's on Friday."

Question one answered. Sabrina *had* made it to her staff dinner.

"How does it work for Crown Counsel? Do they get time off after a trial or is it right back into billable hours?"

She shook her head. "Not much downtime when you're that overburdened. Plus, Sabrina is a workaholic like so many in this field."

"Sadie's friend Emily is interested in becoming a prosecutor." I doubted her fascination would last once she saw it wasn't as glamorous as depicted on television. "You think Sabrina would be amenable to chatting with her one day? It would be great for Emily to speak to a female lawyer at the top of her game. I met Sabrina once briefly, but I don't know her. Would she be open to a meeting?" I flicked my finger against a package of sugar before adding it to my half-drunk coffee.

"You sure Emily wouldn't rather be a drug mule?" Mara said wryly. "Less stress."

"Trust me, I tried to dissuade her." I sipped the coffee, satisfied with the milkiness.

"Well, if the poor girl is determined, Sabrina would be a great resource." Mara rummaged in her purse for a pen and then scribbled a name down on a napkin. "Here. Talk to her assistant, Justin, and tell him I sent you."

Having gotten what I came for and aware of Mara's time restraints, we chatted for only another few minutes. There had been such a huge adjustment and so many revelations once I'd started working for Tatiana that I'd dropped everyone from my previous workplace. Most of them were no great loss, but I'd missed Mara. I promised we'd get together for lunch soon and meant it.

I remained in the café after my friend left, looking up Sabrina's firm's number, but instead of calling it, I put away my phone. I didn't have time to play phone tag. Showing up unannounced was unorthodox, but I had Mara's name to ease the weirdness.

The smell of freshly baked cookies filled the lobby.

Make that Mara's name and a bribe.

Sabrina's office was located near the courthouse in an unremarkable building devoid of the slickness of the private downtown firms. The nicest description was "no nonsense."

Her assistant, Justin Hampton, however, a young man in a skinny suit and bow tie, would have fit right in at those other places. He poked the clear plastic window of the bakery box I'd proffered and sat back in his creaky chair. "Mara may vouch for you, but does she vouch for these lemon bars? Each one of those is another treadmill session and I despise that machine."

"They're worth two sessions," I said confidently.

"You lie."

I tapped the box. "These are the ones that Daniel Shechtman forbade at my old firm."

Justin gasped and lowered his voice to a whisper even though the reception area was empty and the doors to the other lawyers and paralegals were closed. "The infamous crack bars?"

The story was lore in Vancouver lawyer circles. Unable to resist the lemon squares' lure, Daniel had eaten an entire box that a well-meaning paralegal had brought during an all-night session. His sugar crash the next morning had been legendary. He'd kept his meeting with opposing counsel but had been jittery and unfocused, ripping off his tie and jacket to reveal he was sweating like a faucet.

Counsel was so freaked out they called 911 on him and the meeting ended with Daniel being wheeled out on a gurney with everyone convinced he was having a heart attack. It was hyperglycemia brought on by the vat of sugar he'd consumed in those bars. Daniel laughed it off, which was good since he kept getting ribbed by lawyers at other firms sending him "get well soon" deliveries of the treats.

Still, to avoid a repeat, Daniel banned the bars at the office. From then on, as the infamous tale spread, sales skyrocketed at the bakery and most days, unless you got there early, you were shit out of luck.

I waved the lemony goodness under Justin's nose. "The very same."

His fingers twitched. "Sabrina can fit the young woman in." He snatched the box away, clutching it close while he selected a treat.

"Great. Does she have any openings this week?" I rotated my wrist against another warning signal flare-up.

Justin swallowed, a look of bliss on his face. "She's taking some time off after the trial."

I leaned on the high front counter of the reception desk.

"Real time off or lawyer time off where she's already phoned you twice today?"

A list of frequently used phone numbers was taped next to his mousepad, but I didn't want Sabrina's personal number. How could I get her home address?

"Real time off." He reached for another bar and then closed the cover and wagged a finger at me. "You're calorie Satan."

"You're welcome." I winked. "Well, I hope it stays real time off. God knows I had enough lawyers contact me at home when they were supposed to be on vacation." I heaved a dramatic sigh. "No rest for the wicked."

"Too true." He placed the bars in a desk drawer. "Plus, I lost the office pool when she didn't phone me Saturday morning."

"Ouch." I winced.

"Right?" he said. "Five bucks is five bucks."

My reaction had actually been because of the blood oath, but best he have his own interpretation.

Let's see, Sabrina's last sighting was Friday night, and she didn't check in as expected Saturday morning. Excellent. I now had a timeline to follow up and it started with searching her place for any sign of foul play. "It's good that she's resting after that trial. She deserves it."

"Especially after that win."

I shared my contact information with Justin because I honestly wanted Emily to speak with Sabrina. Also, because he entered it in his contacts program on the computer, and while I stood respectfully behind the counter, Delilah may have snooped out the password.

Leaving the office, I got out of eyesight of the glass doors and cloaked, biding my time. Sure enough, Justin soon left with a stack of papers, headed for the copy room down the hall.

I zipped inside, punched in the password, and opened the contacts program. After snatching a Post-it note off the desk, I scribbled down Sabrina's address, but as I clicked it closed, another thought occurred to me. Keeping one eye on the glass doors, not that Justin could see me if he came back, I searched for receipts from the company that ran the parking garage under the building.

Justin appeared on the other side of the glass door with a large stack of collated papers so I shot Delilah over to hold the door closed while I found Sabrina's car make and stall number. The assistant tugged on the door with a frown, the perception filter thankfully keeping him from seeing my shadow, because Delilah would have been incredibly awkward to explain.

Still cloaked, I hurriedly returned the laptop back to its darkened state.

Delilah let go and Justin stumbled inside, losing some of the papers. As he bent over, cursing, to grab them, I slid past him into the hallway, hidden by my magic mesh.

He turned around at the swish of the door closing, but not seeing anyone, finished picking up the papers.

I remained cloaked until I was back in the parking garage. Counting off numbers, I found Sabrina's stall, but her Prius wasn't there. Hmm. I'd been to more than a few celebratory lawyer dinners and the booze flowed. She could easily have left her car at the restaurant and gotten a lift home.

Deciding to check out her condo first, I drove over to her high-rise near English Bay in the west end, located in an older tower. It took five tries before someone took pity on my story that my fob to get into the building was dead and let me in, their lax security working in my favor.

Fortunately, when I reached Sabrina's place on the fifth floor, there was enough of a crack to send Delilah through. I, of course, remained in the corridor under my black mesh.

Other than an open, half-packed suitcase on her sofa with a full laundry hamper on the floor next to it, her two-bedroom apartment was neat, with no sign of a struggle or any foul play. Her bed hadn't been slept in and the coffeepot was clean and dry.

Since I didn't know which parking stall at her condo was hers, I checked the entire parkade, but didn't find her car.

All of that together made it fairly conclusive that Sabrina hadn't made it home after the dinner. Chances were, she'd been the last to leave after settling the bill. Was she attacked at the restaurant? Had she gone somewhere else and run into trouble?

When I got back to my sedan, I made more notes. Why go into hiding when she was supposed to leave the next day, and especially when her fiancé was a rich vampire who could have arranged for protection and gotten her on an earlier flight? I closed my notes app. Unless whatever had occurred had been so quick that she didn't have time to call for help.

Unfortunately, when I drove by the restaurant where she'd held the staff dinner, it didn't have its own lot. Patrons parked on the streets, which they wouldn't have footage of. There was no way to tell if she'd been approached by anyone on her way to her car, nor could I access any cab or ride share records to see if she'd taken one home.

My gut churned queasily. The timing of Sabrina's disappearance after incarcerating Paxton Craig combined with these gangland killings made it unlikely that she'd been targeted because of Vincenzo. She was a young woman who'd taken down a powerful man and had gotten mere hours to celebrate her achievements before she'd been retaliated against.

I'd do everything in my power to find her alive, but even if I did, she'd been gone long enough to have experienced terrible things. Would they fuel her quest as an agent of justice, or would this incident break her?

Scared as I was to be the bearer of bad news, I had to prepare Vincenzo for the worst. He was her loved one first and a vampire second in this case and that's how I'd treat him.

It was late afternoon so he might be asleep, but given how powerful BatXoha was, he might not. Despite bracing myself to make the call, it went straight to voice mail, so I simply asked him to phone back.

I drove home contemplating my next move.

Harry called as I was unlocking my door, following up on my request to meet with a supernatural being in Northern British Columbia who might have intel on the murders of Mom, Dad, and McMurtry. He'd found a raven shifter, not a gargoyle.

I fumbled my keys, catching them at the last second. Raven shifters and I had a complicated history, usually where I got information I desperately needed at a cost I later regretted. The games they play weren't just shooting space aliens and battleships, they were with destiny, bringing something into existence that wouldn't have been there otherwise. It wasn't worth the risk. I'd take the amulet to Nav.

But even if Nav confirmed the amulet was demonic in nature, what were the chances of it narrowing down who killed the Lonestar and my parents? Could I really afford to discount that lead?

I unclenched my death grip on the keys. "I won't play games with raven shifters."

"Relax, luv," Harry said in his broad English accent. "I already sorted that. Nora agreed to accept a gift in lieu of a game. Straight trade."

It couldn't be this easy.

"What does she want?" I stepped into my dim foyer and flicked on the lights.

"She's keen on this specific poison ring that recently resurfaced on the collector scene."

I quickly calculated how much I had available on my credit card, hoping the ring wasn't outrageously priced. "Where do I buy it?"

There was a long pause. Harry cleared his throat. "Um…"

I rolled my eyes. Called it. "Who do I steal it from?"

"Here's the thing."

"Nope. Nothing good has ever followed those words."

"It's Giulia," Harry said.

I tossed my keys harder than I intended into the bowl that

Jude had made me to house them, then quickly checked that I hadn't cracked it. The last time I'd seen the cat gargoyle, I'd destroyed her sweet if impossible fantasy of a happily ever after with Laurent. I'd also perhaps implied that he'd used me for sex and didn't want a relationship. That he was, in fact, incapable of them.

In my defense, the relationship part had been true at the time.

"Miri?"

"I'll figure it out. How do I get hold of Nora if I get the ring?"

He gave me her work address, explaining that she'd recently moved to Vancouver. "She's got a background in mythology and folklore. You'll like her."

I kicked off my shoes. "A veritable font of knowledge."

"Right?" Harry completely missed my sarcasm.

Would it help or totally kibosh my cause to bring Laurent with me on my visit to Giulia? Sadly, I didn't come to any conclusion.

Somehow, I'd missed a text from Sadie saying she'd met up with Tovah and her friends after school, but she'd be home by dinner. She sent a second message that her phone was dying and not to worry if I couldn't get hold of her.

Thanks, Sades. I was only mildly annoyed before but now I was concerned. Sadie's close friends consisted of her cousin and kids she'd known since elementary school, Caleb being the most recent addition to the group. Sadie's description of her new friends painted them as a good bunch, but this was twice in two days that they were hanging out.

I padded into the kitchen. Was I overreacting and this was natural given the newness of her powers? Should I call Romi and ask her about Tovah's friends?

To take my mind off things, I started preparing dinner. The radio broadcast the day's news including a police press conference announcing that the gang murders were targeted and the general public need not be concerned.

I hadn't paid a lot of attention when I'd first heard the story, but this time I listened to the details more avidly because two of the three deceased were members of the Hastings Mill gang, whose leader, Paxton Craig, Sabrina had put away. The group had taken their name from a long defunct sawmill, the area around which became Vancouver.

Metro Vancouver had a history of gang warfare. Targeted hits were, sadly, not uncommon, and they often resulted in innocent people getting caught in the crossfire. I was shaking excess water out of the salad spinner when Vincenzo phoned back.

"Hi." I tore clean lettuce into a bowl, sorting through my next words.

"Did you find her?" His rushed words had a pained edge.

Putting the cell on speakerphone, I set it on the counter. "We've had a series of gangland murders here, including members of the Hastings Mill gang. I'm worried that Sabrina may have gone into hiding for her own protection."

"*I* was her protection." His anger punched into me.

My hands closed on empty air; I'd shredded the romaine into coleslaw-sized strips. "So long as there's even a sliver of hope, I'll find her, but…you need to prepare yourself."

He gave this half sigh, half moan that was heartbreaking— and coming from such a powerful being, incredibly unsettling. "Just bring her back. Even if she's…" He cleared his throat. "You'll still get paid."

He was silent for a moment, and I sensed he was about to hang up, but I didn't want it to end on this note.

I found a Ziploc for the extra lettuce and swapped the bag for a cucumber in the fridge. "I was a law librarian for a long time and my old firm wanted to hire Sabrina. I remember when she came for her interview." I leaned in toward the phone as if I could physically keep him on the line with me.

"You do?"

I smiled. "Yes. A lot of the candidates were pretty cocky, but Sabrina had this quiet confidence to her. When they toured her around the firm and to my library, I felt like she was assessing us not in terms of status or pay but how much good we could help her do."

He chuckled softly. "That's Bree."

Sabrina was a remarkable lawyer, but she had to be a fascinating woman for that warrior of justice to capture the attention of a vampire. I looked forward to meeting her properly.

"I'll get you closure," I said softly. "Hopefully with your fiancée alive and well, and if not, then those responsible. Anything I learn, you'll be the first to know."

"I appreciate that."

A weight lifted off my chest at this turn in our professional relationship. "The Vancouver Police Department is interested in these killings, which may work in our favor."

"Have you spoken to them about it?" So much for our bonding. Suspicious vamp was back.

"You know I haven't." *You blood-oath-forcing bastard, what are you hiding?*

"Good." He hung up.

There was only one way to get answers: I was going to have to play spy in gang territory, and for that I needed Eli's help. Except I couldn't discuss the case with him. Unless... I absently rubbed my wrist. Vincenzo had forced this bond on me, but I'd worked in a law firm for years. I'd obey the letter of the law, the exact wording of the oath to discuss it only with my team.

Cassin & Associates was about to expand by one. Take that, Vincenzo.

8

TUESDAY WAS A BUST.

Unsurprisingly, my online search for the amulet engravings didn't yield anything. I got hold of Nav while he was packing to head out of town on a job for a few days, but he didn't recognize the artifact when I texted him a photo, and while he did a quick search of the Carpe Demon databases, those figures weren't in there.

My failure on that front hammered home the importance of speaking with Nora and seeing if she had any intel about McMurtry's killer. There was no way around it, I needed that ring.

Chugging my fourth cup of coffee to wipe away the memory of the last time I'd pissed Giulia off, I updated my whiteboard to include a sketch of the amulet. Then I switched over to my paying job, starting a proper file on Sabrina instead of notes on my phone and compiling my findings on her disappearance thus far. Well, in between multiple pee breaks from all the coffee.

Once that was done, I phoned Emmett and Tatiana. They were slowly amassing connections to vamps and humans with whom Vincenzo had business relationships. Vendors were happy to deal with him and appeared to be quite loyal. It lent even more credence to this being revenge for Craig's prosecution, but if so, why the blood oath? Why didn't Vincenzo want me speaking to anyone? Was it as simple as maintaining his appearance of power at all costs?

I floated the idea of bringing Eli on board with Tatiana. She didn't love being asked to expand her staff until I assured her it was temporary and would come out of my pocket, then she agreed. Shocker.

Unfortunately, Eli was tied up in meetings because another gang member's body had been found, bringing the total to four. If I couldn't use my homicide detective ex-husband to find out where the Hastings Mill gang congregated, I'd go at it another way.

Ryann might know, but I had no way to ask without breaking Vincenzo's oath.

Old-fashioned legwork it was. Two hours later I had a couple of promising locations, along with a sore back and dry eyes from scanning dozens of newspaper articles. An old story about a slew of murders in the criminal community mentioned the fact that gangs tended to abandon known locales after hits to make it harder to strike at them again.

I grabbed my car keys and headed out to scout Paxton Craig's house, but the driveway was empty and there was a "for sale" sign in front. I crossed it off my list of where the gang had gone to ground and drove to the second address, which was in Burnaby, a good forty minutes away.

Tatiana really needed to pony up for a gas allowance.

The restaurant I found was closed for renovations, with papered-over windows and a heavy locked front door. Going around the corner onto a quiet street, I cloaked myself to check the open door at the back. The place had been gutted. Two tradesmen were plastering walls with nary a gang member in sight. I'd have to wait for Eli for suggestions, though I fired off a text to Vincenzo to say that I was closing in on the new gang HQ. The blood oath didn't act up, so yay me.

While I pondered my next course of action and not the fact that in four hours Laurent would be here to pick me up for our date, Emmett sent me an address for a quick job, because our dybbuk enthrallment hotline was booming. Tatiana had renamed the service as dybbuk bounty hunting and was charging big bucks for it. Huh. I guess she had a point about the importance of branding.

I cracked my knuckles, more than up for destroying one of those fuckers.

At first, all signs pointed to a murderously fun time. A crying mother greeted me at the front door, wailing about how her poor possessed baby would have totaled the car and died had he not wrested back control of his body at the last moment. The car was replaceable but her darling son was not.

She led me out to the garage and left me with a teen whose scraggly beard made me want to shear him to put his facial hair out of its misery.

He sat in a folded-out lawn chair, staring glumly at a luxury SUV. The car's entire left side had been reformed into an impressive modern art sculpture. Even the headlight fragments were embedded in a new and interesting way.

I stood next to the kid and crossed my arms, leaning my weight on one leg as I sent my magic into him to check for the dybbuk. "You sure you're okay?"

He gave me a hangdog look and swallowed, his Adam's apple bobbing. "Yeah. I've been studying pretty hard, and I guess I got enthralled during the last Danger Zone."

"Wow. That's rough." I wandered over to the rack of tools on the side workspace. Ooh. Shiny. I lifted a handsaw off the rack.

"Wh-what are you doing with that?"

"This?" I furrowed my brows. "Didn't anyone explain how I sever the dybbuk from you?"

He scrambled up so fast that the chair fell over. "You use magic."

"Well sure, but also a saw." I mimed sawing off my arm. "Key word being 'sever' and all."

The kid whipped out his wallet, which was several inches fatter than mine, and thrust a bunch of bills at me. "Look, there's no dybbuk."

I bugged out my eyes and replaced the tool. "No way."

"Way. I just said that because my dad will kill me for busting up his car." He shook the money at me. "Take it."

"Thanks." Five hundred bucks. Sweet.

"We're good? You'll tell my mom I was enthralled?"

"Not even a little bit." I stuffed the money in my pocket.

"What? No, then you can't have that," he said.

"Why not? You offered it freely."

"We had a deal."

I raised my eyebrows. "Did you make me a formal offer to which I agreed?"

"Don't be such a bitch," he said.

Oh, you little putz. You saw a middle-aged woman and in your sexist arrogance of youth thought you could bully me. "I wasn't going to actually keep the money, just impart a lesson in the importance of language when striking a verbal contract. But I've changed my mind and will be keeping this. Some people charge sales tax, I charge asshole tax. However, in exchange, you may take this." I handed him a Cassin & Associates card.

"What is it?" He frowned at it.

"A lifeline. Keep it close, kid. I have a feeling you'll need it."

With that I went to rat him out. I left to the dulcet tones of his mother screeching, "Jack, you are in so much trouble!" Even better, my pockets were five hundred dollars heavier because she'd insisted on me keeping the money.

Sadly, there was still one other unpleasant task I had to cross off my list. Hmm, did I want to take my life into my hands and go see Giulia about the ring on the very same day as my date with Laurent?

The answer to that was a big nope, so I did what any woman

going out for the first time with a hot guy did and called my best friend to help me pick out clothes since I had only three hours to get ready.

Jude refused to come over. "No way. I'm familiar with everything in your wardrobe and none of it has that wow factor. We're going shopping."

I tossed a shirt onto my depressingly large discard pile. Would three hours be enough? Maybe we should have started this morning. "He told me to wear stretchy clothes since we'd be eating a lot."

"That's not mood killing at all. Men." She snorted. "Brace yourself, sug. We're going to disregard that memo."

Jude took me on the pub crawl equivalent of glitzy dress shopping. Other than the lack of booze, I felt just as queasy and sweaty as if we were barhopping. I lurched from store to store, contorting myself in and out of clothing.

After the first five shops, I dubbed this outing the Parade of Awful, and the lights outside this current changing cubicle did nothing to sway my opinion. I examined myself in the floor-length mirror, turning sideways to see my butt. "There's such a plethora of options to choose from. Do I go with this King Midas barmaid look?" I ran a hand over the gold ruffled bodice that pushed my girls almost up to my chin. "Maybe go back to the last store for the great lace mishap?"

Jude, sprawled in a chair, tossed a chocolate-covered almond into her mouth. "My vote still goes to the leopard-print number."

"Ah, yes. Mobster's First Wife. A classic." I wriggled a finger under the tight elastic binding my chest so I could breathe properly. "I'm not sure I have time for the spray tan it demands."

"True. Orange is the new black." She snapped her fingers.

"What about the one with the rhinestones? Very *Best Little Whorehouse in Texas.*"

"This is hopeless." I stomped back into the fitting room. "I'm wearing my funeral dress. It's stretchy."

"You are not wearing anything that's seen more coffins than dicks."

The woman in the cubicle next to mine snorted a laugh.

I wrestled the dress off, going very still when the filmy material got stuck around my shoulders. If I had to pay two hundred dollars for this monstrosity, I was going to lose it.

Inch by sweaty inch, I freed myself. I'd pulled it off with a sigh when a mass of slippery purple fabric with no discernable shape was draped over the door.

"Try this," Jude said.

"Is it a body sock?" I peered at it doubtfully. "A bruised sandworm?"

Jude gave an aggravated sigh, signaling I was several seconds away from her barging in and shoving me into the dress.

I grabbed it. "Can't wait to try it on."

It was stretchy, I'd give it that, but I couldn't get a sense of how it looked because my aerial view was of a lot of hills and valleys. Taking a deep breath, I threw the door open to see it in the mirror.

"Nice," said the woman from the next cubicle, stepping out with her arms full of clothes. She flashed me a thumbs-up before leaving.

I stepped in front of the mirror and did a double take.

The dress shouldn't have worked, but *hel*-lo, mama.

The mock-neck halter top reduced my "mannish shoulders" (thanks for that label, Tatiana), while the ruching along the satiny material allowed it to cling to my curves in a flattering way—and not as if I'd been stuffed into sausage casing. It fell to soft pleats along my left calf, the right side cut slightly higher, like a flamenco dancer's dress, and the fabric cupped my ass in a tender embrace.

I grinned. "Oh, this will do nicely."

Jude grabbed the elastic on the leg of my underwear and wrenched it up my ass cheek. "You need a thong."

I slapped her hand away. "That kind of manhandling costs a hundred an hour, and I am not wearing butt floss."

"You're right. Go free under there. But you do need a different bra," she said, nonplussed, smushing my arms against the sides of my boobs to make my girls stand at attention.

I sputtered a cough. "I'm not going naked, either. I have bad luck with gusts of wind at the best of times, and I will not end this date arrested for public indecency." I poked my elastic underwear line and sighed. "I'll wear the shapewear that comes down midthigh, but grant that a new bra is in order."

"Midthigh." Jude whistled. "That'll be sexy fun for Laurent to unpeel later. Maybe you'll even make that sweet, sweet sucking noise when your skin pulls free. Rawr." Leering, she mimed claws.

I narrowed my eyes. "Fashion is a bitch."

"Thong it is." She grinned evilly. "You still have your false lashes, right?"

I dropped my head into my hands with a groan. Sure, they made my eyes pop, but putting them on without wanting to scratch them loose was excruciating. And my child—aka lash specialist, because despite having over forty years of life, I was too chicken to put them on without direct assistance—took a sadistic glee in torturing me.

That said, I still took Jude's advice.

Several hours later I stood in front of the mirror wearing a push-up corset with so much boning in it—and not the pleasurable kind—I swore its design was based off the Iron Maiden. The torture device, not the band. I'd bought a simple black thong, and while there was no panty line, my butt looked like it was nestled in a slingshot, ready for takeoff.

I dropped the dress over my head, slipped into my heels, and faced the mirror again, curling a lock behind my ear. Wow. From my updo courtesy of a blowout salon I'd stopped at, to my outfit, I was a freaking Lamborghini of women. So long as Laurent didn't peer too hard under the hood at the functional but unsexy parts, all would be well.

Between the contouring and the heels, there was an extra sway to my hips that I embraced.

"Ta da!" I struck a pose in Sadie's doorway.

"Whoa, sexy lady." She scrambled off her bed and twirled her finger to get me to turn around. "Oh my God, Mom, you have a butt! I always thought it was just some shapeless dead zone."

"I gave the wrong child away. That's it. Switch back with your sister."

"No can do." She grabbed my hand and tugged me into the bathroom. "She doesn't have my false lashes magic touch."

I sat down on the edge of the tub while Sadie turned my face to the light, studying it with her lips pursed, while she muttered under her breath, "Foundation is good. Blush properly blended."

"I do know how to apply makeup," I said with a laugh.

"Apparently you don't, because you only used one color of eye shadow." She rummaged through a drawer for her large cosmetics case with all her cosplay makeup. "We must create depth. Plus, I've seen better liner jobs on the grade eights putting it on in the girls' bathroom at school."

"Fair." I was happy to endure her teasing because this was the most that my daughter had acted like her pre-magic self in a while.

Once my lips, eyes, and lashes all passed her approval, she smiled. "You look beautiful. Laurent is going to freak out." She shook her head. "Took you guys long enough to finally get together."

I made a vague sound of agreement. Hopefully she had no idea I'd been sneaking off to hook up with him.

There was a loud knock on the front door and I eeped.

Sadie patted my hand. "You got this, Mom." Then with a sly smile, she bolted into the hallway. "Payback is going to be fun."

9

SHE WAS KIDDING, RIGHT? I'D BEEN THE GOOD PARENT when she brought Caleb home. I smoothed down my dress. Of course she was. My darling child loved her dramatic one-liners. I left the bathroom with a wink to my reflection, and sashayed down the stairs, my head held high.

The foyer was empty.

"My intentions?" Laurent said in a pitchy voice.

Sadie, you little shit. I almost broke my ankle jumping the last two stairs and skidding into the living room where my child sat, her back ramrod straight and her arms crossed.

Laurent ran a finger under the collar of his shirt.

"Yo, child, no interrogating my date."

The wide-eyed look of appeal he sent my way turned to something softer, his lips curving into a sweet smile.

Sadie glanced between the two of us. "Fine." She hopped up and kissed my cheek. "Have fun, Mom."

I nodded absently, hearing her clatter up the stairs, but was unable to tear my eyes off Laurent.

He stood up and smoothed a hand over the lapels of his moss green suit that turned his eyes to fiery gems. "You look beautiful, Mitzi."

I blushed. "Thank you. You look gorgeous."

His crisp white shirt and narrow black tie popped under a vest in the same moss green as the suit. He didn't wear socks, just polished black shoes, and to top it off, a black handkerchief was folded into a square in the upper jacket pocket.

"Oh." He picked up a bouquet from the coffee table and held it out. "These are for you."

I expected roses, boring but classic. This bouquet was a hodgepodge: some flowers with delicate petals, others that were spiky blossoms, and a sprinkling of fat, bold blooms in a riot of colors.

"You got me wildflowers." I buried my nose in them.

He rubbed his hand along the back of his neck. "You like them?"

I pressed my hand to my heart. "They're perfect."

The vulnerability in his expression eased. "Good."

We stared at each other, the air curling around us heavy with unspoken promise.

Then it just became heavy, because what if this date jinxed us? What if Laurent and I worked precisely because we didn't label things? I mean, the last official date I'd gone on had ended with me killing the dybbuk who'd fully possessed that sweet man. While the bar was ridiculously low, tonight felt like a turning point in our relationship, a new level of emotional intimacy.

The delicate tissue paper around the bouquet was damp from my clammy palms.

Now a solid minute had passed with neither of us speaking, and if Laurent furrowed his brow any more, he'd have a solid line.

My eyes dropped to my feet, the two of us doing nothing except breathing at each other. I shifted my weight, sweat running down my neck. "Let me put these in water and then we can go."

Nodding, he stepped back, as if to physically release us from the trap we were ensnared in. Better than him gnawing his own paw off.

The night's still young, Feldman.

I rushed into the kitchen, grabbed the first vase I found, and filled it with water, wiping off the back of my neck with a dish towel. This didn't feel like a first date. Those were exploratory, casual, getting-to-know-you encounters to suss out compatibility. We already knew each other's secrets, had exposed our most naked selves to each other, and I trusted him like I did few others.

The pressure suddenly felt too much to bear. Okay, I didn't have to think of it as a date. Just two people going out for a nice meal. There. I could handle that.

I inhaled my wildflowers one last time, grabbed my clutch, and we were off.

Laurent had brought his truck, the more practical choice given our clothing. However, a small part of me mourned not driving to the restaurant on his motorcycle with my arms wrapped around his body and my chest pressed flush against his back.

At first, we didn't speak at all, listening to Wagner's "Ride of the Valkyries" spill out from the speakers. All I could think of was the infamous scene of carnage in *Apocalypse Now*, which was hardly a soothing tonic for my already-frayed nerves.

Laurent drummed his fingers on the wheel almost as rapidly as my leg jittered. Awesome. I was tempted to pretend to nap, but that wouldn't send the right signal for our first date, and his shifter senses would spot the lie in my racing heartbeat and shallow breathing.

He braked hard at a red light, flinging me forward against the seat belt.

"Sorry," he said. "The car ahead stopped at the last second."

"No problem." I pushed a loosened bobby pin back into place. "So, uh, did you get the dybbuk before you came back to town?"

"Yes, though it was a tricky bastard." He turned right, his biceps flexing. "I heard some kid tried to pull a fast one on you with a fake enthrallment."

This was more like it. Regular conversation. "'Tried' being the operative word," I said.

Laurent chuckled, and smiling, I rolled down the window and slung my elbow on the door. "Nice weather we're having," he said.

"No rain yet. Still warm." We passed block after block of condo towers being built. "Lots of construction." My eyes widened. Oh no. We'd invoked the two most clichéd topics any Vancouverite could discuss: weather and real estate. We were one slippery slope away from scoring a hat trick with "hard to meet people in this city."

Alarms wailed in my head; we were flatlining. Death by small talk. How would we make it through a tasting menu that was at least two hours long?

I cast about for another topic like a drowning person flailing for a lifejacket. Ask Laurent to open a portal to Gehenna so I could sneak in and steal the Ascendant back for the Leviathan? I wrinkled my nose. Best to save that romance killer for another day. Desperate, I leaned forward to fiddle with the radio, when, eyes watering, I coughed, making sounds like a cat trying to cast up a hairball.

"You okay?" He thumped me on the back.

"I think I swallowed a fly," I said in a strangled voice.

The Wagner ended and a funereal dirge started playing just as Laurent pulled up to valet parking.

It wasn't an omen.

I was almost positive it wasn't an omen.

I hopefully inspected the friendly young man in the neatly pressed red vest who opened the passenger door for a hint of fang or a peek of demon horn. Anything to turn this date around and give Laurent and me something to discuss over dinner.

Nada.

Sighing, I got out of the car.

Laurent's smile had the same strained, slightly queasy quality that Eli had worn when I'd driven him to his double root canal appointment last year. "Ready?" he said.

I gave it fifty-fifty odds that one of us would "use the bathroom"—i.e. flee the restaurant, never to be seen again.

Fingers crossed it was me.

Steeling my spine, I took his proffered arm. "As I'll ever be."

The well-heeled crowd looked out of place in the homey restaurant, which was studded with photos of the owners meeting famous actors and musicians who'd come through town over the past twenty years. Dean Martin and Frank Sinatra would have made more sense playing on the speakers than Tori Amos.

We were quickly seated and settled into our high-backed booth, studying the drinks menu with an intensity usually reserved for peace talks.

"Would you like wine?" Laurent said.

"Does a dog like to lick its balls?" Oh God. Where had that come from? I wasn't even a dog person. Not that the animal was the problematic element here.

Laurent's eyes widened, a crease once more forming between his brows.

I unfurled my napkin with a violent snap and nodded vigorously.

He called our server over. The celebrity chef must have brought his own staff for tonight, because this guy didn't fit the ambience of this place either. However, for a beefy man with tattoos and large silver circles inset in his earlobes, he oozed disdain like a waiter in the finest French restaurant.

For a moment it seemed as if Laurent was going to order two bottles, one for each of us, which I'd have been fine with, but he went with the less intervention-worthy single one, before pulling at the knot of his tie. "I keep telling myself it's just dinner."

I exhaled. "You too?"

He reached across the table and took my hand. "We'll eat. We'll drink. I will look at a beautiful woman. All good, yes?"

"When you put it that way, I feel like you're getting the better end of this deal." I winked, and just like that the tension was broken.

Our server poured us delicious wine with perfect aplomb, and our first taster dish arrived soon after. "Pan-seared farm-to-table organic pork flavored with garlic and pimento and topped with a raspberry coulis." He set the tiny plates down in front of us, pivoted sharply, and left.

I frowned at the two discs because after that description I expected more than two half-inch-thick wedges cut out of a sausage in a puddle of what looked like blood.

Laurent poked one of the pieces. "It's a meat cupcake," he scoffed.

"A what?" I sniffed it. It smelled grilled and fatty and my stomach rumbled.

"Daya makes them for Evani. She cuts up a sausage, squirts ketchup on the pieces like frosting, and calls it a meat cupcake. The kid loves it."

"That's brilliant." I popped a disc in my mouth, cutting the amount of food on my plate in half. "It tastes good."

Laurent had already eaten his share, turning the plate around like more might appear.

Ninety minutes later we'd consumed—in addition to the aforementioned meat cupcakes—two tablespoons of gray foam, a shot glass of olive oil topped with a sprig of rosemary that I was tempted to eat, and a deconstructed salad. This consisted of two shavings of carrot, a curl of cucumber, a red smear that might have been tomato, and a lettuce leaf that we were sternly informed was for garnish purposes only.

Rebel that I was, I snarfed that puppy down in one bite.

Laurent's eyes looked wild and his canines had lengthened. "This is a joke, yes? They will bring a meal soon?"

I rooted around in my clutch, triumphantly producing a box

of breath mints, which I carefully divvied up, generously giving Laurent the extra one. Never had artificially sweetened peppermint tasted so divine.

He jabbed a shaking finger at the next table, where the diners had just been given their meal. "They have real food," he said plaintively.

I tamped down a frown. If Laurent had gotten desperate enough to believe that the three tortellini swimming forlornly in a huge dish or the brown puddle with a single lamb popsicle constituted "real food," he was moments away from eating the other patrons.

When our server came by with the next course, I pointed at the other table. "Are those the largest portions you have?"

"Yes." He sneered, the stud under his bottom lip catching the light. "They are for the à la carte diners."

"Excellent. We'll take seven of each."

"Impossible. You are on the tasting menu." He marched off before I could protest, and I faced down my next dish with suspicion.

The small knob on my plate was deep fried. That was a good start. I popped it my mouth and gagged. It was deep-fried cream that tasted like slug slime. A delectable visual hiding an unwanted salty surprise. I snorted. Been there.

Just like straight dudes everywhere, Laurent was exempt from that plug-your-nose-and-swallow finish. His cream squirted out the opposite end of the knob, shooting rivulets all over the plate and tablecloth. Small mercies it didn't end up on my face.

Laurent let out a soft wolfy growl, but it was drowned out by my stomach rumble that was so loud, heads turned my way.

My date clenched his jaw. "C'est fini."

The second he stood up, three servers rushed him. I hadn't seen anyone move that fast since Jude and I attempted to leave a multilevel marketing seminar and were intercepted by a phalanx of women who were all named Debbie.

I'd have gotten up to help him fight them off, but I was too hungry to stand.

The staff coaxed him back into his seat, swearing the best was yet to come because it was time for the first of the entrées.

We bravely soldiered on.

Entrée the first involved a dollop of chili sauce the size of my thumbnail, two croutons, and single slice of beef tartare. The second dish topped that marvel with a gherkin sitting atop an empty pea pod next to a sliver of white fish.

Laurent white-knuckled his knife.

Hopefully he wouldn't kill me if he hangrily slaughtered everyone. I eyed the door, wondering if we could make it out without being ambushed, when my phone rang.

I was so excited for a distraction from my near starvation that I grabbed it without checking the screen. "Hello?"

"I have something that belongs to you, Ms. Feldman." Zev's smooth voice slid down the line.

I rolled my eyes. "Yeah. What's that?"

There was a pause.

"Hi, Mom," Sadie said in a small voice.

My phone clattered to the table.

10

LAURENT'S HEAD SNAPPED UP. THANKS TO HIS enhanced shifter senses, he'd heard everything.

Grabbing my phone again, I held up my other hand, control hanging on by a thread. The vampire had come into my home? If she was harmed in any way, I'd destroy him. "Is he at our place? Did he hurt you?"

She swallowed audibly. "Here's the thing."

I closed my eyes. Oh no.

"I went to Blood Alley." It came out as one long rush.

I moved the phone away from my ear. Looked at the screen. Shook the cell phone.

"Hello?" she said.

I placed it once more against my ear. "I was checking that my phone was working correctly because I did *not* just hear you say what I think you said!" Was I yelling by that point? Damn straight I was.

While Sadie nervously babbled at me about how she'd gone there with her new Ohrist friends, but she knew it was safe because Mr. BatKian had promised he wouldn't hurt her, I stood up and snapped my fingers at our server. "Bill. Now."

"Madame has not yet finished the tasting menu," he said with yet another sneer.

"Madame is going to shove the rest of the tasting menu up your ass if you don't bring us the bill," I said in a low voice.

His eyes widened.

Laurent nodded matter-of-factly. "I'd do as you're told."

The server scuttled off.

"And bring us a couple of damn dinner rolls!" I yelled.

Three tables burst into applause.

"Mom?" Sadie said. "How mad are you?"

Leaving Laurent to settle up the bill, I marched to the exit, pausing only to snatch my dinner roll from the server. "Let's see. How mad am I that you decided to impress your new Ohrist friends with how cool you are because of your in with Vancouver's master vampire and sneak into Blood Alley underage?"

"That's not what I said."

"Oh, I know what you said. You are so grounded." I pushed out the door, turning my face to the breeze.

"For how long?" she asked miserably.

"However long I decide with the right to extend it until you're dead. Do you understand me?"

"Yes."

"Good. Now let me speak to Mr. BatKian."

"That was impressive," the vampire said.

"I'm very sorry for any trouble my child caused you. Do you mind hanging on to her until I get there? I'm coming now."

"Of course."

"What about the other kids?" I said nervously.

"They've been sent home. I assumed you'd want to deal with the ringleader yourself."

"Yes. Again, thank you and my apologies." I hung up, leaning into Laurent's touch at the small of my back. "How could she be so stupid?"

"She's young."

86

"I'm sorry our date turned into this disaster." I scarfed down the roll.

"Are you kidding? Your exit was the high point of the meal. Allons-y."

He led me to his truck, but once we were on our way, my fury left me in a whoosh, and I clasped my trembling hands in my lap.

"Even if no one touched her, there are things that happen in Blood Alley that my sixteen-year-old is too young for." Like many her age, Sadie had likely seen porn, but Blood Alley sold desire, honed to a dark sensuality that enticed as much as it unsettled. She was too young to parse its complex nuances.

"Wait to discuss it with Sadie," Laurent said, hitting the gas through a yellow light. "My bet is they didn't get very far inside before they were caught. The Lonestars give BatKian a lot of leeway, but hosting minors is another matter entirely."

"Okay." I stared out the window at the city slipping by, my stomach in knots. My daughter could be super snarky, but she'd never gone through a rebellious phase. She'd never been openly defiant like this. "Sadie hasn't cared about impressing other kids before. Well, not to the extent of doing something stupid. Of all the things I've worried about with her magic, this wasn't one of them." I buried my head in my hands with a groan. "And she pulled Romi's niece into this." How many irate parents was I going to get calls from?

As distraught as I was, I was also secretly relieved that this date from hell was over.

Laurent's expression was inscrutable, so it was hard to say whether he shared my feelings.

Just like that, my earlier set of worries about tonight breaking us came roaring back, fighting with my anxiety over Sadie's actions like two teams in a tug-of-war vying for first place. Could this night get any worse? No, wait, don't answer that, universe.

Since my house was between the restaurant and Blood Alley, Laurent took me home to get my car. He idled the truck at the curb. "You're sure you don't want me to come with you?"

"God no. I mean, I need to talk to Sadie on my own."

"Right." He pulled off his tie and tossed it in the back. "Call me?"

He'd brought me wildflowers and taken me to what he'd believed would be a wonderful meal. It wasn't his fault this date had gone sideways.

"Actually, would you mind helping me with something?" We kicked butt as a team. Maybe that was our way through this awkwardness.

"Of course. What?"

"Giulia has this poison ring and—"

Laurent's face lit up. "I was very clever, non? My olive branch for the strain between us."

A strain that was my fault, but that's not why my face scrunched up in horror. That ring was the one thing that Nora the raven shifter had agreed to accept in trade. A trade that would hopefully buy me information about McMurtry's killer— the same being who either murdered my parents or was tied to whomever had.

Giulia would never give up this ring if Laurent had given it to her, nor could I ask him to sweet-talk her into handing it over like I'd planned.

"You don't think it was a good idea?" Laurent frowned. "You think she was offended? It was rumored to be one of Lucrezia Borgia's, and I thought Giulia would love the Italian history behind it."

"It's perfect for her." Too perfect for that bloodthirsty gargoyle cat. "I, uh, was wondering where you got it. There's someone else who was hinting at it for a gift." I mentally crossed my fingers that there was a duplicate.

He shook his head. "It's the only one of Lucrezia's that's surfaced in years."

It was official. I'd moved from "I can't see how this night can get worse" to "Wow, and yet somehow it did."

I opened the door. "Thanks for dinner."

He laughed, the sound full and rich. "That's like thanking the Wise Brothers for their lovely parting gifts."

I side-eyed him. "Yet it's funny?"

"Yes, Mitzi. That was hands down one of the worst dates ever, and I still enjoyed it because I was with you."

The Laurent of my initial acquaintance would not have seen the humor. He would have used tonight as a whip with which to flagellate himself.

"It was pretty bad." I chuckled. "But it'll make a hell of a great story."

"One of many with us," he said. My insides went mushy at his decisive words. "I was concerned you were upset."

"Only because I thought you were."

"Great minds worry alike." He kissed my cheek. "Go get Sadie."

"Are we platonic now?" I said in a voice lighter than I felt.

He smiled. "No. I want to kiss you properly after our next better date. Is that all right?"

"Tease." He winked and I slid onto the pavement, my cheeks faintly pink. "Oh, one last thing?" I said.

His eyebrows rose in question.

"I'm wearing a thong and a corset. I was hoping you'd help me get them off." I shrugged. "But we'll save it for our next better date."

His nostrils flared and he lunged across the truck for me, but laughing, I slammed the door.

I pressed my fingers to my lips and blew him a kiss, grinning when I heard his truck peel away with a loud revving sound.

Once inside my own sedan, my merriment lasted about three blocks, then I was focused on lead-footing it to Blood Alley before Sadie wore out her welcome. For good.

I made pretty good time downtown, but I got stuck in a snarl of traffic from a car accident, only to clear it and hit three red lights in a row. I was drumming my fingers on the wheel at warp speed at the last one when a familiar figure sprinted across the street.

I honked, causing Ian Carlyle to jump about a foot in the air. Without the Sapien's help, Eli and I might not have learned about the Human Race in time to save Teresa Wong and the other players. Waving, I expected Ian to return the greeting, but he didn't seem to recognize me before he ran off. I frowned, hoping that Celeste BatSila hadn't traumatized her blood donor. Well, traumatized him more than he already was after surviving the Human Race.

The light turned green and I finally made it to the real Blood Alley in Gastown, a wide cobblestoned street, about two blocks long, lined with trendy restaurants. Sprinting from my parking spot, I relaxed my gaze without breaking my stride, allowing the hidden territory to disengage from the physical surroundings like a 3D stereogram coming into focus.

Zev's human henchman Rodrigo, a brick wall of a man with a fondness for this stupid gold braided chauffeur's cap, awaited me just through the spiky metal gargoyle-topped gates.

A group of five vampires were also congregated there. The one in front, a female croupier who I'd seen before, was explaining the history of Blood Alley to the others.

Rodrigo snapped his fingers, and the croupier grabbed the shoulder of a wide-eyed vamp who was wandering off.

"Trainees." Rodrigo shook his head. "Can't take your eyes off them."

Under other circumstances I'd have stuck around to listen to the history and learn more about vamp trainees, but my daughter was in Zev's clutches.

"How angry is Mr. BatKian?" I said, walking as quickly as I could to match Rodrigo's long strides.

"About the fact that you didn't tell him Sadie has magic?" Rodrigo whistled.

"How was that any of his business?"

"When Mr. BatKian agreed to keep Sadie and her friends safe, he assumed he was making the promise about a Sapien child. Not an Ohrist one." He ploughed through a group of dude-bros coming out of one of the rooms.

Each of the black lacquered doors along the four lanes leading up to the nightclub Rome had anywhere from one to three red light bulbs mounted above them. It was a rating system of danger for the Ohrist guests, decided upon by the vampires.

The largest man turned with a loud protest, which he swallowed when Rodrigo, a good half foot and fifty pounds of muscle larger, glowered down at him.

"He did make the promise about a Sapien kid," I said. "As far as we knew at the time. Her magic just got loose."

"Ohrists are born with magic," Rodrigo said in a hard voice.

Wonderful. Sadie crashes Blood Alley and the lord and master gets pissy at me about something else entirely.

Rodrigo stopped suddenly and raised his eyebrows at a weary-looking vampire coming down the crooked lane. "Well?"

The vampire shook his head and Rodrigo cursed.

"What was that about?" I said, once more hurrying behind the Undertaker. When he didn't answer me—big shock—I returned to the more pressing topic. "Did Sadie and the kids see anything...untoward?" My stomach growled again, and I rubbed it. If I didn't get a meal soon, I was going to Hulk-rage.

"No. They spent about five minutes in one of the single-bulb bars before they were discovered."

We hit my second-least favorite place in Blood Alley after the dungeon: Gargoyle Gardens. The large unkempt lawn strewn with creepy gargoyle statues that I was convinced would come alive at any moment had also been the scene of a dybbuk attack. Two strikes; I wasn't looking forward to number three.

I raced through those shadows so quickly that Rodrigo had to keep up with me.

Once we were safely inside Rome, I summoned the courage to ask the question I dreaded the answer to. "Were they taken through the club to get to Mr. BatKian's office?" That place boasted a level of hedonistic decadence that shocked even me.

Rodrigo gave a ghost of a smile. "Yes, thrown over vamps' shoulders and blurred through at top speed. The kids didn't see squat."

I sighed. "Thank you."

I followed him in silence down the levels to the dance floor and the door leading to the basement. Much as I tried not to glimpse the goings-on in the shadowy corners, my eyes were drawn to the couples who writhed and fed in sinuous and blatant sensuality.

I fanned out the front of my dress. This night should have ended very differently for me.

Finally, we arrived at Zev's red office door. Rodrigo rapped briskly and was commanded to enter.

The Undertaker shook his head and Zev frowned.

"How many does that leave?" the vampire said.

"Three."

Three what? Clearly there was trouble in nocturnal paradise. But whatever Zev was glowering distantly about, I wasn't going to inquire. Now was not the time, not when I had Sadie to rescue.

"Very well," Zev said.

Rodrigo left and I pushed deeper into the room. "Hi."

A woman with a bubblegum-pink bob sat in profile to me, and across from Zev.

I narrowed my eyes. Nope, not a woman. A child whose acting out was the gift that kept on giving. "Nice dress, Sadie. You couldn't find a hand towel to wear?" I'd never seen this outfit, but it barely covered her butt.

She wriggled in her seat to try to pull it down.

I grimaced. "Just stop."

My daughter faced me, biting on her thumbnail. She'd gone full anime with liner and shadow to make her eyes look wide, topped with long spiky lashes, and a pink pout of a mouth.

"Good evening to you too, Ms. Feldman." Zev sat back in his chair behind the desk, impeccably turned out as usual. He held a horrifically ornate chalice and there was a smear of blood, hopefully synthetic, on his lip.

A mounted carved clock that I'd never seen before ticked each second off with a ponderous weight. The old-fashioned fussy timepiece didn't fit the rest of the aesthetic with its sleek lines and unusual wood grains. The minute hand hit the half hour and a burst of Bach's "Toccata and Fugue" pealed through the room.

Sadie jumped a good two inches.

The vamp lifted the chalice to his mouth, but not before I saw his lips quirk.

He was messing with my kid, props and all.

I wasn't sure whether to laugh or scream. Perhaps, if he was amused, we'd get out unscathed. Or perhaps we'd have to move into a new place that he hadn't been invited into.

Who was I kidding? He'd find a way to get to us if he so desired.

"Thank you for keeping her here safely," I said. "We won't intrude anymore."

"Allow me a moment of your time to show you a new acquisition." Zev motioned toward the art gallery sharing the space with his office.

"Stay," I hissed at Sadie. "And take off that damn wig."

She pulled it off, her dark hair falling out in a lank ponytail.

I crossed the Persian rug in its deep reds and blues to where art hung on white walls, each piece bathed in its own spotlight.

We navigated several statues to stand before a painting made of shadows and flames depicting a witch being burned at the stake.

I clasped my hands behind my back. "I didn't deceive you. We just learned about her magic a couple weeks ago. My Banim Shovavim magic kept it from being released."

"Regardless, the promise I gave was to protect a vulnerable

Sapien child, which your daughter is not." He sipped from the chalice.

"You saw her magic?"

"I asked and she answered. It's delightfully unusual."

"No disrespect intended," I said through gritted teeth, "but I've had a long and not so great day, so if you'd lay out what you want from me, I'll take my daughter and go home."

What was one more favor that I was threatened into doing? You'd think I could get a rewards card for these things, maybe earn myself a new blender.

"I wish nothing from you." Zev tapped his index finger against the cup. "The colors are so alive in this painting. You can almost hear the wood cracking over her screams."

Not up to a veiled threat masquerading as art appreciation, I gathered the shreds of my patience together. If I didn't get more food soon, things were going to get ugly. "Rodrigo told me you were angry, so just tell me what I have to do."

"It's done."

My stomach stopped trying to eat itself due to starvation and began to ache. "What does that mean?"

"Sadie and I came to an understanding."

My kid was really going to town on that fingernail, but otherwise she had a deer-caught-in-the-headlights look.

"Any understanding with Sadie is null and void. You deal with me."

"As I said, it's done."

"She's a minor."

Zev laughed. "Then sue me. The fact of the matter is that she chose a certain course of action tonight and is old enough to be held responsible for the consequences of that." He adjusted the spotlight on the painting. "This really was a marvelous acquisition, don't you think?"

"Worth every penny." I dug my nails into my palms to keep Delilah from getting loose, the strain of holding back giving me a headache. I was a multitasker. A modern woman. A mom. How ironic that protecting Sadie, my most primal drive, was denied to me. "So, you tried Sadie as an adult?"

"Trust me." Zev flashed his fangs, his voice sending a shiver up my spine. "Were that the case, she would not be sitting in my office."

My baby girl sat fidgeting, obviously trying to eavesdrop and completely unaware of how close she'd come to death.

I shivered. "What was this understanding?"

"Your daughter nulls magic. She will do that for me as a one-time favor at some point. In exchange, there won't be any other consequences for her or her friends due to their actions tonight."

It didn't matter what decisions had led Sadie here or that the one time she'd nulled magic, she'd been psychologically fine with it because she'd saved her father and me. It wouldn't be the same when Zev requested it of her. She'd probably be used as a tool for execution again, but this time, it would change my upbeat child, mark her deep in her soul.

The implacable expression on the vampire's face showed the futility of begging for mercy.

"She can't null demon magic and we haven't dared try on a vampire." We hadn't had the opportunity, but he didn't need to know that.

"Sadie already explained all this to me."

How much had she blabbed? I swallowed the sour metallic taste in my mouth. "Well, then I'm glad that's handled. May we leave?"

He swept out a hand. "By all means. Good night, Sadie."

"Goodnight," she said timidly.

I hustled her to the car, not speaking a word until we pulled into a late-night drive-thru, and I ordered a burger and fries.

"Can I get something?" she said.

"One tap water," I said into the order board microphone. "Tepid."

"Jeez, Mom. We weren't going to get drunk or high or anything."

I inched forward, waiting behind a truck at the pickup window. "Getting drunk is way down the list of dangers you faced."

"Sure, there are vamps and stuff."

"And stuff." I pointed at her. "That's exactly why children aren't allowed there."

"I'm not a child! We were just talking about how wild Blood Alley must be, and when I mentioned that I'd met Mr. BatKian?" She gave a one-shouldered shrug. "I said we should check it out and look around."

"I hope it was worth it," I said darkly.

Sadie threw up her arms. "Sorry that I'm not your perfect daughter all the time and dared to do something that wasn't even risky compared to what some kids at my school get up to. Mr. BatKian had promised not to hurt me or my friends, remember? Besides, you had no problem when I protected you and Dad by nulling some guy's magic, but I sneak out one time and you freak. Make up your mind," she added in a mutter.

I paid for my food and parked in the lot. "Remember that night Mr. BatKian came over to set the ward? At first you thought he was so cool, but then he got mad and scared you." I crammed food into my mouth, speaking over the rumble of my stomach. "Sneaking out, wanting to impress a new group of friends, I understand all that, but you can't apply Sapien laws to the Ohrist world. You haven't even had your powers for a month, and you've known about magic for barely longer than that. Yet instead of thinking through the consequences of crossing someone who you'd seen was dangerous, you chose to impress your new friends."

Sadie toyed with the lid of her take-out cup of tap water, while I barely tasted the meal and had to muscle it down through a chest that felt made of lead.

"Do you understand how badly this could have ended?" I said. "Strike that. How badly it *did* end? You owe him a favor." I wiped my fingers on a crumpled napkin. "Be grateful he sees you as a kid." My voice grew soft and I blinked away the dampness in my eyes. "Don't be in such a rush to grow up, because when magic ends your childhood, it ends it hard."

"Like when your parents were killed," she said snarkily. She put her water in the cup holder. "Maybe if you hadn't kept secrets from me my entire life, I'd make smarter choices instead of doing the best I can."

I dug my nails into my palms at her attitude, but she wasn't wrong. The thing is, she wasn't necessarily right either. Sadie had wanted to impress a new group of kids. This totally normal teen behavior was on her, but maybe if magic wasn't a shiny novelty, this particular situation wouldn't have arisen. *That* was on me and the choices I'd made, believing them the safest—and only—option for my family.

Eli and I had done our best to keep her carefree for as long as we could, but tonight had changed that even more than when she'd nulled the powers of the man from the Consortium. Exhausted, I longed to pull her into my arms and hang on tight.

I dumped my half-eaten burger in the bag and held out my fries for her to share.

Even through the anime makeup her two freckles high on her left cheek peeked out, she slouched in that familiar way with her right shoulder higher, and the part in her hair was as crooked as always, yet when she nodded and reached for the food, her eyes were weary and strained from this new understanding of the world.

She was unhurt and with me. For now, that was enough. Child or adult, she'd always be my baby.

11

I ALLOWED ELI TO LIVE IN BLISSFUL IGNORANCE UNTIL breakfast the next morning. Our family gathered in my kitchen, and Sadie confessed to her misadventures as well as the deal she'd struck with Zev.

Her dad didn't interrupt or comment, he merely sat there with his unreadable Detective Chu face on. Sadie inheriting her Ohrist magic through Eli's bloodline had been a huge shock. He'd asked his mother about it, but she thought he was kidding, which meant that gene had come from his father. His dad had died a few years ago, and he wasn't close enough to any family on that side to ask.

Eli hadn't said much beyond that, but I knew him well enough to know that he felt betrayed to never have known about magic or his genetic legacy before circumstances had sprung it on him.

I was making a second Moka pot of espresso even though we still had some left, because Eli's continued silence was unbearable, and I wasn't even the one in trouble. Also, I hadn't slept well, my lower back was killing me, and the over-the-counter pain meds I'd taken weren't cutting it.

Emmett called midway through Sadie's retelling and I excused myself.

"What's up?" I stepped into the hallway.

"Bad news, toots. Our client is on the warpath."

"Come again?" I said in a squeaky voice.

Tatiana said something in the background and Emmett grunted. "Not against you. Apparently I should have led with that."

I sagged against the wall. "You think? What's happening?" Geez. I really needed to dust my baseboards.

"Some of his business colleagues are being offed. Ohrists mostly, a few vamps. Okay, technically, they're having accidents. It's happening in different places around the world."

"If accidents are happening globally, how do you know Vincenzo is behind them?"

"One of his seconds was killed a couple of weeks ago. It was played off as a fight with another vamp, but Tatiana knows a crooked guy at customs. He verified that one of the Ohrist names on our list arrived in Vegas just before the second bit it."

I paced the hallway. "If BatXoha retaliates with force, word would get out that he's being targeted."

"Seems so," Emmett agreed. "He's being sneaky about his revenge."

Were we back to Sabrina being kidnapped to get at Vincenzo? It didn't feel right in light of the gangland murders, but that would account for the blood oath bullshit. Nope, no feeling sorry for the vampire.

"I'm still going to follow up the gang angle," I said. "Meantime, see if Tatiana has anyone in Vancouver who can check for unwanted visitors. Ohrists can fly on regular airlines, but vamps tend to charter, right?"

"I think so. We're on it. Talk to you later."

As I returned to the kitchen, Sadie dropped her napkin on the table. "Say something," she pleaded.

"I don't want you seeing those kids again." Eli pointed at the Moka pot he'd taken off the burner and I nodded in thanks.

"It wasn't their fault. It was all my idea."

That much was true. I'd verified it with Romi this morning, learning that Tovah was freaked out by the entire experience.

"It's a nonstarter." I paused. "Tovah isn't allowed to see you anymore."

Sadie's face fell. "Oh," she said in a small voice.

She looked so young and vulnerable that it hit me square in the chest. I opened my mouth, but Eli shook his head at me.

"Go get ready for school, Sades," he said gently, and she shuffled off.

A text came through from Vincenzo. *Have you found her yet?*

Would I suffer an accident like his other cronies if I didn't find Sabrina fast enough? Nah, the blood oath would exsanguinate me first. Still, he'd taken my free will in this matter, and I was working as fast as I could.

Will have concrete update later.

Expecting a "You better or else" response, I watched the screen a moment longer, but our conversation was over. I ran my thumb over the screen. I'd said that I was going to treat him as Sabrina's loved one first and a vampire second, yet I wasn't doing so great at that. Asking if I'd found her was a perfectly reasonable question from a worried fiancé. I had to put my anger about the blood oath aside.

Eli pushed his scrambled eggs around his plate. "Stay strong. We need to follow through with consequences, but I feel so out of my depth. How do I parent something like this?"

"If it's any consolation, I feel just as lost." I leaned against the counter, blowing on the steam rising from my drink.

"Our darling child's escapades must have been some end to your date, huh?"

"Actually, BatKian's call was a high point of the evening."

"Ouch."

"Pretty much." Given how jittery I was that Eli would tell me they'd found Sabrina's body, I dumped my coffee down the sink. "Sadie wasn't the only reason I wanted to speak to you." I dug a coin out of my pocket and dropped it in front of him. "This is your signing bonus. Congratulations and welcome to Cassin & Associates."

Eli pushed the coin away with his index finger. "Can't be a police officer and work for that company."

I took it as a good sign that the warning signal didn't jump to life, except this was going to make questioning him *and* keeping the blood inside my body trickier.

"You sure I can't get you another coffee?" I said. "You've been working like mad on those murders. Is it a power grab?"

He scratched his stubbled head. I could always tell how busy he was at work by how much his hair grew in, because he preferred his scalp shiny bald. "While I'm the first to say that nature and gangs abhor a vacuum, these killings aren't from someone trying to take over."

Sadie trudged into the kitchen, grabbed her lunch, and headed for the back door.

"Have a good day," Eli said.

She half nodded, half shrugged.

"Come home immediately after school, okay?" I said.

"Yeah." She left, her shoulders hunched. I almost wished for her attitude back, punctuated with a good door slam.

"I'm so glad it's your week to have her." Eli munched on his remaining piece of toast. "You're way better at dealing with her sad face than I am."

"Maybe if we give Tovah's parents time, they'll come around. Sadie does need Ohrist friends." I joined him at the table, tossing my napkin over the remnants of my now-cold food, as I flipped back to our previous subject. "How can you be so sure these murders aren't a leadership grab?"

"It's not just the Hastings Mill crew that have been taken out."

"I heard that on the radio."

His gaze flitted to the window. "The vics had their necks snapped, but there were puncture marks."

"Shit."

"It's why, as angry at Sadie as I am, part of me is grateful that BatKian offered her that deal, instead of any other consequences." He paused, the half-eaten toast in his hand forgotten. "How fucked up is that?"

I could dance around Sabrina's disappearance with Eli, but if the killer was one of Zev's bloodsuckers and they'd taken the missing woman, then I had to secure his permission to continue pursuing this. However, if it was one of Vincenzo's enemies who'd come to town, that was its own mess, since he wasn't willing to discuss that possibility.

Luckily, Eli was lost in his own thoughts and didn't notice my lapse in conversation.

I rested my foot on my opposite knee and leaned forward to stretch my hip and low back. "Have you spoken to Ryann?"

"Yeah, her dad has me acting as liaison with her. Unofficially, of course." Right, since most cops had no idea that magic existed.

"Are any of the slain gang members Ohrists? Do they have ties to vampires?"

"Why the curiosity?"

I switched sides to stretch the other hip. "You know what gang wars are like, and if magic is involved and someone comes to Tatiana to fix their mess? It's best to be prepared."

"True. Well, one had magic, but none had known ties to BatKian's crew, and none were vamps themselves. The only common denominator between the vics was their rap sheets." He wiped his mouth with a paper napkin and carried our plates to the counter. "Ryann is hell-bent on finding the rogue."

"She's not letting Zev deal with it?" That was unprecedented.

"No way." He dumped his toast crusts in the small compost bin next to the sink. "This vamp is out of control and Ryann wants them brought in by her people. She doesn't trust BatKian to hand them over, especially since he's been turning more Sapiens than usual."

My eyebrows shot up. Was Zev replacing vamps he'd lost to the contagion? It explained the new trainees and why he was bringing more to the dark side. What about the tired-looking vampire and Rodrigo saying there were three left? Three victims of the disease? I shook my head. Kian's blood cured them, so it must have meant something else. Oh well, that wasn't my problem.

Zev wouldn't use Sadie to null Ryann's magic for getting in the way of his plans, would he? No, that would be suicide. He'd never get away with it. I wrapped my cardigan tighter around myself, unable to thaw the icy core inside me.

My thoughts of new vampires triggered a disturbing notion and I frowned. "What if these murders are a power grab, but not between gangs?"

"Meaning?" Eli grimaced at a glob of butter on his hand and rinsed it off.

"Vamps in these parts don't need to go on murderous rampages. They're very well taken care of in Blood Alley."

"Psychopaths are psychopaths," Eli said, drying his hands. "Human or vamp."

"Then why contain the violence to gang members? Those humans carry guns, which can still do a lot of damage to the undead. There's way easier prey for the vamps to slaughter for kicks."

"You think some vamp is looking to start their own crew?"

I shrugged. "Why not? If I was a vamp looking to take Zev on, I'd want criminals on my team."

"They're doing a piss-poor job of it, eliminating some of the best candidates." Eli frowned. "Unless they're taking out the ones that would be hardest to manage."

"Could be," I said.

"Fuuuuck." Eli rubbed his hand over his stubble. "Taking on Zev? Thanks for that totally unwanted angle to pursue." He headed to the front door. "I better give both Espositos the heads-up."

"Wait. Where's the Hastings Mill gang's HQuuuuueeeee—" I bent over gasping, holding my wrist.

Eli dropped his plate in the sink with a clatter. "Did you hurt yourself?"

"Sprained it the other day," I said through gritted teeth.

"You want a tensor bandage?" Off my head shake, he shrugged. "I have no idea where they've set up shop now."

I called bullshit, but the direct approach was out. Stupid oath.

"By the way," I said, "Juliette heard from Daw's healer in Bangkok. She's healing, slowly but surely." The pain dialed down to a mild throb, as if the magic was waiting to pass judgment depending on what I said next.

"That's great." Eli narrowed his eyes.

"Some nights, I lie awake reliving that game and what would have happened if we hadn't saved the players in time."

His suspicious expression softened. "Me too."

"I'd like to think that even with all the details, I'd still have gone after them." The ache in my wrist had disappeared, but I continued to rub it. "Though it would have been good to poke around and eavesdrop on the Consortium beforehand."

Eli took my wrist, carefully turning it over in examination. Looking puzzled, he glanced from it to my eyes and sighed. "Yup. Magic really complicates things."

I shot him a grateful smile.

"But I'd only have agreed to checking the Consortium out beforehand if we'd done it as team," he said, "like we handled the rest of it."

"Totally." I'd never actually been alone dealing with the Consortium, even when I destroyed their game space, because my animated shadow had accompanied me.

He shot me a level stare. "Delilah doesn't count."

I blinked, positive I hadn't spoken out loud.

"Though I'll admit that your cloaking came in handy." He

tapped his finger against his lips. "Sabrina Mayhew was reported missing last night."

"Was she?" Good thing he didn't hear my racing heart. "By a colleague or a partner or..."

"A friend." Eli regarded me with a shrewd expression. "Missing persons is coordinating with us because of the connection to the Hastings Mill gang."

"Makes sense. Well, I'm sure she's got the best possible people on the case."

"I'm sure she does. I have to get to work, but in answer to your earlier question, Hastings Mill has a variety of business interests." He named a café, a couple of bars, and even a bubble tea shop, all of which provided a public front for the organization's activities. With all the cash that poured through those kinds of establishments, they were also a great way to launder money.

"Eli?" I clicked the pen I'd used to scribble down the business names. "I appreciate your confidence in me. On the Consortium case," I hurriedly amended at another achy throb.

He pressed his lips together and looked away. "I wasn't the one who asked for your help finding Teresa Wong. Deputy Chief Constable Esposito suggested it."

"Oh." I'd been ecstatic when Eli wanted to partner up. This respected detective had wanted me to work with him as his equal, but with this admission I felt transformed from a sleek thoroughbred racing alongside him to a donkey he'd been saddled with.

The blood magic warning signal stayed dormant, but my back twinged.

"I was wrong," he said. "Okay, not wrong—"

"No. You were doing fine with that description." I tore off the notepad paper I'd written on. "You saw what I was capable of during Raj Jalota's murder case."

"I saw some of it. The parts you finally shared. And one case didn't equate to years of training and experience. So yeah, I still had some doubts." He nudged my foot. "They were blown away when we worked together to save those players. *You* blew me away."

Blushing, I tossed my hair. "Obviously," I muttered.

"You're more plugged in to the magic community so anything you learn about these murders, I expect you to share. Off the record, of course."

I hesitated, but the blood oath didn't have a problem with that. Noted. Murder intel okay, just keep Sabrina out of it. "Why, Detective Chu, are you using me as a mole?"

"Yup." Laughing, he sidestepped my swat and left.

How did a vampire going after Zev affect my case? Sabrina jailed Paxton Craig, failed to make her wedding to a vampire, and then some fellow bloodsucker started tearing out gang members' throats. I drew fangs on the paper I'd jotted my thoughts down on, unable to find a reason for Sabrina to be caught in that. There was nothing about the Sapien lawyer that could be used against Zev.

Unless this rogue knew that Sabrina was Vincenzo's fiancée, and they intended to set BatXoha on Zev as a distraction for Vancouver's master vamp while they made their power play?

Vincenzo withholding information about his second being killed was understandable; hiring us to find Sabrina and not mentioning a rogue vamp as a potential suspect made no sense at all.

I moved over to the sink and ran hot water over the dirty dishes. Beyond the Vancouver connection, was there any other reason Vincenzo came to us for assistance? He had vamps who worked for him. Was he staying mum about something that directly impacted Zev and using us to sidestep vamp politics? Because if that were the case, Sadie's deal wouldn't be my most pressing concern.

Whether it was the rogue or one of Craig's minions who'd caused Sabrina's disappearance, I'd find them and bring them down. She'd chased her dream of being a prosecutor and successfully put away criminals who had previously evaded justice. It would have been so much easier for her to go into divorce or even corporate law, but she refused that path, striding confidently along the one of her choosing.

It was one thing to brace Vincenzo for the worst, but I'd keep the faith she was alive and act accordingly. Her abductors would rue the day they ever touched her.

After drying off my hands on a tea towel, I looked up addresses and opening hours for the various businesses that Eli had given me. Most didn't open until later, so I phoned Tatiana to update her on our paying gig, speaking over the clacking of her manual keyboard while I ran a lint brush along my precious velvet sofa.

"You're working on your memoirs and not another letter, right?" I said.

"Ye of little faith."

"That's a no, then, is it?" I teased.

While she agreed that a vamp power play was a strong possibility, she didn't like the ramifications any more than I did.

"Hopefully you'll find something useful today," she said, "because Vincenzo phoned. I hear you told him to prepare for the worst." She clucked her tongue. "It's a hell of a thing for anyone to accept, never mind a vampire, but you were right to bring it up."

One thing I loved about my boss was that she didn't often caution me about investigating things on my own. Not because she didn't care about my well-being but because she assumed I could handle myself. It was refreshing to have a person, especially a woman who'd survived in a dangerous field, set the baseline of my capabilities so high.

I wouldn't insult her by asking if she was afraid of repercussions from our client.

"In other news, Nav didn't recognize the amulet." I tore off the lint roller sheet now covered in fuzz and started on the sofa arms with a fresh sticky piece. "Hey, I could go visit the new demon proprietor of Chester's."

That would kill several birds with one stone. If the new owner knew about a demon with fire powers and the ability to manipulate ohr who had been in Northern British Columbia a few months ago, I wouldn't have to get the ring from Giulia for the raven shifter, Nora.

There was a burst of clacking keys and Tatiana groaned, resuming her typing more slowly. "It's between owners."

"Again?"

"Apparently. The latest demon had a run-in with a vampire and it's back in Carpe Demon's hands."

"So much for that." I headed into the foyer and slipped on my shoes.

The keyboard fell silent. "If I'd had any sense that those murders could be part of this case, I'd never have agreed to take it on." She sighed. "Find Sabrina and let's extricate ourselves from this entire mishegoss."

"On it, boss."

That was easier said than done, since neither the café, the bubble tea place, or the one bar that was open yielded anything. To my endless delight, I then got a text ordering me to Blood Alley. Why couldn't Zev sleep during the afternoon like a normal vampire?

Showing remarkable restraint by not firing back *Your wish is my command*, I sent a simple *On my way*, wondering why he wanted to see me.

I'd almost convinced myself that Zev had rescinded the bargain with Sadie and would demand a favor from me, when I stepped into his territory and ducked behind a dolly piled with boxes at the sight of the lethal being headed down the lane.

Yoshi.

Eyes narrowed, I peeked up over the box tops, gauging the odds of backing out through the gates, cloaked, before he gave chase. Our last encounter had ended with him learning my secrets through my blood and I'd intended to give him a wide berth. Instead, he'd blindsided me with this meeting.

I stepped forward to meet him, my chin set at a stubborn angle. Bite me once, shame on you. Bite me twice, prepare to lose your teeth.

12

The ancient vampire had fully recovered since I'd seen him last. His hair was once again dark and lustrous, and his handsome face was youthful and free from the ravages of the disease that had temporarily aged him. He strode toward me with his familiar lithe elegance, with nary a twisted limb. The estrie blood had worked wonders to restore him.

I stood my ground, my magic dancing under my skin. I'd played an integral role in bringing back the demon who'd cured Yoshi, but that didn't mean he'd thank me for it.

He stopped in front of me with a serious look, his sharply structured pants and shirt swirling to settle softly along the strong lines of his frame. "I owe you a debt of thanks."

I silently cursed at his less-than-grateful tone. "Not necessary, considering I had no idea I was helping you at the time."

"Still." He caught a fly by its wings and flicked it away.

Dark shadows snaked around my feet, Delilah alert if not fully animated. "Gift cards are nice."

Yoshi's lips briefly quirked. He tilted his head as if listening for anyone within earshot, then motioned me inside one of the black lacquered doors.

Reluctantly, I followed him. Yoshi was even older than Zev, so I had to assume that he'd see through my cloaking as well.

A quiet hush enveloped the small room. The wood on the poker table gleamed as brightly as the bar set up discreetly in one corner, but the house lights washed everything in a flat glare that would be softened when the lamps with the Tiffany shades were flicked on.

I closed the door at Yoshi's nod but stayed by the exit.

"Tell your ex to stop working with the Lonestars," he said. "In any capacity."

"What?" My pulse spiked and my hand closed over my car keys in my pocket. No vampire had permission to enter Eli's home, but if my ex had to be warned, then I needed to get hold of him stat. "Why?"

"The Lonestars are up in arms about this rogue vamp. Esposito is paranoid they have or will turn criminals and she put an edict out yesterday. That vampire and any accomplices will be incarcerated on Deadman's Island, as will all humans, whether Sapien or Ohrist, turned from the start of the murders."

"That's not fair! Humans aren't at fault for some rampaging bloodsucker."

Yoshi's eyes glinted. "Watch yourself."

I bowed my head in silent acknowledgment. Ryann's decree put a huge crimp in Zev's plans to top up his vamp base due to the contagion. Not that I was dumb enough to voice that. "Isn't it in Blood Alley's interests to also stop the rogue?"

Especially if there was a power play underway.

"Vampires don't answer to Lonestars about our business," Yoshi hissed.

"Fine. What does any of it have to do with Eli?" I said.

"Esposito has assigned the whole force to this. If they identify and capture this rogue before we can bring them in, it'll be war and anyone who's helped the Lonestars will be considered an enemy."

I backed into the doorknob. "Why are you telling me this?"

"I pay my debts. But, Miriam?" In half a heartbeat, he came nose to nose with me. "You didn't get that information from me." He reached out, and I flinched, but he was opening the door. "Come. Zev awaits."

"What does he want to speak to me about?"

"You'll find out."

Gee, thanks. That wasn't ominous or anything. I stomped up the crooked lane past human employees picking up trash. Vacuuming could be heard through several partially ajar doors and the air smelled of lemon polish. If I was being led to the guillotine for some reason, shouldn't storm clouds press down and a rot clog my nostrils? Grave danger would be so much easier to spot if it didn't smell so refreshing and citrusy.

Yoshi ushered me past the basement floor with Zev's office, and down yet another flight.

I had to squeeze past the Undertaker as he marched up the stairs, whistling and carrying a tray holding blood vials, on top of which was a small, bright yellow plastic sharps disposal box. I did a double take.

Did the "three" that Zev and Rodrigo had discussed at my last visit refer to the number of après blood donation snacks they had provided for the estrie? Had that tired-looking vamp's head shake indicated that Kian had drained one to death?

I paused on the bottom step. Was I being brought in as the next tribute? Couldn't they do cookies like a normal blood drive organization?

"Hurry up," Yoshi said.

We bypassed the regular dungeon for the narrow, windowless prison housing the demon, and he nudged me through the gap that was the sole way into the cell.

I peered into the gloom and my mouth fell open.

The space had been transformed. A thick carpet covered the center of the floor, and tapestries hung on two of the walls to hide much of the iron coating and dispel the damp cold. Soft orbs of light stretched across the ceiling, providing enough illumination to read the books piled in one corner next to the heap of large cushions and knit blankets.

Not quite as cozy were the scattered bones that were too large and curved to belong to a human. The one closest to me had a blob of glistening pink meat stuck to one end, but otherwise had been gnawed clean by something with very sharp teeth.

I swallowed and took a step back. "I'm mostly fat," I protested. "You really want a high protein source. May I suggest a nice bodybuilder?"

"What are you going on about now, Ms. Feldman? No, never mind." There was no threat in Zev's voice, merely impatience. The vampire rested on his calves in the middle of the carpet in jeans and a T-shirt that stretched across his broad shoulders and hugged his biceps.

The simplicity of his outfit hammered home the vampire's raw power. Somehow, the less clothing he wore, the fewer layers of civility masked his core primal nature. His expensive suits were as much a cloak as my black invisibility mesh.

Zev cradled the estrie in his arms but he was by no means embracing her. He brushed her hair away from her face and pressed a ceramic mug—that I recognized as one of Jude's—with what had to be blood to the demon's lips, encouraging her to sip from it.

That did not make it less weird. Nor would I have gotten within biting range of the demon even if I were Zev.

"She likes gift cards," Yoshi said from the entrance.

I whipped around. "The estrie?"

Did they want me to go out and buy the demon a spa day?

Yoshi pressed his lips together like he was holding in a laugh. "You. For your role in my recovery."

I snorted. Right, nice cover for my real gift of the heads-up for Eli. I crossed my arms, about to demand the reason for this jail time, when Kian snapped her head toward me, her ancient primal sentience boring into the deepest parts of me, and my brain stuttered.

Her gaze was as sharp as her teeth. It was a promise that she would sever my soul from my flesh, my flesh from my bones, and crush any memory of me to dust.

A bead of icy sweat ran down my back.

"Society has become woefully impersonal." Zev pressed another sip on his maker, unaware or uninterested that I was choked with fear and not contributing to the conversation.

I punched my way through the terror Kian inspired by latching on to facts. Yoshi wouldn't have warned me about Eli if I was being fed to the lions, and Zev wouldn't be droning on about the ills of society if he was going to kill me. Okay, well, he'd totally pull an evil monologue, but it would be more targeted.

The estrie blinked, and I took a deep breath. Now that she'd stopped staring at me, I could take her in properly.

Kian looked deathly pale—undeathly pale? Worse than she should. Being held captive with all the iron in here was taking its toll on the demon, but she was clean, and the rags she'd been dressed in when I brought her out of Gehenna had been exchanged for a long dress in a soft-looking material. Her hair was free of snarls, and on her feet was a pair of slippers that appeared to have been knit by someone's grandmother.

Slowly, I wrangled my breathing under control.

"I remember when people selected a gift perfectly tailored to the recipient and that person was delighted to receive it," Zev said. "Now people are happy with cash to a generic store. No wonder humans are in such a state. Basic civility is a thing of the past."

Civility? I barely bit down my scorn that he could dress this cell up all he wanted, but he still held his sire captive in a prison designed to cause her to suffer and render her too weak to escape.

"Need anything else?" Yoshi said.

BatKian shook his head. "That's all for now. Thank you, my friend."

"I look forward to my gift card," I said.

Yoshi smirked and left.

The estrie reached out for the mug but Zev shook his head. His response was too quiet to hear, but he lay a hand on her cheek and her pinched expression eased.

"Yoshi filled you in on Esposito's little edict about turning humans?" Zev selected a small metal device from a leather sleeve on the carpet. I couldn't see it properly from my angle, but it seemed rather tooth-extractiony in nature.

Damn you, *Little Shop of Horrors*, for making the dentist song so catchy. Cloaking was useless against the vampire as was deploying any magic attack. I couldn't even get into the KH through any of the shadows since Blood Alley was a hidden space.

Zev picked up the estrie's left hand and straightened her index finger.

I ground my teeth together. He'd shown her kindness—the carrot—and now he was going to use the stick. Or whatever that torture device was. Kian was a tool to him, same as Sadie.

The vampire went to town—on the estrie's cuticles. She hummed softly, rubbing against Zev's side like a cat, while I openly gaped at them.

Zev raised an eyebrow. "The Lonestar?"

"Right." I rubbed my arms briskly, but it didn't dispel the cold. "Yoshi told me."

"Good." He snipped away. "I understand Detective Chu is a liaison with the Lonestars."

In light of Yoshi's warning about pulling Eli from that job, I wasn't sure how to answer, but there wasn't any point in lying. "He is."

Zev pointed the cuticle cutter at me. "You will feed me all the information that the good detective learns. As he learns it. Understood?"

Was this Zev's way of offering Eli amnesty in working for the

Lonestars or would Zev seek vengeance on my ex regardless of whether I gathered useful information from him?

It sucked that I couldn't ask because Yoshi could kill me for breaking his confidence.

A hot kernel of anger lodged under my skin, dispelling some of the cold in here. Why drag me into this prison with the demon when Zev's office would have sufficed for this meeting? Had Zev set this scene as theatrically as he had with Sadie? A bit of psychological manipulation to coerce me to agree? My lower back seized up, and when I flinched, something in my shoulder tweaked painfully like a nerve pinched all the way up my neck.

Zev would never give me the full truth, but after everything we'd gone through from the Torquemada Gloves to bringing Kian here, I doubted he'd resort to showy ploys. Besides, nothing about his interaction with the estrie felt staged for my benefit. Zev was tending to his sire, whom he truly cared about. Multitasking with our meeting was merely the best use of his time.

Perhaps once he'd viewed me as much of a child as he did Sadie, but we were beyond that now.

I was beyond that. Zev had given me his word to keep my family safe and I'd hold him to it, no matter what it took.

"I'm not privy to Eli's police investigations," I said evenly.

Zev moved on to his sire's other hand. "Then cloak, go to the police station, and get the details."

Did he even hear himself right now or had he existed in such an exalted place for so long that any nonsense sounded reasonable? "No."

Zev paused his ministrations to raise an eyebrow. "I beg your pardon?"

"No, I won't ask that of Eli, nor will I steal intel from the cops." I held up a hand to cut off his protest. "May I remind you that you're hiding the only estrie on earth? You have a lot of secrets, whereas I no longer have any."

"Is that a threat?"

"Nope, just a reminder that I don't appreciate threats either. I don't want to be your enemy, and should you wish to hire me through the proper channels, I will do my utmost to succeed on your behalf."

Zev's brow furrowed like I had spoken an incomprehensible language, but the estrie narrowed her eyes, an almost thoughtful expression on her face.

"You'll do as I say." He gave a dismissive wave.

"Or what? Will you threaten to come after me and my family? Rescind your promises whenever it's convenient?"

"It's not convenience when it pertains to my well-being." He gave me a wry smile. "You of all people should understand the fine print."

"Oh, I understand a lot of things, including the fact that you have a reputation for your word being your bond, but I guess that's as fake as the trappings in this cell." I twirled a finger at the carpet, cushions, and tapestries. "Dress it up all you want, the cold, hard truth is still there for everyone to see."

A red haze descended over the vampire's eyes. "You forget yourself."

"No, you do." I was playing a dangerous game, but I couldn't stop now. I wouldn't. His manipulations ended today. Ever since I'd reclaimed my magic, I'd given myself props for becoming empowered and ending this years-long feeling of invisibility and helplessness. Yet as soon as there was a threat, I ran to him for protection.

Look where that had gotten me.

Zev hadn't been there to save me from Tatiana's homicide attempt or when Jason Maxwell of the Consortium had come after my family. In the end, his promises hadn't mattered. My relationships with others plus my magic was what kept me safe.

And I'd keep all of us safe now.

I stepped closer to Zev, kicking a bone out of the way. "Touch anyone of mine and I will come after you with everything I've got." I held up a finger for each ally I named off. "Lonestars,

Ohrists, Tatiana, hell, I'll personally rip out the perception filters of every last cop in the Vancouver Police Department to take you down. I'm done being toyed with. And that's a promise you can count on."

Zev blurred to his feet, slamming me up against a wall by my throat. "You bug. You presumptuous nothing. How dare you speak to me that way?"

Shadows swam over my skin, my scythe appearing in *my* hand, not Delilah's, its tip pressed to the underside of his jaw.

Both of us froze.

I no longer needed my shadow to kill vampires? What a lucky day. I smiled.

His breath ruffled a lock of my hair, and while the hand that clutched my neck twitched in reminder that I was at his mercy, he held himself absolutely still as if in acknowledgment that he was also at mine.

I scraped the blade along his throat and his nostrils flared, his eyes flashing in warning. I lowered my weapon to my side.

Zev stepped back.

My heart pounded in my throat as I inched sideways to the exit, but he didn't stop me. I held in the laughter burbling up, but a victory dance was in the very near future.

"You dare speak of a presumptuous nothing?"

My magic shattered at the words that reverberated through the room with the shrillness of a rusty saw, and I turned to the estrie with the same wide-eyed, slack-jawed expression as Zev wore.

"My progeny. A mere child, existing at my whim, forced me from Gehenna to do his bidding?" Kian advanced on Zev in jerky fits and starts. Her footfalls were muffled by the carpet, yet I felt each one shiver up through my feet.

I backed up, but I was already pressed against one of the tapestries.

Were the air not so soaked with a violent current, needing only a single word to make it spark, I'd have relished Zev's hastily sucked in breath and how the corners of his eyes pinched tight, his eyebrows drawing together.

She cracked her neck from side to side, bones popping in a rippling sound like scales on a piano. "Do you think me so easily cornered?"

My brain screamed *Run*, but my feet were too heavy to move.

"No." Zev placed his hands together in supplication. "Mistress, vampires are dying. I called you forth as our only means of survi—"

The estrie flicked her hand and Zev flew across the room, crashing into the pile of books and skidding along the cushions where he fell still.

I pressed a trembling hand against my mouth. I'd intended to get Zev off my back about spying on Eli and I'd succeeded. Allowing me to leave had been his acquiescence on the matter. He wouldn't have come after me.

Now, however? My mouth was dry and my rubbery legs barely held my weight. I'd seen him bested. The vampire who was always so rigidly in control, in power, had been tossed aside like a rag doll, and I'd witnessed his humiliation.

Zev would kill me for it.

If Kian didn't get me first.

The estrie rolled her arm backward over her shoulder to point at the torches in the hallway behind her with crooked fingers. "Leave."

The grotesqueness of her movement spurred me into motion. I sprinted out the door, glancing back for one last look, but the rock panel slid closed with a *thunk,* and a male scream echoed through the stone.

I ran.

13

DINNER WAS A SILENT AFFAIR. SADIE WAS SULKY FROM being grounded while the rush of sympathy I'd felt for Zev since racing out of Blood Alley was messing with my appetite. I pushed my spaghetti and meat sauce around. Loath as I was to admit it, the contagion had placed Zev in a terrible position. First, he'd betrayed Tatiana to save Yoshi, then he'd forced the estrie to do his bidding to save other infected vampires, and now Ryann's directive prohibited him from recovering his population.

Tatiana was rightly pissed off, but Kian didn't even acknowledge that she had any responsibility toward the survival of a species that she'd helped to create. She'd displayed a narcissistic fury on a whole other level, which, worryingly, wasn't as freaky as the way she moved. If I'd been told they modeled the scary girl from *The Ring* on Kian, I wouldn't have been surprised.

I toyed with my water glass. Why did she let me leave? Did I not matter since Zev was the sole target of her anger? Or was the demon seeding chaos, knowing the master vampire would come after me?

Vincenzo, Zev, even Kian. I'd like to tap into their brains and tear out their secrets so I could find Sabrina with minimal bodily harm to any of us.

The buzz of a text made me jump. Shit, Vincenzo was coming to town.

More than one desperate family had gone to the station to ask Eli if he'd caught their loved one's killer yet, their actions sometimes bordering on harassment. As determined as I was to find Sabrina, I felt far more comfortable with several thousand kilometers and a border between me and the accident-causing fiend.

I messaged him that he should stay in Vegas until I got hold of him, but he didn't respond, and the phone call I placed didn't even go to voice mail.

"Damn it!" I threw my cell onto the table.

"What's with you?" Sadie said.

"Having a bit of a day." I forced down another two bites before pushing my plate away. "How was school?" I craved her chatter to anchor myself in the moment instead of all the torture scenarios that ran through my head should I fail to save Sabrina.

However, when I got only grunted responses, I gave up.

After Sadie cleared the dishes, I dumped soap and water on them but didn't wash them. I didn't even wipe down the counters.

What did housekeeping matter anyway?

Grinding my teeth against the pain rocketing along my right hip and up through my neck from all the stress, I popped a "house pill." I'd nicknamed it that because it had the same shape as a child's drawing of a home, but it was a heavy-duty painkiller that my doctor had prescribed several months ago for horrible menstrual cramps due to perimenopause. It knocked the pain out all right, along with my fine motor skills and proper enunciation.

Sadie had retreated to her bedroom, so I curled onto my magnificent sofa, stroking the velvet pile as a calming technique. I didn't have the emotional or physical energy to play spy but sitting here wouldn't accomplish anything other than feeding my fears.

I decided to attempt something less dangerous than a James Bond mission. Potentially less dangerous. I brushed my nose against the velvet couch. Differently dangerous.

Giulia couldn't murder me for asking to borrow the ring Laurent had given her, right? It would just be a little favor.

Since I had about an hour until the house pill made me too groggy for anything other than sleeping, there was no time to waste. I checked on Sadie, who was doing homework, to tell her where I was going.

She looked up, her brown eyes clouded with worry. "Be careful."

"Eh. How much damage can one little cat do?"

"Hmm." She pursed her lips. "Are we talking bashing you with her stone head, ripping you open with her claws, or just crushing you? Because my money's on the gargoyle."

Scowling despite my desire to do a happy dance at her teasing, I chucked a hoodie at her from the pile of laundry on her chair. "You're a brat. And put your stuff away."

"Yeah, yeah." She made a "run along" motion.

Figuring that Zev wouldn't be up to attacking me tonight, and he wasn't about to do anything to Sadie so long as their deal stood, I threw on a warm jacket and hobbled my way into the KH with one hand on my back.

Pyotr was reading to his Chinese evergreen plant, Scarlet. At my entrance, he placed a fat finger between the pages of the final *Lord of the Rings* book, which he'd gotten from his friend Malorie. He looked me over, commented that I was more hunched and twisted than his grandmother—and the sculptor who'd carved her had been drunk—and returned to his place in the story.

With that charming comment, I shoved a sock into a pocket and hobbled along the gloomy path until the exit appeared in the rock, then I stepped onto the downtown street in front of the condo complex on the edge of Yaletown where Giulia lived. I peered in through the wrought iron courtyard fence, but no one sat outside among the softly glowing solar lamps.

Continuing to put one foot in front of the other while in this much pain was overwhelming so I sat down on the stone fence outside the tower's front door. I didn't have the energy to whistle or loudly call out for her, depending on her acute hearing to respond to me saying her name.

It was cool tonight and I hunched into my coat, glad that I'd worn jeans because the cold seeped up from the stone into my butt.

"Ciao, bella."

I gasped, pressing a hand to my heart.

Not even a whisper of wind had presaged her landing on the grass. One blink she wasn't there, the next she sat calmly licking a front paw. A paw whose middle of the three toes sported a gold band with a blue stone set into a carved base.

The cat gargoyle twisted the gem to catch the light.

I sighed. "Nice ring."

"Oh, this?" She preened. "Laurent gave it to me. Though I'm sure he's given you lots of jewels."

"Not a one," I said.

She gave a satisfied purr, the mottled "fur" carved on her seeming to ripple. Giulia knew that Laurent and I were involved, though I was no longer on her hit list.

I hoped.

"I have a favor to ask."

"Will I help you with skin cream?" The cat narrowed her eyes. "Do you not moisturize, bella?" Her Italian-accented English was tinged with disapproval. Tatiana would love her. "You are looking more aged than usual. And why are you sitting funny?" She arranged her limbs into a gross parody of my poor broken body.

"Stress."

Giulia tossed her head back. "Men are very visual creatures. You should take better care, especially given how much older you are than Laurent."

I took the hits with only a minor clenching of my jaw. "About this favor—"

Giulia dropped onto her belly, her head on her front paws and her eyes morphing from jet black to an eerily glowing gold as if lit from behind. Her lids flickered like a movie projector stuttering.

I'd seen this behavior once before when Laurent had questioned her about the whereabouts of a dybbuk. Gargoyles' original function as inanimate objects was to ward off evil. The few who gained sentience and had wings, like Harry, fulfilled that duty by patrolling the city. Gargoyles without wings, like Giulia, found evil by seeing through the sightless. Statues, ornamental facades, any inanimate object with a face in the city became her eyes. However, I'd never seen her drop into this trance unprompted.

Giulia's lashes flickered, but she didn't snap out of her reverie. Her paw with the ring lay a scant couple of inches away from my hand.

I folded my sleeves over my hands to ward off the evening chill, waiting for her to become lucid again so we could speak, but the painkiller kicked in first. My shoulders relaxed, and I took a blissfully full deep breath, bending forward and back, my thoughts now as languid as my movements.

Even if I stole the ring, Giulia couldn't prove it was me. Not steal, obviously, just borrow to get the information from the raven about McMurtry's killer. Then I'd grab it from Nora and return it to Giulia.

I was brilliant.

I reached for her paw.

Her body shook like she was throwing off an itch, and when she resettled her head, the ring now rested under her jaw.

This was a setback but not unsurmountable. I pulled out my phone. I had to stab the home button a bunch of times before it unlocked, my eyes screwed into slits and my tongue stuffed in the corner of my mouth.

Plan, I typed, because lists were important. *Cloak, hold paw, and when she moves, slip off ring.* Brilliant. Phone in hand, I poked her paw, expecting cold, hard stone, but it was warm, and she purred at my touch.

Aww, she liked me. I smiled, my head close to hers. *I like you too.*

No borrowing ring, Miriam. That's bad.

I flicked a whisker, chuckling when she wrinkled her nose, and stroked her back, falling deeper and deeper into the soothing motion.

Her eyes sprang open, the gold glow vanishing. "Ma che cosa? What are you doing?"

"So pretty," I drawled.

Three wicked sharp claws extended from her paw. "Were you petting me like a house cat?"

"Pfft. No. You are a fierce feline. Hear you…" Unable to think of an appropriate action word starting with F, I held up a fist. "Fierce it."

She glanced at her paw. "Were you stealing my ring?"

"No." I bopped her on the leg I'd just petted, hissing when she sliced my finger. I sucked it into my mouth and made a face because blood tasted gross.

"Stealing bad." I explained in detail how I could have borrowed it, but I wouldn't do that.

Her frown grew deeper and deeper. "Basta. You aren't making any sense. Whatever is wrong with you, stop it now."

There was so much bristly irritation packed into her exquisitely carved body that I giggled.

"Miriam!" She headbutted me in the chest. "You must help."

"Ow. You meanie."

She cursed in Italian. "Vamps are headed for some teenagers. Four blocks south. Keep them from being fed on."

I spun around. "Never eat shredded wheat."

"What are you doing?" Her eyes practically bugged out of her head, and I had to remind myself not to laugh.

The scowly face I made felt funny, though, so I made it again. "Finding south. North, east, south, west." I pointed in the direction that south was.

Growling, she nipped my shirt and repositioned me. "Phone Laurent to help. You are useless."

I held up the phone. "Will you give me the ring if I do? Just to borrow." I wagged my finger in her face, but I got distracted by the tracers coming off it and forgot what else I meant to say.

"No." She jumped back like I'd wrestle her for it.

"That's okay. Your ring, your choice. Zev's going to kill me, and I'll never know who murdered my parents, but I'll find another way to deal with the shifter."

Giulia growled. "You cannot guilt me."

I blinked. *Did I use my inside voice outside?*

"Yes! And you did it again. Call Laur—no, there's no time." She lowered herself onto her belly again. "Get on my back and hold on."

She wanted to give me a piggyback ride? Fun. I straddled the hundred and fifty pounds of literal rock-hard muscle.

"Omph. You're heavy."

Not so fun.

Giulia leapt into the air, soaring up to the top of the condo tower.

Shrieking, I flung my arms around her neck and held on for dear life, my eyes screwed tight. Wind streamed across my face.

"You. Choking." She smacked me with a paw.

I loosened my hold a fraction of an inch.

She thudded onto the roof, but her paws had barely touched down before she launched herself again, nimbly hopping along the rooftops, until with a faster rush of air on my feet, she landed on something spongy.

I cracked an eye open. We were on the grass of David Lam Park, which stretched along the waterfront, mere blocks away from Giulia's perch.

She threw me off and sprinted toward two boys with gelled

poufy hair. Their baby-faced teen looks didn't mean shit in terms of age, but the trio of adolescent girls they'd zeroed in on, talking on the playground swings, wouldn't know that.

I jogged after the gargoyle, shivering at the cold breeze coming off the water and keeping other parkgoers away. There weren't any cyclists on the seawall or couples taking selfies in the park itself. Even the boats in False Creek quietly bobbed against their anchors.

The girls hadn't noticed Giulia, but the boys had. They laughed as she pulled up in front of them.

She puffed her body out with a hiss. "Leave them alone."

One of the boys swaggered right up to her and chucked her under the chin. "Whatcha gonna do to us, kitty cat?"

You are going down, bloodsucker. Skipping, I sped up to get a front row seat to Giulia ripping off the offending hand.

"I said, stay away," she said.

I cocked my head. The fiend should have been ash three times over by now.

The gargoyle shot me a pleading look, which my groggy brain failed to decipher.

Girlish laughter rang out from the playground, and I quickly glanced over, but they were oblivious.

The other vamp sneered. "Did you bring your crazy cat lady owner?" He pushed past me. "Move it, grandma."

I tripped him. "Whoops."

He ended up with a mouthful of grass. Rolling up on an elbow, he spat it out with the always original, "You're dead, bitch."

"Language." I tsked him.

Delilah hopped out of the shadows and pressed a foot on his neck.

"The fuuu—" He gulped as the scythe appeared in her hand and she dragged it down the side of his head.

Sadly, in all the fun of scaring this shit, I'd lost track of the first vamp, who now had Giulia in a headlock.

"Think I'm strong enough to snap it?" Grunting, he torqued on her neck.

Giulia's eyes were enormous, her breathing coming in shallow pants. It finally occurred to me that if she wasn't attacking, it was because she wasn't allowed to, not because she couldn't take these prats.

"That's not necessary," I said.

"Get your shadow to step down." He tightened his hold on the gargoyle. "We've heard all about her and that scythe."

Now was probably not the time to boast about reputations. Or magic upgrades.

Delilah stepped off the vamp on the ground and the scythe disappeared.

The asshole on Giulia shrugged. "Eh, I'm a dog person." He torqued up in readiness for his final attack, keeping an eye on Delilah.

My scythe slammed into my hand, and I swung.

His head bounced off the lawn, his mouth agape.

Before his body even hit the ground, I'd pivoted and smashed the weapon into vamp two, catching him in the midsection. Dislodging my scythe with a messy and meaty sucking noise, I decapitated him.

I wiped the blade off on the grass, avoiding the two piles of ash. Killing vamps was more fun than dybbuks, since I didn't have to remember any special words first. Just wham and bam and thank you, ma'am. I screwed up my face. "Did I use my inside voice?"

"Yeah." The tallest of the girls, a lanky blonde, had spoken.

She stood close by with her two friends, a girl of Asian heritage with a nose piercing, and a brunette in an oversize skater hoodie.

"Thanks for dealing with them." The teen with the nose piercing held up a fist. "Vamps are the worst."

"You're Ohrists."

The brunette nodded and crouched down next to Giulia,

who'd been uncharacteristically silent, rubbing her throat with a paw. "You okay, precious?"

Giulia purred, nudging the girl's hand with her head.

This was some cue for all three to descend on the gargoyle, kissing, hugging, and petting her, telling her how brave she was.

I did a little dance around their circle of love, my arms out, ready to grab a human when the temperamental gargoyle hit her limit of physical contact and filleted one of them, but it never happened.

The girls asked Giulia where to find her and promised to come visit. Then, thanking me again, they left, once more chattering among themselves a mile a minute.

Giulia rubbed her ear, watching them leave with a wistful smile and something harder to place.

I screwed up my face, casting about for where I'd seen it before. It finally hit me because both Emmett and Pyotr had shared that expression. "Giulia?"

"Hmmm?" She turned to me. "Sì. Grazie, Miriam. You saved me."

"You don't owe me thanks."

"Good, because it took you forever to realize that gargoyle mediators cannot attack any other supernaturals. I could have been badly hurt."

"I'll try to be quicker on the uptake next time. That aside, would you like to come for dinner sometime? Even if you don't eat, that's okay because my golem friend, Emmett, doesn't either, though Pyotr does. He's another gargoyle friend."

She blinked at me, jerking her head.

Scared I'd offended her, I took a couple steps back.

"We are...friends?" she said carefully.

I winced. I'd messed up the start of our relationship. True, I'd been saving my own ass, but for someone who'd prided herself throughout her professional career on the importance of women supporting other women, I'd been needlessly cruel.

"I'd like us to be friends, if that works for you," I said. "I'm sorry for the way things started, and I take full responsibility for that." I smiled. "Also, I think you'd like my daughter."

Something hit me in the chest and I winced.

Her ring lay on the grass.

"Oh, no." I picked it up, the cunning beauty of the poison ring subsumed by the ugliness of me taking it from the gargoyle, who, despite her flashing eyes and jutted-out jaw, looked achingly vulnerable. "That's not why—"

There was a rush of wind. Giulia was gone.

14

I WOKE UP ON THURSDAY FEELING DULL AND BLURRY thanks to my house pill hangover. I drank a ton of water, knowing from previous experience that I'd feel better within the hour, but as my back and neck were still a knotted-up, throbbing mess, I booked a chiropractor appointment for later today, snagging the last open slot.

Considering that I didn't have any leads on Sabrina and that Vincenzo could already be here in town, I felt like I deserved a break. And thus, I corralled Eli into helping me with a very important task.

"Are you sure about this?" Eli said in hushed tones, skeptically holding the paint chips at an angle. One was royal purple, the other in sunflower yellow.

The employee stood by the mixing machine, which loudly rattled the cans.

"If the last few months have taught me anything, it's that my greatest regret will be dying in a beige void." I added another plastic liner to the pile of brushes, rollers, and other assorted painting supplies.

"And with Sadie grounded, now is the perfect time to force my child into hard labor."

"I didn't mean the colors so much as our child. Twenty bucks says she'll get lost in her playlist and do half the ceiling as well."

"Young grasshopper will learn from her mistakes." I pursed my lips. "But we better get another can of white just in case."

The employee removed one of the cans from the shaker machine and levered it open with a wooden stir stick. The rich purple winked in the light.

I clapped my hands together. "Perfect."

Eli poked me. "Why are you so chipper?"

"I can stand mostly upright, and I've decided not to dwell on Zev having access to my home."

Eli's face darkened into a scowl, and I grasped at the air as if I could physically take the words back. "Why the newfound concern, Miriam?" His bland tone wasn't fooling anyone.

Even the employee raised his eyebrows as he unveiled the yellow for my approval.

I flashed him a thumbs-up on the color. "Let's just say I didn't see Zev at his best and leave it at that. It has nothing to do with Sadie, I swear."

My ex wasn't thrilled about the explanation, but he didn't push me, which was enormous in terms of trust on all things magical.

"You're a good man, Eli Chu." I pushed the cart to the cashier.

"Yeah, yeah."

"You know the list of places you gave me? Was there anything you left off? Doesn't matter how nebulous a connection."

He thought about it. "I've got one more possibility, but it won't be open yet." He gave me the name of a pub located down by the docks on the east side.

After I'd paid, Eli lugged all the paint and supplies to my sedan.

"Buy you second breakfast in thanks?" I said.

He scratched his chin. "This is a coffee payout at best. What's up?"

I'd hoped to do this over food, but Eli held my car keys hostage.

"Here's the thing."

"Nope." He slammed my trunk closed. "Nothing good ever started with those words."

"Right? But still. You need to disassociate yourself from the Lonestars on these murders." I grabbed the keys from his hand and got into the car.

It took him a moment before he followed, and he slammed the door harder than necessary, so I gave both of us until we got back to the main street to continue.

"This goes no further," I said. "Not to the deputy chief constable and especially not to Ryann." I hit the horn and my brakes with equal force, avoiding a car jamming itself into my lane.

Eli grabbed the seat belt, his grip tightening as I recounted Yoshi's warning about Zev going after the Lonestars and any accomplices.

"I thought Ryann was your friend." Eli dropped his hands into his lap and shot me a look of incredulity.

"She is." I inched the car into a right turn, cranking my neck back and forth to check for any cyclists barreling down the hill.

"Then you have to give her the heads-up that the vamps will go to war over this."

A pedestrian cleared the crosswalk and I turned right. "Eli, I realize that you used to babysit Ryann, but you're underestimating her. That woman, sorry, that head Lonestar, is crazy powerful and incredibly smart. She understands every ramification of going after the rogue vamp, and she's got all her officers in her corner. She'll be fine. You, on the other hand, will be a sitting duck. Vamps can't turn Ohrists like Ryann, but you're a Sapien. Step away from the job. Please."

I braced myself for his blustering that he was a trained cop and could handle himself, but he pinched the bridge of his nose with a soft exhale.

"After we survived the Human Race and saved those players, I felt incredible," he said. "The rush was like beating my all-time track record combined with busting open a months-long investigation. Not only had I survived magic, I'd triumphed over it." He chuckled. "Not to be too crude, but I got hard just thinking about it."

"Understandable." I grinned. "I got lady hard."

"But just when I thought the ground beneath my feet was solid, magic-wise, I get knocked upside the head with the reminder of how small a fish I am." His hand dropped to where his gun belt holster would be if he was on duty. "Part of it's ego, I know, but a bigger part is the strain of bouncing between these extremes of utter confidence and powerlessness."

Up ahead, the light turned yellow, and I slowed to a stop. "Being a homicide detective isn't the same?"

"Not really. After all these years, there are patterns. If XYZ, then it's likely a crime of passion. ABC is a targeted hit. Plus, I never had the problem of murderers coming through my walls."

"I'm special that way." I pulled up to the curb outside our duplex and set the parking brake. "Will you resign as liaison?"

He unfastened his seat belt. "Yes. I'll tell Deputy Chief Constable Esposito that I'm feeling pulled in too many directions."

Being the mensch that he was, he carried everything from the car into my foyer. "Gotta book. Want to get a jog in before my shift."

I made the sign of the cross against him. "Begone, fitness freak."

Once he'd left, I retrieved Giulia's ring from my underwear drawer where I'd stashed it and headed downtown.

When I reached my destination, I double-checked the address that Harry had given me against the metal numbers on the brick building because this didn't seem like somewhere a folklorist would hang out. I'd expected the library or some café, but the gargoyle was always reliable, so I shouldered in through the doors and up to the second floor.

The walls not covered in funky mismatched tiles were painted with characters from the game design company's products. There was no reception area, just a huge open space populated by cool toddlers.

Okay, not fair. The twentysomethings couldn't help being dewy skinned and brimming with youthful vitality. Nor was it their fault that the characters and slogans on their graphic T-shirts made me feel ancient and uncool, as did their casually revealed tattoos and piercings.

If Nora was one of this bunch, how could she possibly help me?

I swear my back creaked, my spine hunched into crone formation, and a wart grew at the end of my nose as I tried to get the attention of the two men dueling with pool noodles. They were the only ones not wearing headphones, engrossed in their laptops, and sitting at modular desks or on comfy chairs with their feet on low tables made of slabs of wood.

One of the men spun to block the other's noodle.

The second guy lowered his weapon. His bright orange hair spiked along the crown of his head like stegosaurus spines. "Grayson, dude. How many times can Orion use that move? We've got to reblock this sequence."

Could I train with pool noodles? Fun. I ran a hand over my cardigan. "Excuse me?"

They turned polite faces my way.

"Can I help you, ma'am?" Grayson said.

I winced and refrained from adding a creaky tremor to my voice. "I'm looking for Nora Doyle."

Orange Hair jerked a thumb to the far back corner. "Boots in the red chair."

"Will I be disturbing her?"

"No more than we all usually are," Grayson said. He and his opponent laughed good-naturedly.

Off my hesitation, Orange Hair nodded. "It's fine. Honestly."

"Thanks."

I waded through the smattering of employees. None of them gave me a second look, but that was almost worse because all my old insecurities around invisibility came roaring back. I pinched the inside of my wrist to dispel the negative thinking. These people were busy working. Nothing more. The world didn't revolve around me.

Nora was a petite woman wearing a pair of chunky soled leather boots with heavy silver buckles that weighed half as much as she did. A shock of blond hair fell over her green eyes, her head bobbing along to the music drifting out from her headphones.

"Nora?" I crouched down to eye level to wave at her.

She pulled one side of the headphones off. "Yeah?"

"I'm Miriam."

Nora looked at me blankly for a moment, then jumped up and set her laptop on her red chair. "Seriously? Awesome. Come on." She hurried toward a glass conference room door, egging me to follow her with an impish grin.

We took our seats at the large round table in a room that smelled of coffee.

"If you don't mind me asking," I said, "how did you go from a degree in folklore and mythology to video games?"

Nora smiled. "Spoken like someone who hasn't played one."

"Does *Tetris* count?"

"Sure, but not in this context. Historically, storytelling has been at the heart of a lot of games, and it's gotten far more sophisticated. I'm a die-hard gamer." She laughed at my stony stare. "Shifter ones too, but I meant video games. I love world-building and mythology, so this job? It's a dream. Way better than academia, which is where I'd have ended up with my master's degree. Now." She bounced on the ergonomic leather chair. "You got the ring?"

"Yes." I slid it over to her, and her breath caught.

"Hello, beauty. Show me your secrets." She flipped it over, her bottom lip caught between her teeth, and ran her fingernail along each decorative groove.

A tiny needle shot out, and Nora squealed in delight.

My shoulders slumped. Giulia had handed it over without any expectation of its return, but I couldn't take it away from her. It was from Laurent, and given her reaction to my dinner invitation, the cat gargoyle didn't have many friends.

The trouble was, I couldn't give it to Nora and then steal it back either, because that was all kinds of shitty.

The raven shifter used the hard case of her phone to push the needle back in, a sheepish expression on her face. "The rumors of this being Lucrezia Borgia's poison ring are likely just that, but better safe than sorry."

I placed my hand over the ring and sighed. "I can't give this to you."

Nora sat back in her seat. "You want the information first? No prob."

"It's not that. I'm sorry. I shouldn't have gotten your hopes up for the ring. It's not mine to give, and I was wrong to come here." I put it back in my purse.

She cocked her head, studying me. "We can play for it."

"God no." I stood up. "No offense."

"Why not? It's easy enough to get the information that way."

I snorted. "I know how playing shifter games brings things into existence."

"So?"

"Not interested in complicating my life that way." I turned around to leave, the ring in my pocket, but she stuck her leg out, blocking me.

"It doesn't have to be connected to you."

I planted my hands on my hips. "I'm not playing a game and shuffling the consequences onto someone else."

She dropped her foot abruptly and shrugged.

I studied her for a long moment. "How about a different trade?"

"Like what?"

"A puzzle."

Nora rubbed her chin. "Keep talking."

Sitting down once more, I pulled the amulet I'd gotten in Vegas out of my purse and slid it over to her. "Any clue what this is? It may be connected to a fire demon."

"Oooh." She leaned in, her eyebrows raised and her eyes wide. "May I?"

"Go ahead."

Nora examined the amulet, muttering to herself. "Not Mesopotamian. Egyptian? No, that doesn't feel right either. I don't recognize it from any tales I've studied in ancient cultures." She pulled out her phone. "Mind if I draw them for further examination?"

"Do we have a trade?"

"Hell, yeah." She quickly sketched them in a drawing app.

I tapped the middle figure. "My favorite is the one that looks like a wingless duck."

She nodded. "It's pretty good, but I like this figure on the left. Poor dude is just the number seven with legs. Doesn't even get a head."

"You wouldn't happen to know anything about the angels Senoi, Sansenoi, and Sammaneglof, would you?" I said casually, over the pounding of my heart. "Like maybe if these engravings are of them?"

Nora began the third drawing. "I don't know about those three in particular, but angel sigils tend to be abstract. These engravings are crude, but these guys have legs and the two bird-like ones have heads, so they do convey a physical form."

"When you say sigils, you mean pictograms to summon angels?"

"Summon or invoke their powers. There was this grimoire called the Key of Solomon, thought to belong to King Solomon, who had a bunch of them." She tapped the amulet. "It's likely these three are demonic in nature."

I wasn't sure if that made me feel better or worse.

Once she was done copying images, she gave the artifact back. "Harry said you wanted to know about a recent supernatural event, but he didn't specify. Which one?"

I wrinkled my nose. "You seem like a bright young woman, but I'm unclear how you're possibly plugged in enough to help me."

"Ah." She swung one leg over the other, her foot bobbing. "My mom is an archivist. And…" She bit her bottom lip, studying me, then exhaled. "She works for the Library of the Arcane."

"That's a thing?" I slapped the table. "How do I get a card?" Why hadn't Tatiana told me about this place?

"It's not open to the public and it's a highly guarded secret." She gave me a pointed look and I nodded, even though I had a million follow-up questions. "Archivists document all things supernatural. Events, important people, that kind of thing. The records are filed in the library. I've been helping my mom document things in our community for years."

"I'm archiving and cataloguing Tatiana Cassin's documents for her memoirs."

"Wow, Tatiana's a legend. That must be fascinating."

"It is." I was reassured by this random similarity between Nora and myself. Still totally wanted into that library, though. "Fred McMurtry's death. What do you know?"

Her face shuttered.

Oh crap.

I rolled my chair back a couple inches into a shadow. "Touchy subject?" I said blithely.

"What's your interest in it?" she asked.

Shoving aside my natural inclination to make up some excuse, I folded my hands on my stomach. She'd shared the secret of the library; I could reciprocate. "I want the name of McMurtry's killer."

Her eyes narrowed. "He died in a house fire."

"No." I leaned in, spreading my fingers over the table. "He really didn't."

She rocked back on her chair, her gaze drifting to the window. "It's a bummer about the ring, but I like your moral code. You know how many people have turned down my offer of an easy way to get what they want with no repercussions to themselves?" She held up one finger. "Take my advice. You don't want to poke around in McMurtry's shit. Hell, I certainly wouldn't."

I held up my hands before she could rise, trusting my gut that now was the right time to share. "Twenty-seven years ago, my parents were murdered. Their necks were snapped before my home burned down. McMurtry covered up the truth, and when I got close to him to demand answers—"

Nora paled, the chair thunking back down on all four legs. "Someone took him out the same way."

I leaned closer. "Did you know him?"

Shaking her head, she raised stricken eyes to mine. "My dad was a Lonestar. He died a couple years ago. Heart attack."

"I'm sorry. He must have been young."

"Late fifties." Yikes. That was young. "He investigated your parents' case."

A shiver skittered up my spine. This was one coincidence with the young woman too many. Had he aided McMurtry in covering things up? Was that why Nora had warned me off? I fiddled with my purse strap, my gaze on my lap. Was my gut wrong about her or was I lapsing back into paranoia and her dad being on the case truly was a coincidence?

"Actually," she amended, "that's not entirely correct."

I tensed. This was where she said that there was nothing nefarious to look into.

Nora traced her finger around one of the wood tiles that made up the tabletop. "To be more specific, Dad tried to investigate, but he was shut down."

"Oh." I untwisted the purse strap from my fist.

"I didn't know about any of this until Mom turned to McMurtry's funeral. Dad hadn't liked his former boss, but I figured small town and all, she had to pay her respects. I was home visiting so I went with her, but when we got graveside to pay our last condolences, my incredibly polite mother muttered that he'd finally gotten what he deserved."

"How much did she know?"

"Not as much as you'd probably like. Dad was convinced it was a cover-up, and he hated that a magic family in our community wouldn't get the justice they deserved. Also, McMurtry had been sick before the fire, then he went away on vacation and came back healthy."

"I suspect a demon had a hand in that."

Nora whistled. "Can I tell my mom that to add to the archive?"

"Go nuts."

"That's about it. The current head Lonestar who took over from Dad when he died was one of McMurtry's people." She spread her hands wide.

"He helped write off their deaths as house fire victims."

She nodded. "You're sure McMurtry's neck was snapped?"

"Positive."

Nora tapped her phone. "And you think this amulet is connected to it?" She bounced in her seat when I nodded. "My mom is going to freak when she hears all this. I can tell her, right?"

"Yeah. Especially if she's willing to help me figure out what it all means."

"She will. Mom loves her puzzles even more than I do."

Smiling, I stood up. "Nora, I think this is the beginning of a beautiful friendship."

Despite the fact that our meeting had gone wonderfully, by the time I got to the chiropractor's office for my much-needed appointment, I was still so knotted up that the doctor kept murmuring "Oh my" as she worked on me.

My body felt somewhat better after the treatment, though it hadn't boosted my mental state. Well, I had four hours to get my head in the game. With Vincenzo somewhere in the city impatiently waiting and Sabrina's life on the line, failure was not an option.

15

I SWUNG BY GIULIA'S TOWER ON THE WAY TO THE gang-owned dive bar to return her ring.

She took it back with a sad smile. "Grazie, Miriam."

What had I done wrong? Did she believe that all relationships existed as quid pro quo and now she felt compelled to do something in return? I frowned. Gargoyles were go-to creatures for information and golems performed tasks, but in my experience, they were treated as tools more often than friends.

Jude, Laurent, me—we were all good people, and yet all of us were guilty of the above. Emmett, for all he was loved, had huge insecurities about how he fit in and his worth, Pyotr, despite all the Banim Shovavim using the KH, was comically excited when I'd become his first real friend, and now here was Giulia, another lonely supernatural.

"Giulia." I jangled my car keys to get her attention. "You're still invited for dinner because you're my friend. It was wrong of me to ask you to give up your gift from Laurent and I'm sorry."

She slid the ring onto her paw, her expression brightening. "You are forgiven." She licked my chin with her raspy tongue and I squirmed. "But if he ever gives you a better present?" She snicked out her claws.

I took a step back, then narrowed my eyes. "What happened to not hurting other supernaturals?"

She scratched her face, her gaze briefly darting away before she gave a forced laugh. "Kidding."

"Uh-huh."

"Or am I?" She sailed back to her rooftop.

Awesome. She'd almost crushed me once over Laurent. My boyfriend was sooo making it up to me for placing me in a "do not injure" exemption.

I backed up to my sedan, keeping an eye on her, but before I got there, the world swung sideways with a sickening lurch, depositing me back in the underground grotto. The brilliant turquoise waters rippled, casting rainbows on the stone walls, and the Leviathan raised its armored head above the surface to train its dark, vast gaze on me.

"Hello." I gave it a feeble wave.

There was a rumble, and Smoky took shape, its socket-less stare sending a second wave of goosebumps over my skin. "Have you found the Ascendant?"

I fiddled with my car fob. "I'm working on it, but it's only been three days."

"Four." Smoky gave me a grim smile exposing far too many pointy teeth.

Everyone wanted things to happen right away. Tough, the world didn't work like that, and being badgered by a phantom smoke face was not helping tonight's mission.

"I'm doing my best," I snapped. "And considering I'm your only option, don't antagonize the person doing you a massive favor."

Smoky's eyes, such as they were, widened comically and its entire face stuttered.

"Not used to people talking back, are you?" I planted my hands on my hips, unleashing my sternest mom face and voice. "Look, I'm in full agreement that Senoi, Sansenoi, and

144

Sammaneglof were total dicks for exiling you here, and I'm happy to get you out, but don't harass me."

Smoky's gaze dipped down to the rest of the Leviathan and it nodded.

"Good." I flipped my hair off my shoulder. "Now return me to my car."

———

The final Hastings Mill business that Eli had directed me to was a classic dive bar with scuffed floors, gloomy lighting, and a plethora of beer signs nailed to the walls.

Thanks to my invisibility mesh, I waltzed past the gruff bartender and the few day-drinking patrons into the back office without incident. No one was in there, allowing me to thoroughly search all the drawers and the battered old computer on the desk. There was a ton of porn but no useful information.

I sat down on the chair that was more duct tape than fabric at this point. Gangs in Vancouver were smart and ruthless, and this one didn't keep incriminating material at this particular property holding. I smoothed down a frayed edge of duct tape. With their boss in prison, someone on the outside had to be running the show for him. As I pulled out my cell to call Eli, two men entered the office.

I fumbled the phone, managing to catch it before it hit the ground—which would have alerted them, cloaking or not.

The older man, with a pot belly and a grizzled ZZ Top beard, slammed the door, causing the nudie calendar on the back to bounce against the wood.

I tamped down my snort. Phrasing.

Scrambling out of the chair before Old Guy got the surprise of his life, I backed into the corner, standing in a handy escape shadow.

Despite Old Guy taking the seat behind the desk, it was the

other man with his flat dead eyes and scarred hands that made me shiver.

He checked under the skinny cactus, behind the calendar, and even unscrewed the light bulb. When he examined the stack of old car magazines tossed on the filing cabinet, he was so close that I had to suck in my gut and wrap my arms tightly around my midsection to keep from brushing against him.

"We're clean." Old Guy swung his booted feet onto the desk. "Charlie already swept for bugs."

"Can't be too careful," Scary replied. Even his voice was devoid of emotion. Not robotic, more as if normal rhythm and cadence required energy he couldn't be bothered to expend.

I swallowed a few times past the dryness in my throat.

"Is it on or not?" Old Guy said.

"It's on. One man each." Scary succinctly gave details of a meeting with the leader of a rival gang. He pinned Old Guy in his gaze. "Don't fuck this up, Tom."

The other man's sneer came off as a grimace. "Fuck you, Harley. I outrank you."

Harley smiled thinly. "Of course you do."

Tom thudded his boots back on the floor. "It's that bitch's fault. If she hadn't put Paxton away, we wouldn't be dealing with this shit."

I perked up. Yes. Keep talking.

"Pax got careless." Harley rubbed the twisted scar tissue on his left hand. "All that matters now is that Mayhew was found this morning and will be back in our hands tonight. Provided you don't botch the meeting."

Back in their hands? They'd had Sabrina and lost her? No matter. She was alive and their loss was my gain. New plan: crash the meeting, grab Sabrina, and get her to safety. Easy peasy.

A truck rumbled up outside.

Tom glanced out the window, smoothing his beard down with one hand. "Booze is here." He headed for the door.

Harley followed but paused in the doorway.

I edged one foot into the in-between space between here and the Kefitzat Haderech, the air turning spongy beneath my feet as I balanced on one leg on solid ground.

He glanced back into the corridor, then blinding light shot from his palms, turning the room into a bright white void.

Cracks appeared in my cloaking.

Harley narrowed his eyes and flexed his fingers.

I envisioned my giant crochet hook, patching up the mesh as quickly as possible, but for every hole I closed, another two opened.

An Ohrist whose powers were wrestling mine into submission? Holy hell! Of all the ways my spy mission could go sideways, I'd hadn't remotely considered this.

The light intensified and my shadow magic melted off me in long drips. The mesh still covered my face, protecting my identity, but my cloaking magic was a giant bull's-eye. How long before Harley identified and tracked down the lone Banim Shovavim in the city?

I flung myself backward into the KH, but Harley's eyes met mine for a horrifyingly long moment before I vanished.

The pain of landing on my ass on the stone floor paled in comparison to my tight chest and racing heart. He'd seen me. Fuuuck! Did the others know he was Ohrist? Would he show up at the meeting?

Pyotr wasn't in the cave reception area, so I grabbed a sock and got myself back to my car in record time, very glad that I'd parked several blocks away from the dive bar.

First up? A text to Vincenzo saying that I'd have Sabrina tonight. I scratched my wrist, which throbbed sharply as if to hold me to that, but the vamp didn't reply. I hoped he was busy and not on a plane. Should Sabrina's anxious fiancé demand continual updates, or worse, micromanage this operation, things could go horribly wrong.

I'd deal with any Harley repercussions once Sabrina was safely in my keeping.

When I got home, I put a few pieces of my rescue plan into place. Luckily, Tatiana had convinced Laurent to be on staff so I didn't bleed out like a slaughtered cow when she enlisted him to come with Emmett and me.

I served Sadie her favorite fish tacos for dinner to get her in a good mood, then unveiled the paint cans and plastic tarps.

"Ta da!" I pulled the lid off one can, revealing the brilliant purple color.

My daughter bounced on her toes. "Are you having the place painted? Finally! I won't have to live in tapioca pudding."

"I *am* having the place painted." I nudged a plastic tray liner against her foot.

She frowned at it. "What am I supposed to do with this?"

I snapped a foam roller onto the metal frame. "I refuse to believe that your critical thinking skills are that poor."

Her face screwed up, then her eyes widened. "You want me to paint?"

"I knew you could get there, honey." I pressed the roller into her hands. "Start with the living room. Tape along the ceiling and make sure you use the angle brush for the seams. Then start with a coat of primer."

"Bu-bu-but—"

"Use your words."

"This isn't fair! I'm already grounded."

"Aw, poor baby. You have to spend more time in your room with all your devices, which I kindly did not take away." I dumped the rest of the supplies out of the large plastic bag. "You snuck into Blood Alley and then made a deal to help Mr. BatKian at his discretion. So you're going to repaint the living room and the kitchen, and if you whine about it, you'll find yourself doing the entire house." I balled the bag up. "Am I understood?"

My daughter nodded meekly.

"Good."

Hey, if Harley showed up, maybe I could just mom voice him into submission. Heh.

"I'm working tonight." I ignored the throb in my wrist, hating that I couldn't tell her exactly what I was doing since I'd promised to be transparent whenever magic was involved. We hadn't sworn a blood oath, but I took that vow more seriously than anything. "I've let your dad know so he'll keep an eye on the place, but if you hear anything or get weirded out at all—"

"I'll sic my magic on them."

"That's one option. The other is run next door."

Sadie dropped the roller in the paint tray. "You think Mr. BatKian will show up?"

"Nope." Well, maybe, but he wouldn't terrorize Sadie. She was safer without me home. I kissed the top of her head. "They're 'just in case' instructions. Now." I swatted her butt. "Go change and start working, my little minion."

"You're the worst," she muttered and stomped out of the room.

"Yes, but I'll be the worst in my beauuuutiful purple living room. And cover my couch before you start. I love it more than you right now."

She slammed her bedroom door, and I laughed, my spirits restored. Maybe tonight wouldn't be an unmitigated disaster.

16

It was, of course, an unmitigated disaster.

Laurent, Emmett, and I arrived at the small parking lot above the train tracks by New Brighton Park for the meeting to return Sabrina to the Hastings Mill gang. In summer, it served as overflow parking, accessed from a quiet service road, but on this drizzly September evening, it was deserted.

The sun had already set, and the overcast sky cut down on the moonlight. There weren't many streetlamps along the road either, providing plenty of shadows, but Emmett and I still hid behind a high clump of prickly blackberry bushes, both of us cloaked. Harley the scary guy couldn't nix my magic if he didn't have a line of sight.

The wolf made himself scarce elsewhere.

Emmett nervously fingered a capped syringe. Assuming that Sabrina would be traumatized, Tatiana had obtained a sedative for her from "her guy." Other than checking that this concoction wouldn't kill the lawyer, to which I'd received a scoff, I'd chosen not to inquire about the details of what we were giving her. Plausible deniability and all.

Juliette was on standby back at my boss's home. Hopefully BatXoha would allow Juliette to treat Sabrina before he showed up because it wasn't fair to expect the young healer to do her best with a powerful vampire menacing over her shoulder.

I shook my head. We'd deal with that if it came to it.

Emmett's fidgeting was causing his leather jacket to rustle, so I pressed a finger to my lips, scanning the lot.

According to the information I'd overheard back at the dive bar, each of the two men meeting would have one person as backup. If Tom brought Harley, that complicated things. It was worse if Harley surprised us midway through the rescue, though Laurent had thoroughly checked the area and conveyed with a low yip that we were alone.

For now.

We'd get Sabrina back. I could feel it.

Just when I was ready to hold Emmett down to keep him from fidgeting, two vehicles pulled up within minutes of each other.

Tom and some thug with a shaved head got out of a pickup truck, while two men in complementary track suits exited a sports car that had been blasting a bassline through closed windows.

I peered through the bushes, tensing because there was no sign of Sabrina. Did those asshats have the poor woman stashed in the trunk?

Believing themselves alone, the men didn't bother lowering their voices, and since they stayed a good twenty feet apart, their conversation was loud and clear.

"Well?" Blue Track Suit, the leader of the other gang, stepped forward. BTS. I smothered a laugh, imagining him doing snappy choreography.

Tom crossed his arms over his denim-encased beer belly. "It's not us and it's not Suresh's crew. There's a new player."

The track suit dudes exchanged looks.

"Bullshit. No one else has the muscle for this." BTS ran a tongue over the gold grille on his teeth. "I lost a good man."

"We both did."

"No, you lost a couple of lowlife pieces of scum who'd been causing trouble for your people." BTS moved his jacket away, resting his hand on a gun in his waistband.

The others immediately followed suit, the air sharpening and strung tight. One wrong finger twitch would unleash a maelstrom of violence, but none of the men even blinked.

Emmett grabbed my hand and I held on tightly. Neither of us were bulletproof, and while we could get into the KH, I wasn't leaving without Sabrina.

"How do we know you weren't covering up a hit on your own by taking more out?" BTS said. "With Craig gone, your guys are running wild."

Tom notched his chin up. "You threatening me, son?"

"I've got eyes, old man."

"So do we," Tom said with a smirk. "In places you can't imagine." He let that sit for a moment. "Where's the bitch?"

A shot cracked through the night and Tom fell backward onto the ground, blood dribbling from his head and down his cheeks to stain his beard.

I swallowed a scream while Emmett slapped his hand over his mouth. BTS's minion had executed Tom.

The minion trained his gun on Tom's buddy next, the one with the shaved head.

A muscle ticked in the targeted man's jaw—his only recognition that his weapon was still holstered and he was basically fucked.

Track Suit Minion motioned for the lone Hastings Mill member to get onto his knees.

I eyed the sports car, running the odds of getting to it undetected to search for Sabrina while the men were preoccupied. Cold? Yes. But it was the only place she could be, and two gangs set on offing each other wasn't going to keep me from finding her.

Shaved Head lowered himself slowly as a motorcycle zoomed into the lot and skidded to a stop.

Harley whipped off his helmet and jumped off the bike.

Adrenaline coursing through my veins, I yanked Emmett further down behind the bushes even though there was no way the Ohrist could see us.

Harley thrust out his hands and blasted a wave of light magic at the other humans, who covered their eyes.

The skin on BTS's face turned red and raw. He gave a pained exhale, fumbling for his weapon, which he immediately dropped as his hand bubbled into a mass of ruined flesh.

A train whistle and the rattle of cars from the rail line that ran through this part of East Vancouver didn't drown out the anguished cries of Harley's victims, all of whom were incapacitated by the light, though only BTS was being barbecued.

"What do we do?" Emmett whispered.

These men weren't innocent. Their deaths would improve society, and I had to locate Sabrina. Still, I hesitated before I grabbed the syringe from Emmett's hand, hissing at him to stay put, and skirted the shadows along the far edge of the parking lot, determined to get to the sports car.

A wolf's howl rent the night. It was the cry that villagers wove stories about when safe behind thick locked doors, while still speaking in whispers, desperate not to draw that attention their way.

Harley flinched, his magic dimming for a precious moment.

Shaved Head whimpered, and even I broke out in a cold sweat, reassuring myself that Laurent wouldn't hurt me.

Harley whipped around, firing balls of light into the darkness.

BTS fell to his knees, his burned arm hanging uselessly at his side. The minion propped his shoulder under his boss's shoulder, half dragging him to their vehicle.

A banging sound started from the trunk. Still invisible, I sprinted toward it, keeping one eye on the action.

Shaved Head pulled his weapon. His hand trembled at the wolf's next howl, but he raised the gun to the back of Harley's head and—

The trunk flew off the sports car and hit the concrete halfway across the lot.

Something blurred past me, and by the time I spun around, blood arced from Shaved Head's throat.

A vampire licked red streaks off her fingers. Her suit was tattered and filthy, her blond hair was matted, and her green eyes bore a crazy glint.

Eyes that I'd seen flash in triumph on the news.

Sabrina Mayhew.

The gasp that punched out of me felt as loud as an explosion.

Track Suit Minion almost dropped his boss, and even Harley visibly trembled, his light magic flickering and dimming.

Sabrina swiped a finger through the blood, sucked on it, then kicked the body aside like a bottle containing a cheap vintage not up to her standards.

I swallowed a scream.

Swearing loudly, Track Suit Minion dragged his boss to their car.

Laurent tore out of the darkness, two hundred plus pounds of lethal muscle and emerald eyes that burned with an unholy fire against his white fur.

Harley pitched orb after orb, alternating between the blood-sucker and the wolf with increasing desperateness, but Sabrina barely spared the new predator a second glance. She stalked the Track Suits.

I was forced to stop and look away or be blinded, but the sizzle of flesh and the thud of two more bodies were more than enough clues to the state of things.

Don't let it be Laurent. I dug my nails into my palms. Normally, the wolf would make short work of a new vamp, but Sabrina was unhinged. Clearly in need of blood, she'd been abandoned by her sire and left to go rogue instead of being brought in for care at Blood Alley. Now she was a marauding loose cannon.

Harley's magic abruptly stopped, and I blinked away the final traces of dazzling light.

A swathe of fur along Laurent's right flank was scorched but otherwise he was unhurt. My gaze jumped from body to body, sifting through the carnage, and I gave a strangled wheeze, my magic falling away.

Harley's head had been flung aside like a discarded soccer ball, leaving Sabrina to feast on the stumpy neck still attached to his torso. She clutched his chest, his ribs cracking like dry twigs.

Harley had been the wild card I was most concerned about tonight. He had magic, he knew I was there, and he could have done serious damage to everyone on my team, but Sabrina disarmed him in a flash because she was peckish.

I gagged, muscling down bile, while she squeezed his body like it was a cheese tube and she had the munchies.

Dark crimson was smeared along her mouth and up one cheek, a chilling accompaniment to her closed eyes, flushed cheeks, and slight sway.

The wolf knocked into the vampire, dislodging her. He bared his fangs and she bared hers, growling with such ferocity that it turned raspy before she blurred off down the service road with Harley's desiccated corpse.

Laurent was in hot pursuit.

I should have been as well, except I couldn't make myself go into the dark night with the smell of hot copper clogging my nostrils.

Staying firmly in the light, I inched closer on wobbly legs to the dead men, hypnotized by the blood sprayed over the dirty cracked concrete like graffiti.

Distant traffic, voices, a wolf's growl, all sound blended into a buzzing noise that made as little sense as the four bodies, three of whom had no heads.

My stomach lurched and I spun, vomiting into a rain gutter.

The syringe fell from my grasp and rolled away, mercifully intact.

Rock-hard clay hands clomped down on my shoulders and I screamed.

"Get hold of yourself." Emmett was wild-eyed. In all the chaos, I'd completely forgotten about my partner.

I clutched his biceps, resting my forehead to his.

"It all happened so fast," he whispered.

I nodded. All these lives extinguished in an instant, the world already moving on. Violence begetting more violence; was fighting the good fight as deluded as trying to slap a Band-Aid on a bullet wound?

Emmett scooped up the syringe, and we made our way back to my car on the service road in silence. I couldn't stay with those bodies, and not just because any Sapien cops or Lonestars might show up.

We sat on the hood, waiting for Laurent's return. Guilt at leaving Sabrina to him when she was my responsibility was buried under a layer of numbness so profound that I kept flexing my fingers and toes to make sure they still worked.

Sapien, Ohrist, vampire—there was no winner tonight. Sabrina, in particular, had lost so much: her career. Her marriage? Her sanity?

Emmett paced up and down the road, peering intently into the gloom for any sign of the shifter and vampire, while I tried to put the pieces together in a way that made sense.

Whoever was behind this had miscalculated badly. Was I back to an attack against Vincenzo using his human lover to weaken him, or was this truly a strike at Zev by turning the lawyer and abandoning her, leaving the master vampire to deal with the fallout?

I stared up at the dark clouds, wishing for pinpoints of starlight to break up the heavy gloom. Anyone loyal to Zev knew better than to abandon a Sapien after siring them. A coldly logical part of my brain wondered if alerting him about tonight's events could get Sadie out of her bargain, but without concrete answers I had no leverage.

Snarling and the patter of claws alerted me to the wolf's

return. He had one of the vampire's sleeves grasped none too gently between his teeth, prodding her forward.

Sabrina hobbled along with a funny bent-over limp. She passed under one of the few streetlights, showing the twisted bloody foot that she dragged.

The wolf bore bloody gashes down his front and under one eye, and he was breathing hard, but his gait appeared normal.

Emmett and I ran to meet them halfway.

Sabrina snarled and lunged at us, but Laurent yanked her back, allowing Emmett to jam the syringe into her neck. Barely ten seconds later, she was unconscious.

Well, I hoped she was, because young vamps were cold to the touch, and it wasn't like I could check her breathing.

The golem helped Laurent drag her to my car and lay her in the trunk with a snort. "Finally," Emmett said. "Shotgun."

I opened the back door for Laurent to retrieve his clothes and go shift, but he hopped inside and lay down, licking my hand before his eyes closed. His fur was matted with blood and sweat and I let him be.

Emmett was already making a big production of settling into the passenger seat, so I shut the back door and went around to my side.

"Fasten your seat belt." I jerked my chin at Emmett while clicking mine in. My car stank, mostly of wet wolf, so I cracked a window. I left the radio off so I could hear any thumps coming from the trunk, but other than the wolf's soft snores, all was quiet. Even the streets were relatively free of traffic.

"Why'd you bring me tonight?" Emmett said, fiddling with all the buttons on the dashboard. "You could have jabbed her yourself. Am I on a pity retainer from Tatiana?"

"Don't be ridiculous. You man the enthrallment hotline and I couldn't have stolen the Torquemada Gloves without you."

An ambulance siren grew closer, so I pulled over to the shoulder of the road.

"Because I don't have a heartbeat, not because of anything I actually did."

"That's not true. When we were ambushed by that guy with the poison needles, I'd have died without your quick thinking. Same for getting into that pod unscathed when we took Route 666 into the Human Race. And you helped Tatiana get the lowdown on Vincenzo."

"The only thing I've ever had going for me was my prophecy ability and now I'm not supposed to do that."

I tightened my grip on the wheel. I wasn't at my best to handle his existential crisis, but I'd be a shitty friend if I wasn't there for him now, especially since he'd also voiced these feelings back in Vegas after Vincenzo froze him.

The ambulance whipped by and I resumed driving.

"Emmett, you're not even a year old."

"What does that have to do with anything? I'm not a kid."

"No, you're not, and a lot has happened to you in your very short life. But humans don't just burst out of the womb as action heroes."

He crossed his arms, staring sullenly ahead.

"Even as a librarian, I had to work my way up."

"But you started solving kidnappings and murders as soon as you got your magic."

"After *hiding* my powers for almost thirty years, I reclaimed them with no clue what I was doing. Thanks to all my other life experiences, I could apply them to the new situation I found myself in. Give yourself time to learn and live. As for tonight?" I did a quick shoulder check before merging into the right lane. "Other than chase after Sabrina, which I didn't do either, there wasn't much else you could have done."

"You gonna say the same thing to our client? Shit happens, sorry. You think that'll make him feel better? If all his *life experience* didn't keep that lady safe, what hope do I have? Bad things happen to good people all the time, but if being magic can't stop them, what's the point?" He slumped down in his seat.

He wanted to protect his loved ones, the same as I did. "We do the best we can in every situation."

"That's not always enough." His frustration was palpable.

"No, it's not. Sometimes life kicks you in the teeth." My hands tightened on the wheel. "We can't always protect people, hell, we can't always protect ourselves, no matter how hard we try. Maybe our greatest asset isn't our strength but our perseverance. Our ability to remember even in the face of tragedy, or especially in the face of tragedy, that life is worth living to its fullest and to help others remember that."

Emmett was silent. Hopefully he was digesting my words, but in case he was sinking deeper into depression it was better to keep him busy.

"Call Tatiana for me."

"Why?" He dug his phone out of his leather jacket.

"Change in plans." I turned off Cordova into the Railtown neighborhood. "Have her bring Juliette to Laurent's place. It'll be safer." The healer was already on staff for Tatiana so the blood oath wouldn't be an issue.

The design firms and microbreweries that populated this tiny neighborhood were closed for the night, which meant there was no one around to see us unload a body.

Laurent went to shift and dress, and I slowly opened the trunk in case the sedative had worn off and a very angry vampire lunged at me.

Emmett had opted to sit in the car.

Sabrina lay still, her eyes closed. Was this a fake out or was she still under the influence?

I ghosted a fingertip over her arm, but she didn't move.

Damn, breathing was a handy checkpoint.

While I'd adopted Tatiana's motto of "assume the worst, prepare for the worst" lately, Sabrina had to be alive. Undead alive. She hadn't turned to ash, and that had to count for something.

Except, as I looked over her body in my trunk, it didn't feel like much.

Sabrina had been a tireless fighter in life, a defender of justice. Where was the justice for her being tossed into this immortal nightmare? The careful decision-making that I'd sensed when I briefly met her likely extended to all areas of her life, so what a bitter irony that she'd ended up with no say in her eternity.

Bad enough she was a vampire, but with the Lonestars bent on protecting the prime directive and the vampires in an uproar, would she be tossed on Deadman's Island? Was there such a thing as mitigating circumstances or was the worst outcome assured?

Sighing, I brushed a muddy strand of hair out of her face. She'd killed multiple times. I had my answer.

Vincenzo loved Sabrina enough to stay by her side, watching her age and die, honoring her choice to remain human. Now she'd been changed against her will, and Vincenzo was going to destroy whoever had done this.

I doubt he cared if he burned the world down in the process.

But his actions would spring the Lonestars and Zev's crew into action. We had to keep her condition a secret until we made certain she wouldn't end up on Deadman's Island. However, this decision would put the entire team at risk and wasn't mine to make alone

My hip buzzed. *Coming home soon, Mom?*

I snorted. *Well, honey, I've got a vampire in my trunk, multiple murders I need to steer clear of, and an undead about to burn our city down.*

Yeah, that wouldn't fly. I simply replied that I was going to be a while longer. After a quick check-in with Eli, I sent another message to Sadie instructing her to stay with her dad because after what I'd just witnessed, I wanted them together.

I rested against the bumper, rolling my shoulders out to loosen some of my stiffness and fatigue.

A cloud passed by, allowing moonlight to filter down, and I blinked.

The exterior of Hotel Terminus, the small three-story hotel that Laurent had appropriated as his home, had been power washed. The black horizontal chevron pattern running between stories had been touched up and the rust removed from the wrought iron balcony railings.

Sure, the front entrance remained boarded up, but the sign with the hotel's name in flaked-off letters was gone.

Warmth bloomed through my chest. My first impression of the ramshackle exterior was that it was a calculated look to make people undermine the shifter. The more I got to know Laurent, however, the more I worried that this was how he saw himself, rather than as a reflection of the main floor interior, which he'd so lovingly restored.

This transformation said more about the success of us being together than the most romantic night ever. I smiled.

Laurent took longer than I expected, returning in jeans and a sweater. His hair wasn't wet, so he hadn't stopped to shower, but he walked stiffly, cradling his right side.

I cupped a hand to his cheek. "Are you okay?"

He leaned into me, his shoulders dropping. A bruise bloomed along his jaw and tight exhaustion pulled at the corners of his eyes. "Our date is looking pretty good in comparison to tonight, so there's that."

"Look at you, becoming all Mr. Positive."

"Wait, you mean that wasn't part of my attraction before?" He staggered back with one hand on his heart, before his expression grew serious. "How are you?"

I mimed a bomb going off complete with a whistle and boom sound.

"I'm great, thanks," Emmett said testily, getting out of the car.

I put my hand on the golem's arm, but he shrugged it off and grabbed Sabrina's ankles.

"Let's get the vamp inside," he said.

Laurent raised his eyebrows in question at me, but I shook my head and mouthed "Later."

The two of them carried Sabrina into the hotel, but before I crossed the threshold my phone rang with a call from Vincenzo.

Great. Just what I needed to top off the night. But with no passing car I could fling myself in front of to avoid answering it, I hit the green button and accepted the call.

17

"DO YOU HAVE HER?"

I pulled the phone away from my ear as if that could lessen the intensity of the vampire's question. "Yes."

"Put her on," he snapped, his Spanish accent growing heavier.

"She's not awake yet." I chose my next words carefully. "We sedated her so our healer could examine her without further trauma."

"*Further* trauma?" he said in a low growl.

Grimacing, I banged my free hand against my forehead. "We simply want to make her as comfortable as possible. As soon as she's been checked out and is awake, I'll tell her you wish to speak to her."

Sabrina should decide if she'd break the news to Vincenzo or if she wanted us to—and when.

"You have one hour." He hung up.

Sixty whole minutes before the vamp went batshit to find her. How long before the Lonestars found Sabrina and arrested us all under Ryann's edict for assisting the rogue?

I took an extra deep breath, my head throbbing like a son of a bitch, my body in knots, and all the fine work of my chiropractor undone.

Boo, Laurent's gray cat, rubbed against my ankle, and I picked her up, nuzzling her fur against my cheek. My racing heart slowed to match her comforting purrs, and I closed the side door behind me without slamming it.

The warm lighting turned the checkerboard parquet floor of the former lobby into a gleaming expanse, inviting people to curl up in the cushy furniture. One day I'd have the time to pluck a title from the neat stacks crowding the length of bookshelves and get comfy in front of the large fireplace, while the 1940s-style radio crooned jazz. Laurent would lay his head in my lap, my fingers idly scratching through his curls, both of us absorbed in our books in perfect contentment together.

"Mitzi?" He poked his head around the curved staircase leading to the boarded-off second floor, carrying an armful of clean sheets.

I patted Boo on the head and deposited her on the floor. "Is Sabrina secured?"

He nodded, holding up the linens. "She won't have to sleep on the floor either." At least vamps weren't affected by iron like their demon sires.

"I'll help." I strode past the upright piano and vintage alcohol ads on the wall with nary a floorboard squeaking. Laurent had carefully crafted many details of this space yet denied himself in other ways that were painful to behold, like the single table and chair in the gorgeous kitchen.

I followed him to the large elevator, which was situated to the right of the staircase. Its iron gate and old-fashioned copper doors carved with diamonds and swirls were partially ajar and we slipped inside.

Sabrina was propped up, her head slumped forward and one of her hands cuffed and attached with a heavy chain to the iron-lined wall.

Emmett knelt beside her, washing her face off with a small cloth. "I found it in your bathroom and figured…" He shrugged.

Laurent arranged the bedlinens on the ground. "Good call."

I'd been through a lot with them since I reclaimed my magic, and I'd seen them exhibit a gamut of emotions, but never had I felt this level of helplessness stemming from all of us.

I settled my hand on Emmett's shoulder. "We're going to find out who did this to her."

"It's unthinkable. They left her to fend for herself as one newly turned." Laurent had difficulty speaking through the canines that had descended. "The murders of those gangsters are on her sire." He made Sabrina as comfortable as possible with a pillow and a soft blanket.

Emmett grimaced. "This needs to be rinsed out."

I took the cloth from him. "I'll do it."

"I'll fill a bowl with water," Laurent said.

We walked to the kitchen in silence, my heart heavy.

He got me a bowl, which I filled before rinsing the cloth out with hot water until it ran clean.

Laurent stood behind me, his hands on the counter and his chin resting on my shoulder.

I stepped back into the comfort of his arms. "Emmett's not doing great."

"Not surprising after tonight."

Dropping the cloth in the bowl, I turned to face him. "It's more than that."

I bit my lip, finding the line between expressing concern and betraying a confidence. The shifter had been in the car with us when Emmett had spoken about his feelings, but he'd been asleep so I wasn't sure if that counted. "He's struggling and your approval matters to him."

Laurent ducked his head, briskly rubbing a hand through his curls. "I know," he said quietly.

"Okay." I didn't want to guilt him out. It was on him to change his behavior.

There was a loud knock on the side door and I jumped, thinking Vincenzo had tracked us down.

When Emmett called out that he'd get it, I bolted after him, but Laurent caught me.

"Vamp!" I tugged free.

"They can't get in uninvited, and it's not Vincenzo." He sniffed the air to show how he knew.

"Let me see her," Tatiana demanded, entering the hotel with a soft slapping sound.

"You need to let me examine her first," Juliette said.

I sagged in relief, because I'd feared the two women would run into BatXoha. I headed back to Sabrina with the bowl of hot water and the cloth.

Tatiana and Juliette stepped inside the elevator, and the young healer let out a soft whistle. Juliette was dressed in yoga pants and an oversize sweater, the most casual I'd ever seen the Frenchwoman, while Tatiana was in men's pajamas with her swirling chiffon robe thrown over top. She hadn't bothered to change out of her slippers.

Tatiana stroked her chin, her eyes narrowed. "Mishegoss," she huffed.

I snorted, setting the bowl and cloth on the ground. The craziness of this situation had barely begun.

"The Lonestars will throw Sabrina onto Deadman's Island when they learn she's the rogue vamp behind all the murders," my boss said. "We can forget payment if that happens." I glared at her, and she waved a hand. "And her imprisonment would be a tragedy," she said with no real concern.

If Sabrina's only crime were being made into a vamp when Ryann had issued her ban, we might have successfully pled her case. Add in these murders, though? I clenched my fists at how unfair this all was.

"We have a decision to make as a team," I said. "Once Vincenzo discovers that Sabrina was turned, he'll go ballistic."

"Which will bring the Lonestars and Zev to our door," Laurent said.

"But if we don't tell the Lonestars," I said, "we're culpable under Ryann's edict and could end up on Deadman's Island as accomplices."

"Because Sabrina is the rogue," Emmett said glumly.

I nodded. "I'd like to keep this a secret from everyone, including Vincenzo, at least until we've spoken to Sabrina. She should get to decide what happens next."

Everyone, even Tatiana, agreed with the decision. It wasn't even a debate.

"Now leave me with her," Juliette said in her French-accented English.

I escorted Tatiana to the kitchen, where Emmett and Laurent were rattling around.

"I'm making tea," Laurent said.

Tatiana eased her bony frame into a chair and smothered a yawn.

I frowned at the kettle heating up on the stove because a hefty slug of bourbon would have been preferable.

Emmett sat in one of the extra folding chairs that Laurent had unearthed from somewhere, tapping a small spoon against a jar of honey.

I glanced from him to Laurent and raised my eyebrows in question.

Laurent shrugged and rolled his eyes, and I tamped down a smile. Okay, I wouldn't make a big deal of it, but I glowed with satisfaction. Huff 'n' Puff hated tea, but Emmett couldn't drink alcohol because of the dangers of falling into—and getting stuck in—a prophecy state. Which begged the question of why Laurent had a familiar-looking Jude Rachefsky teapot?

Tatiana smirked. "I told you you'd use it."

"This is my first time." Laurent puttered around, distributing mugs and placing the teapot on the table.

His aunt tossed her head back like she'd still won the point.

"Maybe we could smuggle her to Vincenzo to take to Vegas with no one the wiser?" I poured the fragrant Darjeeling—Tatiana's favorite blend—for Emmett, my boss, and myself, since Laurent hadn't bothered with a mug of his own.

"I'm sure he'll be the picture of graciousness when he learns about this," Tatiana said sarcastically, adding a second heaping teaspoon of honey to her drink, "and be delighted to take Sabrina home without retaliating."

Laurent sat down and hooked a foot around the leg of my chair, pulling me close enough to drape his arm over the back of my seat.

Pretending the rosy flush on my cheeks was from the steaming beverage, I checked my phone. "He's calling back in fifteen minutes. What are we going to do?" My head throbbed harder. "Would you be dissuaded from reuniting with someone you loved? He's a vamp. They're already territorial. He won't be put off."

"True." Tatiana took a sip and smacked her lips together. "But he didn't come to town when he hired us. He had us come to him."

"You think he has a problem with Mr. BatKian?" Emmett tried the tea, then grabbed his throat, making exaggerated choking noises. At least he'd stopped his incessant spoon tapping.

"Not necessarily." Tatiana elbowed the golem and he shut up. "But there are protocols for when a vampire shows up in another's territory. If he didn't want Zev to know about his business to begin with then I'm willing to bet he still doesn't. We can use that to our advantage."

"You're gonna rat him out?" Emmett nodded in approval.

Tatiana threw him a fond smile. "We're going to stall, tattele."

"What if Mr. BatKian is behind this?" the golem said.

"If it was the gang murders, I might believe he either condoned this or deliberately turned a blind eye to something his vamps were up to," I said. "But why turn Sabrina? Even if she's Sapien and he's allowed to, what's the point?"

"To strike at Vincenzo," Laurent said.

"If he knew about the two of them," I said.

"Zev might have," Tatiana said thoughtfully, "but he'd also know the consequences of such a move and that it would directly tie back to him and his people. If he wanted to attack Vincenzo, he'd be sneakier about it, and I didn't uncover anything about the two of them dealing with each other before."

"BatKian also wouldn't let a newly turned vamp roam around unchecked and get the Lonestars all up in his business," Laurent said. "Unlikely that his bloodsuckers would do that either."

Emmett unscrewed the jar of honey, sniffed it, and grimaced. "So, who turned her?"

"There's a good chance that some unknown vampire has come to town," Tatiana said. "Are they going after Vincenzo or Zev, though?"

"Or both," Laurent said.

Tatiana jabbed a finger at him. "That's all we need."

"You can't ignore the possibility," he said. "Vincenzo's vampire nature will make him attack Zev since his fiancée was changed in Vancouver, and Zev will retaliate in kind. It's a good ploy to set them against each other while the mastermind swoops in."

"Plus, Vincenzo will be out of his mind with grief and in no state to think logically about why Zev would have left Sabrina unchecked." I ran a finger around the rim of my cup. "It could be one of Zev's own people making a move against him."

"Stop talking," Tatiana pleaded, massaging her temples.

I glanced at my phone again. "Ten minutes," I said softly.

Tatiana pinned Laurent, Emmett, and me in her gaze. "Is there any trace of evidence that can tie you to the human deaths?"

We shook our heads.

"That's something. All we need is Detective Chu getting his

panties in a twist that you're involved in another of his murder cases."

"He knows I'm involved," I said, "and even if I don't tell him what happened tonight, his top suspect will still be a vamp. I mean, they'll realize that the Hastings Mill guy was shot, but the others had their heads torn off. It's pretty clear-cut."

"Wait." Tatiana startled and jostled her mug, spilling tea onto the table. "Torn off?"

Laurent grabbed a napkin and blotted up the mess.

"Tell me exactly what happened tonight," she snapped.

Keeping an eye on the time, I narrated the story.

Tatiana's hands closed into tighter and tighter fists, which chilled me, because she'd taken the news of a human heart on her car seat in stride.

Boo was chasing a pine cone around the kitchen. There was a loud snap and she mewled.

The pine cone had exploded into fractures.

"Careful of my cat, tante," Laurent admonished in a mild voice, squatting down to check his pet for injury.

Tatiana shot Boo a concerned glance. "Sorry, minou."

The cat nipped Laurent's finger and squirmed away to bat at the largest chunk, unharmed.

Emmett poked Tatiana's arm with a teaspoon. "What's got you so hot under the collar?"

"Sabrina worked to take down gangs as a lawyer," she said. "Now she's a newly turned vamp who's been abandoned and left to survive on her most primal instincts."

"Sure," Laurent said. "That's why she murdered those men tonight."

"Our assumption is that she murdered all of them," Tatiana said.

"Okay." I sipped my tea, wrinkling my nose at the bitter taste. "So?"

"Why the escalation in violence? You said the others had their necks snapped."

"She was found this morning, which meant she was sleeping." I shrugged. "Whoever grabbed her might not have known she was a vamp, but they must have drugged her hard because it was well past sunset before she blasted out of that trunk."

"She was pissed off," Emmett said.

"Yes, but if she was changed without consent, she'd have been furious before." Laurent shook his head. "Tatiana's right. Why weren't all the kills this savage? Those first ones were more controlled…" He paled and shot to his feet. "Merde!"

I glanced up in alarm. "What?"

Laurent grabbed my wrist, hauling me out of my chair. "Juliette! Arrêtes-toi!"

Juliette glanced up as he tore inside the elevator, dragging me behind him, her hands on Sabrina's chest. The lawyer's exposed skin had been cleaned of dirt and blood, and her suit jacket had been removed, leaving her in her grimy, torn blouse. "C'est quoi le problème?" Juliette said. "I was just about to clear the sedative from her system."

"Dybbuk," Laurent said grimly.

Juliette dropped her hands to her sides while I gaped at him. A dybbuk had inhabited a vampire? My brain reeled. How was such a thing even possible? And just how fucked did that make us all?

18

"MIRIAM," LAURENT SAID, "CHECK SABRINA."

Icy tendrils snaked through me. It was terrifying to contemplate, yet a dybbuk gaining the upper hand went a long way to explain Sabrina's extreme violence tonight.

"Are you sure?" Juliette said. "There's nothing inside her other than vampire magic."

"You're not Banim Shovavim. You can't sense them." I nudged her aside and dropped to my knees.

Tatiana and Emmett crowded into the space with us.

Closing my eyes, I sent my magic out over her.

Inside Sabrina, a storm raged. It was like being in the destructive inner rings of a hurricane: violent twists and seemingly limitless power all hell-bent toward destruction and set to an unending howl. Her mind must have been in chaos. Still, I concentrated, looking for that familiar pulse of endless darkness.

There.

Then I was yanked to my feet, and my eyes snapped open as Laurent furiously balled up his sweater sleeve to wipe my lip. "You're bleeding."

I touched my tongue to the spot and winced. "I didn't realize I bit down on it."

"Is she possessed or enthralled?" Tatiana said.

"Enthralled," I replied.

The collective tension deflated.

"Was Sabrina Ohrist?" Emmett said. "How did she become inhabited?"

"She was definitely Sapien," Tatiana said. "Vincenzo had no reason to lie about that, nor would Sabrina have hidden it from him. She must have a recessive gene that allowed her to become enthralled Friday during the Danger Zone." She paused. *"Before she was turned, since vampires can't be possessed."*

That was a relief, though it made Eli with his recessive gene susceptible. I rubbed the back of my neck. The list of worries was endless. At least he could behave appropriately during the Danger Zone and not fall prey to a dybbuk.

"Talk about the world's worst night," Emmett said.

"She was probably exhausted from the trial." I shook my head. "Add a celebratory drink or two at her staff dinner and she'd have been primed for being inhabited." I refastened my ponytail. "I'll get it out of her and then you can wake her, okay?"

Juliette nodded.

I made everyone leave the elevator before manifesting my shadow scythe. "Mut!" The Hebrew letters for "die" shimmered onto the blade, and I swung the tip into Sabrina's shadow, severing it.

An angry crimson mass exploded out of her body to dive-bomb me, but I made short work of the spirit, cleaving it in half. It leached of all color and imploded, dead. Oh for the days when dybbuks were the worst of my problems.

The vampire didn't fall into convulsions, which was good, but again, breathing would have been a handy clue that Sabrina had come through the dybbuk removal unscathed.

"One freaking thing gone right tonight," Emmett said.

"No kidding." I flung a strand of hair from my face, my scythe vanishing. "She's all yours."

Juliette took my place while I crowded against the back wall with Laurent. As soon as Sabrina woke up, we'd determine if she was in compos mentis. If she wasn't, then we'd protect her until she could make informed decisions. We also needed a description of the vampire who'd turned her and if she had any theories about why this had happened. I tapped my foot, impatient to speak with Sabrina and put a solid plan into action.

Laurent nudged me, his gaze fond. "More lists?" he murmured.

I stuck my tongue out at him and he chuckled.

Juliette swore and shook out her hands, bending over Sabrina so low that her nose almost touched the vampire's body.

Next to me, Laurent tensed.

His niece swung around to face us, concern etched into her delicate features. "I don't understand it. I've already healed a cracked rib and her abrasions. Her blood is circulating as expected, and according to the vampire physiology I studied, she's fine, if a bit malnourished." She licked her lips nervously.

Tatiana crossed her arms, fixing the young woman with an impatient look. "But?"

"All sedatives are gone from her system, but I can't wake her." Juliette turned worried dark eyes on me. "There's some kind of interference that wasn't there before."

I looked at the floor, where Sabrina's shadow should have been. "Does it feel like Banim Shovavim magic?"

"No. Can you sense dybbuk residue inside her?" She blotted her forehead with the back of her hand. "That's normally not a thing, but with a vampire?" She shrugged helplessly. "We're in uncharted waters."

I checked, but there was no trace of any.

"I'm sure it's just the result of a vampire losing its shadow, and she'll wake up when it grows back." Juliette did a pretty good job selling her theory but couldn't completely keep the strain from her voice.

"*If* her shadow grows back." My voice was steady, but it sounded very far away, like someone else was speaking. Ohrists lost their magic and even went into convulsions when I severed their shadows, but this was the first known vampire shadow sever. It was a whole other ball game.

We'd been so caught up in removing the dybbuk from the feral vampire that we hadn't considered this could play out differently than usual. I could say that was on all of us, but in the end, my scythe had dealt the blow.

Something flickered over Laurent's features, then he shook his head, placing a steadying hand on the small of my back. It barely registered.

By saving Sabrina from dybbuk possession, had I thrown her from the frying pan into the fire? I felt like I'd been taken apart and rearranged in a way that was all sharp angles and raw edges.

A buzzing noise started up in the kitchen like an angry hornet.

I flinched and Laurent bunched my shirt in his fist like he could physically keep me from the next thirty seconds, but this was one call I dare not miss—almost as much as I feared answering it.

Tatiana elbowed me aside in the kitchen and swiped my cell from my hand before I could answer. "Hello?"

My stomach plummeted. Her concern in sparing me was sweet, but I would have rather spoken to Vincenzo directly than wait to have it conveyed.

She narrowed her eyes at whatever Vincenzo was saying, his voice too low for me to hear, but Laurent had his head cocked, eavesdropping.

I tugged on his sleeve, my eyebrows raised in question, but he held up a finger.

Emmett and Juliette had remained with Sabrina.

"Your fiancée is with us but we're going to keep her sedated for a while longer," Tatiana said, cool as a cucumber. "She's been through a lot and needs to sleep. Meantime, you need to present yourself to Zev BatKian, which you have yet to do. Or should I personally let him know of your visit?"

There was silence on the other end, and I threw her a thumbs-up, receiving a smirk in return. Zev loved his protocols so whatever "presenting himself" to our master vamp involved for Vincenzo, it would buy me—us—time.

Sadly, my triumph was short-lived. This was merely a stay of execution unless—until—Sabrina woke up. I braced my forearms on the counter, my head bowed.

"Tell me where she is!" Vincenzo's voice boomed out of the phone.

Tatiana's eyes went glassy. "She's—"

Fuck. She'd been compelled. I snatched the cell away. "You have to follow proper protocol." My words came out in a rush. "Don't force Sabrina to go up against Mr. BatKian's wrath over something so easily avoided." Some sliver of self-preservation made me shut up before I babbled out the full predicament that Sabrina faced, and I snapped my mouth shut.

Laurent wrapped a struggling Tatiana in his arms. She wasn't compelled anymore, she was swinging for the phone like she could send her magic down the line and fry Vincenzo.

Vincenzo let out a harsh breath. "You are right. Mi amor, she's been through enough."

I turned my strangled laugh into a cough. *You don't know the half of it.*

"Who took her?" he said.

"We're working on that."

"Work faster," he growled.

Vincenzo was systematically going after those who'd killed his second, but his insistence on my help meant he truly had no idea who had done this. Whomever had changed Sabrina hadn't done so as a direct attack on him, though that didn't preclude Vincenzo and Sabrina being used as pawns in an attack on Zev.

"I'll go see BatKian," Vincenzo said, "as soon as I've checked on Bree. Tell me where you are."

His soft command burrowed into my skull. Gritting my teeth, my defenses hanging by a thread, I hung up and exhaled in a long, exhausted breath. Really, dude? I do the impossible, find your fiancée, and this is how you repay me? By backseat driving my head?

I wrung an invisible vampiric neck and then turned my phone off for good measure.

Tatiana tore free of Laurent's hold. "That bastard," she hissed.

The full weight of Laurent's gaze rested on me. "You can't just avoid him."

"I know." I rubbed my wrist, assuring myself that blood oaths weren't tracking devices. "Sabrina's vampirism, the murders, all of that is going to be horrible enough to share with Vincenzo." I pushed the phone away like it was cursed. "But we must protect Sabrina until she wakes up, and that means putting Vincenzo off from freaking out that she's a vampire and I put her in a coma. People do rash things in the name of love."

"You don't know that you're responsible for her condition," Laurent said.

Tatiana wrapped her chiffon robe around her. "Now isn't the time for delusions, Lolo. Juliette only sensed that interference after Miriam removed the dybbuk, so we make a plan to keep Vincenzo away from all of us until Sabrina's shadow has grown back, she can be roused, and Miriam goes back to being the fixer who successfully reunited Vincenzo with his fiancée."

Tatiana always acted like she could bend the universe to her will, but right now, the combination of her no-nonsense tone and a plan allowed me to stand a little straighter. Plus calling me a fixer in my own right. Hell yeah, that felt good.

"Then it's settled," I said. "We stall until Sabrina wakes up and can choose for herself how we proceed." I grabbed my phone. "Start throwing out ideas, people."

Since Sabrina was as stable as possible, and it was after midnight, Juliette opted to grab an Uber and go home to sleep. She promised to come back later in the day to check on the patient.

Emmett had passed out on one end of Laurent's sofa, snoring away with his dying bagpipe wheeze, and Tatiana was clearly fading, her lids half-closed as we discarded idea after idea.

I rested against Laurent's side, both of us sitting on the floor. He'd built a fire to ward off the chill, the flames dancing and the wood crackling, but as calming as it was, the best we came up with involved all of us hiding out here in the hotel until Sabrina's shadow grew back.

I scraped my fingers into my hair. "This is hopeless."

Laurent shifted his weight to stretch out his back, but when he settled himself and I didn't return to his side, he pulled me against him, resting one hand on my hip to keep me close. "There is one move we haven't discussed," he said. "BatKian."

Tatiana slammed the arm of her chair. "No."

"You know I'm right," he said reasonably.

She glared at him.

A piece of wood popped sharply, and Emmett snorted.

Zev had compelled Tatiana to hand over the Ascendant, and I didn't want to be around him for a number of reasons. Yet he'd soon know the other vampire was here to collect his fiancée and wouldn't take kindly to Tatiana and me stalling that reunion for no discernable reason beyond Sabrina needing to rest. Plus, he'd been invited into both our homes. I snuggled closer to Laurent. At least Eli's side of the duplex was off-limits to him.

The smart thing to do would be to tell BatKian about Sabrina, since shit would fall on Blood Alley when Vincenzo learned of her undead state, but I clenched my jaw and Tatiana's clenched fists had gone white.

My boss finally conceded Laurent's point with a defeated nod. "Go to Blood Alley, Miriam. Zev is the only one who can hold Vincenzo off, and it's in his interests to work with us."

I tapped my wrist. "You realize I'll have to get him on staff first, right?"

"I do."

I toyed with my cuff. "There's one other potential hitch."

"What?" Laurent's growl rumbled through me.

"Still tired, pussycat," Emmett slurred sleepily and rolled over.

"I saw something I shouldn't have," I hedged. Much as Laurent and Tatiana would relish hearing about the vampire's humiliation at his sire's hands, my gut screamed that sharing this knowledge would get all of us killed.

Tatiana gave me a piercing stare, and while Laurent had to fight from shifting his fingers to claws, I kept my chin up resolutely, and they finally backed off.

The trouble was, although Zev's anger made my life a million times more difficult—or just shortened it entirely—it didn't change the fact that he was still my best option for dealing with Vincenzo.

The devil I knew or the devil I kind of knew?

"I'll go," I said softly, wringing my hands. I flashed back on the empowerment I'd felt when I'd stood up to Zev before the estrie humiliated him. The certainty that I was stronger than I gave myself credit for and that my strength stemmed not simply from my magic but from my relationships.

Zev had betrayed Tatiana once and he might do it again. He might even go so far as to compel her into killing me. Yet, his desperation during their last visit had been because his best friend was dying of a vampire contagion. Zev and Tatiana had history that might tip the scales in my favor.

I shot my boss a hopeful look. "Would you come with me?"

She opened her mouth, then sighed. "Yes. We'll get him to swear a blood oath not to take his displeasure out on you for Sabrina. Or for anything else."

Laurent's finger brushed over my skin where the puncture marks had been. "You think he'll agree?"

His touch sent delicious shivers up my arm. Well, Laurent's touch and the thought of making Zev swear a magic vow. How much could I get him to agree to?

Tatiana fiddled with her bracelet. "We'll force his hand."

"How?" Laurent said.

"With a good plan," I said.

"And an insurance policy," Tatiana added. "Between us, we'll make sure Zev doesn't hurt you."

"Damn straight he won't hurt her." Laurent waved a hand loftily. "You're not dying before experiencing my excellent dating skills."

I hiccuped a laugh.

Once we had both those items in place, Laurent stood up. "That's enough for tonight. Tatiana, you can have my room, and the rest of us will bunk out here since my place is the only one Zev can't access."

"Don't be ridiculous." She pushed herself off the sofa with a yawn. "I'm sleeping in my own bed."

We argued with her, but she was adamant that not only would she sleep at home, but she was perfectly capable of driving her and Emmett back. She roused the grumpy golem, and I bid them goodbye with a knot in my belly.

Laurent and I opted to stay by the fire instead of moving into his bedroom, since the sofa was more than wide enough for the two of us to lie side by side, and it was cozy and warm here.

I pulled off my socks, rolled them into a ball, and tossed them onto the floor. "You got injured when you went after Sabrina, but you didn't let Juliette heal you."

"I've had worse." He pulled me into the crook of his arm and threw the blanket he'd grabbed over us.

I poked his biceps. "That just means you're stubborn, not that you aren't hurt."

He burrowed his nose into my hair. "Then you should do whatever I want to make me feel better."

Snorting, I relaxed against him, drowsily watching the flames.

The list-making part of my brain kicked into high gear as it always did right before bedtime: get the Ascendant back from Gehenna for the Leviathan, find a way to wake Sabrina up, and touch base with Nora.

Laurent turned onto his side and tucked his arm under his head, causing a curl to fall into his eyes. He puffed out his cheeks and blew on it, looking like an annoyed little kid when it fell right back into his face.

I pushed the stray lock off his forehead and was rewarded with a sleepy smile. For once in my life, I didn't want a list. I wanted to take casual touches for granted and not memorize them in case they were my last. I wanted to put my freezing feet on Laurent's ridiculously warm legs when they got cold, shrieking in laughter when he retaliated with tickling and kisses. I wanted to sit here painting my toenails while Laurent played DJ and Sadie lounged on her phone with Boo snuggled against her.

All of it was possible, offered up on a silver platter even, so long as we made it past vampires and Lonestars to the finish line.

Lulled by Laurent's slow, deep breathing, I let sleep pull me under, settling for sweet dreams until they were made reality.

19

I WAS ON A TROPICAL BEACH, SWINGING IN A hammock. I didn't know how long I'd been there, but time had stopped mattering. The ocean was infinite, but some idiot was banging their surfboard against a rock or something. I didn't know much about surfing or how this was helpful, but it was damn irritating. I was on my way to tell them off, when I fell out of the hammock, realized it was actually a sofa, got tangled in a heavy body, and figured out that the knocking (still real) was coming from Laurent's front door.

Muted sunlight slanted through the frosted front windows of the hotel. Was it late enough for any powerful vamp to be awake?

I spat hair out of my mouth and shook Laurent. "Go see who it is," I whispered.

Boo mewled angrily from the cushions.

The loud knocks continued.

The shifter rolled over, pulling the blanket over his head. "It's Harry," he mumbled.

I poked his shoulder. "Shouldn't you answer it anyway? What if something's happened?" Gasping, I jumped up and ran for the kitchen where I'd left my phone. I'd turned it off last night but what if Sadie had tried to contact me?

While Laurent greeted the gargoyle, I muttered at my phone to hurry and boot up. At the flurry of texts that pinged, I mashed my finger against the screen to open the app and flew through the messages.

I only pried my hand off the counter's edge once I'd determined Sadie was fine, but she was wondering where I was because she was home from school. I'd swear I'd only been asleep for twenty minutes, not hours. I phoned her to say I'd crashed at Laurent's since work ran late and told her to finish painting the living room. She wasn't happy that I wouldn't let her boyfriend keep her company, but she agreed. Not like she had a choice.

By the time I returned to the main room, Harry, the stocky gargoyle, sat on the sofa, twisting a cap between his broad fingers. His manbun was half-unraveled with his stubby horns peeking out, while his misbuttoned shirt exposed gray stone skin. The second he saw me, he shot to his feet. "Something's up with Nora."

Laurent was forcefully reshelving his perfectly ordered books. Was he upset about Nora as well? He didn't know the raven shifter, did he?

"What happened?" I glanced warily between them.

The man who'd held me all night stared at me with his lips pressed into a thin line. "You stole Giulia's ring? Is that why you asked me about it?"

My heart dropped into my toes. "Not exactly." I rolled onto the outsides of my feet. "She gave it to me."

"Brilliant. My mistake. Don't care." Harry gave a defeated sigh and I sat down next to him, while Laurent turned back to his task like it was the most fascinating thing in the world.

"I gave it back safe and sound," I said.

Laurent glanced at me, his lips pressed tightly together, and shook his head, but didn't reply.

The gargoyle gripped my shoulders, his fingers biting into my flesh. "What did you ask Nora to do?"

I struggled in his grasp, my heart racing. "You're hurting me."

Laurent smacked two books together, his canines elongated, and Harry released me, scrubbing a hand over his wide face.

"I'm sorry, luv, but Nora's in a state. She called the Bear's Den because your phone was off, mumbling about an amulet." He tugged on one of his large ears. "If something magic's got her in its grip, we have to help her."

His teeth normal again, Laurent stilled, a fat hardcover in his hand. "What amulet?"

I clasped my hands behind my back, not up to dealing with him getting any pissier. "Short version? These whack jobs kidnapped Emmett when we were in Vegas, wanting me to answer some summons. They had an amulet and I think it's tied to the Ascendant. I asked Nora, who is a raven shifter friend of Harry's, to look into it."

"Oh well, if that's all." He slammed the book onto the shelf.

"Laurent!" Harry snapped.

The shifter shot him a contrite look. "Sorry, mon ami."

"Hey." I caught Harry's arm. "Nora called and then what?"

"She wasn't making much sense." He shook his head, his expression pinched tight. "I went to her place to sort it out, but she wouldn't let me in."

"Could the amulet be enchanted?" Laurent said.

I tugged my socks away from Boo, who'd been batting them around, and yanked them on. "I wondered if it was demonic in origin, but I didn't have any sense of it being enchanted." I turned a stricken gaze on Harry. "I swear, I wouldn't have given it to her if I thought it was dangerous."

He nodded. "We need to get inside her place. Maybe she'll speak to you and you can get the amulet away from her. If that doesn't cure her, I'll whisk her over to the Carpe Demon lot. Let them examine her."

"You can get there?"

He shot me an "obviously" look. Guess his neutrality allowed him access to their secret HQ.

Shoving my phone in my purse, I jammed my feet into my shoes, and flung open the door.

"I'm coming," Laurent said.

"No, mate," Harry said. "I can't fly both of you."

"Fl-fly?" My mouth fell open.

"I get carsick," the gargoyle said sheepishly.

That seemed to settle the matter—at least for him—because he snapped out an enormous pair of wings, tossed me on his back between them with a "Hold tight!" and shot out the door.

We flew straight up into the sky. I was screaming and hanging on for dear life, my arms wrapped around Harry's neck, my legs cinched around his waist, and my eyes screwed shut. Not this again.

"Choking!" He tried to loosen my fingers, but I gripped him tighter, my screaming growing louder.

I felt his sigh rumble through him, and we tilted forward. The wind was no longer rushing down over the crown of my head, so I cracked my eyes open.

Harry had turned horizontal, streaking across the sky like Superman. We weren't at airplane altitude, more like very high treetops, but I preferred to travel looking up at roofs, not down.

My head swam and I moaned.

"Don't hurl," he ordered. Now that I'd stopped screaming, I heard the leathery beat of his wings propelling us in strong strokes through the air.

"Someone will see."

"Nah. My magic prevents that. You're good."

"No! I am the furthest thing from good!" It came out as a high-pitched jumble. I grabbed his collar, tugging upward like it was a bridle on a horse. The material ripped under the force of my movement, fluttering free before blowing away. Whoops.

Harry groaned.

The warm breeze streamed through my hair and the sun kissed my skin as we soared over the water toward the North Shore mountains, the waves twinkling like precious jewels. It was one of those perfect September days where summer had yet to end.

"Kill me," I whimpered.

He pointed at one of the backyards up ahead. "Almost there."

"How are you going to laaaaaaaaa—"

Harry dove for the ground.

My stomach fell clear out through the soles of my feet at his suicidal rush to pancake us against the earth. I couldn't even scream through my final moments.

Mere feet before impact, he pulled up sharply and smoothly touched down. "See? Safe and sound."

I let go, staggering backward before my legs gave out, and I fell onto the ground, rolling over to kiss the grass. There was not enough Ativan in the world to make me repeat that journey.

Harry tugged me up before I'd finished blessing terra firma, and I took stock of my surroundings. We were in the pocket-sized backyard of one of the ubiquitous Craftsman bungalows built here in the 1920s and '30s.

He strode up the rickety back stairs and knocked briskly. "Nora," he called out. "I've brought Miri."

The curtains were drawn tight. Pushing my snarled hair out of my face, I pressed my ear to the door, but didn't hear footsteps.

Harry had decided to break it down when the door opened a crack and Nora peered out.

I raised a hand in greeting. "Can I come in?"

Her eyes didn't blaze red or slither with shadows, but their fervent gleam was far more unsettling. She held up a red permanent marker. "He can't have one."

I exchanged a baffled look with Harry.

"I wouldn't dream of it, luv," he said.

"Wait out here?" I asked.

He nodded, making himself comfortable on the patchy grass.

Nora led me into her kitchen, which smelled of pine and lavender from the dozens of candles placed on the counters and table. They gave off a lovely warm glow, but I shivered at how out of place they were in the middle of the day.

Had I brought whatever weirdness was back at that Vegas wedding place into Nora's kitchen by giving her the amulet?

She sat across from me, popped off the marker cap, and began coloring something on the table. I couldn't see what it was because my sightline was blocked by a wall of unwashed coffee mugs, but this wasn't normal host behavior. Also, Harry had said Nora was in a state when he spoke to her, but she was so chill right now, engaged in her coloring like a happy child.

Or someone under a compulsion.

"You've got some intel for me?" I kept my posture relaxed and a friendly smile on my face, but I let my magic dance under my skin. "Did you learn anything about the amulet?"

She looked up. "Yes. I need the pink."

Grabbing the marker, I stood up to lean over the table and hand it to her, and gasped.

The edges of the amulet had been scorched and the three figures defaced in felt pen with devil horns, mustaches, and giant penises.

"Nora, what are you doing?" I touched the amulet and she smacked my hand. "Sorry." I rubbed soot off my finger. It was a miracle she hadn't hurt herself or burned down the house, because it must have taken multiple attempts to blacken the artifact that thoroughly.

And what was with the crazy graffiti? I could almost understand a creepy summons from an unknown supernatural being, but this made no sense.

Delilah twined around my feet. "Why did you vandalize those figures?" I said.

"They're evil asshats," Nora said matter-of-factly. "Steer clear of them."

I narrowed my eyes at the crude engravings. "Who are?"

"You know who." She drew slitted snake eyes on one of them. "After darkness comes the light."

The hunters' motto? What did that have to do with anything? I clenched my fists against the urge to punch a wall. "I don't understand."

"Follow the whispers." Her words were so quiet they barely carried above the hum of the old yellow fridge.

I froze, goosebumps breaking out over my body. Learsdon said he'd found me by following whispers, but there'd been no mention of them in any of his papers. I'd have remembered something like that. Still, my neck prickled, my researcher sense screaming at me that the amulet was tied to the Ascendant, but otherwise, I was so lost.

Nora hummed under her breath, happily defacing away.

"What are the whispers saying?"

"I can't understand them, silly. That's your job."

Could I get a training manual? I exhaled. Okay, whoever was behind this wasn't directing Nora to do anything specific. That was good, wasn't it? Now, were these whispers separate from the evil figures, who were either demons, hunters, or something else entirely, and oh my God, my head was going to explode.

I crouched down beside her. "Who's whispering?" When she ignored me, I placed my hand over the amulet. "Nora. This is important."

Crossing her arms, she heaved a sigh. "Not whispering."

"You're not making any sense. You just said I had to follow the whispers, but now you're saying they aren't whispering? Did the whispering stop?"

She shook her head.

Nora had the presence of mind to call Harry because she couldn't reach me. There must be something she wanted me to understand. Follow the whispers, but not whispering. I turned the words over and over, growing more and more frustrated until a thought hit me.

When Eli and I had been searching for Teresa Wong, a missing person, we'd initially mistaken a reference to the Human Race as metaphoric instead of literal.

Did "whispers" have a definite article, not an indefinite one? Was it, perhaps, the name of a demon complicit in my parents' and McMurtry's deaths?

"Nora, it's the Whispers? Like with a capital W? A name?"

"Yes!" She clapped her hands together. Great, but why couldn't she say that in the first place?

"Good. Is the Whispers a person?" No reaction. "A demon?"

She unfurled a smile that was too wide, too manic, and her eyes gleamed. "It's a broken hallelujah."

"Enough cryptic bullshit." I slammed my fist on the table, rattling the coffee mugs.

Nora's smile turned sly, but she didn't offer any other clues.

Shadows swirled up my body like a whirlwind and I turned my face to the sky. "You want me? Then talk to me. Quit hiding behind others."

At the very least, I could stop it from using any more people as puppets. Grabbing the artifact, I ran out the back door, yelling at Harry to stay with Nora.

He caught her around the waist on the porch, the woman bellowing that she wasn't finished with the amulet yet, and shut them inside the house.

Going deeper into the backyard, I phoned Nav. "If someone had the impulse to burn and deface the amulet I showed you because the figures are evil, would destroying the thing free that person from any compulsion?"

"Most people start a conversation with hello," he said dryly, right as a muted boom echoed through the phone.

I flinched. "What was that?"

"We tracked down a nest of demons and I promised Clea she could blow their home up after we killed them," he said.

I shrugged. Sure, why not. "About the amulet?"

"It didn't affect you at all?"

"No. It compelled its previous keepers into kidnapping Emmett, but I felt nothing when I took it from them. They were Ohrists, like this person."

"It's not the amulet. Something is communicating through it. What else was this Ohrist told?"

"It said to follow the whispers, but I'm pretty sure that part was for me." I tracked an airplane streaking across the sky, wishing I was flying somewhere tropical with frosty alcohol-laden drinks.

"Quite the special little lamb, aren't you?" Nav said.

"I am, but the clock's ticking. How do I help her?"

"Find out who's using other people to give you messages," Nav said. "Although, it's rather odd the sender isn't sending these charmingly creepy little communiques to you directly."

"Maybe because I'm Banim Shovavim and they can only speak to Ohrists?"

"Maybe," he said doubtfully.

"Doesn't matter, there isn't time to find them. I need to help her now. What do I do?"

"My best guess," he said, "is—

There was another boom and the line went staticky.

"Nav? Hello?"

"Can you hear me?" he said.

"Yes."

"Destroy the amulet, and if this person doesn't snap out of it, bring them to Carpe Demon. Bloody hell. Clea! Enough!" The line went dead.

I called Harry outside. He brought Nora with him, his large hand over her mouth, smothering her screams.

After kicking away some grass to make a circle of dirt, I lay the amulet down. The gargoyle stomped on it, smashing it, and then I burned the dust with a book of Bear's Den matches that Harry had.

Nora slumped in his hold, shielding her eyes, even though she was in the shade. "I feel like I went on a bender."

I scanned her carefully, but she seemed compulsion-free. "It was the amulet," I said. "I'm so sorry. It didn't do anything to me and I had no idea you'd be affected."

She tugged free of Harry, skirting away from the ash, and examined her hands stained in a rainbow of colors. "Why do I have felt pen all over me?"

After giving her the synopsis of what had happened and thanking her, I left Nora with Harry, opting to Uber home despite the cost, because I had to get ready to see Zev and the ride would give me time to think.

What was a broken hallelujah? A hallelujah was a form of praising the lord, but if it was broken, was it a curse against God? Could it refer to something celestial, like the Ascendant that was used then tossed into Gehenna, perhaps breaking it in the process?

I hoped it was intact because I needed that sucker back in one piece for the Leviathan.

I rested my head against the seat. Every Banim Shovavim entering the KH for the first time was fed propaganda about how our damnation was a foregone conclusion because of Lilith, but I'd assumed that beyond telling that lie, Senoi, Sansenoi, and Sammaneglof were hands-off until we let our own doubts and self-judgment convince us that we deserved to be damned. Only then did they follow through with eternal torture.

According to the Leviathan, however, those angels were far more active—and pernicious. That story was magically set in our minds to prey on us, meaning that very few Banim Shovavim saw through the lie. Then the three angels carried out our eternal damnation.

Judge, jury, and executioner. Talk about a purity complex. I was happy to undermine them and help the sea monster escape.

Except it didn't make any sense for them to be communicating with me via the amulet. Maybe they couldn't snatch me out of the KH since I'd seen through their propaganda, but why bother with human middlemen? Just show up.

I fanned out my shirt, letting the air-conditioning flow over me.

When I got home, I'd strike the Consortium off my board as having anything to do with my past or my parents. They had their own people to come after me; they didn't need that cocka-mamie amulet.

Except once again, that left me with some demon as my prime suspect, a fiendish being who was hardly conflict averse, and wouldn't bother to cover up their nefarious deeds. So not them either.

Not only did I not have any suspects for my parents' murders, I had no clue who'd summoned me, warning me off the evil those three figures represented and alerting me to follow the whispers.

My head pounded in a tight throb that stretched down my neck and into my shoulders. I rifled in my purse for some Tylenol and dry swallowed two pills, falling back against the seat.

The driver was listening to some rock station's '70s hour and the upbeat tone took a mellow turn as "Bennie and the Jets" was replaced by "Wish You Were Here." Exhausted from my thoughts going in circles, I half dozed in a pool of sunshine, singing along in my head. Eli had introduced me to this album in university, both of us stoned and lying on his futon, with candles flickering around the room, and the guitar washing over us.

The Uber sped through downtown to "Let It Be" and headed up Main Street to some song by Fleetwood Mac called "Angel" when my head snapped up, lyrics tumbling through my mind.

Heaven and Hell, the wish that you were here, those whis-pered words of wisdom, it was like the radio was speaking to me. In a crazy person conspiracy theory way sure, but while the thought that hit me was absolutely bonkers, it made perfect chilling sense.

The song wasn't called "Angels," it was "Angel." Singular.

The second I got home, I ran upstairs into my office and started furiously writing everything down on the whiteboard.

The Ascendant opens riffs to Gehenna.

Monsters should stay in the dark.

Dybbuks aren't the only monsters there.

Follow the Whispers. James had.

When I opened the rift, I heard a wash of whispers and felt something watching me.

My parents were killed even though they didn't have the Ascendant.

McMurtry was killed because he knew who'd ordered their deaths.

A broken hallelujah.

What if all those facts didn't point to a demon acting uncharacteristically, or a celestial trio, but the most broken being of all —a fallen angel in charge of torturing evil spirits?

Dumah could release dybbuks to earth on the Sabbath and blow his trumpet to call them back to torture time, but no one ever mentioned his presence here.

What if he couldn't leave, because like the Leviathan, he'd been imprisoned? It wasn't a stretch to believe that, like another famous fallen angel, he'd been banished to a realm where he tortured the wicked.

Perhaps Dumah's only way to communicate was via the amulet. I hadn't had possession of it long enough to know whether he would have "whispered" to me directly. He'd summoned me, though, and when I hadn't responded, passing the amulet to Nora, he had gotten her to lead me to him but by piquing my curiosity with "the whispers."

Another point in favor of this hypothesis was that Senoi, Sansenoi, and Sammaneglof saw Banim Shovavim and the Leviathan as abominations. They wouldn't exactly think highly of a fallen angel either, and when I'd asked Nora who those evil figures were, she'd said that I knew, then quoted the hunter motto.

Since the three angels weren't as passive in their hatred of Banim Shovavim as I'd thought, it was entirely plausible that they'd founded the hunters to kill us as a backup to their plans in the KH. "After darkness comes the light" made scary sense if I framed it as the angels coming after Banim Shovavim.

Dumah, a fallen angel, and another abomination in their eyes, wouldn't have any love for that sanctimonious trio and would plausibly deem them evil. How long had he been spying on me to know that I didn't care for them either? Since the night he murdered my parents for not having the Ascendant?

My hands shook so much that I dropped the cap of the marker twice before I popped it on. If I was right, I was the latest pawn in a long con by the fallen angel Dumah to get the Ascendant and attain his freedom. But unlike everyone else?

I'd succeeded.

20

IF I HADN'T GONE POKING AT THE PAST LIKE A KID taking a stick to a snake, the angel would remain locked up nice and tight forever. Clearly Dumah hadn't staged his jailbreak yet, otherwise we'd be flooded with dybbuks. So, what was he waiting for?

Would I go down in history as the person who'd doomed us all? Would there be anyone left to record history when an angel with a grudge and control of all dybbuks returned on a massive revenge quest? Even if he had nothing against humans and merely wanted to visit hurt upon all his smarmy angelic brethren, we'd be the casualties.

Shivering, I wrapped my arms around my thighs, but there was no time to curl up paralyzed with a blanket thrown over my head because someone started banging on my front door.

As my distress was using up most of my brain function, I didn't immediately process why some high-powered female lawyer in a sharply tailored navy pinstripe suit stood on my stoop, until she barked at me in a raspy New Yorker accent to get a move on already.

No oversize red glasses, outlandish outfit, or black leather? "Am I missing some psychological gambit?"

"Are you going to stand there blabbing or are we going to deal with Zev?" Tatiana said.

My head was reeling, I was in pain, tired, and still wearing yesterday's clothes, but the stubborn set of her shoulders said it was now or never. "Sabrina's shadow?" I said, needing one piece of good news.

Tatiana shook her head.

Right. I crawled into the front seat of her car, happy for once with her lurching, overbraking, traffic-lights-are-just-a-suggestion driving, because it was a much-needed distraction.

Then Ryann's call came in. I debated ignoring it, but really, how much worse could this conversation be than handing a fallen angel the key to his prison?

My sigh turned into a cough. Did Dumah still need me, or, rather, my Banim Shovavim magic to call him forth? Was that why he'd summoned me, and if I kept refusing to meet, would he send assassins after me like he'd done with Mom and Dad?

Had Arlo been working for Dumah? Was that why the three angels tortured the Banim Shovavim man? Had freeing Dumah been Arlo's way of "flying with the angels" since he'd never specified it was Senoi, Sansenoi, and Sammaneglof whom he'd wanted to fly with?

I dropped the phone before I hit answer.

Tatiana looked over at me. "What's wrong with you?" She didn't just glance like a normal driver, she kept staring until a honk forced her attention back on the road.

Numb, I rested my head against the glove compartment.

Would the agony of being torn apart and reformed into a twisted tangle of light like Arlo be the thing that drove me mad? Or would the angels ensure I kept just enough presence of mind to feel every second of that torment?

Maybe Pyotr could give me a plant?

A strangled laugh caught in my throat. Could angels cross wards?

The shrill ring of my phone threw me out of my head. I

checked the screen and reluctantly scooped it off the floor mat. "Hi, Ryann."

"Want to tell me the real reason why Eli quit as my liaison on these murders?" Her voice had an uncharacteristic edge to it.

I twisted a lock of hair around my finger. "He was working with you? I had no idea."

A door slammed on her end. "Are you involved in this? Is your new client, Vincenzo BatXoha, up to something?"

"Vincenzo wasn't here when the killings started."

"Don't play stupid. He has plenty of accomplices to carry out orders, and he's hardly a pillar of society."

"There's not a ton of career choices for vamps, though, is there?" I smacked my hand against the dashboard. "Zev was a rabbi before he was turned. Vincenzo could have been a heroic firefighter for all we know, but none of that matters because those doors are closed to them once they change." Sabrina's career was definitely over. "Imagine the world we could live in if Lonestars helped magic be accepted instead of hiding it?"

Tatiana rubbed my shoulder, miraculously keeping her eyes on the road.

Ryann sucked in a sharp breath on her end of the call. "So help me, if you're protecting him from facing murder charges—" She broke off with a frustrated snarl so loud that, even though she wasn't on speakerphone, Tatiana hit the brakes.

In the middle of the street.

We were flung against our seat belts to a screech of brakes behind us, and I braced for impact.

It didn't come. Well, not from the car.

"Consider this your one and only chance to save yourself," Ryann said. "I've got dozens of Lonestars hunting for the killer. It's Deadman's Island for anyone protecting that rogue."

Tatiana resumed driving.

"How big is that place anyway? Because it's going to be pretty crowded with everyone you're tossing there." I held the phone so tightly that the plastic case bit into my fingers. "The rogue, accomplices, any turned humans. I mean, I'm all for densification but this is sounding a little too cozy for my tastes."

Tatiana flashed me a thumbs-up at the snap in my voice. Some of it was bravado, but I was angry at the Lonestar's black-and-white thinking that put me into this position when all I wanted to do was save Sabrina from a horrible fate. More horrible than she'd already endured. And yes, I also wanted to come out unscathed. Sue me.

"Really, Miriam?" There was a quiet resignation to Ryann's words.

My relationship with the Lonestar hadn't been easy, but I'd impressed her to the point where she unofficially subcontracted me to take on jobs she wasn't allowed to. Yelling I could handle, but disappointment was another story.

I opened my mouth, wanting to assert that the murderer was a victim too, a human changed without consent and left to fend for herself. That the one Ryann should go after was whomever turned Sabrina against her will in the first place and then abandoned her, but the words stuck in my throat at the unfairness and futility of having to explain this, not to mention the blood oath sending hot shafts of pain up my arm.

When my silence went on several beats too long, Ryann sighed and hung up.

"Don't beat yourself up," Tatiana said. She jammed her beast of a car sideways into a parking spot, bashing the vehicles both in front and behind her so violently that they bounced. "She wouldn't have listened."

"I know," I said, tracing a finger along the window, "but we were becoming friends."

Uninterested, Tatiana was already climbing out of the car. She left me to pay for parking, striding on ahead to the gates of Blood Alley.

Most of the doors to the rooms were open, though the bulbs were off, and our walk up the lane was accompanied by the sounds of clanking bottles and the whir of card machines. Only human employees were about, but the sky was growing dark, and the vamps would be awake soon.

Were the trainees working tonight? Had they found others for Kian to snack on?

My heart pounded in my ears, my mouth was dry, and I would rather have faced the collective undead minions of Blood Alley than their leader. Depending on Zev's mood, I might have to do both.

Tatiana would do her best to prevent Zev from hurting me, but she was compellable, and my magic was laughable in the face of his powers. I'd seen that lethal predator be taken down; how could he possibly let me live?

Did we have enough to persuade him to swear the blood oath —and would he give us a chance to speak or was my death warrant signed the second I stepped into his office?

At the top of the lane, I eyed the stretch of unkempt lawn between us and the front doors of Rome with trepidation, my arm out to assist Tatiana. She ignored it, striding shakily on her heels over the uneven ground, her head high.

I kept pace with her, not wanting to insult my boss by walking behind her in order to catch her. We were in enemy territory, after all. Still, I sighed in relief when she made it to the concrete outside the front doors without breaking a hip.

Instead of entering, though, Tatiana went around to the side and flipped open a small metal panel. She fit a gold key into it and the wall slid away, revealing an elevator.

Look who had intimate access to someone's club. My jaw fell open a further thousand feet or so at the discovery that there was only one button inside the car. Zero guesses for where it led. My curiosity about her and Zev reached new heights, but at her granite expression as we descended, I wisely kept silent.

The elevator deposited us in Zev's art gallery, the vampire on hand to greet us. There was no sign that Kian had hurt him: no bruises marred his pale skin and there was no stiffness in his movements, though he wasn't wearing a suit jacket.

"Tatiana. I wasn't sure I'd see you here again." He tugged on his perfectly straight shirt cuffs, and my eyebrows shot into my hairline. Was he nervous?

They stared at each other, not with longing or even sizing each other up; the look was far more complicated than that.

I cleared my throat. "We have business to discuss."

A muscle ticked in his jaw when he flicked his gaze over me, and I dug my nails into my sides to keep from protecting my throat, but he didn't attack. "Indeed."

Tatiana motioned for him to lead the way back to his office area, but he didn't move.

Zev sliced the plastic on a pallet open with a fingernail and the packaging slipped to the floor revealing a bubble-wrapped painting. "Your client formally greeted me and asked my permission to conduct business in my territory. I've granted it. Now, return his fiancée at once."

Tatiana shrugged. "As you wish. Good day, Zev."

His expression turned wary at her automatic capitulation. "Wait," he commanded, but Tatiana was already halfway back to the elevator while I scrambled after her.

The vampire sped to block us. "What are you up to?"

"I'm just doing as you asked." Tatiana raised her eyebrows. "Are you going to compel me into behaving otherwise?"

Zev exhaled.

"The Lonestars are on a rampage to find the vampire behind all the gangland murders," I said.

"Did you learn that from Detective Chu? Perhaps before he suddenly stopped working with them?" Zev snapped his fingers. "I wonder why that was?"

Tatiana squeezed my shoulder, reminding me that I wasn't alone, whereas Zev, for all his minions, mostly was. I was swamped with a rush of sorrow because for the vampire, survival meant secrets, and relationships were weaknesses, something I understood far too well.

Except all my secrets had crumbled into dust and here I

stood, smarter and stronger, thanks to those I'd decided to trust. Resilience wasn't a singular oak tree, it wasn't even a willow tree, able to bend and sway, it was a garden of companion plants where each had their own unique characteristics and needs yet they thrived better together.

"I know you want to kill me," I said. "Recent events and all."

Zev's glance flicked to Tatiana, who shook her head.

"I heard there was an incident, but Miriam refused to share the details."

His surprise flashed over his face for a second before he schooled his features. "Your point, Ms. Feldman?"

I kicked some of the plastic wrapping out of the way. "It's nothing compared to how much I want to kill you."

The vampire barked out a laugh and tilted his head jauntily to the side as if daring me to try. "Please. I would enjoy the spectacle."

Asshat. "Despite my wishes, we came here to help you." I unclenched my jaw. *Hold your horses, stupid oath.* "And in the process, solve our own problem. No more compulsions, no more threats, no more broken promises. We either ally ourselves or we all burn." I spread my hands wide. "Welcome to the new world order, Zev."

He gave two fast blinks at my use of his first name, which was deeply satisfying. "How dramatic," he scoffed.

"Which you'd know nothing about." Tatiana stepped sideways, catching the edge of a spotlight that shone on a marble bust of Medusa. "'Love me Sweet, with all thou art,'" she recited. "'Feeling, thinking, seeing; Love me in the lightest part, Love me in full being.'" She smiled. "Remember the moonlight on the steps of the Paris Opera house that night, Zev?"

Holy hell! I released the breast of the statue I'd grabbed hold of in shock, waving at the marble figure in apology, while not taking my eyes off the drama going down before me.

The vamp seized Tatiana by the throat and pressed her against the marble Medusa. "'Nay, I have done, you get no more of me; And I am glad, yea glad with all my heart, That thus so cleanly I myself can free.' Also dramatic, but more apt."

My scythe manifested in a second, but before I could intervene, Tatiana calmly peeled his hand off her neck and pressed it to her heart. "My first statement stands."

I froze, torn between making sure my elderly boss was safe and not wanting to draw attention to myself, but damn did I have questions.

Zev snatched his hand away. "You were terrified of what I offered you, so you threw away all our years to remain with your *normal human*." He sneered that last part. "Yet despite all that, I allowed him to live, so tell me, Tanechka, who truly loved whom?"

Feeling like the worst kind of voyeur, I cloaked myself and tiptoed backward to the office door, taking great care not to stumble into any of the artwork.

Tatiana planted her hands on her hips. "Samuel was a wonderful man, but the only reason you left him alive was so every day I'd torment myself with what I'd given up. And you're wrong about why I left. Your love was couched in secrets and barbed wire, just like everything else in your life, and it was destroying me." Her lips parted slightly like she hadn't meant to admit that last part.

"And now?" He flicked a piece of lint off his sleeve like the answer was of no concern.

She jabbed him in the chest twice, pushing him out of her personal space. "As tempting as it is to watch you self-destruct, *yet again*—"

Zev flinched and I bumped into a painting with my hip, scrambling to catch the heavy frame before it fell.

"I don't enjoy your pain," she said. "So, will you actually listen for once in your damned life?"

Zev chuckled without any humor. "It is damned, isn't it?" He spun around, his glinting eyes locked on mine through the invisibility mesh. "Enjoying yourself, Ms. Feldman? You do seem to be privy to so many of my private moments."

"No." I stood on the carpet with all my shields down. "I just feel sad."

A red haze washed over his eyes and his fangs descended.

"Do you remember when I almost gave up in Paris and went home?" Tatiana said, stopping Zev in his tracks. "I stayed because you convinced me I didn't have to keep playing the part that others expected of me. I could rid myself of the path that strangled me even though it was the only one I knew, and live life the way I wanted to."

He ran his tongue over his teeth. "You fought me hard before you saw it my way."

"True, but you enjoyed that." She grinned wickedly, and I grimaced because I preferred to keep any vision of her love with Zev as a platonic ideal. Like really, really preferred. She grew serious. "Take your own advice now, l'vionak, and hear us out."

21

ZEV BLINKED SLOWLY, HIS EYES RETURNING TO THEIR regular brown color. "By all means." He motioned us back to the chairs and sat on the edge of the desk with his legs brushing ours.

I slapped a five-dollar bill down. "Should you accept your employment with Cassin & Associates, your business cards will arrive in five to ten days."

He picked up the bill and dropped it to the floor. "You're testing my patience."

From out in the hall came the clatter of glass and a muffled curse.

Tatiana cleared her throat and tapped her wrist.

Zev turned his head like a lion who'd scented prey, his eyes glittering, and pocketed the money. "And I would be delighted to join your organization. It wouldn't be the first time." So. Many. Questions. "Debrief me, will you? Succinctly," he added when I opened my mouth.

"Sabrina Mayhew was turned against her will and is the rogue vampire killing gang members." *That succinct enough for you, jerkwad?*

Zev leaned so far forward that he was nose to nose with me.

"Who sired her?" The barely leashed violence in his voice made me shudder.

"I don't know yet," I said. "What I do know is that Sabrina didn't want to become a vampire, but someone did it and left her to fend for herself. She also killed three men in front of me. I could be wrong that she's behind the rest of the murders, but I doubt it."

Zev gouged the desk with his fingers like it was butter, strips of wood curling around his hands. It was scarier than if he'd destroyed it. "That's why you've been stalling Vincenzo."

It was a bit more complicated than that, but I nodded. One dilemma at a time.

"Yet he made you swear a blood oath of secrecy instead of calling in all possible resources to find her." Zev pulled a two-inch splinter out from under his fingernail without even a wince, but I grimaced enough for both of us. "He's in a precarious position right now, isn't he?"

"Hypothetically, if he were," Tatiana said in a warning voice, "he's handling it with no one the wiser."

Zev smirked and steepled his fingers under his chin.

"Who was Vincenzo?" I said. "Before he was turned?"

Zev always insisted he hadn't lost his humanity when he became a vampire, and despite much evidence to the contrary, I also had proof that he'd loved deeply—both Tatiana and his wife, whom he still mourned hundreds of years after her death.

Vincenzo also loved Sabrina. Maybe I could appeal to his humanity?

"Who knows?" Zev toyed with the pearl-handled letter opener on his desk. "Digital records have made hiding one's past more difficult, but Vincenzo was changed long before that technology. He's a vampire, he's possessive, and his mate was turned by someone else. That's all that matters."

"He loves her," I said. "That matters too."

Zev darted a glance at Tatiana. "That makes it worse."

"We want your permission to find whoever did this to his

fiancée," Tatiana said in a matter-of-fact tone, "and hand them over to our client."

"You think that will satisfy him?" Zev ran a finger along the letter opener's blade, drawing a single crimson bead against his pale skin.

Tatiana looked away.

"I doubt you need my permission," he said, his finger already healed, "since none of my people would dare leave a new vampire alone. That means someone else has come to town and you may do whatever you like to them." He stood and started pacing alongside us like a tiger in one fluid motion.

Tatiana shot me a pointed glance and I scowled at her. *Thanks for making me the messenger.*

"Well." I fidgeted on my seat, drawing Zev's predatory stare. "It could mean that one of your people is making a power grab." I shrugged my shoulders up to my ears to protect my neck.

Zev laughed. "A good leader knows if their crew is unhappy enough to mutiny. Trust me, Ms. Feldman, I am an exceptional one."

"With an exceptional ego," Tatiana said.

I smothered a grin.

"True," he said. "But I take excellent care of my people, and I have eyes and ears everywhere. Anyone thinking to challenge me would have come to my attention already. Now. Where is Sabrina?"

I believed in Zev's paranoia enough to decide he was right and knocked a power grab for Blood Alley off my list of motives for turning Sabrina. If her sire hadn't done this to go after Zev or Vincenzo, then why? I drummed my fingers on my thigh. Sabrina had been turned into a vampire on Friday night, before Ryann's edict on Tuesday. Yes, she now fell under it, but her sire wouldn't have been worried about repercussions at the time, so why abandon her? What an incredibly stupid and pointless thing to do.

"Sabrina is safe," I said, answering his question.

Zev stroked his goatee, his eyes on the ceiling. "At Amar's then."

I kept my expression impassive. He didn't get a gold star for figuring it out.

"Regardless, that's not good enough," he said. "I want her brought where I can guard her."

"First, swear a blood oath that you will never compel me, my people, or any member of Miriam's family." Tatiana rummaged in her purse for a tissue, then sneezed into it. "When's the last time you vacuumed this carpet?"

Zev curled his lips at the aspersion cast upon his precious Persian rug, and I glared at my boss. Maybe don't antagonize the bloodsucking fiend while we're trying to strike a deal?

"My family includes Jude," I clarified, back on topic. "Also, you won't harm any of us either directly or indirectly. Ever."

"Any second cousins you'd care to include? Sadie's third-grade teacher, perhaps?" He sounded amused.

"Well, if you're open to suggestions," I said.

"I'm not," he replied flatly. "Nor do I agree to a blood oath. You shall have my word—"

"Like I had your word to never compel me?" Tatiana snorted. "Your promises are worth less than this tissue these days," she said, stuffing it back in her purse. "When did you become that person?"

"Watch yourself, Tatiana, for I've not agreed to anything yet," he growled.

"Everyone take a breath." I pushed my chair back, the better to keep them both in view.

Start negotiations for more than I'd settle for—the lawyers had taught me well. Laurent hadn't wanted Zev's protection in the first place, and it wasn't in BatKian's interests to take out a police officer. That left Jude, Emmett, and Sadie who were vulnerable. I doubted the vampire would go after my best friend, and the golem never went anywhere on his own, so we'd have his back. Our relationships plus our magic would keep us safe, and I'd steer the discussion around to my daughter and me in a moment.

"We all want the same outcome," I said, "which is to avoid Vincenzo's wrath and any altercations with the Lonestars." Before Zev could go all alpha vamp about how he'd take his chances, I threw him a bright smile. "Oh, I'm being so rude. I haven't even asked how Yoshi's doing? Am I getting my gift card soon?"

Zev's eyes narrowed.

That's right, hot shot. You can't afford to fight on multiple fronts when you have this vampire disease to contend with. Too bad Vincenzo didn't seem to have to deal with it, given it had hit other vampire territories, like Dagmar's in Boston.

"I have yet to hear anything that's in this for me," BatKian said.

"How's this?" I ticked items off my fingers. "You can refuse, you can kill us, you can frame some other vampire for the Lonestars, but it doesn't change the fact that you can't get to Sabrina without our cooperation."

Zev rested his hands on the chair along either side of my head, penning me in. "And should Vincenzo declare war even if it was an unknown vampire who did this simply because it occurred in my territory? Your plan does nothing to address that."

"Sure it does." I pressed my hands to my cheeks. "How noble you were to defy the Lonestars on his behalf and let him deal with the vampire who attacked Sabrina."

Tatiana clucked her tongue. "I told you to leave the theatrics to Sadie."

Zev stepped away with a dismissive flap of his hands.

"Explain Vincenzo's choices to him," I said, ignoring her. "He can rage out and deal with all your crew *and* the Lonestars, or he gets Sabrina back as well as whomever changed her. The same vamp who'll take all the blame for Sabrina's killing spree. Even Vincenzo has to admit that Sabrina as a vampire is better than her imprisonment on Deadman's Island."

My boss placed a hand on my shoulder. She now stood next to me, beaming and dabbing at her eyes. "My little girl is all grown up. I'm verklempt."

I shook my head but gave her a fond smile.

Zev stroked his goatee. "It will be unfortunate when the rogue vampire dies during apprehension and can't be handed to the Lonestars to make a confession."

Some of the tension left my body, my shoulders descending a whole quarter inch. "Right? So sad."

"This is all provided nothing goes wrong." The vampire tapped his finger against his lips.

"Then make sure it all goes right." I picked my purse up off the floor. "Look, the bottom line is if we don't walk out of here with a deal, or fail to walk out of here at all, a number of people have letters they're to deliver to Vincenzo and the Lonestars stating that we kept Sabrina isolated on your orders because one of your vamps was very naughty and you were trying to hide it."

"Do they now?" he purred.

Suddenly the devil I knew seemed like the wrong choice, but I held out my phone, my hand steady. "Who do you want to ask first?"

I kept the cell extended with a bored look on my face, waiting for Zev to call my bluff. Except it wasn't a bluff. This was the insurance policy we'd put into place. My chance to be free and clear of the threat he posed to me once and for all.

Would it be enough?

"Well?" I prompted. "Will you swear the blood oath and take this deal?"

"Tanechka, leave the room for a moment," Zev said. "Ms. Feldman and I have something to discuss."

I lowered the phone. "It's okay."

Tatiana gave me an uncertain smile but did as we asked.

Zev slid into her vacated seat. "You are correct that I'm in checkmate as far as Sabrina is concerned, but you and I have unfinished business."

I couldn't come up with a response that tiptoed around the subject, so I went for it. "That wasn't your finest moment, but Kian's your sire, and I kind of assumed all estries have more power. Seems to me your only error was forgetting that." I shrugged. "Either way, I promise not to bandy it about. Besides, it's nowhere near as revealing of your vulnerabilities as the story you told me about your wife, and I really should have shut up ten seconds ago."

He made a sound of agreement. "Regarding Sadie," he began.

Shadows whipped around me like a tornado in the blink of an eye. "Don't touch her. Swear to it in blood."

"In exchange for your vow not to interfere with the bargain your daughter made with me and keep my secrets?" He gave a one-shouldered shrug. "If you want me to swear an oath, the reverse seems entirely fair."

I teetered precariously on a razor's edge. Realistically, short of the witness protection program, there was no way to prevent Sadie from fulfilling her end of their bargain. She'd gotten herself into this situation, and much as I wanted to take this burden from her, I couldn't.

My daughter had loved swings from a very young age. I'd stand behind her, telling her over and over to hold on to the swing chains, until one day, I gave up. The swing went up and Sadie went down hard, badly skinning her knee, arm, and right cheek. She'd screamed bloody murder, tears and blood pouring down her face. The guilt that I'd let her get hurt had strangled me like barbed wire, but I'd made sure she wasn't swinging too high when it happened. She didn't break any bones and she always held on tight after that, able to soar.

We can't always protect people, hell, we can't always protect ourselves, no matter how hard we try. Maybe our greatest asset isn't our strength but our perseverance. None of my magic or life experiences would free Sadie from the consequences of her actions. I couldn't stop this bargain, but I could mitigate the circumstances to make it as safe as possible. Physically and emotionally. Sadie would learn from this and survive to make better choices.

"I gave you my word not to break any confidences or to interfere in your deal with Sadie," I said. "And I've proven that I can be trusted. You don't require magic to force me to keep my promises."

The vampire crossed his legs and let out a loud breath. "Which of your friends or loved ones have I harmed since I first agreed not to? Tatiana's compulsion aside."

He'd threatened to attack them to get me to do his bidding, but… "You haven't," I admitted.

"Yet you insult my character and demand blood oaths."

I traced the mitered grooves in the armrest, unable to meet his eyes. He could have forced a blood oath on me when he told me the tragic story of the Torquemada Gloves, but he hadn't. And all this time, his word had remained his bond.

"You're right, and I apologize for that," I said. "Though your constant manipulations are insulting to *me*."

"A thought you would never have dared voice previously."

"Are you taking credit for my growth? Is that why you didn't murder me after I saw what Kian did? Some kind of mentorly goodwill?"

Zev grimaced. "Ascribe such sentimental rubbish to me and I will dismantle you. You have worth. I've seen it, Tatiana's seen it, and most interesting of all, you are finally seeing it."

That sounded suspiciously like a compliment. From the ancient vampire.

I turned it around for the dig that had to be buried in it somewhere, but try as I might, I couldn't find it. There'd been a shift at our last meeting when I had my scythe at his throat. It was less about strength than stature, but I still couldn't wrap my head around the fact that Zev found that praiseworthy, instead of deeming me an irritant or a foe to be snuffed out.

"Thank you." I crossed my legs, swinging a foot nonchalantly.

"So, you agree we either ally ourselves or we go down in flames together?"

"I agree that we either treat each other with respect, free of magic bindings, or we go to war."

Ah. There it was. Threat equilibrium restored.

"Fine. No blood oaths." I shrugged. "It'll be more fun to destroy you myself should you break your promise."

"To use one of your phrases, 'back at you.'" He chuckled darkly and went to fetch Tatiana. "Miriam and I have come to an agreement," he told her.

I did a double take at both his use of my first name and my colloquial phrasing. Had the apocalypse started? I glanced around the room. Had one of his paintings been even an inch crooked or the corner of his Persian rug been folded up, I might have decided that yes, yes, it had. Instead, I chalked it up to me growing on him.

Tatiana sat down. "What did you two decide?"

"I'll swear a blood oath to never compel or harm only you, Tanechka."

"I don't want that," she said. "I want you to be the person I know you can be."

"You don't trust that person." Zev sat down in his desk chair and neatly folded his shirt sleeves up, exposing a dusting of dark hair on his muscular forearms. "What would you have me do?"

My enjoyment of his physical prowess was short-lived when I noticed Tatiana ogling him as well. Nope. Any vague attraction to the vampire was well and truly dead.

"Become someone I do trust again," my boss replied archly.

They exchanged a loaded look while I shrank against the chair and tried to make myself invisible instead of appearing like I was hanging off every word and glance.

Zev inclined his head at her, and Tatiana returned the gesture. That wasn't as good as a kiss, but it also wouldn't scar me for life as the sight of any lip-lock between them would.

The events of the past few days had left me exhausted, but

this mutual respect that Zev and I had come to was worth it. Then I remembered that Dumah had the Ascendant thanks to me, and my foot hit the ground, all satisfaction gone.

Tatiana and Zev stared at me with similar curious expressions.

I flexed my foot. "Muscle cramp," I lied.

I dug my nails into my palms to keep my magic from breaking free because that situation wouldn't have occurred if the two of them had been honest with me—and each other— from the start about that damned amplifier.

The thing is, in the end, it had been my choice to throw the Ascendant into Gehenna, so I could hardly throw blame around. Until I'd met the Leviathan, I hadn't even thought of that place as Dumah's prison since the angel was in charge of torturing souls. Apparently, no one else in my circle had either, including Laurent, because no one had raised the issue after the artifact was gone.

Perhaps it was a carefully guarded secret to make Dumah and the threat of eternal torture for the wicked appear more dire. As Tatiana always said, branding was everything.

"Our business is concluded," Zev said. "Bring me Sabrina."

I stood up. "You'll talk to Vincenzo?"

Zev nodded. "Once I have Sabrina where he can't get to her until a deal is struck." He slid his phone out and sent a series of texts. "Have Amar deliver her here tomorrow at 9AM."

When I hesitated because Laurent was compellable, the vampire eyed me. "Doubting me already?"

"Nine AM it is," I said.

"Rodrigo will meet you at the gates." Would Zev be asleep at that time? I'd never seen him in the morning so maybe that was our best window of opportunity to avoid Vincenzo as well. "Until then," Zev continued, "I'll send my people to guard both your places. And if you find her sire before I do, tell me. Immediately."

"Absolutely."

Tatiana nudged me. "Tell him about the shadow."

Zev blurred in front of me, blocking my way. "What shadow?"

I scratched my arm. "It turns out that before Sabrina was turned, she was enthralled."

Zev pinched the bridge of his nose. "You did get it out of her, correct?"

"Yes."

"Why do I sense a 'but'?" he said in a tight voice.

"She's dybbuk-free but she isn't waking up. There's nothing wrong with her," I said, "and once her shadow regenerates all should be well, but I'll look for a way to make it happen sooner. Just keep Vincenzo from seeing her until then." I held a fist up in solidarity as Zev ground his teeth. "Mutual respect for the win."

22

Tatiana did her best to use the crowds in Blood Alley to keep us separated on the way back to her car. It wasn't even 9PM, so the popular attraction was nowhere near as crowded as it would grow later, but there were enough people to carry out her plan. Her behavior was hilarious, but she wasn't deterring me from my many follow-up questions about her love affair. Besides, if I couldn't tail an eighty-year-old, I had other problems.

I sidestepped two men coming out of one of the bars where a small crowd of humans and vamps were "interacting." Compared to the nightclub, this was tame: some of the undead fed off their companions, but others just chatted. One of the parties caught my attention and I backtracked to the door.

Celeste sat chewing gum and perving on some other vamp feeding from a blond guy. The vamp lifted his head and my eyes widened.

Ian Carlyle had quite the set of new fangs. Good for him, but wow, of all the people I'd expected to jump at an offer of immortality, Ian wasn't it. He'd even admitted to being too much of a coward to go for it, too scarred from his time in the Human Race. Something must have changed.

Celeste laughed, removing a smear of blood from Ian's mouth with her thumb with the look of a proud parent. Creepy as fuck, but pretty much what I expected from a siring vampire caring for their new charge.

Blond Guy swayed toward Ian with a dreamy look. Carlyle looked at Celeste uncertainly, but at her nod, he grabbed the man and bit down once more with a ferocity that made me and Celeste flinch.

She put her hand on Ian's shoulder, but before she could say anything, Ian threw the human aside, and smashed his own head into the table.

Celeste's mouth dropped open and her gum fell to the floor as all the patrons turned to stare.

Two other vamps were immediately on them. One strong-armed Ian toward a back door, Celeste trying to stop them, while the other checked on the young man.

An older female vampire close by me smirked. "I told Zev she was too young to sire anyone. So, there's a few less vamps? So what? Better that than scrape the dregs to join our ranks."

Her companion applied some lipstick. "He already did that when he turned his granddaughter."

They laughed cruelly.

Celeste stiffened and glared at them, then at me too, when she saw me.

I turned away with a pang. Poor Ian. Was he stable enough mentally to survive this transition? Either way, I was glad he had Celeste taking care of him, though I wished that Sabrina had a mentor in her corner.

Even with my delay, I caught up to Tatiana before she made it back to the car, however, I paused before getting in because a thought hit me. Did every Sapien who was turned survive the transition? Statistically they couldn't, especially not if in the rush to create more vamps, the vamps weren't being as picky about their candidates as usual.

Had one of Zev's replacement vampires not made it, leaving

"the three" that Rodrigo had mentioned? With Ryann's edict, he wouldn't be able to make any more, at least not for a while.

I opened the car door. I'd been so busy ascribing violent motives to Sabrina's abduction that I'd missed an important alternative. What if Sabrina's sire changed the lawyer because they wanted to curry favor with Zev? Sheesh. Talk about backfiring.

When I clicked my seat belt in and stretched my legs out with a sigh, Tatiana narrowed her eyes.

"No third degree?" she rasped.

"Really?" My mood improved eighty-seven percent. "How'd you meet? How long were you together? Did Samuel know? Hypothetically, do vampires make good lovers?"

Tatiana turned on her ignition with a grunt. "Aren't you seeing my nephew?"

"Don't deflect."

"Quid pro quo. If you're not going to comment, I don't have to either." She jerked the gold monstrosity of a vehicle back and forth even though there was no longer anyone else parked on the block before pulling onto the road.

"Yes, but your story is ancient hist—ouch!" I rubbed the arm she'd smacked. "Not current. Mine is. Plus, you're his aunt so that's weird." I opened a browser on my phone, trying to find what she'd called Zev.

"L'vionak," she snapped and plucked the cell out of my hands, since keeping her eyes on the road while driving was, once again, optional.

I snatched it back, before grabbing the "oh shit" handle above the door. "Car!"

She swerved sideways back into our lane.

"If you're going to kill me, then at least satisfy my curiosity before I die so tragically young. What does 'l'vionak' mean?"

Tatiana heaved a sigh. "Russians use animals as terms of endearment. It means 'little lion.' That's all you get, so stop bothering me or I'll magically seal your mouth shut."

I wasn't sure she could do that, but I wasn't not sure either. I folded my arms and stared out the window, listening to the jazz station she put on.

We were halfway home when Tatiana piped up. "He knew."

It took me a moment to put that in context, but when I did, I screamed *Holy crap* in my head. However, I kept my body language and voice casual, not even turning from the window to look at her. "And Samuel didn't mind?"

"I loved my husband," she said with a glare.

"Tatiana," I said gently, "I've seen the letters between the two of you. I have absolutely no doubt of that."

She relaxed, her shoulders dropping.

"And there's nothing wrong with an open marriage when all people consent to it. It just surprised me given the time period and the fact you came from a religious family. Was that why you were estranged from them?"

She uttered a mirthless laugh. "No. Running away to be an artist in Paris instead of getting married was enough." She remained quiet for another few blocks. "I wouldn't say Zev consented, but he had no choice if he wanted to keep me."

"Did you know he was a vampire from the start?" My fingers twitched; I longed to take notes and put this all in her memoirs. The publishing house she was negotiating with would have a bestseller on their hands. But alas, that could never be. Oooh. Unless we put out an Ohrist edition. We were totally discussing that later.

"I had no idea. I was sixteen and sneaking out to attend artist salons while he was a well-known and charming patron of the arts."

I shuddered. I couldn't help it. "Sadie is sixteen and Zev was about forty when he became a vampire."

She clucked her tongue. "My parents hired a Shidduch to matchmake me at her age. Don't apply today's standards to my life, Miriam."

"Sorry," I said, abashed.

"Besides, Zev didn't do anything inappropriate. We didn't even interact much for the first few months until I brought some of my paintings to one of the salons. He commented on my talent, which was a big deal to me." A smile flitted across her face. "I worked up the nerve to ask for help finding an art teacher, since I'd been self-taught to that point. My parents hadn't been religious prior to their rise in fortune, and they'd always taken me and my siblings to museums. They didn't take issue with me painting as a hobby, though it was understood I'd stop all that when it came time to produce children and run a home."

She stopped halfway through the intersection at a red light, her arm flying out to block me from going through the window.

I barely even registered the cars honking at us. "What happened?"

"Zev was good friends with my instructor and was often there for my lessons. We got to know each other." The years seemed to fall off her wrinkled frame as she spoke, lost to these happy memories.

"Green light," I murmured.

She hit the gas and we jolted forward. "When I was seventeen, I got engaged and my art lessons came to an end. My parents watched me like a hawk, and if I wasn't with them, then I was with my betrothed, Shlomo, and his family."

I twisted around in my seat. "Did you make it to the chuppah?"

"Absolutely not. About a month into my engagement, I ran to Zev and declared I'd rather die than get married."

"Not dramatic at all," I said wryly.

"That's why I'm such an expert." She winked at me. "That's also when he showed me what he was."

"Were you scared?"

"I was young, with a head full of dreams, and the person I'd begged to take me to France turned out to be a handsome vampire. What do you think?" She turned onto my street. "So began a new chapter of my—" She stiffened. "Miriam."

My argument that this was no time to go all Scheherazade fled because all the windows and the front door of my home were open.

I'm not sure I even said goodbye before bolting out of the car and onto the sidewalk.

An unfamiliar vampire peeled away from the shadows in my neighbor's yard and intercepted me before I got to the protective wards around my property. Luckily, she penetrated my adrenaline-addled brain enough for me to understand that Zev had sent her.

Tatiana's vehicle blocked the street, the artist watching the two of us with a steady gaze.

I rested my scythe on my shoulder, attempting to think logically. Zev was the only one who could get through the wards. That was the entire point of them. Even a human with intent to harm would have the strongest urge to move along. Sadie had been painting. She must be airing the fumes out.

Waving at Tatiana that all was well, I allowed her to drive off, but if she thought her storytelling was over, she was deluded.

"You need anything?" I said to the female vampire. Coffee I could do, blood not so much.

She scanned the neighborhood. About my height, she had the broadest shoulders I'd ever seen on a woman. Her biceps were the size of my thighs while her torso tapered down to a narrow V at the waist. A former bodybuilder or could the undead gain muscle mass?

"I'm good," she said. "But there was another vampire prowling around outside your wards. I never saw their face and they're gone now."

"Tell Zev, okay?" It had to be Vincenzo, looking for Sabrina. Until we determined whether he was awake during the day, we'd have to be careful leaving the house.

Heading inside, I called out Sadie's name, but receiving no

answer, I beelined for the living room where I halted in the doorway.

My daughter rolled on another coat of paint, drops splattering onto her skin as she sang along loudly to the K-pop blasting out of her earbuds. The plastic sheeting on the floor looked like a Kandinsky painting, and I wasn't sure how she'd managed to get a smear of paint on her butt, but the purple on the walls cleanly met the white ceiling paint, and the room didn't stink too badly.

I waved my arms until she noticed me and shrieked, pulling the earbuds out.

"Geez, Mom."

"How much did your father do?" I motioned for her to stay back because I was already sweaty and gross in two-day-old clothing. I didn't need paint spatter to complete my look.

"None of it."

"Yeah, right."

She shook the roller at me, sending paint into her hair. "Why have me do this if you assumed I'd do a bad job?"

"Because you were grounded, and I wanted to punish you. I figured you'd do an okay job, but I'd have to help on the corners and seams." I crossed my arms. "Was it Caleb?"

"No." Huffing loudly, she shoved one of her earbuds back in.

Hmm. Tatiana would have mentioned if Emmett had come over and I'd have gotten a text from Jude, so who... "Did Laurent stop by?"

She froze and gave a half shrug. "He might have checked if you were back from the vampires. And helped. A bit."

I twirled my finger around the room. "Which bit?"

"The edges," Laurent said from behind me. He held an angled brush with traces of white paint on it, and there was a smudge of purple on his arm, but he hadn't gotten a single drop on his clothes. "And the kitchen."

With his biceps straining tight against his faded T-shirt, the dust of stubble along his jaw, and the paintbrush in his long, elegant fingers, he was a sexy handyman fantasy come to life. Honestly, at this stage in my life, I got hotter for a man who could fix things than a man who just looked the part.

As hot.

Regardless, I currently looked like a swamp witch and was never getting my second date. Which didn't matter right now because he shouldn't have taken over. "Laurent," I sighed, "this was supposed to be her punishment. You shouldn't have stepped in."

He set the brush down on the painter's tray. "I know, ma chèrie, but it was so horrible. The walls, they wept." He shuddered theatrically and I laughed. "The only one it would have punished was you, and you'd been through enough."

"Oh my God!" Sadie stamped her foot. "Wept? Could you be more of a drama queen?"

"My mistake," he said somberly, though his eyes twinkled.

How was I supposed to stay irritated with a man who came to check I was safe from vamps, put his extensive renovation experience to use so my house looked pretty, and called me "ma chèrie"—which was a total step into romance-land from ma chèr?

Who was I kidding? I was already so settled into romance-land with him I'd thrown away my tourist visa.

"Let's see the kitchen." Head held high, I strode past him.

23

THE WINDOWSILLS AND DOORFRAMES WERE PAINTED in the sunflower yellow I'd chosen. It was bolder than I anticipated, and had the entire room been that color, it would have been overwhelming when combined with my red maple shaker cabinets.

Laurent, with his decorator's eye, had seen that and diluted the yellow down to a more of a light sunny kiss that warmed the space and made the cupboards glow. It turned the room into the kind of place where I could do the dishes in the middle of the brightest day feeling like I lived inside a sunbeam, yet on gray and rainy winter days, steal away to read a book at the table with a cup of tea in a slice of summertime.

"It's beautiful," I sighed dreamily. "Thank you." I motioned him to the table, taking a seat across from him in case I stank. Then I remembered he was a shifter and he'd probably smelled me when I came up the front walk, but I still arranged my arms elbow out to air my pits. "I'm sorry about Giulia's ring."

He pressed his lips together, and I thought he was still angry, but his shoulders shook, and I dropped my arms.

"Yeah, yeah, wolf smelling abilities." I paused. "I'm kind of surprised you came over at all, never mind did something this lovely for me."

He shrugged. "I spoke to Giulia, who set me straight. Sort of. Apparently, you were drunk?"

"Very strong painkiller," I mumbled.

"Ah. I also realized that if I'd taken a moment to think instead of jumping to the worst conclusion, I'd have known that the ring must have been crucial to get hold of."

"It was, and I'd resolved not to steal it, but I confess that was my intention when I saw Giulia."

"Can you tell me why?"

"I'm done." Sadie thumped over to the sink with all the grace of a herd of elephants and rinsed the foam roller out. "I'll pull up the tarps once it's dry, then have I suffered enough?"

"You barely painted," I said.

"It was a bunch more than barely, and Laurent also made me wash all the kitchen cupboards inside and out." She glared at him.

Grinning, I nudged his foot under the table.

"I offered you a choice," he said mildly. "We could have gone for a ten-kilometer run instead. Your father approved the options."

"You all suck."

My eyebrows shot up. "Sadie May Chu."

"Sorry." She ducked her head. After turning off the tap, she squeezed the water out of the roller. "I'm going to bed." She wiped her hands off on a tea towel and then looked around the room. "It's really pretty, Laurent. Thank you."

"You're welcome," he said.

She'd screwed up and would have to live with the ramifications of her deal with BatKian. Plus, my home was starting to transform into the jewel I wanted to live in. I could cut the kid a break.

"Sades?"

She stopped in the doorway, her shoulders slumped. "Yeah?"

"You can hang out with Caleb or Nessa tomorrow provided you've done your homework." I didn't even finish before she was squealing and hugging me, bouncing like a puppy. She even hugged Laurent.

"Thanks, Mom. You're the best. Night!" She raced out of the room.

"Teen girls are very…" He furrowed his brow.

I smiled. "Yeah. They are."

"Will she be okay? She told me what happened when she snuck into Blood Alley."

"That wasn't a high point." I shrugged. "I don't know, but I'll be by her side to help her through it. A lot of people will."

"She has good parents. That's important."

"Speaking of…" I wiped a breadcrumb off the table. "That's why I wanted Giulia's ring. To get the name of my parents' killer."

"And?"

"I got it, but…" What was the right opening line for this conversation? *Hey, did you hear the one about the fallen angel and the Banim Shovavim?* I stood up. "Come with me."

I led him upstairs into my office, where I used my whiteboard to lay out everything I suspected about Dumah: from Arlo to Learsdon's whispers, Nora and the amulet, and most especially the murders of Fred McMurtry and my parents.

My throat was dry after all that, so I got a glass of water, drinking it at a snail's pace at the kitchen sink. I hadn't dared look at Laurent's face while I told him the story. I'd deserve his anger for giving Dumah and the dybbuks free rein, but if all I saw was disappointment? My stomach ached.

"The angel now has the means to escape Gehenna," he said upon my return. "So why hasn't he?"

"My assumption is that he needs my Banim Shovavim magic in conjunction with the Ascendant to free him." I stood by his chair, studying the whiteboard. "I thought I was being so clever tossing it in. What have I done?"

He pulled me into his lap and wrapped his arms around me. "I fear that it was always going to come down to you procuring it for Dumah. If you hadn't handed it over, who knows what would have happened? He'd already started using others to get to you, Professor Learsdon, the ones who kidnapped Emmett, Nora."

I absently traced hearts on my yoga pants. "Dumah can coax people via whispers into doing his bidding, but if he could grab me himself or personally rough me up, he would have."

"He outsourced killing your parents and McMurtry."

"Yeah." I shivered and snuggled back against Laurent's chest. "There's no evidence that Dumah has consorted with demons, though as a fallen angel, it wouldn't surprise me that he has access to them." I shrugged. "It doesn't matter who or what he used to kill Mom and Dad. It was his call."

"McMurtry was a loose end," Laurent said. "But why murder your parents and not Calvin Jones, who hired them to steal the Ascendant from Tatiana, since Jones was the one who ended up with it?"

"He wasn't Banim Shovavim." I twisted around in Laurent's hold. "Arlo's attempt to free Dumah must have been aborted by Senoi, Sansenoi, and Sammaneglof, and if my parents"—my voice cracked—"refused to help Dumah, they were put on his hit list."

I gripped his hands. "We have to get the Ascendant back."

Laurent laughed, then at my expression, stopped. "You're serious."

"Dumah hasn't used it yet. He needs me to use my magic with the Ascendant to free him. I feel it in my gut. If I get it back and destroy it, it's over."

Laurent ran a hand through his hair. "Even if that's the case, hell, especially if it is, you can't just waltz in and hand yourself to him."

"I won't be caught. Dumah is focused on me, either because of my parents or because I gave him the Ascendant, but how long will he wait now that he has the magic amplifier? What's to stop him from finding a willing Banim Shovavim to break him out? What happens to the dybbuks then? Are they still imprisoned, or do they all come with the angel, free to roam the world until every last one has found a host?"

"Merde," Laurent said softly.

"That's not all." I buried my face in his neck, breathing in his cedar scent and wishing I could get my erratic heartbeat to slow down and match his steady one. "I kind of promised to get the Ascendant for the Leviathan to escape the Kefitzat Haderech where he's been exiled by Senoi, Sansenoi, and Sammaneglof for being an abomination."

Laurent groaned, his hands loosely clasped at the base of my spine. "Unpromise him."

"He's stuck there and Pyotr's been telling him about our visits. I think he's lonely. And he did heal me. Twice. He could have left me to die."

Laurent ground his teeth together.

"Now you're mad because I keep getting into these lethal situations," I said, not lifting my head. "But it's not as if I have a death wish. Honestly, it's the opposite, but back to the Leviathan. If Dumah hasn't used the Ascendant yet, then I can use my cloaking to steal it back. And sure, if Zev can detect me under my cloaking then Dumah has a damn good shot, but you need to consider the fact that Gehenna is a real place, not a hidden space, so the KH should get me there. If I get the lay of the land, then conceivably I can enter close to the most likely hidey-hole Dumah has stashed the amplifier."

Brushing my cheek against the shifter's shoulder, I sighed. "Which is where you point out that Gehenna isn't on Google Maps, and I say that we don't need that because there's an estrie who just spent who knows how long there." I propped a hand under my chin. "Though you'll rant, rightfully so, about trusting an estrie, especially one that I helped lock up, but I'll reply that we don't have a lot of choice and maybe there's something I can offer her. To which you counter that the KH doesn't go to hidden spaces, so why would it go to a place only the dead can access? And even if it does, should I really be alerting those three Banim Shovavim–hating angels where I'm going? No, I shouldn't, but we can avoid all that if you'd just open a portal to Gehenna, which is what I wanted to ask you to do in the first place except for the fact that you'd freak out."

Laurent's jaw hung open, his brows furrowed and a look of fascination on his face.

I dropped my voice into a growly impression of his. "I refuse to send you on a suicide mission. Non, Mitzi. I will not help you steal from the angel who killed your parents. You're insane for even considering it." I sat up, shaking my head. "Forget it. The amulet was destroyed so I have some time before Dumah contacts me again to come up with another plan."

Laurent's snort turned into full-on belly laughs, his giddy mirth lighting me up like the brightest August day, except for one thing.

I punched his shoulder. "This isn't funny."

He crossed his arms. "No, because I do not sound like Pepé Le Pew. How vile."

"Why aren't you Hulk raging right now? I just asked you to open a portal to Gehenna so I could steal the Ascendant back. But I want to help the Leviathan, and then I'll destroy the artifact once and for all. It's the only way I see out of this madness."

"Yes, I heard both sides of your argument," he said, chuckling. "Did you ever consider a career in law?"

I narrowed my eyes. "You'll help?"

"I will and if you ask me why, I'll be insulted."

I mimed zipping my lips. Then cracked two seconds later. "Why?"

He flexed his biceps. "Because I am a paragon among men."

I lowered his arm. Laurent had deviated from his expected part in a huge way, but then again, I had as well. I wasn't scared anymore, the woman keeping all her secrets close. "You are, aren't you?"

"Oui. You're very fortunate to have me."

"Do I have you?" I toyed with my old engagement ring. "I'm guessing you haven't been in a relationship with anyone since Delphine, and if you want to go slowly or see other people, then tell me."

Because I may need to excuse myself very quickly afterward.

"Mitzi, I wanted to take you on a date because you deserve fancy nights out, not because I need to go slow."

"Oh." I glanced up in case hearts were dancing around in the air.

He placed his hands behind his head, regarding me with a cocky grin. "That ship sailed when you barreled into my life and wormed your way under my skin before I knew what had hit me."

"I'll hit you again if you like," I said sweetly.

"Non, I cannot take that much foreplay after painting your house. I am only one man. Better than others, yet still human." He stood up, steadying me on my feet as he did.

"So, we're officially in a relationship now?" I threaded my fingers through his.

He brushed his lips over mine. "Yes. A fact we'll celebrate when your child is not around."

"Does that mean you'll help me move something tomorrow?" I checked the time. It was after midnight. "Or, rather, later today."

"Like a dresser?" He walked out of the office. "Depends when. It's a supermoon tomorrow evening."

I hopped down the stairs behind him. "It would be at nine in the morning. Take Sabrina to Blood Alley."

His shoulders tensed briefly, stemming from his dislike of Zev, not fear.

"You're a veritable paragon," I said. "And Rodrigo is meeting you. I'm not sure that even ancient vamps are awake that early."

He shoved his feet into the sneakers by the door, then

speared me with a wicked look. "You're going to owe me. The second all this is over, we're having our next better date."

"Even if it's the middle of the afternoon?" I teased.

His lips quirked. "Did you not realize adults could *date* during daylight hours?"

I lightly punched him in the arm. "I was going to demonstrate how grateful I was for all your help, but—"

"But are you thong and corset grateful?" Laurent retrieved his leather jacket and motorcycle helmet from the closet.

"Possibly even thigh-high stockings and heels grateful," I said in a sultry tone.

He pulled me to him for a brief, hard kiss that left me mindwhacked and clutching his shirt.

Neither of us moved for a moment. This was real. Holy hell was it real. The Laurent I'd first met would have been a disaster in a relationship, but I would have as well. I'd had to find my feet in this magic world first, find *myself*. We'd changed each other, but more importantly, we'd chosen to change ourselves.

I shook my head sharply to clear it. "We also have to plan the Ascendant heist."

"Non. Go back to the corset." Laurent shrugged into his jacket, rustling the leather.

"And be on the lookout for Vincenzo."

He squashed his curls under his helmet. "Never a dull moment."

24

SABRINA WAS DELIVERED INTO ZEV'S CARE WITHOUT incident, though the handover involved two large golf umbrellas and a heavy blanket covering her. A sensible precaution even if it was raining. That good news was followed up by the even better news that her shadow had regenerated, but my happiness crashed down upon learning that Juliette still couldn't rouse her.

"We've decided the best use of your time is to find a way to wake Sabrina," Emmett said on the phone after the update.

I jammed the nozzle into my gas tank, one eye on the dollar amounts creeping higher on the pump, and the phone cradled on my shoulder. I agreed with Emmett, but his high-handed directive put me off. "Who exactly is 'we'?"

"Not me. I'm not that foolish," my boyfriend called out on the other side of the line. His shifter hearing rendered speakerphone moot.

Also, boyfriend? What was I, fifteen? My partner? Eh. Regardless of the label, Huff 'n' Puff was a smart man. And mine. I smiled dreamily.

Emmett snorted and made the sound of a whip. "Me and Mr. BatKian decided it."

"Wait, what? Laurent took you with him to Blood Alley?"

"Obviously," Emmett said. "Why else would I be in his truck now?"

"Rodrigo conveyed the orders," Laurent said. "The vamp wasn't there and Emmett had no part in it."

"I'd just been about to suggest Miri work on waking her," Emmett protested. "It's like I'm in sync with Mr. BatKian."

"Uh-huh." The pump clicked off. Emmett had done a one-eighty from being down on himself to issuing orders; a way of feeling in control. "Where are you now?"

There was a blast of a rock song through the phone followed by the golem's "Ouch!" and the music changing to a classical piece.

"Following Rodrigo," Emmett said.

"Following him where?" I replaced the nozzle and tightened the cap on my gas tank.

"He and a bunch of vamps spent the night tracking down Vincenzo and his goons to a place in Southlands." There was a noise like Emmett had cracked his knuckles, which was weird because he didn't have bones, did he? "We're gonna stake them. Pay that asshole back for freezing me."

So much for any midafternoon date today. Also, was taking Emmett along a wise idea? I punched the button on the gas pump for my receipt. "Put Laurent on."

"No, because you'll tell him I can't do it. The wolf said that I survived the Human Race and I'm tougher than I give myself credit for. Smarter too."

Laurent had a heart-to-heart with the golem?

A fizzy warmth whispered through me. I was going to lavish that man with gratitude the next time I saw him.

"Don't call him the wolf." I shoved the receipt in my wallet and got in my vehicle.

"Wolf is my nickname for him," Emmett protested. "He also said you need to stop mothering me because I can handle myself."

"I did not," Laurent said.

"You implied it," the golem said breezily.

It wasn't easy to correct my original impression of him as having the emotional intelligence of a young child, but he'd matured a lot in our short friendship. "You're right. You are a very capable and valuable member of this team. I won't mother you anymore, but that doesn't change the fact that this doesn't make any sense. Killing Vincenzo will start a vamp war. Zev had no interest in that last night, so what changed?"

"Rodrigo said—"

Emmett was cut off by Laurent speaking up in the background. "Vincenzo won't turn the other cheek when he learns about Sabrina, and with the assassination of his second, his death can be played off as a successful hit by his enemies."

Wrenching on the ignition, I pulled away from the pump. "So, Sabrina wakes up and she's got nothing? Not her humanity, not her career, and not her fiancé? You can't do that to her."

"It's not your call," Emmett said.

"Did you check in with your actual boss, Tatiana, about killing her client? She's not a big fan of losing her paycheck," I said icily.

"You talk to her," Emmett muttered.

He must have given Laurent the cell because the shifter's next words were spoken directly into the phone. "Tatiana isn't happy, but she agreed. The vampires will be asleep, and this is the safest way to stop them. Are you willing to risk Vincenzo turning his wrath on you or Tatiana? On Sadie?"

I merged into traffic, a light drizzle of rain hitting my windshield. "You're playing the guilt card."

He sighed. "I'm playing the reality card."

"Then admit this isn't about me or Sadie. Zev's protecting his own ass." I manually turned my wipers on and off because the mist setting wasn't fast enough, but the regular setting was too much. I hated this weather so much.

"It's both." He paused. "You're too emotionally invested in their relationship," he said gently.

Everything he said was true and logical, but this entire situation made me want to curl up under the covers for a week.

"Why bother waking Sabrina up at all?" I said bitterly. "It's more compassionate not to."

"The Lonestars will require it."

"No," I wailed. "She'll end up on Deadman's Island."

"You can't keep Mayhew hidden. Ryann is too smart for that. There's no happy ending to this love story, Mitzi." His reluctant words were punctuated with a sigh.

I was surrounded by loss: Laurent and Delphine, Tatiana and Zev. Hell, I thought I'd found my happily ever after with Eli, and instead I was another divorce statistic.

Yes, I was embarking on a new relationship, but my new circumstances were more complicated than when I'd fallen for Eli. We'd both been young, had both wanted kids, but even though Sadie was my everything, I had zero desire for more. Laurent had lost his chance to be a father and he was younger than me. I would never begrudge him wanting a child, but did that mean we were over before we'd truly begun?

Had I been invested in Sabrina and Vincenzo's happily ever after because their relationship was as unlikely as I'd judged mine and Laurent's to be? I shook my head. We'd figure this out, same as everything else. Together.

Women were told so many limiting stories. Tatiana's parents had reduced her world to being a wife and a mother instead of an artist. I'd been a sad divorced single mom making stultifyingly safe choices.

Tatiana had rejected the choices offered to her and I'd reclaimed my life. Now here was Sabrina, who'd chosen an unconventional happily ever after, with everything about to be torn away from her.

"Please don't do this," I said.

"Even if I don't," Laurent said, "Rodrigo will. This way, I watch his back. There's no stopping this. I'm sorry."

Something in my chest dropped. I sighed. "Me too."

What else was there to say? I cleared my throat, but before I could say goodbye, Laurent spoke up.

"I'm also sorry we won't have our date this afternoon." He injected some lightness into the mood.

Emmett's "Ew, gross" was followed by a grunt and a "Sorry, toots."

"Does the supermoon tonight mean you'll be affected earlier?" That hadn't occurred to me when we'd discussed our second date, but Laurent wouldn't be in wolf form for that. This vamp attack was another matter. I peered up at the sky. "Even though it's overcast?"

"It's supposed to clear up later," he said. "But I won't be affected until dusk, around seven thirty, same as any full moon."

"Good. Still, wrap it up quickly and safely."

"I will. À bientôt, Mitzi."

"Later, Huff 'n' Puff."

Nora was supposed to be my first stop today to find a way to wake Sabrina up, but after that call, I was tempted to go home because I didn't want to drag the lawyer into a waking nightmare.

Call me naïve but I'd been rooting for Vincenzo and Sabrina, despite the odds. A vampire loved a human enough to remain by her side, knowing he'd have to watch her grow old and die if she didn't give up her humanity. That was tragedy enough so why couldn't they have this lifetime?

I passed the turnoff for the bridge to the North Shore where Nora lived, aimlessly driving through Burnaby while I figured out what to do.

How truthful had Tatiana been about the nature of Zev's love? Or, rather, how much had that contributed to why she'd stayed with Samuel? She'd been with Zev before she met her husband and given the impression that affair with the vampire had gone on for decades. Had she really had enough? Had Samuel known and given her an ultimatum? Or was it something else entirely?

Did Tatiana worry that an elderly woman with a younger-looking man (vampire) would be considered a sugar mama? Did her unassailable confidence not extend to bucking the stares and going out in public with Zev when she grew old?

Pulling a U-turn, I headed back to the bridge, because despite my misgivings, I couldn't let Sabrina remain unconscious. I didn't have that right. Still, when I got to Nora's place, I sat in the car, gathering my courage to go inside.

I'd inadvertently caused the raven shifter trauma and wouldn't blame her if she refused to have anything more to do with me, but I also had no one else to turn to. Sabrina was the first enthralled vampire that any of my team, including Zev, had heard of. Even stopping enthrallments was brand-new territory. Our knowledge was predicated on my experiences with Ohrists, all of whom awoke immediately after I applied CPR compressions. We'd assumed it was the shock of severing their shadow and losing their magic that sent them into unconsciousness and convulsions in the first place.

As a healer, it should have been a piece of cake for Juliette to wake Sabrina up. Yet her shadow had returned, and Sabrina was still out, so why the holdup?

A curtain twitched in Nora's front window, so I exited the car, grabbing the gift basket filled with teas, macarons, shortbread, and fancy chocolates from my trunk. I didn't bother with an umbrella, using the basket as cover.

Amazingly, she answered my knock without hesitation.

"Harry told me you were taking a few days off," I said. "How are you?" Her color was good but that didn't speak to her emotional state.

"It's all faded like a fuzzy dream, which is for the best. Come on in."

"Thanks." I slipped off my shoes and followed her into the kitchen. With the curtains wide open and the warm-toned lights on, it was a much cheerier room even on this gray day. Plus, all those creepy candles last time had been a real mood killer. I set the basket on the table. "This is for you. It's an apology gift but I'm afraid it's going to come off as a bribe."

"Hmm." She tore off the cellophane wrapping. "On the one hand, chocolate, tea, and treats. On the other, supernatural invasions of my brain. Ooh, shortbread." She ripped the package open. "Screw it. Bring on the voices."

"Not that kind of favor."

She brushed crumbs off her lip with the back of her hand. "Even better."

I rubbed a finger over my wrist. "If I had a question and the only answer might be in the Library of the Arcane, could you research it? I know you said it isn't open to the public, but I have a problem I need answered immediately."

"It depends on the question. Archivists work in cells so that no one person becomes too knowledgeable and thus too powerful. I don't even know who oversees the whole thing."

A fat bumblebee walked up the outside of the window before shivering its wings and lifting off.

"Could I get access to the library?" My wrist tingled. Not so much a warning as a reminder that the blood oath would know if I'd been bad or good. My own personal Santa.

"Tea?" Nora stood abruptly, took the basket with her to the counter, and busied herself filling a kettle.

"Not an option?"

"Technically, one-time visitor passes exist, but you're not going to like the cost."

It had to be better than Vincenzo's wrath if I couldn't wake his fiancée. I'd even considered having Sadie give it a go and null whatever this interference was, but she wasn't trained enough to separate out magic and if she nulled vampire magic, Sabrina would die.

As would Sadie.

"Is it a raven shifter game?" I said.

Nora put the kettle on the burner and flicked on the heat. "You wish."

My eyebrows shot up.

"All kinds of Ohrists work there," she said, "but the pass is determined by a test."

I brightened. "I'm excellent at tests. Give me the topic and I'll rock studying it."

"You are," Nora said.

"I'm what?"

"The topic. The library will read you and if you're interesting enough or your brain contains enough knowledge that the library wishes to obtain, then you're issued a pass."

"Because I passed. Cute," I said in a flat voice. "And if I fail?"

"You get weeded." At my look of utter confusion, she continued. "Weeding is when—"

I held up a hand. "I know what it is, but it's one thing to judge a book on variables like condition, accuracy, and whether it gets checked out to keep it in circulation. I'm a person and I'm not in your library's circulation, so how exactly would that apply to me?"

Nora rolled onto the insides of her feet, her gaze on the linoleum floor. "For the purposes of the test, you're a source of knowledge, same as a book. If what's inside you isn't relevant to the collection..."

"I get recycled?"

Nora removed the whistling kettle from the stove. "In a manner of speaking. Black or herbal?"

I'd bypassed tannins to a straight-up slug of whiskey mood. "That's preposterous."

Nora shrugged. "Library rules. You want to go ahead with it?"

I very much did not.

"Decaf Earl Grey might be best right now." Nora placed a mug in front of me, the string from the tea bag hanging over the rim. "Milk, sugar?"

"Milk," I murmured.

Vincenzo might already be destroyed, and with Sabrina's

fiancé removed from the equation, that left the Lonestars. If Sabrina didn't wake up, would Ryann blame me? Too bad. It would have been worse to let the dybbuk gain control of Sabrina's body. I clinked my ring against the mug. Assuming Ryann didn't blame anyone, that still left Sabrina unconscious. Would she be sent to Deadman's Island? Would they just kill her?

Even if neither outcome transpired, I couldn't leave Sabrina like that indefinitely.

But I couldn't be weeded either.

25

I TOOK A SIP OF MY TEA, WHICH I HADN'T ADDED MILK to, and which had gone tepid while I'd been thinking. With only Ohrists working for the library, my odds of passing the test were pretty good. Not only was I Banim Shovavim, I'd figured out the riddle in the Kefitzat Haderech to avoid eternal damnation. That right there had to count for something. Plus, the library was interested in important people, and I doubted it knew about Tatiana and Zev's epic love story.

I took a piece of shortbread from the plate Nora proffered, not feeling guilty in the slightest about passing my boss's love story on like cheap gossip. It's not like anyone could just wander into the library and learn about it.

"Let's do it." I inhaled the cookie in two bites.

"All right." She fired off a quick text and nodded as she read the response. "You'll get confirmation in a second."

"The test is here?"

"It's everywhere."

Did she mean the testing locations or the library itself? A sentient library watching us like Big Brother? Best not to think about it.

My phone pinged. "It's happening in two hours in my living room. Not where I expected."

"FYI, this is a one-time deal," Nora said. "And don't be late. If you miss the start time by even ten seconds, you don't get to take it."

"Understood."

We chatted for a while, then I took my leave to allow plenty of time to arrive home and psych myself up for the test. Maybe read some stuff off the dark Ohrist web in case anything there caught the library's attention.

Even though it remained overcast, the clouds had lightened, and the rain had let up. Taking that as a good omen, I drove home singing along to some breezy pop song and feeling confident about what I had to offer.

A call came in as I pulled up to the curb. An innocuous, old-school ring.

Knocks convey tone. Is it a furious banging on the door? A playful rap? They can be brisk or ponderous. Insistent or meek. Fast or slow. They're a heads-up to what awaits me on the other side of that door.

But a ring tone? It didn't matter if someone programmed their partner's number with the sweetest love song, it wouldn't alert them they were about to be dumped. This call could have been anything, including a bot, which was what I initially thought when my hello was met with silence. I'd almost disconnected when static crackled down the line.

"...wrong..." Emmett said.

"I can't hear you properly." I stuck my finger in my other ear.

There was another loud burst of static, but it was the single word before the call cut out that made my blood run cold.

"...trap..."

Fumbling with my seat belt, I almost fell out of the car, my return call already ringing in my ear.

And ringing.

And ringing.

A car backed out of a driveway startling a bird, and a garbage truck beeped in the distance. Just another mundane day.

Yet, I stood on the sidewalk, listening to Emmett's snarky voice mail greeting, feeling oddly disconnected, my plea to call me back inadequate.

I multitasked at Olympic levels and my list making was second to none, so why was I totally blank about what to do next? A breath shuddered out of me, but it kicked in enough basic intellect for me to remember that Laurent had a phone. Before I could punch in his number, someone gripped the fleshy underside of my arm.

Where was my nosy neighbor Luka when I needed him? He wouldn't have detected that Vincenzo's grip was so tight that my eyes watered, but even seeing a man, not a vampire, with a torn jacket, and blood streaked along his forehead grab me had to send up a red flag, right?

"Is she alive?" Vincenzo hissed in my ear.

"Yes." My eyes darted to my property line, safety a mere ten feet away.

The vampire spun me around and frog-marched me down the block. "Take me to her this instant or watch me destroy everyone you care about."

My blood boiled, my desire to unleash my magic physically paining me. But the stupid fucking overcast weather kept me from animating Delilah to rip off his head or summoning my scythe to stab him a dozen times in his most vulnerable bits.

He shoved me inside a high-end sports car with tinted windows. "Where to?"

"Blood Alley," I said in a croak.

The vehicle peeled out with enough force to slam me back against the seat.

I gripped my seat belt, praying he didn't hit anyone because from the set of his jaw, telling him to slow down would be a death sentence. Same with feigning ignorance or asking what had happened to him.

How was Vincenzo even here? Laurent and Emmett—a scream wailed in my head, and I twisted my fingers together like that could physically shove it away—*my team* would have gotten there before the vampire or his minions had woken up.

The clock on the dashboard showed it was after noon now, but they'd driven to Vincenzo's place a few hours ago. Zev would have known when it was safe to send them in, and it didn't make sense for him to betray my... I swallowed. Them. He wasn't working with Vincenzo to take those two out, was he?

I forced away the image of the gash along Laurent's side courtesy of BatKian. The vamp knew damn well that...*harming*... those two would hurt both me and Tatiana. I almost laughed. "Hurt." Four letters wouldn't encompass our devastation.

But it would violate our mutual respect agreement.

This wasn't Zev. I glanced at Vincenzo. So, who'd given him a heads-up? Or, rather, protected him, since I doubted he could be roused early?

My abductor had wicked good fortune going for him: no construction slowed our progress, no cop clocked us for going way over the speed limit, and we hit every green light.

Vincenzo swerved into a parking spot in front of the real Blood Alley and forced me out of the car. My stomach twisted, because I still couldn't access my magic.

Zev was my best option to help.

Or the best shield to hide behind when Vincenzo saw Sabrina.

New plan: as soon as Zev showed up, I'd race home. There was still plenty of time before the library test.

BatXoha quickly walked us through the invisible demarcation line into the hidden space and tensed as we stood outside the spiky gates. The gargoyle statues that normally sat on either side of the metal sign were gone, and a dense fog cloaked the entire territory.

Vincenzo shoved me into the entrance and I screamed, caught in a ward whose electric magic flared sharp and strong, wrapping me in sticky tendrils. I manifested my scythe and cut myself loose, but my skin throbbed bright red.

Weapon aloft, I faced my captor. "There's no way through."

He glanced at the fog. "Has he done this to keep me from her?"

I didn't even see him close the space between us. Suddenly, he gripped my shoulder, and my scythe grew too heavy to hold. It fell from my hand onto the concrete and shattered, the pieces vanishing.

"I don't know," I squeaked.

His fingers were bruising, forcing me into a hunched-over twist, while magic dripped down my left side, weighing me down into paralysis. "Best guess."

"M-maybe that other vamp was really after you and Zev both?"

Vincenzo frowned and I sucked in a breath, my eyes briefly closing at the huge misstep I'd just made.

"What other vamp?" His compulsion pushed at my brain, and although it didn't work on me, his magic had cemented both of my feet to the ground and locked my knees stiff.

I dropped my head, exhaustion and defeat sweeping away any ability to formulate a plausible lie. "The one who turned Sabrina."

The vampire staggered back, his hand on his gut as if he'd been punched, his face crumpling. A feral cry burst out of him, his features contorted. "You lie!"

I shook my head, deafened by his roar. "It's why we didn't want you to see her."

"When?" He touched his ring finger. His unfettered grief was as raw as a live wire, and it sparked goosebumps that skated over my skin.

"Friday night, when she went missing, but I only learned of it when we found her."

Lost to fury and heartbreak, he slammed his hands against my chest and I stumbled backward, cold heaviness blossoming over my sternum, then my ribs, and then out through my limbs. It was like frost carried via arteries, blood vessels, and capillaries, and I gradually numbed out, white snow eating at the edge of my vision until everything telescoped to a single figure amid the white.

And the last thing I saw was a man or a monster, hunched over himself in grief, rage, or some other emotion too vast and horrible for a body to hold.

The only good thing about nightmares was that they ended. Eventually. Sometimes, though, I'd get trapped in this in-between space I couldn't wake from. The problem had started after my parents' murders, yet I hadn't suffered from it in years.

Here's how it happened. I'd wake up from a terrible dream and see my room, just like I'd left it. Except I couldn't move. I couldn't get out of bed. At some point, I'd realize I was still asleep and would tell myself to wake up. Sometimes it would work. Sometimes it wouldn't, and I'd be stuck just as paralyzed and unable to do anything as I had been before, repeating the cycle over and over and screaming silently at myself to just wake up. When I did finally come to, it was always with a hard jolt. And when I finally pressed my bare feet against the ground, everything was real.

I couldn't tell what this was.

The sandstone tile in this room was cold and hard under my back, and when I moved my arm, pain blazed down from my shoulder. It wasn't broken but the vampire had pulled something.

Those clear sensations should have indicated I was awake, but that was impossible because the Undertaker lay crumpled a few feet away, his lifeless eyes devoid of their usual intelligence and his stupid gold braided chauffeur cap nowhere in sight.

Oh please. He loved that hat like Linus loved his security blanket. Can't trick me, dream.

Wake up. I scrunched my eyes closed, then snapped them open again when someone nudged my leg. Sitting up with a flinch, I smiled because it was Emmett, and I was so happy to see his friendly faaaa— My breath stuttered.

Wake up. I dug my nails into my sides.

One of the golem's arms had been snapped off above the elbow, and part of his neck up to his left ear was gone, his face misshapen.

I smacked my head. *Wake up. Wake up.*

"Mir." He scrabbled at my sleeve, my name almost too garbled to understand.

"Wake up!" I screamed.

Emmett hid his head.

"No, buddy. I'm sorry." I wrapped my arms around him, holding him tight.

He squeezed me back so fiercely that a hot blaze rumbled through my shoulders, but I didn't pull away.

"Who did this to you?" I said. "Are you in a lot of pain?"

He buried his face in my neck like Sadie used to as a baby and said something that sounded like "Vincenzo."

"Hold on a bit longer, I'll get you out of here. I promise." I released him and swallowed a couple of times past the thickness clogging my throat. "Where's Laurent?"

Emmett gave a helpless shrug.

The wolf was a crafty fighter who could take care of himself. Emmett and I were getting out of here and we'd all find each other. I fixed that thought in my brain like a commandment etched into one of Moses's tablets.

"Are we at the place in Southlands where the vamps were hiding?" It made sense given the blackout fabric duct taped over the windows.

Emmett nodded.

Juliette didn't live far from here. I pulled out my cell, but there was no reception.

"Did Vincenzo kill the Under…" I swallowed.

The deceased hadn't exactly been a saint in real life. I'd wished him dead on more than one occasion and working for a vampire had more than its share of risk, but his death, like the tragedy of this entire case, felt…

Sighing, I crouched down next to him and closed the man's lids. Rest in peace. "Did he kill Rodrigo?"

This time Emmett shook his head.

"One of the other vampires?"

Another head shake. The answer went into the "later" pile because I didn't have time for charades. I had to focus on the living.

"We'll retrace your steps and find Laurent." I stepped into a shadow but couldn't access the KH. Was this a hidden space? I tore a corner of the blackout fabric free, revealing the sky darkening over an ordinary backyard.

My relief turned to a tight ache. I'd missed the test, my one-time chance to check the Library of the Arcane for the means to wake up Sabrina. *Later.*

A flash of gold through the trees caught my attention. Rising onto tiptoe, I shuffled to my right, only to be rewarded with the edge of an enormous gold moon beaming serenely down.

Laurent. *Later*, I snarled at myself.

I strode across the room. Emmett and I were in the real world, but I couldn't sneak us out via the KH. I jiggled the knob, but it was locked, so I pressed my hands to the door to determine if we could kick it down.

A hum rolled along it, buzzing through my palms, and when I pushed against it, it pushed back. The buzz extended along the walls on either side of the door.

"We're magically locked in."

Delilah appeared and I rubbed my shoulder against hers,

delighted that at least this particular magic worked. "Let's try green vision," I said.

Her shadow vision displayed the ward as a pulsing band running the circumference of the room, which was cool but also hammered home that we were well and truly trapped.

Just then, the door opened and both Delilah and I were blown back against the far wall. My shadow lost her animation and crumpled to a puddle of black at my feet.

I dragged in a shaky breath, holding my poor shoulder, ready to take Vincenzo on. Except he wasn't our new visitor.

Kian, the estrie, the *demon* who should have been imprisoned in Zev's dungeon, strolled in carrying a huge bloody monstrosity like he weighed nothing. The beast shifted in fits and starts, a grotesque dance between fur and flesh set to the crunching of bones and a low, pained wail. If Hell had a melody, this was it.

This may have been the real world, but the nightmare had just begun.

26

————————

THE DEMON TOSSED LAURENT DOWN LIKE A PIECE OF trash.

My—the wolf faced away from me. I curled my toes under in my shoes like I was taking root in the floor, so I didn't give in to my screaming need to help him, because I refused to hand Kian any weakness.

Emmett scuttled over to the shifter.

The estrie swiveled her head one hundred and eighty degrees to face him. "Stay," she said in a bored voice.

Emmett froze and I swallowed down a whimper.

We had to get past Kian and through that open door. The odds of besting her physically, even with my magic, weren't great, but I had a better tool at my disposal.

"You fucked up, demon." I stood up, pleased to note that at least I was taller than her.

Kian narrowed her eyes. She wore the same dress she had in the cell, and while still pale, there was a palpable strength that flowed off her now that she was free from all that iron. Or maybe she'd had her recommended serving of bodybuilder. "The human who wrenched me from Gehenna." She stalked toward me, like bad too-fast stop-motion animation. From one blink to the next she'd narrowed the gap between us, her head askew and her shoulders crooked, and then suddenly she was in front of me, her eyes glinting with vicious glee. "Do you regret your actions? You should."

I willed my breathing to remain even. "No, but you will."

She blinked at me with an amused expression. "Why, pray tell?"

"Didn't you hear? I gave Dumah the Ascendant."

Kian tossed her fall of black hair off one shoulder. "A nothing trinket from a nothing human."

Laurent's left leg was stuck in a loop shifting from foreleg to forearm, fingers to claws, pallid skin to matted fur, while Emmett remained rooted in place, his face slack from the estrie's magic command.

I mentally gathered up every shard of my heart, imagining them pounding into my body like spikes and embracing the pain. "I gave Dumah the keys to his jail cell. Given the messages he's passed along, he's very anxious to make my acquaintance. As powerful as you are," I continued, "do you want to risk angering an angel with eons of torture expertise? I have no clue why you got tangled up in Vincenzo's business, but I suggest you walk away and let us do the same."

The demon furrowed her brow like she was doing complex math equations in her head.

Come on. Put two and two together and let us out.

There was a series of sharp snaps, and I slid my eyes sideways to catch the wolf's head morphing into a lumpy man's skull. The animal's howl died as a human whimper, and Laurent scratched a matted furry foreleg over his lank, dark curls.

I gnawed on the inside of my cheek hard enough to draw blood. Why couldn't he shift out of this hybrid form?

"You're lying about the angel," Kian said. She now hung upside down from ceiling in front of me, her hair brushing the floor. I yelped, because she had not been that way a second ago.

"Dumah has no interest in you." She swayed like a giant spider about to pounce, her knobby fingers twitching.

My terror was knocked aside by the memory of Mom's huge eyes, brimming with tears, and how she'd positioned herself so I couldn't see my dead father before imploring me to hide on the night she died.

"Trust me," I said icily, backing up, "his interest goes back years."

The estrie landed on her toes, nose to nose with me. "This is so much better than I expected." Huh? "I merely wanted he who is no longer of my line to suffer an unexpected change in plans."

No longer because she'd stripped Zev of his name? Or of his life? I shoved the question away.

She wagged a finger. "But you believe you fly with the angels."

I shivered, as frozen to the spot by those words as if Kian had glued me there. "I never claimed that."

Delilah snuck up behind the demon with the scythe.

Kian did her creepy head swivel and blew on Delilah. Both my shadow and the scythe dissolved into waves, which rippled away. "You've done nothing for Dumah."

My throat was dry and icy sweat crawled down the back of my neck, but I dared not show fear. "You're wrong. Dumah is imprisoned in Gehenna, is he not? And the Ascendant brings the monsters out of the dark via *my* Banim Shovavim magic." I cocked an eyebrow. "You'd know."

"You are correct."

Her pronouncement confirmed that I'd finally solved the most important puzzle of my life: Dumah had killed my parents.

There was no swell of joy, no trumpets pealed across the land, and my chest felt hollow.

Laurent's shifting had slowed from a rolling boil to a simmer, no longer transforming, merely alternating patches between fur and skin, but that was scarier, because it was like his body was giving up. From the shoulders up he was human. His torso was a misshapen hybrid, while his left arm and leg were wolf, and his right limbs those of a man's.

I clenched my fists. I had a second chance and no one, not a demon, not a vampire, and not even a fallen angel was going to steal it. *Hang on, Laurent.*

"Why say I haven't done anything for Dumah?" I said. "It seems to me that I've done everything."

Kian stroked my hair, her lips teasing up, and I fought off a flinch. "It would seem so," she said, "except for one thing. Dumah has no desire to leave Gehenna."

"Of course he does," I snapped. "He's imprisoned there."

"True." She wrinkled her nose. "But he never was as fallen as his punishment implied. Merely poorly allied. One thing Dumah does have plenty of? Guilt. You may have handed him the key, human, but he exults in being imprisoned."

"You're lying," I hissed.

"I don't care enough to bother with fabrications," she said flatly.

I pressed my fist to my mouth like I could physically staunch the air that punched out of me. It was horrible enough if Dumah had murdered my parents in pursuit of his freedom, but if it wasn't that, then what did that leave? Some twisted game to pass the time?

Wake up.

A snarl escaped my lips; I'd never been more awake.

Kian lay her hand on my cheek like a caress, her eyes glittering maliciously, and magic exploded out of me, darkening the entire room for a split second. The demon gasped, her hand falling away.

I'd rammed my scythe right through her center.

Freed from the demon's magic hold, Emmett whistled.

Wrenching the blade out with a twist to inject one more millisecond of pain before the demon dissolved into ash, I met her eyes and smiled. "Just a nothing trinket from a nothing human."

"Miri." The golem pressed his hand to Laurent's forehead and made a sizzling noise.

Laurent's half-closed lids showed only white behind them, and his face was flushed.

I sank to my knees. "Open your eyes right now, Huff 'n' Puff," I cajoled. "You've got to shift so we can get out of here." The ward was gone, but Laurent couldn't go into the KH and I wasn't leaving him. I lightly slapped his cheek.

He was unresponsive, his pulse sluggish.

Emmett wasn't faring much better. His eyes were glassy and his messed-up jaw kept spasming, not to mention he had only one arm. He couldn't carry Laurent on his own in his condition.

"Can you hang on long enough to help get him outside?" I said. "I should have cell reception again and we can hide until Juliette comes."

"Yes," he slurred.

I was running on fumes, held together by willpower no thicker than Scotch tape. Delilah flickered and fell apart when I called her up, and cloaking us was out of the question. Should Vincenzo be upstairs and attack us, we were screwed.

Cell range. Focus on that.

"Be quiet and stay alert in case Vincenzo shows up." Ignoring the pain in my shoulder, I grabbed Laurent under his armpits, using my thigh to elevate his head.

Emmett took his feet and we carried him out the door. Unfortunately, being quiet flew right out the window about halfway up to the ground floor. Emmett kept dropping Laurent's legs because of his short arm, and the shifter's hybrid form was so awkward that there was no way to prevent his middle from bumping loudly up every stair.

Poor guy was going to be a giant bruise, but on the upside, no one came to check out the commotion.

"We seem to be alone." I mopped the sweat from my cleavage and checked my cell phone, but there still wasn't any reception. "You know what'll help? Music." I discarded my first choice of "I

Will Survive" in favor of an enthusiastic rendition of the Bee Gees' "Stayin' Alive." Yes. There was a theme. Whatever.

I even encouraged Emmett to hum along, our voices growing louder as Laurent grew stiller. By the top, I was using my good shoulder to shove him onto the landing, while Emmett heaved from the other side.

By the time we got Laurent across the kitchen, Emmett was swaying and the pain blazing down my arm from my injury made me nauseous. I wasn't sure how much more any of us could handle, but if we waited here in the kitchen until our help came we'd be exposed.

"We stick with the plan," I said.

The moon was higher now, hitting us like a spotlight the moment we stepped outside. I let it bathe Laurent, but he didn't shift to wolf form like I'd hoped. Instead, he let out a low moan that didn't let up.

Sweat burned my eyes, and I had to keep taking breaks, but we got most of the way down the back stairs. Our hiding spot in the bushes was close enough to taste.

Suddenly, Emmett lost his footing on the final stair, rolling his ankle.

I carefully set Laurent down, but he flopped limply into the dirt, still moaning. His closed lids fluttered madly, his face was flushed, and he was perspiring. I pressed my lips to his forehead to check his temperature and my heart sank.

"Don't you dare die on me," I snapped. "I did not buy that corset for nothing."

Emmett hissed, attempting to stand up. Even with my help, he couldn't put any weight on that foot, but more worrying was the gray sheen covering his red skin.

I hid my clenched fists behind my back and shoved down a scream. "Crawl over to those bushes, okay?"

He got onto all fours as best he could but limp-crawled in the other direction. "Wolf," he mumbled.

"Don't ever doubt yourself or your ability to keep people safe, all right?" Hopefully this stubborn, wonderful golem hadn't heard the shakiness in my voice. "You're a survivor, my friend."

He nodded.

I positioned Laurent over Emmett's back, once again carrying the shifter's shoulders and head.

About twenty feet from our hiding spot, a car crunched up the gravel out front of the large house.

Emmett and I exchanged panicked glances, and he hauled butt to the bushes, collapsing as car doors slammed.

Gritting my teeth, I tugged Laurent far enough behind the brambles that none of him stuck out, then I kissed Emmett's forehead, mindful of his mangled jaw. "You're the bravest partner ever," I whispered. "Can you muffle Laurent?"

He nodded weakly and fell onto his back, one hand over the shifter's mouth.

Keeping one hand on Laurent's chest to make sure he was breathing, shallow as it was, I grabbed my phone, my eyes welling up at the sight of those two beautiful bars. Emmett needed Jude stat. I'd call her to meet us after I phoned Juliette.

"It's over," Ryann called out, coming around from the side of the house. Her pink leggings and oversize sweater with a unicorn on it did nothing to diminish the power she projected. "Show yourself."

I dropped the cell into the dirt. Was she here for me?

"Copy that."

I'd heard that man's voice before. Frowning, I peered through the bushes.

Hawaiian shirt Lonestar touched his ear. "The house is empty. Did BatKian get to Vincenzo or did the other vamp get away?"

Ryann swore, which was so unlike her that I flinched. "Have they broken the ward across Blood Alley yet? Do we have Sabrina in custody?"

My pulse spiked. Holy fuck.

Emmett dropped his hand because Laurent's face was

shifting into a deformed muzzle. He'd stopped moaning, but white foam leaked from his mouth.

Wiping Laurent's fur with my sleeve, I called up my contacts with a shaking hand, almost missing Ryann saying my name.

"No," Hawaiian shirt Lonestar said. "Detective Chu would have checked in if he'd found her. Same with Tatiana if Miriam had called. Last I heard, her phone hadn't been turned on for Anna to track."

I slapped the power button off. Could I make one quick call without tipping off the Lonestars? Even if Juliette answered on the first ring and ran every red light, would she make it in time to save Laurent?

There was only one thing I could do.

Emmett scrabbled weakly at my leg as I stood up, shaking his head.

"It'll be okay," I lied.

I stepped out of the bushes with my hands up. "Help us. Please."

An unreadable expression flashed over Ryann's face before she schooled it into a cold mask. She strode toward me. "Don't move."

"Laurent's dying and Emmett might be too. They're innocent —" I broke off with a yelp because she'd wrenched my arms behind my back and slapped nulling cuffs on me.

"Miriam Feldman, you're under arrest for accessory to murder."

It hadn't been Dumah or Vincenzo or Kian who'd stolen my second chance. It had been me. Every nerve ending in my body flared as if someone had taken a grinder to the exposed ends and I trembled, my soul ground to dust.

And Sadie? I'd vowed never to abandon my precious girl like my parents had done to me. Yet here I was.

"Do you understand the charges?" Ryann peered into my eyes.

I nodded, tears rolling down my cheeks. "I do and I'll tell you everything. Just save them."

"Already on it," Hawaiian shirt guy said.

I had one final glimpse of Laurent and Emmett being carefully carried out of the bushes, then Ryann dragged me away.

27

THEY LEFT ME TO STEW IN A CONFERENCE ROOM AT Lonestar HQ. I wasn't offered a lawyer, and when I demanded a phone call, the Hawaiian shirt Lonestar chuckled, not unkindly, and said I watched too much television.

By the time Ryann joined me, I'd bitten my nails to the quick, and was on my third run-through of every way I'd blown up my life. I leaned as far forward as the chair bolted to the concrete allowed. "How are Laurent and Emmett? Can I speak to Sadie or Eli?"

The thought of never seeing my daughter again was a physical ache that clawed through my chest.

Ryann slapped a folder with a pen clipped to it down on the table. "You could have avoided this."

When former magic cop Oliver Anderson had looked at me, all he'd seen was a despised BS, but I'd have taken his derision over the utter impersonality Ryann pegged me with. Her blue eyes weren't a summer sky, wide in wonder, they were glacial cold and calculating.

Void of magic due to the nulling handcuffs, I reached for anger to cloak myself in, but found only sorrow. "I could say the same thing about you."

"What's that supposed to mean?"

I stroked a finger over the spot where Vincenzo had bitten me. With my luck, these cuffs worked on only my magic, not the blood oath. "Sabrina was turned against her will and left to fend for herself." With that one measly sentence, a pressure built on all my tendons and muscles like they were about to snap. I fell to my knees, gripping the table so hard that my knuckles turned white.

Ryann frowned and then grabbed my wrist. "You know," she said, "you don't have to do all the hard things by yourself."

"It wasn't a choi—fuck!"

She'd dug her finger into the skin and electrocuted me. I collapsed forward onto the table, light-headed and dizzy, my powers still nulled thanks to the cuffs.

"You can speak without consequence now," she said.

I weakly raised my head. "You broke a blood oath?"

"I'm the head Lonestar," she said evenly.

Dragging in a breath, I hauled myself back into the chair. "You know what else you are? Powerful and smart. You also bake cookies, which you give away on a regular basis instead of keeping them for yourself, and you know how every single person in this building is doing, whether their kid just won a swimming match or their dog has fleas." I grabbed the ballpoint pen from the file and dug its tip into the wood, my grip so tight that my knuckles turned white, my eyes locked on hers. "Someone had to be on Sabrina's side, but you were uttering edicts and threats without a whole hell of compassion. Had you been acting like the person I knew you were, I'd have confided in you in an instant."

"The prime directive was being threatened. I was doing my job."

"Yeah, but you've never lost yourself doing it before." I dropped my cuffed hands into my lap with a sigh. "I said I'd tell you everything, Officer Esposito, and I will. What do you want to know first?"

A muscle ticked in Ryann's jaw. She stood up abruptly, her metal chair scraping back like nails on a chalkboard, and marched out.

The door slammed behind her.

I was too wrung out to care one way or the other. I tipped my head back and counted the perforations in the ceiling tiles, making a game out of how far I could go with nothing in my head except numbers before my worries came crashing back.

Most of the time I didn't get past ten, so I was annoyed when my winning streak of twenty-three was broken by the door opening again.

A Lonestar wheeled a whiteboard with a jumble of markers on its ledge into the room.

"Do you know how my team is doing?" I said.

"No, but I'm sure Ryann will fill you in soon."

The old Ryann would have. "Right."

Speak of the devil... She entered the room and shut the door behind her departing colleague.

Ryann leaned over the table. "Who sired Sabrina?"

"I have no idea." I crossed my arms, then winced because no one had treated my shoulder yet. "Trust me, Officer Esposito, if I knew, I'd hand that asshole over to you in a nanosecond."

She winged a marker at me.

"What's your problem?" I snapped, throwing my hands up over my face and almost taking my eye out with one of the handcuffs.

"Call me Officer Esposito again and I'll throw you on Deadman's Island."

"You're already throwing me there. Can't do it twice."

She drew a timeline on the board. "Start at the beginning and lay your investigation out."

I slumped down. "Last Sunday, Vincenzo BatXoha contacted Tatiana from Vegas about a case."

The left end of the line got marked with last Sunday's date. Above the date she wrote "hired." The longer I spoke, the more the board filled up. A missing person. Blood oath. My fears of gang reprisals. The meeting between Tom and BTS. The revelation that Sabrina was a vampire—and the rogue killing gang members. Taking her to Laurent's hotel. The dybbuk and Sabrina's inability to wake up after.

Ryann bent down to retrieve the dry erase brush that had fallen on the ground. "She was enthralled?"

"Yeah."

She removed some crime scene photos from the folder and carefully compared the ones from before the parking lot murders to the ones that night while I used the hum of the furnace as white noise against my own thoughts.

Finally, she pulled a small key out of her hoodie pocket and uncuffed me. "Consider the charges dropped."

The cuffs fell to the table with a soft clank.

"What?" I rubbed my chafed wrists, my head reeling, and Delilah exploded out of me.

Ryann didn't bat an eye at my shadow looming over her. "If you hadn't captured Sabrina and gotten the dybbuk out of her, how much further would she have escalated? A possessed vampire is a terrifying thought." She tapped a photo of a severed head. "You didn't abet murder; you prevented it."

I understood law and order. Due process. Was I glad it could be bypassed so easily in my favor? Sure, but I wouldn't have been locked up in the first place if the Lonestars didn't have unlimited power, and there was a legal code they had to adhere to with provisions for this type of situation, instead of making decisions as they saw fit.

Take the win, Mir. I wrestled my magic down.

This next part of my story was tricky. Zev had made new vampires to replace those struck down by the contagion, but I wasn't sure I should tell the Lonestars that. Things were so fraught between the vampires and Lonestars that I didn't want to be the match on the pool of gasoline. Or violate the mutual respect pact with the vampire.

"Miriam?" Ryann prompted.

I faked a yawn. "Sorry. Tatiana and I went to see Zev because I was scared that Vincenzo would do something rash." I flinched, remembering Kian's comment about Zev no longer being of her line. "Is Zev alive?"

"As far as we know." Her answer filled me with a complicated set of emotions, but oddly, mostly relief.

"We wanted to buy time for Sabrina to wake up and have a say in her life," I said, "so we enlisted BatKian's help. He didn't want a war, not with you guys already breathing down his neck, and when I saw him last night, he wanted her sire found. Laurent and Emmett took Sabrina over to Blood Alley this morning at nine for safekeeping. Rod-Rodrigo met them."

Ryann sighed sadly at my stuttered pronunciation of the Undertaker's name. "We haven't told Zev about Rodrigo yet because Blood Alley is still on lockdown." She paused. "Juliette has been working on Laurent nonstop and Judith has Emmett. Their situations are…" She gathered the photos up and stuffed them in the folder. "I don't know anything concrete."

I swiped at my eyes. "Do Sadie and Eli know I'm here?"

"Yes. Did the handover go smoothly?" The Lonestar was all business again, back at the board, marker poised.

I took a breath to compose myself. "As far as I know. Emmett called to say Zev had found out where Vincenzo was hiding with his other vampires. He and Laurent were to follow Rodrigo there and kill them, while I'd try to wake Sabrina up before she was given to you."

But nothing had worked out. Sabrina was still comatose and, given that Emmett and Laurent hadn't been successful—I sucked in a breath—Vincenzo was still alive. There was hope for Sabrina to have something of a life she could choose herself.

Provided Ryann agreed not to prosecute her.

"That gels with Zev's message to us. I didn't believe it when I heard it." Ryann scraped her fingers through her Easter egg blue and purple buzz cut and sank into a chair. "What happened between that and Blood Alley going into lockdown?"

"Kian."

Ryann did a double take. "His estrie? She came back?"

"Short answer yes. Long answer, talk to Zev." She nodded reluctantly and I continued. "Kian foiled Zev's plans. I don't know what happened on his end because I was kidnapped by Vincenzo, who I didn't see again after I was imprisoned."

"Where's the demon?"

"Dead."

Ryann nodded in approval. "We have everything except whoever kicked this into motion." She stretched out her legs, surveying the timeline. "Tatiana told us about Vincenzo's trail of payback."

"She did?"

Her lips quirked. "Not me personally since I wasn't going to get near her after arresting you, but yes."

I refused to smile. "I believe that Sabrina was changed by one of Zev's people before being abducted by gang members."

Ryann drummed the marker against the table. "Zev really didn't know who did it?"

"Not when I spoke to him."

We studied the typed murder reports like they'd yield some vital clue to the sire's identity. Well, Ryann studied them. I was still wrapping my head around the fact that I wasn't headed to Deadman's Island.

"What gang did the first victim belong to?" I said.

"Hastings Mill. He was killed Friday night."

"The night Sabrina was turned. Ryann, what if the first deaths, the ones where their necks were snapped, weren't because Sabrina, as opposed to the dybbuk, was in control? And her sire was with her teaching her how to hunt and feed?"

"Good thought, but even a human who *asks* to be turned isn't in any condition to learn to hunt and feed at first." Ryann pursed her lips, a thoughtful expression on her face. "It does beg the question of how Sabrina was able to successfully pull off those first murders if she hadn't been taken care of through the change and taught what to do. Newly turned vamps are like baby birds. Leave them alone and they die."

That twigged a memory of Sadie's fascination with this nest of baby chickadees at our local playground when she was little, and how she insisted we go visit them and make sure the mama was feeding them. We had to go every day but one morning they were gone. Sadie was devastated until we saw them flitting in the trees, healthy and able to care for themselves.

"What if her sire knew they'd screwed up by changing Sabrina without consent?" I said. "Even if she was Sapien, she'd been all over the news and was a high-profile figure."

Ryann nodded. "They couldn't bring Sabrina to Blood Alley but felt guilty enough to take care of her. They stashed her somewhere."

"Then the rival gang found her while she was asleep during the day, drugged her, and brought her to the handover."

"Which is when the dybbuk took charge and Sabrina slaughtered those men. It fits," Ryann said. "Her sire wasn't brilliant at evasion, they were scared of getting in trouble with Zev and tried to hide it." She snorted. "Just like a child."

I gasped. That was it. Four simple words that finally allowed all of this to make sense. The vamp *was* like a child, but only because they themselves were newly made.

A Sapien who'd been traumatized before their change and wasn't handling this transition well.

"I know who turned Sabrina and killed the first four men," I said.

Excitedly, I explained my hypothesis. Celeste had turned Ian and taken care of him, but when Ian was deemed capable enough to hunt on his own, things went horribly wrong. Terrified of what he'd done on that fateful Friday night—changing Sabrina instead of merely feeding from her—he took care of the lawyer as best he could, until she was captured by BTS's people and brought to the handover meeting.

Ian hadn't been the most stable person after his experiences in the Human Race, and it was no great stretch to posit that being changed had unmoored him.

No wonder the original Hastings Mill dude had lost Sabrina —he was Ian's first casualty. A random thug would be a better target for Ian to hunt than a well-dressed woman, but we might never know who he went after first.

"That's brilliant, Miriam, except for one thing," Ryann said grimly. "Zev's change of heart to kill Vincenzo. If he planned on pinning all the murders on the sire once he learned their identity, why take out your client?"

I scrubbed a hand over my face. "Celeste must have found out."

"Or she was complicit."

"No." I flashed back to Ian's freak-out. "Ian had an incident at Blood Alley the other night, and Celeste was gobsmacked by his violent outburst. I really doubt she knew, but if she discovered it last night with everything going down, she might have begged Zev to help Ian. She was fond of him."

Ryann looked off into the distance. "Some days I hate my job."

"What about Sabrina? Don't throw her on Deadman's Island and victimize her even more. She deserves better. Please."

She nodded. "The world needs more woman fighters."

"Does that mean you won't prosecute her?"

"It does. But I wasn't just talking about Sabrina." She clapped me on the shoulder. "Go home."

The compliment would have been absolutely perfect with an apology or her homemade cookies, but I wasn't about to push my luck. I went.

28

I CALLED ELI TO PICK ME UP IN THE AQUARIUM parking lot at the real Stanley Park. It was a bit of a walk, but the fresh air would do me good. However, I blinked at the sunlight like it was a cruel tease, not trusting the hope that a new day brought because this nightmare wasn't over yet. Not by a long-shot. Laurent hadn't recovered, Sabrina hadn't woken up, I didn't have the Ascendant, and Dumah...

Later.

I got to the meeting place first, sitting on a bench and clocking every vehicle that entered the lot. When Eli pulled up and Sadie bounded out, I launched toward her faster than an Olympic sprinter off the starting block and hugged her tight.

Eli scratched his stubbled jaw, yawning. "I know you want to check on Emmett and Laurent first, but you need to rest. That's a direct order from your boss, your healer, and your family."

"I better do as I'm told." I opted to sit in the back seat with my kid so she could lean against me. "How are they?"

"Emmett will be fine." Eli wove through the park back to the exit. Sunshine filtered through the trees and happy music played over the speakers. "Jude said the damage was mostly cosmetic."

"Is she sure?" I put my arm around Sadie. "He looked like he was coming apart."

"Fatigue and stress. Once he's whole again and rested, he'll be good as new."

I clamped my lips together but couldn't prevent the weird sob that escaped.

Sadie squeezed my hand.

"And Laurent?"

My daughter turned earnest brown eyes to mine. "Juliette is working really hard on him."

"I know, and she's very good at what she does." Sometimes, though, that wasn't enough.

"What's the latest update?"

Eli merged into the lane leading to the west end. "It's complicated. The demon infused magic into Laurent making it impossible for him to shift."

Whitecaps danced on the waves in English Bay, and the seawall was filled with people enjoying the beautiful weather, but the sight of my favorite beach left me cold.

"Juliette can't get it out?" My voice was strained.

"The supermoon is screwing everything up." He zipped through a yellow light. "She can only remove the demon's magic out of him a bit at a time. Trouble is, once, say, Laurent's hand is free of the demon magic, the moon exerts its pull and he shifts. A wolf part turns human and vice versa. She's worried about the strain on his heart with this constant transformation, and he needs to be in one unified form to heal."

"It's going to be this way for the next two nights?" Technically, the full moon was only one night, but it took three for its effects on shifters to wane. "He's at least in a magic coma, right?"

There was a long, weighted pause, then Eli met my eyes in the rearview mirror. "No."

"What? She's doing this while he's conscious?"

"Not exactly," Sadie hedged.

I rested my forehead against the cool glass, torn between wanting to be by Laurent's side and not leaving my daughter. I tried to tell myself that he had Juliette and Tatiana and he wasn't even awake, but I still felt like shit.

"Putting him into a coma might be one magic too many for his body to handle," Eli said. "For now, it's a waiting game." He whipped past the enormous silver globe housing Science World and turned onto Main Street for the final stretch home. "Hopefully tonight, he'll shift fully to wolf. That's the sign he's out of danger."

My family wouldn't let me phone anyone until I'd showered, eaten, and slept. I figured I'd humor them, but the hot water felt so divine, unlocking knotted-up muscles, that I stayed in there until it ran cold.

Eli had bought matzoh ball soup from one of the Jewish delis and warmed it up before he left. When I smelled the chicken broth, I devoured three bowls and was starting to doze off on the sofa when Sadie poked my arm.

"Mom?"

"Yeah, sweetheart?"

She sucked her top lip into her mouth. "Can we talk about my grandparents?"

I frowned, wondering if something had happened to Eli's mom, when it hit me. "You mean my parents?"

"Yeah." She shrugged, looking down at her feet. "What they were like and what exactly happened to them and stuff?"

"Absolutely."

I spent the next two hours answering all her questions and sharing memories like when a squirrel got stuck in our house and my dad turned into a crazed man opening walls to find the squeaking, or my mom calmly dished dirt out of a potted plant as dessert one night and started eating, keeping a completely straight face and not letting on that the soil was cake.

"You think this angel, Dumah, killed them?" Sadie was curled up against my side on the sofa.

"It's the most logical explanation, but I keep getting stuck on the fact that he doesn't want to leave Gehenna." I yawned.

"The estrie could have lied."

"She could have, but she had no reason to."

My daughter stood up, stretching. "You'll figure it out. Get some rest now. Sorry I kept you up."

"I'm not."

"Yeah, I'm not either." She kissed the top of my head and left.

I didn't even hear her get to the top of the stairs because I crashed hard.

I woke up in an unfamiliar room and panicked, sure that I'd been kidnapped and attacked again. Then I realized it was just my newly painted living room. The curtains had been drawn tight and a blanket was draped over me. I relaxed against the sofa pillows.

The room was actually a very comforting shade of purple even in the dim light.

Sadie wandered in wearing pajamas and eating a bowl of cereal. "Good morning. Feel better?"

"Much." I flicked on a standing lamp.

She sat down beside me and held out her spoon. "Want some?"

I shook my head. "How long was I out?"

"Hours. It's Monday morning." She slurped down the milk.

"And school is now optional?"

"Pro D." Ah. Her teachers were taking the day for professional workshops. She made a face. "I've got a history paper to finish."

"Any more training sessions set up? Does Nav plan to check if you can null vamp magic?"

"I couldn't on demons," she said glumly.

"That doesn't mean you're doomed to fail with a vampire."

She pressed a hand to my forehead. "You're giving me permission to go all Buffy?"

I smacked it away. "No, I still want you to run first, but I was damn lucky the vamp who kidnapped me didn't go after you, and if that ever happens, then I want peace of mind that my baby girl stands a chance of getting away."

Sadie plucked out the lone flake sticking to the bowl and ate it. "Wouldn't they be dead? Like dead dead? Take away a vamp's magic and what's holding them together?"

"That's what I want to find out. Demons initially created vampires. If estrie magic still runs in their blood and fuels their reanimation, maybe you can't kill them outright, but what about their strength and speed? At the very least, if a vampire was an Ohrist in life, you'd be able to null those powers."

Sadie placed the bowl on the coffee table. "It's like a Jenga game."

"Holy shit, kid. You're brilliant." I tossed aside the blanket and raced up the stairs to my bedroom. "And put the bowl in the dishwasher," I called out.

A couple of minutes later, she ambled into my bedroom. "I know I'm brilliant, but why specifically?" She crawled onto my bed, avoiding the clothes I was flinging out of my closet.

"When Juliette first started working on Sabrina, there was no interference," I said. "Her magic was stable, made up of dybbuk and vampire blocks. To use the game metaphor."

"Who's Sabrina?" Sadie seated herself cross-legged.

"A woman I was searching for. She was turned into a vampire against her will."

"That's awful."

I nodded, hopping into a pair of wide-legged black pants. "Then my Banim Shovavim magic added another couple blocks to the tower. Just momentarily until I severed her shadow and killed the dybbuk."

"That left only the vamp blocks with huge gaps in the structure," Sadie said.

"Not only that." I shrugged into a sweater. "We assumed we were dealing with three kinds of magic inside Sabrina. There were four. She had a recessive Ohrist gene that allowed her to get enthralled while she was still human. That's the interference."

"Why didn't Juliette sense it?"

"Because it's recessive. A discoloration on a building block, not a separate one. Juliette has the basics of vamp magic, but vamps don't use healers, they depend on their own recuperation abilities. Juliette would have no way of detecting something this slight when it wouldn't feel like regular Ohrist magic, just part of the vamp landscape." I twisted my hair back and secured it with a clip. "I need to speak to her."

"You do that. I'm going to go back to perspectives on nationalism."

"Good luck." I pulled on some socks.

"You too. And Mom?" I glanced up. "If my magic won't null vampires," Sadie said, "remember, there's always Phoebe."

"You can't carry a flamethrower with you everywhere. Even a mini one."

She grinned. "Tell yourself that."

Ten minutes later, I'd thrown on makeup, scarfed down a piece of toast, and was out the door, sorting through a flurry of texts. There was nothing from Zev, though a call came in from my old law firm.

"Hello?"

"Miri?" Mara sounded uncharacteristically subdued.

"Are you okay?"

"Sabrina Mayhew is dead."

I stumbled off the curb, crashing my hip into the front of my car. "Say what? How?"

"Heart attack. She was found in her car." The older woman sniffed. "Can you imagine? She'd been there since Friday night. How could the universe be so cruel?"

"That's horrible." I unlocked my door and got in the sedan. "They're sure it was her?"

"Yes, her friend said the police confirmed identification

before releasing the body to the funeral home. Apparently, Sabrina wanted to be cremated."

No one would ever learn the truth. Ryann, you sly devil. I mentally saluted her, though her dad must have helped pull this off. "Is there going to be a memorial?"

"That's why I called. The funeral itself is private, but there's a public service for her next week."

She gave me the time and the place, and I assured her I'd be there. If Sabrina attended her own memorial, would that give her closure?

I called Jude on speakerphone while I drove.

"Hey, toots. Deadman's Island has cell service?"

"Emmett! I'm afraid you're stuck with me."

"Aw, man."

I laughed. "How are you?"

"Bored. Jude's asleep from her all-nighter fixing me and there's nothing on television."

A knot in my chest eased. "You were a rock star the other night. I hope you told Marjorie all about it."

"You bet your sweet ass I did," he said proudly. "She was worried about how dangerous my job is, but doing what I do is how I want to live, even when it's dangerous or I feel helpless, because maybe I can help someone else remember what they have to live for when life knocks them down. Help them persevere."

"That's pretty wise of you."

"Yeah, I'm kind of brilliant on the life insights," he teased.

I rolled my eyes though I was grinning. "Are you staying with Jude for a bit?"

"She wants to keep an eye on me, then I'll go back to Tatiana's." He paused. "I heard Laurent didn't shift yet." It was a measure of his concern that he used Laurent's first name.

My amusement vanished. "He will. Meantime, I'm pretty sure I figured out how to wake Sabrina."

"Anything I can do?"

"Not on that front, but you have a way to contact Pyotr, right?" They'd become buddy-buddy after their garden store jaunt together.

"Yeah. Whaddya need?"

"Get him to visit you and ask if there's a sneaky way into Gehenna from the KH." Hopefully Sabrina would be awake soon and then Vincenzo could have her. I knew who'd killed my parents, and after everything I'd been through, the why didn't matter. Even if their deaths had saved the world, it wouldn't have eased the ache in my heart.

It was time to move on because I had so much to live for, and that meant this one last promise to fulfill: getting the Ascendant for the Leviathan.

"Done," Emmett said.

I promised to keep him updated on Laurent's condition.

Tatiana answered my knock at Hotel Terminus. My spritely boss was stooped with fatigue, and when she pulled me into a hug, her arms trembled.

"It's good to see you too," I said, "but when's the last time you slept?"

She put finger to her lips, motioning to Juliette, who was crashed out on the sofa. "I've napped."

"That isn't enough." I took off my shoes. "Did he shift?"

She shook her head. "He's in the bedroom. Talk to him. It'll help." Tatiana sat down in one of the chairs and pulled a blanket over her lap.

Most of Laurent's body was covered, but his tail stuck out at the end of the bed. His human face wasn't flushed or sweaty, his breathing was steady, and his fever was gone.

I took a seat by the bed and smoothed out the blanket, making silent wishes for him to shift like the wrinkles in the fabric were pennies cast into a magic wishing well.

"Hi, Huff 'n' Puff. It's been an eventful night." I fought to keep my voice light, his hand clasped in mine. "Did you know Blood Alley has this super creepy fog and an electric ward? Oh, and my permanent excursion to Deadman's Island was canceled, so how great is that? Also, I killed an estrie. Bet none of the Carpe Demon people can say the same."

He didn't respond. Not a single flicker of his lids, not the tiniest twitch of a finger.

"You have to shift, baby." I smoothed his hair off his forehead. "There's this fancy cocktail lounge I was thinking we check out for our second date and you need a suit." Nothing. "I've made a new list. You'll like this one. It's all the creative ways I'm going to pay you back for safely delivering Sabrina just like I promised, but you'll need your strength for them. Especially items three and seven." My voice cracked and I bowed my head. Had Laurent's death wish finally been granted and I'd have to watch him burn out like a dying star?

Several times his fingers twitched, and once I thought I heard him whisper my name, but it was just wishful thinking and a rasp in his chest.

"Delphine."

I'd been dozing, but at his whisper, my eyes snapped open. "Laurent?"

Still unconscious, he repeated his wife's name followed by something slurred in French.

Laurent had become playful recently, but was his newfound joy in life stronger than the death wish he'd lived with since the deaths of Delphine and his unborn child? Would he fight for his life or fall back into his ingrained desires and give up?

I stayed with him until dusk, occasionally checking in with Sadie and Ryann. Blood Alley was open for business again, but there was no sign of Zev, Vincenzo, Sabrina, Ian, or Celeste, and no one else, not even Yoshi, knew where anyone was.

Laurent repeated Delphine's name, lapsing again into French, however, it was too garbled for me to even write it down and ask anyone what he was saying. And a small part of me was scared to decipher it and find out he was begging to be with her.

"Miriam?" Juliette showed up during one of his silent phases to check his pulse. "You wanted to speak to me?"

I explained my Jenga theory.

"I didn't sense Ohrist magic, but you're correct. The recessive gene wouldn't have registered." She caught her bottom lip between her teeth with a glint in her eyes, the last foggy remnants of sleep disappearing. "My uncle is stable for now. He'll either shift soon or remain this way another night. Take me to Sabrina. Tatiana will call if anything changes."

"I wish I could, but I have no idea where she is. I'll leave Zev a message and hopefully he'll call back soon." Unless something had happened to him and he couldn't. Did Yoshi really not know where his best friend was, or had Kian's betrayal allowed Vincenzo to get the jump on Zev? I stood up. "I need some air."

The master vamp didn't answer my text or my phone call. I stood in the doorway behind the wards, breathing in the night air and rocking my pelvis back and forth to stretch out my tight lower back.

"I want to see him." Giulia stood on the patchy lawn, her eyes blazing.

I jumped, giving a little shriek. "Don't sneak up on me. Geez. Come inside."

"We'll root out the one who did this to him and then?" She swiped a claw across her throat.

Giulia was treating me as a friend, not a threat, and it felt good to be on the same team.

"Laurent's attacker was a demon and I killed her," I said.

"Did she suffer?"

"Not nearly enough."

"I'm sure you did your best." Giulia padded into the hotel then sat on her back haunches, her eyes wide. "Meravigliosa," she whispered, trying to take in everything at once.

Tatiana plodded over to greet her. "Ciao, Giulia."

"Ciao, Tatiana." The cat gargoyle rubbed her head against my boss's side and the artist scratched between her ears. "Where is Laurent?"

"I'll take you." I headed back, Giulia silently stalking along beside me. "I haven't forgotten I owe you dinner. Soon as things calm down a bit."

"Laurent will come as well."

"Sure."

She stopped at the bedroom and waved a paw. "You are not needed."

Uh-huh. I peeked in, but he hadn't moved, so I left her to it.

Tatiana was in the kitchen, making sandwiches. "Laurent will shift tonight and this will all be behind us."

After my boss and Juliette ate, I made them go home to shower and sleep, promising to call the second there was news on any front. Sadie had finished her history paper, so I asked her to stay at her dad's again tonight for my peace of mind since I'd be keeping watch here.

While Giulia visited with Laurent, I cleaned up the kitchen and tidied the blankets and pillows that had been used in the living room, then with nothing else to do, I played a few games of *Tetris* before checking on the gargoyle.

She was asleep on the floor at the foot of Laurent's bed. It was peaceful with the moonlight filtering through the curtains, though the room was hot and stuffy, so I opened the window wide.

Laurent began mumbling more French, yet he wasn't shifting. I sank into the chair by his bed and clasped his hands as if my touch would keep him with me.

One second I was watching him, and the next I was sleepily opening my eyes at a cat's meow.

The bed was empty.

I ran to the window in time to see the gargoyle leap onto the high back wall. "Giulia!"

"Non preoccuparti, Miriam. He shifted." She waved a paw and leapt into the night.

I flopped onto the bed, clutching the pillow to my chest. Laurent was going to be all right. I texted everyone with the good news, adding for Tatiana and Juliette that he'd gone for a run so not to bother coming over. I'd have him call tomorrow when he was rested.

Boo joined me from wherever she'd been all this time, crawling onto my chest and purring. Between her comfort and my relief, I relaxed, my lids falling shut.

"Mitzi?" Laurent's hoarse voice sounded like I'd dreamed it up, like he couldn't possibly be calling me by that nickname with that amount of tenderness, not after everything he'd been through.

But it was him, and he was real and whole and okay, kneeling on his bed, alive and awake.

He looked like a college kid who'd come home to stay with his family after a long semester and had just woken up after sleeping fourteen hours: dazed, a little disoriented, but refreshed. Brighter than he had been.

Without thinking, I launched myself into his arms, colliding with his chest and the mattress. I didn't miss his abrupt flinch.

"Oh my God, I'm so sorry. Did I hurt you?" I pulled away.

"No," he said, raking his damp hair with one hand, eyes wary.

Confused, I sat up. "What's wrong? Is it Vincenzo?"

He turned away, grabbed a T-shirt from a drawer, and tugged it down over his shorts, his back to me. "You should go home and sleep."

Guess again. You'd fought this much, Huff 'n' Puff, now it was time for one last battle.

29

I crossed my arms. "No."

The look on his face was priceless. "No?"

"Are you going to stop being friends with everyone who saw you all halfsies or is it just me?"

"The others aren't going to remember what a monster I was every time we have sex," he snapped.

"Dude." Grimacing, I shook my head. "Two of those people are your family. Watch the phrasing. Plus, sex? You're getting ahead of yourself here."

His nostrils flared. "You're enjoying this."

"Immensely, but you know my sense of humor. It's one of the things that attracted you to me most."

"Not at all," he said haughtily.

I dragged my fingers down his chest, relishing his hiss. "Sure it is. Just like how your grumpy outer layer hiding your enormous heart did it for me."

He caught my hand and bit my index finger, his lips teasing into a wicked smile at my inhale. "My enormous heart, was it?"

"What else could it be?" I blinked at him innocently and laughed as he pushed me onto my back and pinned my arms against the mattress.

He licked his bottom lip. "What was number seven on that list of yours?"

"You heard that?" I made a sad face. "But you've already taken a shower."

"Hmm." He leaned over and brushed his nose against mine. "I guess we can wing it this once, but we'll be revisiting this."

"Yes, because lists are..."

Laurent's breath was hot in my ear as he sucked on my lobe. "Are what?"

I shivered, tangling into the twin scents of cedar and soap. "Important."

"Oui. Your exceptional list-making skills have become a turn-on." He straddled me, rocking forward to press his erection against my body, his eyes sliding along my skin with a fierce hunger.

"Wait till you see how I color-code an Excel sheet." A wild restlessness built inside me, and I grabbed his hands and thrust them under my sweater and up to my breasts, needing his touch more than oxygen.

Laurent flicked callused fingers against my nipples, capturing my moan with his mouth. He tasted like mint toothpaste and kissed with the abandon of a lover who had nothing left to hide.

I threaded my fingers into his damp curls and swept one hand to the nape of his neck to pull him closer, reveling in the almost vicious crest of our kiss that ebbed to a teasing, soft caress, the two of us floating lazily in these new waters.

He tugged my sweater off, and I yanked on the hem of his T-shirt impatiently, pulling him close to feel the heat and slide of our skin. He nipped and licked along my neck to my collarbone, popping open my fly, while I flexed my bare feet against his in giddy delight.

I sat up onto my elbows and Laurent cocked an eyebrow. There were stray wolf hairs on his left biceps from the sheets, I had stretch marks on my belly, yet all I saw were the stories that had led us to this moment. I cupped his cheek and brushed my lips against his.

His eyes darkened and he pounced, shucking off my jeans while I pushed his shorts to the floor. My hands suddenly didn't move fast enough to touch him as much as I craved: a stroke along the divot in his hip, my nails rasping across his back, and my thumb slipping over the head of his cock.

Laurent nudged my legs wider, one hand pleasuring me, and grinned.

I sucked on his neck, snaky tendrils of lust flaring up at the pads of his fingers pressing against me one by one as if he was playing Chopin on my skin. Wrapping one leg around his waist, I arched against him and his fingers slipped over my clit and inside me.

His quiet moan was barely more than a breath. "I can smell your desire." He pressed his index finger to my mouth. The taste of me on his skin made me clutch my thighs, and I bucked up to meet his hot, messy kiss, growling when he broke it to grab a condom.

"Attends," he muttered, before tearing the package open with his teeth.

I flipped over onto all fours, throwing a saucy grin over my shoulder.

"Is that how we're playing this?" He knocked my legs wider and gripped my hips.

"Wait," I said. "We need lube."

"We were fine a moment ago."

"Yes, but I switched positions. Things change." Sitting back on my calves, I waved a hand around my vagina. "This is its own microclimate."

Laurent grabbed a bottle of lube from the bedside table and applied a generous amount to the condom. "Then we'll have to do some geoengineering."

"That's a fine multisyllable word." I swooned.

"Book learned, Mitzi. How quickly you forget." He slapped my ass. "Back into position."

"Aye aye." I sighed as he entered me, our connection soul deep and perfect.

He bowed his body over mine to press a hot kiss to the back of my neck. His left hand on my hip flexed with each thrust, while he raked the fingers of his right down my spine.

I stroked my clit faster and faster, my cheek resting against his bed and my breasts brushing the mattress with each bounce. God, friction was a marvel.

A sigh of pure bliss escaped Laurent's lips and that was it. My orgasm shattered me, Laurent coming soon after, and we collapsed on the bed.

He scooted over to kiss me, his hands tangled in my hair, and my fingers splayed against his chest. "Stay," he barked.

I raised an eyebrow. "Care to rephrase that?"

He made this adorable, flustered motion. "English."

I smiled. "You're forgiven." I paused. "I was scared you didn't want to come back."

"Why?"

It was suddenly very important to inspect the fitted sheet for tears. "Well, you called for Delphine a couple times and seemed to be talking to her in French." I hazarded a glance at him.

He got a pensive look on his face. "I was. I saw her again. I didn't realize I was speaking aloud."

Last time he'd seen Delphine was during a hallucination while we were in the Human Race and it had done quite the head trip on him. He'd survived Kian's attack and we'd made love, but was there still a part of him that wanted to die and be with his wife? "What did you say?" I flapped a hand. "Never mind. That's personal."

"No, it's not because it involves you."

"It does?" I clutched a pillow to my chest.

Laurent slung his leg over mine. "Back in the game, I was confused about what was real or what I wanted to be real, but this time, I was completely clear." He rubbed his hand over his heart. "I needed Delphine to know that thanks to you, I'd found a life worth living and that I forgave her for what she'd done." Turning onto his side, he linked his fingers with mine. "I finally forgave myself for not protecting her. No more guilt. I want this life. I want us. And I want the ghosts of my past finally at peace."

Clasping his face in my hands, I kissed him, infusing all my gratitude for what he'd done and my love of what we were slowly building together.

When I pulled away, he smiled. "Attends." He hopped off the bed to disappear into the bathroom. I didn't hear the shower or sink turn on, but he was gone a very long time.

It didn't matter. Laurent had found closure, and we had all the time in the world.

When he returned, he held out a hand. "Come with me."

"Naked?"

"Yes." He led me into the bathroom and out the sliding door to the patio area. I shivered, almost running back inside, because it was night and the crooked flagstones underfoot were freezing, but the goosebumps that broke out on my arms weren't because of the cold.

Tall candles in glass holders flickered around the enormous copper soaking tub, their light bouncing off night-blooming flowers crawling up the high back wall.

Squealing in delight, I hopped along the path of smooth river rock to the tub and dipped my finger in the scalding water. Perfect.

Laurent turned off the tap and sat down with a splash, steam curling off him. My entry was far more gradual with a lot of yelping and turning on the cold water to splash on parts of me until I immersed myself with a sigh and settled back against my man.

He wrapped his arms around me, nuzzling my neck.

I tilted my head to give him better access, glancing up

through the cedar slats of the gazebo roof above us. "I wish we could see more stars here in the city."

"I slept out in the Sahara once," he said.

"You did?"

"Yes." He stiffened. "It was with Delphine," he mumbled.

I patted his hand. "You can talk about her."

"But this is the second time in less than an hour that I've been naked with you and speaking of her."

"Yeah, we'll work on your timing." When he laughed, I told him to carry on.

"It was in Morocco. We'd ridden camels into the desert."

I used my toe to nudge the cold water tap on for a moment. "Only you would sound grumpy about camels."

"They're not fun to ride, but the desert is incredible." He played with my hair. "It was this endless sea of rippling dunes and so humbling. All these tiny grains of sand amounted to something so much more majestic and timeless than us. Tents had been set up, but what was the point of sleeping inside them? No."

I chuckled at his definitive stance on the matter, and he tugged on a lock.

"We dragged our bedrolls out." His voice turned pensive. "I remember thinking that I'd never known silence until that moment."

"And the stars?"

He dragged his fingers through the water. "When I was little, Tatiana used to give me small canvases to paint on. She didn't care if I used my fingers or a brush or even if it looked like anything, she just wanted me to create." The smile in his voice was evident. "My favorite thing to do was to splatter paint on them. That's what the sky looked like. A million white droplets spattered against the night, so huge and close that I swear I could have reached out and smeared one."

"Did you shift?"

"Oui." It came out as a dreamy sigh. "I ran through the sand for hours. Terrified the stupid camels." He chuckled.

My back rested against his chest and his legs were over top of mine, both of us content to laze in the water to the play of candlelight and darkness.

He poked me in the back. "Would number seven work in a tub?"

That's when Zev poked his head up from behind the high fence. "Where is your daughter?"

First lovemaking while officially in this relationship and a vampire shows up to blow away the afterglow.

Laurent covered my breasts with his arms. "Get the fuck out."

"Technically," Zev said, "I'm not in. I can't see anything personal, nor do I want to."

I shrank lower under the waterline. "Are you hovering above the ground?"

"Sadie," he repeated. "Our deal. Now. She's not answering her phone."

"Because you use an unlisted number and she's probably asleep."

"Turn around," Laurent snarled. "Or should I just call the Lonestars?"

"Do you want a matching scar to remember me by?" Zev said.

Laurent shot to his feet, splashing water over the sides of the tub and sputtering out several candles. "Try it."

Zev shot him a cold smile. "Go ahead."

I sent Laurent a pleading look. Also a longing one because holy shit, the angle from here was spectacular.

He smirked and reached for one of the folded bath towels on the ground and wrapped it around his waist. Too bad.

Zev disappeared behind the wall. "She's not in her bed. I checked. I also checked Detective Chu's place."

"You can't get in there." I scrambled out of the tub, taking the towel that Laurent held out.

"There's this marvelous resource called windows. Perhaps you've heard of them." I didn't have to see Zev to know he was sneering. "For the last time, where is your daughter?"

I had a couple of ideas, neither of which I was going to share with the vampire. "Tell me where and I'll bring her."

"Just the two of you," he said.

Laurent pulled the stopper out of the tub and winged it at the wall.

I shrugged. I was in no danger from Zev. "Is Vincenzo secured? Because if not, how are you going to protect us?"

"He's with Sabrina. Trust me, you're of no interest to him right now."

"Can Juliette come?" I said. "I figured out how to wake Sabrina."

"I'll send her the address." There was the sound of a text being sent. "Now you have it as well. Don't make me wait."

I marched inside, muttering about anatomically impossible things that I'd like to do to vampires, and got dressed. When I got hold of Eli and told him the situation, he explained that he'd been called into work and driven Sadie to stay with his sister. Grinding my teeth, I informed him that he could phone Genevieve and give her a reason why I was doing a curbside pickup of our child in the middle of the night.

My perfect boyfriend—I'd decided I really hated the word "partner"—had made me coffee.

I slugged some back, then handed him the mug. "Duty calls."

"I know you'll win. You and Sadie both." He walked me to the door, stealing one last kiss.

I stepped outside. "Talk to you later. Oh, and for the record? Number seven definitely could be achieved in a tub."

"I despise vampires," Laurent said, and shut the door.

30

MY HOPE THAT I'D SNEAK IN, GRAB THE KID FROM HER sleepover, and leave was thwarted by the sight of my sister-in-law staring out her living room window. I sighed. Genevieve wasn't an evil or bad person, but she was just so awful to deal with, and I already felt tired. Why couldn't she be asleep like the rest of the block?

Wave, don't wave? Which would encourage her more? I gave a halfway sort of wave, more of a finger waggle that probably couldn't be seen in the darkness of my car.

Wrong move. The porch light snapped on and she escorted a dopey-looking Sadie in pj bottoms and a hoodie down the front steps.

Yawning, Sadie slid into the passenger seat, mumbling hello before burying her face in her sweater and curling up against the door. She had dropped her backpack onto the floor mat and a sock fell out.

I rolled down my window, braced for disapproval—and not for my ex-sister-in-law to lean in to hug me. Dear God, Eli. What did you tell her? But damn, she always had the nicest perfume. This one hinted at roses drifting on the breeze on a warm summer's night.

"My deepest condolences." Genevieve zipped her expensive running sweatshirt up over her slender frame.

"Thank you." I put on a somber expression.

"Had you been working together long?"

"Long enough to become dear friends," I said, having no clue who we were discussing.

"Obviously, if he'd been given uncle status." Ah, okay. "That's not just something one hands out, but I guess when you're all alone like you are, you have to make your family wherever you can." Genevieve patted my hand, her skin springy and supple with proper moisturization.

I surreptitiously pulled my slab of sandpaper away.

Sadie snorted and I jabbed my elbow in her side.

"Emmett was a good man. I need to..." I waved my arms around because again, no clue what I was supposed to be doing for the pretend deceased.

"Of course. Good night, Sadie."

"Night, Aunt Gee."

Genevieve tucked a strand of fashionably gray streaked hair behind her ear. "Hopefully her sleep disruption doesn't impact her academic performance. I know you don't care about that like I do, but teens need their rest."

"Yup." I was already rolling up my window.

She kept her hand there like she expected me to stop, only yanking her fingers back at the last second. Her tasteful diamond ring clanked against the roof.

I waved through the glass and zoomed off. *I hope you choke on my exhaust.* "That was nice of her to take you tonight."

Sadie laughed, her sweater sliding off her face.

"Shut up," I said, joining in until I remembered the real reason why I was here. "Did Dad tell you where we're going?"

"No. I figured it out from the texts when I woke up." She plaited her hair into braids. The smaller they were, the more anxious she was, and these were tiny. "Whose magic am I going to have to take?"

"I'm not sure. Not anyone you know."

"Okay." Still her leg bounced all the way to our destination.

I pulled up at the address and frowned at the funeral home.

Sadie darted a nervous glance my way.

"I'm sure there's a reasonable explanation." I drove around the back to the large garage door and texted Zev that I was here.

The door rose up and I backed into the bright space. A shiny black hearse was parked next to us, while a refrigeration unit hummed in the back corner next to stacks of long, flattened rectangular boxes.

Yoshi met us. Hello, liar who didn't know where his bestie was.

"Why are we at a funeral home?" Sadie squeaked.

"Mr. BatKian owns it and the location was convenient," Yoshi said. Right. More like the Lonestars don't know about this place.

The chill and mechanical buzzing from the garage was replaced by a delicious warmth and somber hush as we entered the main building.

"Did Juliette arrive?" I said.

"She's already with Sabrina." He escorted us down a hall and past a door with a "Caution: Flammable" sign on it as a cry came from within.

Sadie froze, and Yoshi sighed as I entered, but he didn't stop me.

My pulse spiked at the sight, and I motioned for Sadie to stay back. Thankfully, she didn't argue, turning away to the stairwell before she'd gotten close enough to see anything. I hovered in the doorway, my hand over my nose against the stench of bloodied meat.

Ian lay on the concrete floor in a puddle of blood with his throat savagely torn. Intestines spilled out of his torso in a glistening, gloopy mess, and one of his eyes had been plucked out. The handles of the cabinets had been ripped off and embedded through his hands and feet into the concrete. *Crafty Ideas for Psychopaths.*

What a way to die. Then it hit me that Ian was a vampire, and if he was dead, he'd be a pile of ash.

A strangled sob tore from my throat.

"My daughter isn't going in there," I said to Yoshi over my shoulder.

"That person is not who Sadie is here for," Yoshi said serenely. "They merely exist at the whim of Mr. BatXoha."

Celeste knelt beside Ian, her puffy red eyes rimmed with blood, but her fangs descended at my voice. "Get out of here. All you ever did was cause Ian pain."

Had I contributed to Ian's instability by forcing him to relive the trauma of the Human Race? I forced down the magic that had flared to life at her fangs. "If I did, I'm sorry, but he helped save lives."

Ian's remaining eye blinked and an inhuman wail escaped him, capturing Celeste's attention.

Yoshi pulled me back into the hallway, the door swinging shut, but not before Celeste tossed out her last words.

"The wolf should have died."

I spun around but Yoshi had a firm grip on my arm. "How does she know about Laurent?"

"Leave it alone, Miriam."

"Tell me."

Sadie poked her head out from the stairwell where she'd been waiting, but I held up a hand and she disappeared back onto the stairs.

Yoshi pressed his lips into a thin line.

My eyes widened. "Celeste freed Kian. That's why she knew about the attack and who'd be involved. I'm right, aren't I? Celeste found out what Ian had done to Sabrina and asked Zev to protect him." My tone hardened. "And Zev said no."

"Very good," Yoshi said. "You figured everything out."

"Not everything. When did Zev learn about Ian?" Shadows swam over my skin and my scythe slammed into my palm.

"Celeste approached him after you and Tatiana left, but he

didn't send your team into a trap. Zev had no idea what she'd done until Kian got loose and started slaughtering vampires at Blood Alley."

"Why refuse Celeste if Zev planned on killing Vincenzo and pinning Sabrina's change on him?"

"Just because Ian would have been safe from the Lonestars or BatXoha didn't mean he wouldn't pay," Yoshi said coldly.

"Zev's little plan to make more vamps really worked out great for everyone, didn't it?" I pictured Emmett's mangled face, Laurent's constant shifting, and Rodrigo's dead eyes, and flung my scythe across the hallway into the wall with a curse. Drywall crumbled to the immaculate beige carpet.

"Mom?" Sadie stood in the hallway. "Can we get this over with?"

"Yeah."

"Zev is upstairs in one of the viewing rooms," Yoshi said.

That's where Sadie and I found the oddest tableau.

Chairs were grouped along either side of a row leading to a gurney where Sabrina lay like Sleeping Beauty with Juliette working on her. Zev sat on one side while Vincenzo sat in the front on the other side, leaning forward and twitching at Juliette's every motion.

Vincenzo didn't spare us a glance, but Zev made his way over.

Sadie sucked in a breath and tucked up against my side.

"Thank you for coming." Zev extended his hand for Sadie to shake like this was a real funeral.

Confused, she did.

This was a travesty. "I killed the estrie," I said.

"Yes, I felt the moment Kian died." He said it without any emotion, but he'd cared for her. I'd seen it and my stupid heart felt bad for him.

I sighed, wrung out from this day. "Is this going to be a problem because of the…" I glanced at Vincenzo then mouthed "contagion?"

"I took precautions for that situation."

The Undertaker and those vials. My face fell. "Rodrigo—"

"I know," Zev said softly. He cleared his throat. "Tell the golem I'm in his debt for trying to save my friend."

Emmett hadn't mentioned that at all. No boast? He was definitely growing up. "I will. Feel free to reinstate BatKian as your surname after Kian's decision to strip you of it."

"I'm going back to my human surname. Toledano."

"Much like in a divorce," I said, and he chuckled. Okay, this congeniality was disconcerting. "What about the rest of her line?"

"They can decide what they want to do." Zev turned to Sadie. "Have a seat. I'd like to see the outcome of Juliette's efforts."

Sadie sat down, her leg jittering once again.

"I'll be back in a sec." I met her eyes, waiting until she nodded to make my way to Vincenzo. "Are you sure you want to wake Sabrina?"

He hissed at me, flashing red eyes that matched the diamond pattern on his linen shirt.

"Obviously you do." I held up my hands. "I mean no disrespect, but you haven't been human in quite some time, and Sabrina has lost everything she's ever worked for, not to mention her friends and family, who she'll now have to hide from. I want to make sure you've got resources in place to help her through that."

"Why do you care?" Vincenzo stared at me like I was an alien doing some space dance.

I frowned. "Why wouldn't I?"

"She's a vampire now," he said defensively.

"Ms. Feldman can be surprisingly compassionate to our kind," Zev said, having overheard us from the other side of the room.

I remembered my manners enough to keep my mouth from falling open at yet another compliment.

"Then I thank you for your concern," Vincenzo said. "I will

do everything to assist her through this transition and ensure her life is as happy as it can be."

"There's going to be a memorial for Sabrina. It might be good for her to secretly attend. Get closure."

"Yes, her friend contacted me and I thought the same thing."

Juliette stepped back, shaking out her hands. "It's done."

Vincenzo shot to his feet, pushing past the healer to be at Sabrina's side and pull his fiancée into his arms.

Sabrina let out a sob. "It's true, isn't it? I hoped it was some nightmare but—" She took a shuddery breath and pressed her face against Vincenzo's chest. He murmured into her hair, running a hand comfortingly along her back.

A crescent of light flared up beside Juliette and I cried out, Delilah flying across the room to save the young woman from the blind spot.

She didn't make it in time.

But Sabrina did. She moved faster than I could track to knock Juliette to safety and the blind spot winked out without a victim. The vampire looked down at herself, her mouth open. She held out her hands, a look of wonder on her face.

Sabrina had lost her friends and her old life but in the first seconds after being healed, she'd saved Juliette. She was still a fighter. She'd survived the curveball of becoming a vampire under unimaginable circumstances, yet with her intelligence and experience, she could carve out a different yet equally impressive life for herself.

Just like so many of us women did.

"Is that going to happen to me?"

At my daughter's bleak tone, I spun around. I'd promised not to lie to her, but now was not the time for her to process the danger of blind spots.

"Possibly. If you continue to use your magic," Zev said. Great. Mr. Secrecy decided to be blunt now. "This one time, however, your mother is here and will protect you from any blind spot."

Juliette brushed past me and I called her name, but she shook her head wearily. "Not today, Miriam." She continued out the door. "We'll speak later."

Sadie tugged on my sleeve. "Who do I have to null?"

Did Zev know for sure that her magic worked on vampires? Was he going to make Sadie null Vincenzo's powers for being part of Kian's attack? Except anything Vincenzo had done, and I wasn't even sure how large a role he'd played in things, had been in self-defense. Zev had struck first.

Yoshi entered the room and Zev's features twisted. I did a double take because that was impossible. Zev would never betray his best friend. Then Yoshi stepped aside and a soft "oh" slipped from my lips.

"Celeste," Zev said with a tenderness I'd never heard from him but knew well as a parent.

Sadie's eyes widened. "But that'll kill her, won't it?" she squeaked. "Mom, please don't make me."

I thought the worst scenario would be Sadie facing off against some incredibly lethal foe who'd fight back with everything they had. Not someone, who until recently, had been a young woman not much older than my daughter, and who stood there, her body stooped in defeat.

Celeste wouldn't fight Sadie.

I would rather have carved out my own heart and presented it, dripping, to Zev than make my baby go through with this, but I dug my nails into my palms, my stomach tied in knots. "You wanted to be treated like an adult," I said softly. "You screwed up. That means accepting that your actions have consequences and doing stuff you don't like in order to fix things."

My daughter rounded on Zev. "Why don't you kill her yourself? You don't need me."

Braced for the vamp to snap something about their deal, I put my arm around Sadie's shoulder, but she shrugged it off and Zev heaved a sigh so full of sorrow that I shivered.

"He doesn't want to hurt me," Celeste said in a resigned voice. "But I betrayed him." She cocked her head. "Give a condemned woman her last meal?" she said flippantly. "I still haven't tried Banim Shovavim blood."

Lost to my shock and despair, I could only gape at her.

She rolled her eyes and jerked her chin at Sadie. "Let's get this over with."

"Wait. You want to do this here? How about somewhere nicer like a mountaintop?" I said. Anything to postpone the moment marking the end of Sadie's childhood, even if I was complicit in it.

"This is as good a place as any." Celeste wiped the blood from her eyes and then licked her finger.

Sadie had bitten her lip so hard she left teeth marks, but she took a deep breath and pulled her spine straight. She nodded, a cold mask of determination falling over her young features, and something inside me broke, bleeding out.

I sat on the edge of a chair, breathing shallowly.

Zev moved to one side next to Yoshi but remained standing.

Sadie unfurled her shadow, which grew larger, rising off the ground until it stood on its feet. I squeezed my eyes into thin slits against the dazzling light, the white of my child's eyes morphing to a jet black.

"Ready?" she said.

Celeste nodded. "See ya, gramps. Thanks for letting me see Ian." She snapped off a salute.

Zev pulled out a kippah from his suit pocket and began to pray. *"Yitgadal v'yitkadash, sh'mei raba b'alma di v'ra chir'utei; v'yam-lich malchutei b'hayeichon u-vyomeichon…"* The vampire fell away to reveal the rabbi he'd once been, Zev rocking back and forth, his Hebrew uttered in a rich baritone.

Sadie's shadow reached out its arm made of hard light and touched Celeste's shoulder.

"Y'hei sh'mei raba m'varach l'alam u-l'almei almaya…"

Celeste stiffened, her face turned up to the ceiling. Black threads of magic streamed from her body into the shadow and a pained cry tore from her throat.

"...b'rich hu, l'ela min kol birchata v'shirata, tushb'hata v'nehemata da'amiran b'alama..." Zev kept his eyes locked on his granddaughter. He shouldn't have been saying the Mourner's Kaddish while she was still alive, or without a minyan, but he wasn't reciting it as a comfort. His voice was raw, his chant more a whip than a prayer. This wasn't meant in supplication to God, Zev was branding this moment on his very soul.

Celeste's magic slowed to a trickle, her features twisted in an exaggerated grimace.

Vincenzo and Sabrina observed the death with a solemnity I hadn't expected, though he kept his arm tightly around her.

"Y'hei sh'lama raba min sh'maya, v'hayim..."

Celeste's corporeality dissipated, her form became translucent, and her voice died out.

"...shalom aleinu v'al kol yisrael, v'imru amen."

Sadie screwed her face up, her soft grunt crashing into the ensuing silence as she tried to remove the final strands of the vampire's magic.

Celeste was barely visible and yet her look of terror forced me to turn away. That didn't help because it would be forever seared on my brain. I just prayed this wouldn't destroy my daughter's soul.

Sadie strained forward, her arms outstretched. Her light filled the room so brightly I was scared that all the vamps would be turned to ash, but it died in a snap.

I blinked my way through the black dots swimming in my vision.

Celeste stood there, fully corporeal and still undead, patting herself down, her mouth hanging open.

"Our deal is fulfilled," Zev said to Sadie.

"You used her?" I lunged at him, but it was my daughter of all people who pulled me back.

She jutted her chin up, her chest heaving. "Did you know that it wouldn't work?"

Zev hesitated then shook his head. "Not conclusively."

"Take me home, Vincenzo." Sabrina's muted plea broke the stare down happening on my side of the room.

I should have checked in with the female vampire or introduced myself or something, but the only thing I cared about was Sadie.

"Sades?" I was almost scared to speak and have her cold stare turned on me.

Her granite expression softened somewhat when she faced me, but not enough.

I held out a hand and after a moment, she took it.

"Let's go, Mom," she said quietly.

The case from hell was over.

There was just one thing left on my plate: steal the Ascendant back from Dumah to free the Leviathan and destroy it once and for all. If the Ascendant even existed anymore. It could have been broken in transit or Dumah might have destroyed it as part of his penance if he was as guilt ridden as Kian claimed.

I stuffed a handful of chips in my mouth, staring at the board where I'd laid out my case for Dumah having killed my parents. The facts all fit, but if Dumah had no desire to escape—and I believed Kian on that score—then there was no motive for any of the murders.

He could just be cruel, but now that I was able to think logically about it, why go to all the trouble of arranging the killings, since he hadn't done them himself? The fallen angel had scores of souls to torture. He didn't need to send proxies after a few humans to get his kicks.

If I excluded all evidence from the past and stuck only with what had transpired in the past week or so, what was I left with?

An amulet that Dumah had used to summon me, and which Nora had felt compelled to deface. It was tied to the hunters and the figures on it had to be Senoi, Sansenoi, and Sammaneglof.

Was Dumah trying to warn me about the three? Why? I already knew how awful they were.

Next up were these Whispers, though technically, they'd shown up in the past as well.

Last, but not least, a broken hallelujah.

I licked chip crumbs off my fingers. Who wanted to meet me if not Dumah? I munched on another handful, the vinegar flavor puckering my mouth.

I spun my chair from side to side, repeating, "Senoi, Sansenoi, Sammaneglof. Senoi, Sansenoi, Sammaneglof. Sen san sam. Sen san sam." When I said them softly like that, it kind of sounded like...

Whispers.

Who would have murdered my parents if not Dumah? How about the three angels who'd created the hunters to do the dirty work of murdering more Banim Shovavim?

I choked on my mouthful of food, coughing and pounding my chest.

Senoi, Sansenoi, and Sammaneglof hated Banim Shovavim—and the Leviathan. Did they classify the fallen angel as an abomination and despise him too?

The chip bag hit the ground with a rustling sound. "Did Senoi, Sansenoi, Sammaneglof want Dumah out of Gehenna so they could destroy the angel or exile him in their own territory like they did to the Leviathan?"

I paced the room, refitting the facts to this new theory. Dumah had the means but no motive for the murders.

What about the other three angels? They weren't imprisoned, and while I had no idea what celestial beings were capable of, I'm sure they could both snap necks from a distance and start very contained and considerate fires that never harmed anyone else's property.

Okay, they had the means, what about motive?

They were the ones who tortured Arlo. That was a fact. Was it because he'd helped Dumah or because he tried but Dumah didn't take the bait? Was that when the trio went after my parents, not to kill the latest Banim Shovavim with the Ascendant, but to convince them to do their bidding? Except by the time the three caught up with Mom and Dad, Calvin Jones had the amplifier, not them.

I crushed my chip bag underfoot, a sob catching in my throat. Were Mom and Dad condemned to die because the angels were pissy the Banim Shovavim they required for their plan no longer had the amplifier?

Magic poured out of my skin, encasing me in darkness. I gripped the table, my head bowed, taking deep breaths until I'd forced it all down and locked it away with my rage.

The bitter irony was that Dumah didn't even want to leave Gehenna. If the angel *had* wanted out, it would have been a disaster, but he didn't. My eyes widened.

The other three angels didn't know that.

"Angels aren't omniscient, are they?" I said in surprise.

An answering trumpet blast almost made me wet myself.

Just like when I'd opened the rift with the Ascendant, a crack of light appeared in my office like a crooked smile. It grew wider and wider, filling the room, then a backlit figure appeared, careful not to breach the boundary into my home.

I fanned away the sharp, fetid stink of rotting onions.

A familiar older woman with frizzy gray hair, shapeless jeans, and purple socks with plastic clogs batted a couple of stray dybbuks back into the darkness, before firing finger guns at me. "What's crackalackin'?"

"Goldie?" I crashed back onto my chair hard enough to make the seat bounce. "You can't be an angel. I'm going crazy."

She laughed, a booming, warm sound that had come to represent home. It hit me in the heart. Damn, I missed her. "Breathe, matzoh ball, you're freaking out."

Matzoh ball, that had been Goldie's nickname for me. M.B., the same as my real initials, Miriam Blum. For a moment, I felt like a teenager again.

Then I vowed to never let Emmett or Laurent hear it.

"I'm woven from your memories because my true brilliance would knock you flat on your ass," she said. "Worse than the time you mixed all the booze in my cabinet together into a shit mix after Darren what's-his-face dumped you."

"Oh, good," I said faintly. "You have access to all my memories."

Dumah-Goldie sniffed the air. "You should get some scented candles in here. They really freshen up a place."

"Uh-huh," I said, massaging my temples. The angel looked and sounded like Goldie, but I couldn't get past the sense of something primal and ancient peeking out at me, even while chatting candles.

"I have a fabulouso collection of them," she said.

"Does Gehenna have direct shipping or do you use a post office box?" Were these words actually coming out of my mouth? Yes, yes they were.

Dumah-Goldie wagged a finger at me, still not entering my living room. "Don't be ridiculous. Dybbuk-possessed hosts like to give me offerings so I don't blow my trumpet and drive them out of their new body."

I jumped to my feet. "You could do that?"

She shrugged. "No clue. Never tried."

My headache worsened. That right there was why I didn't want to meet with any angel. I missed what the angel said next. "Sorry, what?"

"I said that next to candles, my favorite offerings are hard lemon candies." She looked around hopefully. "You wouldn't happen to have any?"

"No." I rocked back on my heels.

"Too bad. Oh well, we have a lot to talk about."

"Do I have a choice in this chat or will you compel me into becoming another hyped-up puppet?"

Dumah-Goldie placed her hands on her hips. "It takes a lot of effort to catch a human's attention from my home base. Sometimes, I may go overboard in my hold and the humans get…excitable."

"Excitable? You practically break their brains."

"Is that really important in light of everything else?" She held out a hand. "Come on."

"Where to?"

She shot me a look like my low intelligence was exactly what she expected, but she'd do her best to work with it. "Gehenna."

Thank you for reading Bent Out of Shade!

Are you ready for Miri's final adventure? Then get **Ace of Shades now!**

Gehenna isn't on Google Maps and there's no *Angel Annihilation for Dummies*. To Miriam Feldman, list lover extraordinaire, this is an irritating oversight.

It's fine. She's got this mission under control. Sure, her instructions are vague, and her team is trigger-happy, but she's got plenty of motivation to carry them to victory.

Vengeance counts, right?

Plus, if ridding the world of celestial menaces doesn't top up Miri's karmic bank, then stopping a vampire contagion will definitely earn her some good will.

Unless it gets her killed. That's a distinct possibility.

One which she refuses to worry about since she's got her shiny new relationship with a sexy wolf shifter to enjoy. And honestly, his family dysfunction is making hers look pretty damn insignificant.

How's that for positive thinking? She's going to nail this.

Happily-ever-after, here she comes.

Ace of Shades, the thrilling finale, features a later in life romance, a heart-pounding mystery, and a magical midlife adventure.

Get it now!

Every time a reader leaves a review, an author gets ... a glass of wine. (You thought I was going to say "wings," didn't you? We're authors, not angels, but *you'll* get heavenly karma for your good deed.) Please leave yours on your favorite book site. It makes a huge difference in discoverability to rate and review, especially the first book in a series.

Turn the page for an excerpt from *Ace of Shades*...

EXCERPT FROM ACE OF SHADES

"Celestial beings are colossal dicks," Dumah, the angel currently presenting as my cousin Goldie, said. Her plastic clogs slapped against the rough-hewn paving stones of an enormous courtyard and orange blossoms fluttered into her frizzy gray hair from surrounding trees. "Present company included."

One second, I'd been in my living room, having the shock of my life realizing that the three angels Senoi, Sansenoi, and Sammaneglof had been the ones who killed my parents and Fred McMurtry. The next, Dumah-Goldie had appeared in a blast of trumpets and was ushering me into Gehenna. If only solving my jigsaw puzzles earned me this same kind of fanfare.

Hummingbirds in a rainbow of iridescent colors dipped and soared between patches of swaying wildflowers, while the air was fresh and sweet. I spun slowly, eyes wide. This was the land of the dead where wicked spirits resided?

"Stop." I pinched myself, half convinced this was some go-into-the-light scenario, especially since my magic was gone. A distant part of me freaked out at my helplessness, but most of me fell into line with the chill vibe exuded here.

Not once in my life had I been described as chill.

"Are you compelling me into being calm?" I said, abruptly becoming even less calm.

"Compulsions are so passive-aggressive. If I wanted you calm, I'd say so." The older woman tugged up her shapeless jeans with a little hip wriggle. It was such quintessentially Goldie behavior that I squeaked, plowing my fingers into my hair. Though my real cousin, who lived in Florida, veered less to jeans and more to floral capris these days.

At least the angel didn't smell like tea tree oil, that fresh camphor scent from my cousin's favorite lotion. It might have sent me over the edge.

"You look like you're gonna plotz." Dumah-Goldie jerked her chin at two elaborately carved chairs on the grassy bank overlooking the water. "Sit. Take a load off."

Fumbling for the armrest, I crashed into the seat then squinted up at the sun, shielding my face with one hand.

The storm clouds and fog that were visible every time Laurent tore open a portal to this place were notably missing, and the fluffy cloud drifting overhead looked like a bunny rabbit. Not even a bunny rabbit with fangs or rabies of the damned. Huh. I peered into the crystalline depths of the meandering river, but unless the fat koi sunning themselves were repositories for especially malevolent souls who'd been terrified of water, I had nothing.

Where were all the tortured dybbuks? It was one thing for Dumah to assume my cousin's image to accommodate the limits of my brain in looking upon the angel, but either the angel had done a massive cleanup campaign before I got here, or… I shook my head. Nope. I had nothing.

"Shouldn't it be black and ringing with tortured screams?"

She scoffed. "Oy. Who wants to listen to that 24/7? This is Ḥaẓarmavet, the Courtyard of Death, also known as my happy place."

"Wait! So, I *am* dead?" I half rose up off my seat, feeling for a heartbeat.

She lowered herself into the chair next to mine, leaned over, and smooshed my cheeks with her hand. "Ah, matzoh ball, always with the worries. Stress and lack of fiber: they'll do you in far too soon."

I wrenched free, massaging my aching cheeks, because for a celestial being, she had a wrestler's grip. "Please don't call me by Goldie's nickname." My cousin's way of keeping my real initials —M.B. for Miriam Blum—alive after I took her surname; this was the second time the angel had used it in our brief acquaintanceship, and it was getting weird. "Also, being dead is a pretty fair thing to worry about."

"You're alive and kicking." She snapped her fingers and a black smudgy shadow appeared.

The demon was both too large and too small, had too many horns and too few limbs, but mostly I couldn't process the sight because its utter malevolence was causing my brain to curl into a quivering lump. I looked away.

It growled something, to which the angel replied, "Prosecco, I think. Thanks, Tad."

The air pulled taut and Gehenna's stench of rotting onions that had been missing from this courtyard suddenly wafted in, then with a sproingy snap, all was serenity and orange blossoms once more.

I cautiously looked back, but we were alone. "The demon is called Tad?"

Was that the most important question right now? Of course not, but my mind was screaming at me that I was in Gehenna and that angels had murdered my parents, and I could grasp only the low-hanging fruit of knowledge.

BECOME A WILDE ONE

If you enjoyed this book and want to be first in the know about bonus content, reveals, and exclusive giveaways, become a Wilde One by joining my newsletter: http://www.deborahwilde.com/subscribe

You'll immediately receive short stories set in my different worlds and available only to my newsletter subscribers. There are mild spoilers so they're best enjoyed in the recommended reading order.

If you just want to know about my new releases, please follow me on:

Amazon: https://www.amazon.com/Deborah-Wilde/e/B01MSA01NW

or

BookBub: https://www.bookbub.com/authors/deborah-wilde

ACKNOWLEDGMENTS

I would never have made it through this book without the incredible love and cheerleading of my husband and daughter. I love you both impossible and ridiculous amounts.

Dr. Alex Yuschik, my phenomenal editor helped me take this story to the swooniest highs and most nail-biting lows and deserves all the appreciation.

As yet another book written during these strange times, the support and good humor of all my Deborah's Wilde Ones kept me going. You are all the best.

And thank you to every reader who's taken a chance on Miri and Laurent. <3

ABOUT THE AUTHOR

A global wanderer, former screenwriter, and total cynic with a broken edit button, Deborah (pronounced deb-O-rah) writes funny urban fantasy and paranormal women's fiction.

Her stories feature sassy women who kick butt, strong female friendships, and swoony, sexy romance. She's all about the happily ever after, with a huge dose of hilarity along the way.

Deborah lives in Vancouver with her husband, daughter, and asshole cat, Abra.

"Magic, sparks, and snark! Go Wilde."

www.deborahwilde.com

27425889R00184